I hope you enjoy reading my book as much as I enjoyed writing it!

Mr. and Mrs. Darcy

Mrs. Bennet's Solace

Bridgetta

BRIDGETTE BRUCE

BALBOA.PRESS
A DIVISION OF HAY HOUSE

Balboa Press books may be ordered through booksellers or by contacting:

Balboa Press
A Division of Hay House
1663 Liberty Drive
Bloomington, IN 47403
www.balboapress.com.au
AU TFN: 1 800 844 925 (Toll Free inside Australia)
AU Local: 0283 107 086 (+61 2 8310 7086 from outside Australia)

Print information available on the last page.

ISBN: 978-1-5043-2497-7 (sc)
ISBN: 978-1-5043-2498-4 (e)

Library of Congress Control Number: 2021906414

Balboa Press rev. date: 05/05/2021

Contents

———•———

.

Chapter 1

It is a truth universally acknowledged that a single man in possession of a good fortune must be in want of a wife.

However little known the feelings or views of such a man may be on his first entering a neighbourhood, this truth is so well fixed in the minds of the surrounding families, that he is considered as the rightful property of some one or other of their daughters, and now there were to be two less such single men of good fortune to be sought after.

Such were Lizzy's thoughts as she walked towards the altar on her father's left arm, her dearest sister Jane on her father's right arm. She was definitely relieved to have gotten thus far, ending what could only be described as a somewhat emotionally uncomfortable, but thankfully short, courtship.

Mr. Darcy had been exposed to the overly deferential treatment of her mother, though fortunately she was too much in awe of him to speak to him the way she spoke to Mr. Bingley, Jane's betrothed. Her cousin Mr. Collins had also paraded and treated Mr. Darcy with obsequious civility in his efforts to ingratiate himself with his current patroness's nephew. He had obviously taken to heart Mr. Bennet's advice to stand by the nephew rather than Lady Catherine, since Mr. Darcy had more to give with his extensive patronage in the church. Lizzy had tried to shield Mr. Darcy as much as possible from as many of her relations as could not be counted on to behave with decorum and civility, without being vulgar. Her father, Jane, and Bingley were the very few she could feel at ease with to converse with Mr. Darcy, without causing mortification on her part, until the arrival of her aunt and uncle Gardiner, who would not have missed the marriages of their two favourite and most deserving nieces, for the world.

In spite of her mother's most earnest desire that she be married by special license, Lizzy and Mr. Darcy were being married at the same time as Jane and Mr. Bingley, through the more conventional path of having the banns read in the parish church three times before the wedding. It was also their own clergyman, Mr. Powell, a gentleman of some venerable years and great learning, officiating in spite of Mrs. Bennet's efforts to get at least a bishop or even the archbishop for the wedding of her now favourite daughter, to Mr. Darcy, and Mr. Collins' unsubtle hints on the appropriateness of himself, a relation of both of the brides and a properly ordained man of the cloth, as having the best right. However, Mr. Collins then recollected, with his wife Charlotte's assistance, that his illustrious patroness, Lady Catherine De Bourgh, most definitely did *not* approve of her nephew's marriage to Miss Elizabeth Bennet, and thus he refrained from further hints, for fear of offending her ladyship, should it come to be known that he had had *any* part in the joining of his cousin Elizabeth to Lady Catherine's nephew.

Jane looked radiant, dressed in a pale blue satin gown trimmed with pale gold lace, the hem was scalloped in flounces with gold ribbon bows. She also wore a gold velvet spencer lined in the finest woven cream wool, trimmed with blue braid, to keep off the chill of the late November morning, and a bonnet trimmed in blue and gold. Lizzy felt her sister had never looked more handsome or happier than when they stepped into the carriage with their father earlier. She could not now see her dear Jane; the bulk of their father walking proudly between them down the aisle, flanked by the pews decked in flowers and ribbons, provided an ample screen, allowing Lizzy to collect herself and to stop smiling quite as much as she had been. This was supposed to be a solemn, albeit happy occasion, and her smiles were taking on a joyous life of their own, which if left unchecked, would burst into nervous giggling which she would be unable to hide behind her bouquet of flowers.

Lizzy herself had chosen a peacock green-coloured silk for her own gown, trimmed with exquisite black lace, the flounces at the hem exposing a warm black velvet underskirt, a similar velvet spencer to Jane's, but in black, trimmed with black swansdown and buttons, a wedding gift from Mr. Darcy, made of silver gilt inserted with emeralds. Her bonnet was simple but adorned with a gossamer-like peacock-blue veil, attached to her bonnet with diamond and sapphire pins, another gift from her soon-to-be husband.

The ceremony was simple, apart from the fact that it was a double wedding. Jane, being the eldest, was married first, both she and Mr. Bingley smiling brightly, as they pledged their troth to each other, and then the clergyman, Mr Powell, turned to Lizzy and Darcy.

Lizzy thought she had never seen Darcy smile with such warmth; his eyes filled with such tenderness as they gazed at each other at the altar: he was so absolutely the handsomest man in her world. He was dressed in a superbly cut blue jacket, a waistcoat made of the same green silk as Elizabeth's gown, with identical gilt and emerald buttons as on her spencer, a cravat of the finest white linen, and a diamond and sapphire white gold pin. Polished black boots over his dove-coloured breeches finished the ensemble. Darcy himself was equally emotional, thinking she had never looked as beautiful as now, on the point of making him the happiest of men, by becoming his wife.

After the moving ceremony, the family party returned to Longbourn, where the wedding breakfast was prepared for the happy couples and their guests. Jane and Charles Bingley leading the way in their new barouche, by right of Jane's seniority, and Lizzy and Fitzwilliam Darcy following in theirs, then the other guests. The Gardiners and the Phillips' in the Gardiner carriage followed the Bennet carriage, that carried a very proud Mr. Bennet and Mrs. Bennet, who was alternating between tears of happiness and absolute pride at the beauty and the success of her daughters in having married such rich men, as well as Kitty and Mary, finely dressed in new white gowns, as the attendants to their two elder sisters. Georgiana Darcy was accompanied her other guardian, Colonel Fitzwilliam, in the Darcy family carriage, Miss Bingley and the Hursts were also present, all dressed in their finest clothes, but none outshining the brides and grooms. These were the guests invited to the wedding breakfast, but the church had been quite full with friends and well-wishers, and the local gossips from Meryton, eager to have something so splendid to relate through the town.

The breakfast was beautifully prepared and presented, with as many of the favourite dishes and delicacies Mrs. Bennet could get her cook to contrive that she thought her two new sons would like. She had done credit to her housekeeping, though she had had Jane to keep her in check during the planning and preparations - otherwise the wedding breakfast would never have fitted in her dining room, ample as it was, with all the guests around the table.

The wine was of the best available, sent down from Pemberley, Mr. Darcy having a cellar which was only *just* surpassed in size and excellence by his library. Flowers had been procured from London and also Pemberley, where the conservatory and hothouses could provide many blooms and fruits, exotic or out of season, at a moment's notice.

Dahlias, chrysanthemums, orange blossom, lilies, carnations, roses, autumn berries and brightly coloured leaves produced a profusion of colour in two silver gilt centrepiece vases on the table and vases on the sideboards and occasional tables.

The centrepiece vases were a gift from Bingley and Darcy to Mrs. Bennet, who had never received anything so splendid in her life, sending her into a state of profusive thanks, which the gentlemen received with more composure than Lizzy had thought they were capable of. Mrs. Bennet had mostly recovered from her emotional effusions after receiving them the week before, but it was now Mrs. Phillips who was sent into paroxysms of admiration, determined to regale her acquaintance with the details of the most splendid wedding breakfast she had ever seen or heard of in her life, surpassing possibly even Rosings in its elegance and grandeur.

Chapter 2

The weeks between their coming to an understanding, their engagements and the wedding were mercifully short, but very busy for the two happy couples. Between them they had agreed that Jane would organise the details for the wedding breakfast and Lizzy would go to town to organise the purchase of any finery that they required for their wedding gowns, which she would also procure in London. Lizzy knew her sister's taste in style and colour, so Jane had no qualms in entrusting her with such an important gown.

"I know, Lizzy," said Jane smiling, "that you will possibly make a better choice than I would myself; I would hesitate so much more than you, with so much to choose from."

Lizzy's main concern was in how to prevent their mother from ordering far more than they actually wanted, her idea of elegant weddings being so more in the quantity of clothes and linen, rather than in the quality.

Mrs. Bennet was quite determined on making the wedding as grand as possible, having waited for this moment since Jane was fifteen, and also having missed out in the arranging of Lydia's rushed and hushed nuptials, whereas both Jane and Lizzy wanted a quiet, private wedding with just their close friends and family. The Gardiners were of course invited, having been so instrumental in bringing Lizzy and Darcy together, but the girls preferred to keep the ceremony small and simple.

After breakfast one morning, to which the gentlemen had been invited, as they would be spending the whole day with the ladies they each felt were to make them the happiest of men, the subject of the wedding, uppermost in all their minds, but none more so than in Mrs. Bennet's, was raised again. Jane gave her opinions and wishes and Lizzy's, the gentlemen sensibly remaining silent.

"But Jane, Lizzy, this is to be the most important day of your lives" Mrs. Bennet cried, her thoughts running on those elegant nuptials she read about from town "I must ensure that you both have a proper wedding, unlike poor dear Lydia, for whom I was allowed to do nothing! She did not even have wedding clothes for her marriage with dear Wickham and the notice in the paper was most shabbily done, no mention of her father or where she came from. But I was over-ruled, as I always am. Nobody knows what I suffered, there is never any compassion for my poor nerves, but those who do not complain are never heard." Mrs. Bennet was most unhappy at missing such an opportunity of showing off her well-married daughters and suffered another attack on her poor nerves before Bingley came up with an original idea.

"A mere suggestion, Ma'am, why do we not have a small wedding, with just our family for the wedding breakfast here at Longbourn, where everyone will fit around your magnificent table, Mrs. Bennet, and then a wedding ball and supper the following day at Netherfield, where so many more people could be invited? I am certain that my dearest Jane," looking at her lovingly," yourself Mrs. Bennet, and my housekeeper could easily organise such a thing between you."

Mrs. Bennet was in raptures with the idea.

"Oh Mr. Bingley, what an excellent idea! Nobody else hereabouts has ever done such a thing, 'tis as good as a lord! Such an opportunity to show your wedding finery, girls! Such gowns, such jewels! I shall go distracted! Mercy me, how jealous Lady Lucas will be; she did not even have a wedding breakfast when her daughter Charlotte married

Mr. Collins: they scurried away, straight from the church door, and Mrs. Long, her nieces are so plain, not at all pretty and very good sorts of girls, I like them immensely. What a shame that poor dear Lydia cannot attend, for she likes nothing better than a ball, but dear Wickham has been sent so far away. A wedding ball at Netherfield!"

Her two daughters were relieved that a source of fretfulness, agitation, and querulous complaints had been so skilfully removed, however they took the first opportunity thereafter to leave the room with Bingley and Darcy, to walk around the grounds whilst the weather held fine, leaving Mrs. Bennet to her raptures with Mrs. Hill, the housekeeper, and Mr. Bennet retreated to the haven of peace that was his library.

Even Darcy was happy with the idea, walking down the little wilderness, holding Lizzy's arm in the crook of his.

"I confess that I am looking forward to dancing with the most beautiful woman in the room, with the advantage of knowing her to be my wife!" looking at Lizzy with absolute devotion in his eyes. Lizzy smiled teasingly back at him.

"Do you now think that I am tolerable enough to dance with sir?" Her teasing tone was part of her charm for him, and he was learning to take the words in the non-critical light in which they were spoken.

"Indeed, I find that Miss Elizabeth Bennet is tolerable, very tolerable, in fact one of the handsomest women of my acquaintance, but she will be utterly surpassed by the soon-to-be Mrs. Darcy." Lizzy's heart was bursting with the love she felt for him, reflecting on how she had lost so much precious time with this wonderful man, due to her previous prejudices and misconceptions. Mr. Darcy was also thinking of the same period of time, but blaming himself for his arrogance and pride at the time, which had made him totally unacceptable to a woman like Elizabeth; a woman worthy of being pleased. They both kept their thoughts to themselves however, having agreed not to go over those difficult and painful moments again.

"I have been thinking about it, Jane" Mrs. Bennet later declared over dinner, "with so much to organise, you will most certainly need my advice on how best to go about things. I will show you how to organise everything, indeed you could leave it all to me; a mother must make sacrifices of her time and energy for her children, no matter how hard. It is difficult at our time in life, to take on new responsibilities, but we willingly do so for your sakes."

Jane and Elizabeth looked at each other, horrified at the thought of leaving Mrs. Bennet to organise 'it all', and then at Bingley and Darcy, who looked equally disconcerted at the idea. Turning to her mother, Jane spoke tactfully.

"Perhaps my dear ma'am, that as a young woman about to go out into the world as a married woman, I would benefit from trying to organise the events, but of course with my mother's invaluable guidance to help me." Mrs. Bennet surprisingly conceded with little argument, simply saying that she felt content that she had raised her daughters properly, having taught them how to run a household competently and would be there to advise Jane with any details that her own wiser head might assist her with.

Mr. Bennet, who sat with them but had said very little until then, swallowed down a splutter into a cough before speaking.

"Mrs. Bennet, I believe our eldest daughter is learning to be wise; she realises that she will need to be able to run a large household and there is nothing like the challenge of a ball *and* a wedding breakfast to start her off on her responsibilities. Let her attempt it, my dear, and I am sure she will not hesitate to ask you for advice on anything she is unsure of. I admire your fortitude Madam, in accepting to guide our eldest in her first marital housekeeping venture, much may she learn from you."

Lizzy and Jane almost gawped in surprise; they had hardly ever heard their father compliment his wife and certainly never on her intellectual capacities. Mrs. Bennet was equally surprised and basked in this unexpected approbation of her capabilities from her husband.

9

In this frame of mind, Mrs. Bennet was even able to be persuaded, with not too much effort, that she would be so much needed at home to help Jane organise all the details for the wedding breakfast and the ball, she would not be able to go with Lizzy to Town, to order all the clothes, linen, muslins, calicos and cambric etc., for her sister and herself, which had been so sadly lacking with Lydia's wedding, making it hardly a marriage at all! Mrs. Bennet had been more alive to the disgrace, which the want of new clothes must reflect on her daughter's nuptials, than to any sense of shame at her eloping and living with Wickham for a fortnight before they took place. It was therefore agreed that Lizzy should go with her father, for which Lizzy was most relieved. She felt more at ease at being in Mr. Darcy's company with her father, rather than with her mother. It also gave the opportunity for the marriage settlements to be made, at Haggeston's, for which Mr. Bennet had to be present.

Mrs. Bennet did however give Lizzy and Mr. Bennet an extensive list of the best merchants, shops and modistes, jewellers, goldsmiths, silversmiths and so forth, before they left with Mr. Darcy in his coach, which was to convey all three of them to London. Mr. Bennet and Lizzy were to stay with the Gardiners and Mr. Darcy would go to his town house in Grosvenor Square.

"Be sure that you go to the warehouses that I have written down for you, for you will not know which are the best places." was Mrs. Bennet's parting remark as the carriage set off from Longbourn. Mr. Bennet had no intention of abiding by the list, preferring to be advised by his much more sensible brother by marriage and his wife, Edward and Marianne Gardiner, and also in keeping the expenses down. Not that he objected to spending the money on his eldest and most deserving daughters, but two daughters at once was a strain on any man's income, especially with such a spendthrift wife as Mrs. Bennet; it was only due to his determination to remain independent that Mrs. Bennet had been restrained from systematically exceeding his income, with some extravagant and vulgar displays of taste, behaviour and dress, having no turn for economy herself.

Mr. Darcy was going to Town also, to arrange his affairs now that he was to be married, and to get his town house made ready so that he could invite his future wife and father-in-law and the Gardiners to dinner, thus introducing Lizzy to one of her new abodes. He also wished to buy a new carriage on the occasion of their marriage, but more importantly for him, to buy gifts for Elizabeth: he wanted to shower her with jewels, gowns, new silverware and china, anything he thought her heart could desire. However, the main reason he was in town was simply because Lizzy was going to be there; he could not bear to be apart from her so soon after having finally had his proposal of marriage accepted.

While Lizzy set off with her aunt the following morning, with the enormous lists her mother had made, trimmed down by her own taste and her aunt's assistance, the gentlemen spent their time together, accompanying Mr. Darcy to the carriage-maker, which they all enjoyed, Mr. Bennet being able assist with what he thought Lizzy would like when it came to deciding the interior furnishings of the new landau. They then proceeded to the bank to recuperate the Darcy family jewels and then on to a well-known court jeweller, depositing the jewels there, to await Mr. Darcy's return with Lizzy at a later date to decide what she wanted and how they were to be reset. This was quite enough shopping for Mr. Bennet and Mr. Gardiner, so they then retired to the gentlemen's club of which Mr. Darcy was a member, for a nuncheon served with an excellent wine.

The ladies were more valiant, having so much more to acquire. "My dear aunt" said Lizzy "I am so happy and relieved that you are helping me with this, for I had not realised just how many things we had to purchase!" Her aunt smiled and squeezed her arm.

"My dearest Lizzy, I am delighted to assist you with shopping for yours and Jane's weddings, especially since your mother could not be spared from Longbourn. I know she would have come if she possibly could; she has been planning weddings since Jane turned fifteen!" With a chuckle, Lizzy then admitted to her aunt how she and Jane had manipulated their mother into staying home and letting Mr. Bennet come to town in her stead. In turn Mrs. Gardiner had to quietly laugh too, imagining Mrs. Bennet helping, or more likely hindering, Jane in the preparations of a wedding, the wedding breakfast and a ball.

"All credit to your dear mother, Lizzy, she may well have some small faults, as we all do, but she has only your wellbeing at heart. I do however agree with your reasoning in preferring your father to accompany you here"

Having been to some warehouses and selected quantities of linen, lawn, cambric, calico, muslins, satins, silks, ribbons and lace, they retired to a tea-room for much needed refreshment, before setting off to a well-known modiste to discuss the all-important wedding gowns for Jane and herself.

She and Jane had different tastes in gowns, but Lizzy knew her sister's preferences and also had her measurements. Their mother had wanted them to wear white muslin, since only the wealthy could afford to always wear white, not having to concern themselves with the laundering of such garments, but both Jane and Lizzy preferred coloured gowns of sturdier fabric, more in keeping with the late autumn weather, to which they could add velvet spencers, to keep warm in the cold stone church in which they were to be married.

Jane, with her fair colouring was going to look even more handsome in the pale forget-me-not blue satin that Lizzy had selected for her, to match her blue eyes. Mrs. Gardiner had suggested a wide, pale gold lace trim, matching gold coloured ribbons on the scallop-flounced hem, and a gold velvet spencer, trimmed with blue braid and gold buttons. The dressmaker totally agreed with the choices and commenced a design that would make even Mrs. Bennet gasp at Jane's beauty as she became Mrs. Charles Bingley.

Lizzy, being of darker colouring with her dark brown tresses and dark, blue-green eyes, felt that a peacock green silk was more to her taste. She hesitated between a silver trim or more unconventionally, a black trim, asking her aunt her thoughts. "Well most ladies would choose the silver trim Lizzy, but I think the black would be more striking on you"

The dressmaker fetched a selection of silver and black lace of varying widths and laid them on the shimmering silk. Her assistant then draped the silk over Lizzy's shoulders and laid a broad length of silver lace over one shoulder and black lace over the other.

"Oh my, Lizzy" exclaimed Mrs. Gardiner, "I think the black looks so beautiful; it stands out on the green silk whereas the silver is blending in with the sheen. What do you think madam?" turning to the dressmaker.

"I have never made a wedding gown with that combination of colours, but you are right madam, the beautiful delicacy of the lace does stand out better in the black"

Deferring to her aunt's good taste and the superior knowledge of the dressmaker, Lizzy chose the black lace trim, a black velvet spencer, lined in fine black wool, to be edged with black swansdown and silver buttons.

The ladies then decided to return home to rest a little before preparing for dinner; tired, but very happy with the day's proceedings, leaving the bonnets and ball gowns to be decided upon another day.

Chapter 3

———•———

At dinner with the Gardiners, the party compared their respective days, the gentlemen being less interested in the haberdashery, but Darcy's attention was caught by her aunt's description of the colours for Lizzy's gown.

"It sounds like a beautiful combination Mrs. Gardiner." he replied "Do you think it would be possible to have a waistcoat for myself made up in the same silk?" Mrs. Gardiner looked surprised, but Lizzy pointed out "Mr. Darcy has been Miss Darcy's guardian for many years, so of course he will have an idea on gowns and fabrics, since I very much doubt Miss Darcy is wearing the same gowns she wore as a child!"

Mrs. Gardiner laughed, saying "I should have thought of that, how remiss of me, I know myself how fast little ones can grow! Miss Darcy is always so beautifully dressed so I cannot doubt your good taste sir."

"Perhaps it would be simpler if I had a length of the silk so I can take it to my tailor, who is making my wedding coat. I am sure the dressmaker will not mind, having two wedding dresses to make already." said Darcy. Unbeknownst to Lizzy, he had an ulterior motive for his request. If he knew the precise colour, he could have some buttons made at the jewellers, to match the silk. He also liked the idea of having their outfits somewhat coordinated, an idea his valet had come up with.

Thinking of his valet, he must find a moment to speak with Lizzy about a lady's maid. Till now she had been served by Sarah, one of the Bennet family servants, sharing her with Jane and her other sisters. As Mrs. Darcy, she would require the dedicated services of a lady's maid, skilled in the arts of hairdressing and sewing, so that she could step into the highest circles, perfectly groomed and dressed. Not that he did not think she looked beautiful as she was, but he knew of how critical the Ton could be and he did not want his wife to feel in any way inferior.

Bringing his thoughts back to the present, which was not so easily done, he found himself gazing lovingly at Lizzy until a remark on his inattention from Mr. Bennet brought him back into the conversation. "I was explaining to the ladies, Mr. Darcy, that the carriage interior was to be done in a brown leather, but you seem to have wandered on to happier thoughts." quipped Mr. Bennet, smiling at his future son's discomfort at having been caught out being inattentive.

"I was indeed far away in my thoughts, Mr. Bennet, so thank you for reminding me." said Darcy, smiling at Lizzy. "Elizabeth, we thought that you would prefer dark green for the landau, with dark brown leather upholstery, but if you prefer any other colours, I shall have the changes notified tomorrow." Lizzy was somewhat in awe of the fact that a carriage was being made specifically for her, with her taste being consulted.

"From what my father and my uncle have been saying, Mr. Darcy, the colours are perfectly to my taste, thank you."

She was beginning to fully realise what her marriage to Darcy entailed: a step into a higher sphere where luxury was the standard. She started to feel that her current wardrobe was totally inadequate, and was concerned at the cost of refurbishing it. Her father had funds, but they were not limitless. It was something she would have to discuss with Mr. Darcy at some point, though she knew not quite how to speak to him about it.

After dinner, the ladies left the gentlemen to their port and retired to the drawing room, fitted out in fashionable colours, with furniture that would not disgrace a gentleman's abode, certainly not reflecting the Cheapside address which had made Caroline Bingley and her sister Mrs. Hurst, laugh at Jane's expense. Whilst waiting for the gentlemen to join them, Lizzy consulted her aunt about her concerns for her wardrobe. Being far more sensible and practical than Mrs. Bennet, her aunt was able to allay Lizzy's fears.

"Lizzy, Mr. Darcy knows that your father will not be able to buy everything you think you will require, especially as he has two daughters to provide for at once. Realise that once you are his wife, he will provide you with all you need. Apart from your wedding gown, you really only need a new ball gown for the ball at Netherfield, and perhaps an outfit for travelling to your new home. Other garments can be made from the vast quantities of linen you have ordered. As for gloves, bonnets, reticules, pelisses, and so forth, your uncle and I have planned on offering them to you and Jane as our wedding gift."

"Oh! dearest Aunt Marianne" cried Lizzy "I am so glad to have you give me such sound advice! I am afraid my mother would have simply told me to buy more!"

"More than likely that would have been her advice, my dear Lizzy, but I don't think your father would have thanked her for it! By the by Lizzy, have you thought of what your new position as Mrs. Darcy entails as to social responsibilities?"

Lizzy looked at her somewhat perplexed, then realised that she had not given much thought to the social part of her new duties as Mrs. Darcy, wife of one of the wealthiest men in England.

"Oh, my goodness! Another thing I must ask advice about!"

"Well, I was thinking that since you were concerned about gowns and other such things, you will also have to consider getting a lady's maid to take care of your gowns, your jewels, and your hair.

You will not have the time to take care of these things yourself, and however well done your hair has been in the past, you will need more intricate styles than what is considered sophisticated enough for Hertfordshire"

Before Lizzy could answer, the gentlemen joined them in the drawing room, so she settled down to serve the tea and coffee. Darcy came up to her straight away, with a slightly concerned look on his face, which worried Lizzy, not being used to see that look on his face when he was in the company of her aunt, uncle, and father.

"Is there anything wrong, my dear Fitzwilliam?" she asked hesitantly.

"Oh Elizabeth, I am sorry if I have troubled you with my mien, I was in fact trying to arrange my thoughts in order to ask you a question which I thought you might possibly consider impertinent."

"What can you mean? We are to be married, so everything about me concerns you, surely?" she replied, wondering what it could be that put that troubled look on his face.

"It is somewhat delicate, Lizzy, and I am not sure how to discuss it, without possibly offending you, but have you considered getting a lady's maid to assist you with your hair and clothes? The expense is of course covered by the Pemberley household, but I thought we could arrange something, whilst we are here in town. Georgiana has her own lady's maid so it is only proper that you too should have such a person to assist you"

Lizzy laughed at such a coincidence: her aunt and herself thinking the same thoughts as Darcy, with the same reticence, and explained the source of her mirth to him. They were both relieved that they were able to talk about relatively intimate details of their future life together, both realising that their intimacy would increase even more so after their wedding.

Having gotten past the delicate subject of her maid, Lizzy was then less uncomfortably able to broach the question of the number of gowns she was expected to have as Mrs. Darcy.

"There is something else I wished to speak to you about Fitzwilliam: I am not sure as to what the expectations are of me in that regard, but I think that my current supply of gowns will be insufficient" she said, still somewhat shy about talking of money with the man she was marrying for love, not his fortune.

"That is something which I also wished to speak to *you* about my dearest Lizzy" he replied "As Mrs. Darcy, you will be invited to the highest spheres, including the Ton, which I personally prefer to avoid, but it will be expected of us to appear in society, so of course you must have the clothes that you need, to be perfectly attired. I will arrange with your modiste, and any other suppliers of your choosing, to have accounts opened for you so you can buy whatsoever you need, whenever you need, without regard to the expense. As the handsomest woman of my acquaintance, and my soon-to-be wife, you deserve only the best"

Lizzy's face broke into an unladylike grin, thinking of how Mrs. Bennet would have reacted to such a declaration, and then started to laugh, enlightening Darcy as she did so. His mirth was not as great as Lizzy's but he could certainly imagine the spectacle, having gotten to know his future mother-by-marriage somewhat better over the past weeks since his engagement to Elizabeth.

Whilst they all talked with ease over tea and coffee, Elizabeth felt blessed that she had some relations for whom she need not blush, and watched with pride and love as her father conversed with Darcy with no appearance of his frequently used irony.

Chapter 4

The following day, whilst the gentlemen passed by Mr. Darcy's tailor and then on to other activities more suited to them than going through shops and warehouses, Mrs. Gardiner and Lizzy continued their shopping.

They returned to the modiste to order the ball gowns for the ball. They selected pearl white damask, which would delight Mrs. Bennet, to be trimmed with the finest Brussels lace and trains of diaphanous silver silk. The gowns were identical in the fabrics but different in styles. They also ordered Lizzy's travelling costume, in a cerise coloured velvet, the pelisse lined in the finest wool, trimmed in black braid: the intent being to be warm, as well as fashionable, whilst travelling in the winter.

Their next destination was to a milliner, frequented by the Ton. In addition to their wedding bonnets and headwear for the ball, Lizzy ordered lace caps for herself, Jane, and Mrs. Bennet for wearing indoors, and a ravishing creation in cerise, dove grey and a black ostrich feather to go with her travelling outfit. She had never in her life spent so much on a bonnet, but felt that it would be something she would have to become accustomed to as Mrs. Darcy. She was torn between not spending too much, and the obligations of being Mrs. Darcy, but her wise aunt talked her through her hesitations, besides pointing out that the bonnets were being bought as a wedding gift from herself and her husband, and therefore she was not to worry about the cost.

Going on to a prominent shoe maker, who apparently served the royal family, she ordered a pair of black lamb skin boots for herself and blue boots for her sister, who fortunately had the same size and shape foot as herself, to complete their wedding ensembles. White satin dancing slippers were also ordered for the wedding ball, sturdy black travelling boots lined with fur for her travelling outfit and other footwear for wearing indoors.

"But Aunt, you are not purchasing anything for yourself!"

"That is because I ordered everything I required, as soon as I knew about the wedding ball from yours and Jane's letters! I had organised my outfit for the wedding as soon as I heard of Jane's engagement, little thinking, but hoping, that you would be marrying too, in the not too distant future. I had noticed that Mr. Darcy was very much in love with you when we met in Derbyshire in the summer, but since I did not know of your feelings in the matter, and with the ensuing event of your sister's elopement with Mr. Wickham, I did not like to ask, in case I raised hopes to a level that was not reasonable."

"Speaking of letters, my dear Aunt, I expect we shall soon hear from Jane, to let us know how she is proceeding, with my mother's help, with the plans for everything" replied Lizzy. They both smiled as they both imagined how much actual help was occurring, knowing the mildness of Jane's temper, but they also knew she could be firm when she felt herself to be right.

They returned to Gracechurch Street early, after having booked tickets for the theatre that evening, and there they found the expected letter. They ordered tea and settled in the small parlour to read the letter together.

"My dearest Lizzy and Aunt Marianne, since I am certain you will both be reading my letter, all is well here at Longbourn and Netherfield. We have been most industrious in our labours, my

dear mother giving me the kindest advice in whatever matters we have been engaging, as have also my Aunt Phillips and Lady Lucas. Knowing your wishes Lizzy, I have managed to contain her in her efforts to get a bishop, or possibly the archbishop, to perform the marriage ceremony. Our own Mr. Powell will be doing the honours and he was most profusive in his thanks, since he seemed to think that you would prefer the bishop ... I think we can guess where that idea was started and by whom the rumour had spread.

I have left my mother to speak with Mrs. Hill and Cook for the wedding breakfast, though I shall speak to them myself when Mama next goes to Meryton, to ensure that all is to our taste and not too elaborate. You know how she likes to indulge our palates when she is trying to impress anyone.

My mother came with me to Netherfield to speak with Mrs. Nicholls, the housekeeper and the cook, Mrs. Duce about the ball, and it was not without great effort on her part that she did not step into my place and make the event into something far more grandiose than we would want, something that perhaps she has always dreamed of doing; organising a ball, but had never the opportunity of doing so, since Longbourn might accommodate a dance but never a ball. We managed to agree for the supper, with only the addition of a wedding cake, to be cut and distributed to the guests after the desserts. Knowing it to be a favourite with you Lizzy, there will be a syllabub amongst the choices.

Whilst you are in town, I will ask you to arrange for some flowers to be sent down to decorate the wedding breakfast at home, the church and the ballroom. Late November is a difficult time to find a wide array, but foliage can fill in gaps between the flowers. *Do not get too many, because flowers are expensive at this time of year and I do not wish to distress my dearest father, since he also has to come up with the monies for our wedding clothes, and as you can imagine, two daughters at once would strain any father's purse.*

What else is new since you went to town? We have had some heavy rains, preventing much exercise, so Mary spends much of her time studying, as usual, but I am trying to get her to rest her eyes. Kitty is in raptures at being your bridesmaid, Mary seemingly less so at being mine, but she has resigned herself to what she feels is her social obligation, though I suspect she is privately flattered that I asked her.

If my father had wanted the horses used on the farm during his absence, he would be sadly disappointed because we use the carriage every day. Less for myself, but my mother needs to go to Meryton on most days, to organise her bonnet and caps for the wedding events, but I suspect it is more so that she can regale her friends and my Aunt Phillips with the details and progress of the preparations. I think Lady Lucas is paying dearly for getting a daughter married before my mother did.

Everyone sends you all their love, none more so than Mr. Bingley and myself.

Your loving sister and niece,
Jane"

"Well Jane certainly seems to be managing very well,' said Mrs. Gardiner, "it must have been difficult for her to curb some of your dear mother's more extravagant ideas, such as the call for a bishop for the wedding"

"Indeed, she has," replied Lizzy "I would not have had her patience, though I do often sincerely try to emulate her example."

The gentlemen having also returned, they all discussed their day's activities and Jane's letter was read to them.

Mr. Darcy took Lizzy aside and spoke to her quietly. He told her that she should order whatever flowers she wanted, and that if she wished, he would have vast quantities of blooms sent down from Pemberley or London. He would have a list drawn up of what was available, from which she could make her selection, and they would be sent down to Longbourn or Netherfield. He also mentioned that he had spoken with Mr. Bennet and that he was most obliged at Darcy's offer to send down the wines for the wedding breakfast.

The evening passed very pleasantly at the theatre which was showing a new play which none of them had yet seen. An equally pleasant supper followed and Lizzy went to bed feeling both grateful and fulfilled with her future husband's tact and understanding.

Chapter 5

Having purchased almost everything she felt was required, Lizzy was at liberty to accede to Darcy's request that she accompany him to the goldsmith and jeweller the following morning. Her aunt accompanied them as her chaperone, Darcy's sense of decorum not allowing him to go about alone with Lizzy.

They arrived at Storrs in Dean Street, a firm so reputable that it was a place that Lizzy had read about in the Court section of the papers, but never dreamed of visiting, and were shown in to private rooms at the back of the shop, where they were seated in comfortable chairs around a large table. The table was loaded with an array of jewel boxes, rising like a pyramid in the centre, and plates, platters, bowls, cups, vases, goblets, centrepieces, candelabras, and candlesticks in a multitude of old-fashioned styles, were displayed on another long table against the wall.

"My dearest Elizabeth, we are come here so that you can go through the family jewel and plate collection and select any pieces that you desire, which I will have reset to your taste." explained Darcy. "It is a large collection because it has been acquired over many generations, so do not feel overwhelmed. This is simply what is currently superfluous to our current needs and taste, but should anything please you, then just mention it; please do not feel that you have to be parsimonious with your choices."

The business owner, Mr. Paul Storr himself, was attending to them, since he would be responsible for any changes that would be requested and he had few larger collections in his keeping than the Darcy one. Elizabeth and her aunt were astounded at the display. As the craftsman opened box upon box in the order of the category of the stones involved, they became positively awestruck. Diamonds, sapphires, rubies, emeralds, amethysts, pearls, opals, more stones than they had ever seen before, set in brooches, necklaces, earrings, bracelets, tiaras, rings etc.. They had to force themselves from gaping in astonishment: such unladylike behaviour. The silver and gold plates, etc., on the table against the wall were simply what were superfluous to the requirements of the family, since Pemberley and Darcy House were fully equipped with the best and more modern wares.

Reminding her niece of her future social obligations, Mrs. Gardiner was able to guide Lizzy in her initial choice, a string of perfectly matched pearls, several beautiful pearl drop earrings and a multi strand pearl bracelet with a diamond clasp. Emeralds and sapphires were then selected, to be made into parures, and a diamond necklace, bracelets, a tiara with drop pearls, and hair pins for the ball. Lizzy then chose a stunning ruby brooch and some diamond and ruby earrings, to be reset, to complement her travelling costume, as Darcy sat and just smiled at her with the smile, she now knew, was specifically for her; a smile of utter and complete devotion.

"Please, Fitzwilliam, let that suffice for the moment" pleaded Lizzy "I am totally overwhelmed by it all. We can go through them another time perhaps, but I am more than satisfied with what I have already selected"

"Very well then, my dear Miss Bennet, that will do for now, but I do wish to consult you on another matter," taking her gently by her arm. "Bingley and I have decided to offer Mrs. Bennet a gift, as a gesture of our appreciation of her providing us with our brides, and we thought that she would perhaps like some silver gilt table centre pieces, since we know that she does like to entertain."

"She would be delighted with such a gift" cried Lizzy "I do not think she would ever recover from the delight in fact, but perhaps, vases with the candle sticks incorporated would be of more use for her table setting, for you know that the table at Longbourn is not as large as your dining table at Pemberley."

"*Our* dining table at Pemberley," corrected Darcy teasingly "my table is your table too"

Mr. Storr showed them an array of designs, astounding Elizabeth with their intricacies, but with the craftsman's suggestions, and Darcy's insistence that the cost was not to be regarded, Lizzy made her choice, Mrs. Gardiner agreeing that Mrs. Bennet would be more than delighted with such a gift.

When the ladies had finished, they were offered tea while Darcy went off with Mr. Storr to finalise matters. It took him rather more time than they expected; they had finished a second cup of tea before he returned to them, Mr. Storr thanking him and saying that all would be ready, and that he would send everything down to Netherfield by the second week of November.

After an emotional morning, they returned to Gracechurch Street, to rest before dressing for dinner, which was to be at the Darcy town house in Grosvenor Square.

Arriving at an imposing building in his family carriage, Darcy assisted the ladies out and led them up the wide stone steps, flanked by bronze chains and conifers, in large stone pots, clipped into perfect conical shapes, where the housekeeper and butler awaited them.

"Miss Bennet, Mrs. Gardiner, may I present to you Mrs. Clayton, the housekeeper, and Mr. Parsons, the butler." Elizabeth and her aunt bowed their heads as Mrs. Clayton dropped a curtsey and Mr. Parsons bowed low.

"Welcome to Darcy House, Miss Bennet, Mrs. Gardiner." proffered Mrs. Clayton civilly to the ladies, as Mr. Parsons took their cloaks, gloves and bonnets. Mr. Gardiner and Mr. Bennet followed behind, and were relieved of their outer attire by a liveried footman.

They were led into a beautifully fitted out drawing room where refreshments were available for those who wished to partake of them whilst they waited for dinner to be served. The room was neither gaudy nor uselessly fine, with less of splendour, and more real elegance, than that which Lizzy had observed at Rosings. Rich burgundy, pine green and cream striped satin curtains were draped to great effect over the windows, trimmed by fashionable braids, cords and tassels. The fireplace was large, made of creamy white marble and housed a noble fire. The mantelpiece displayed some beautiful pieces of china, from the Worcester and the Wedgewood factories, far removed from the indifferent imitations of china found on her Aunt Phillips' mantelpiece.

Mr. Parsons knocked and opened the door to announce dinner. Although it was an informal, family dinner, it was with a sense of pride and immense gratification that Elizabeth was led in by Mr. Darcy, followed by Mr. Bennet and the Gardiners.

Dinner was excellent, though not as excessive as Lizzy thought it might have been. Had Mrs. Bennet been the lady of the house, responsible for ordering the dinner, the sideboard would have groaned under the weight of dishes that would not fit on the dining table, large as it was. An excellent soup was served, followed by a leg of pork, partridges, venison pies, several side dishes, and then a superbly crafted iced dessert, the like of which Lizzy had never seen before, and all accompanied by excellent wines. Darcy House obviously boasted an extremely creative cook, whom Lizzy was looking forward to meeting in the future, when discussing future dinners, that she would be hosting when 'Mr. and Mrs. Darcy' were in town.

The gentlemen did not linger long with their port after the ladies left the dining room, and they joined them in the drawing room where tea and coffee were being served. Being such a small family group, no-one felt the need for the more formal behaviour decreed by a first dinner engagement and were happy to sit together to discuss events in general. Long gone was Mr. Gardiner's former apprehension that Darcy could possibly be a little whimsical in his civilities, as great men often are, changing his mind and warning him off his grounds or out of his house. The three gentlemen were in fact becoming firm friends, with sense enough to recognise each other's finer qualities of character, as they became better acquainted. Lizzy saw this with delight and relief, since she knew that her father had initially only given his consent to Darcy's request for her hand, because he did not dare refuse such a man of his standing, to whom he should never have dared to refuse anything, which he condescended to ask.

Mrs. Gardiner was speaking to Darcy about the magnificent flowers that had adorned the dining room, as well as the small vases of posies dotted around the sitting room.

"Mr. Darcy, for a man who allegedly spends so little time in town if he can avoid it, you have such beautiful blooms here, one would be convinced that they are freshly picked!"

"As indeed they are Mrs. Gardiner: I am fortunate enough to have extensive grounds, for a town house, and my gardener is very proficient in the use of the hothouses, cold frames and glasshouses at his disposal, so we can have flowers ready at a moment's notice, most of the year round." He turned then to Lizzy, fetching a paper from his pocketbook and handing it to her.

"My dear Elizabeth, with regards to our conversation of yesterday, concerning the procuration of flowers for the wedding, I took the liberty of asking Mr. Betts, the head gardener here, to draw up a list of what is and what will be available should you wish to avail yourself of my offer of providing as many as you should desire. Just as a matter of interest, Mr. John Betts is the twin brother to my head gardener, Mr. Colin Betts, at Pemberley!"

The list was longer than she had anticipated: lilies, roses, carnations, tulips, narcissi, hyacinths, freesias, orange blossom, gypsophila, dahlias, antirrhinums, zinnias, chrysanthemums, even orchids were on the list, to be provided whenever requested. Jane's suggestion that the floral displays be filled out with berries and foliage seemed to be unnecessary with such a profusion of available blooms, although Lizzy was not going to put away Jane's idea, since she herself liked the idea of greenery, autumnal leaves, and berries in the displays.

In a corner of the room was a magnificent pianoforte, decorated with a silver rose-bowl, filled with beautiful red roses, gypsophila and trailing ivy. It seemed to beckon to Lizzy and her aunt asked her to play, since she herself could not. As she sat down, she perused some of the music sheets, possibly chosen by Darcy for his sister, since they were more modern than anything she had played, and she knew that Georgiana was very accomplished on the instrument, from what she had heard Miss Bingley mention in the past, and from what she perceived in Darcy's pride of her talents. Darcy came over to her and found some sheets of music that Lizzy *did* know and stood behind her to turn the sheets as she required.

Lizzy's performance was not capital, but most pleasing to the ear, her voice reaching the notes in an unaffected manner, and her audience all determined in her favour. Darcy selected a ballad, asking her if she knew it, and as she started to play, lifted his voice in a wonderful baritone, which sounded delightful to Lizzy's ears and also to the others.

"Now if only our Mary's singing could attain this level of accomplishment," said Mr. Bennet, "I shall not despair of disposing of her yet." Although this was quite derogatory with regards to his daughter Mary, the present company forgave him the slight, realising that Mr. Bennet was becoming more at ease in this grand setting, and returning to his more usual ironic and flippant remarks. Mr. Bennet was in fact becoming very happy with Lizzy's choice of mate, seeing how they complemented each other, how she respected and looked up to him, and also how he respected his dearest daughter. Mr. Darcy was now the only man in the country to whom he would willingly relinquish his precious Elizabeth.

Chapter 6

Lizzy awoke the following morning, stretching in her very warm and comfortable bed, a maid having remade the fire earlier and her aunt's maid had now brought her some tea.

"Thank you, Dorothy" she remarked as she sat up in bed and the maid draped a shawl around her shoulders. The maid dropped her a curtsey and made to leave the room, but she then hesitated before reaching the door, turning around to face Elizabeth.

"What is it Dorothy? You seem to have something on your mind."

"If you please Ma'am, I know it is very brazen of me and the mistress would not be pleased, but as you are soon to be married, I was thinking that perhaps you will be requiring a maid. It is not for me you understand; I am very happy here as Mrs. Gardiner's maid, but for my cousin … "answered the girl, with a downcast face so that perhaps the young lady she was so impertinently addressing would not see her blushing from acute embarrassment.

"Your cousin? Is she seeking employment? What are her skills, what is her background?"

"Oh Ma'am, I am sorry to speak so, but my aunt made me promise to help find a situation for my cousin! My aunt married a French refugee and Madeleine is their daughter and my cousin. My uncle's sisters taught her their skills as a seamstress and then in caring for and dressing ladies' hair, things they themselves had learned before they had to flee from France. I have now kept my promise to my aunt, so please forgive me, I will not trouble you again Ma'am. Please do not mention this to my mistress" before curtsying again and bolting towards the door.

"Wait Dorothy! Come back, do. Please tell me a little more about your cousin; you say she can sew and dress hair, does she have any other skills that sets her above any other maid?"

With a look of surprise, Dorothy turned back and explained that her cousin was five and twenty, very skilled with her needle and most dexterous with creating hairstyles for all occasions. She was currently seeking employment because her husband had been killed in Waterloo, leaving her with nothing. She had been educated at a seminary in London, paid for by some of the better fortuned French refugees, with the idea that she would be thus fit to be an upper servant or even a merchant's wife.

Lizzy thought that this was indeed a fortuitous moment: she had been intending to find a lady's maid and here seemed to be a person who might be acceptable in the role.

"Can your cousin come and see me before I leave town, Dorothy? I will tell my aunt that I made enquiries of you, should she ask. I would like to see her."

"Oh ma'am! How kind of you! I will send word to her at my aunt's and she will be here at your convenience!" she cried, before adding "will that be all ma'am?" as she curtsied again and almost skipped to the door.

"Well that was easily sorted" thought Elizabeth as she drank her tea, "Hopefully she is as good as her cousin claims."

Over breakfast she mentioned to her aunt that she had enquired of Dorothy whether she knew of anybody suitable or desirous of being a lady's maid, and that she had mentioned her cousin.

"I have asked her to arrange for me to meet her, I thought here would be best, and I would like you to be present my dear Aunt, to help with any advice or questions I might fail to consider. It still seems strange that I am to hire a maid for my own personal use!"

"I will be happy to assist you Lizzy, Dorothy has always been an excellent servant, so if her cousin is anything like her and is as skilled as she says, you could not do better, although I must admit that I have never had any experience in hiring a proper lady's maid myself"

Mr. Darcy, also present with the other gentlemen at breakfast, said nothing, but just smiled his approbation of Elizabeth's assuming her new role as Mrs. Darcy, mistress of Pemberley and Darcy House. Mr. Bennet also smiled, but then wickedly suggested that her getting a lady's maid would give Mrs. Bennet even more ideas on how to spend his income. Mr. Gardiner, in an attempt to defend his sister, tried to remonstrate with his brother but a big wink by Mr. Bennet to Lizzy simply made them all laugh, instead of frowning upon his language about his wife.

After breakfast, the gentlemen set off together on their morning pursuits and the ladies returned to the modiste for the first fitting of Elizabeth's wedding and ball gowns. One of the modiste's assistants was the same size as Jane, so Jane's gowns were fitted on her. Lizzy also had the first fitting of her travelling clothes, the beautiful red velvet feeling warm and soft, the matching redingote fitting her perfectly. She was to have a warm flannel petticoat to wear underneath, so with the fur-lined boots, woollen stockings and probably fur blankets in the carriage, she was going to be as warm as toast. Some of the other garments were already finished, fine lawn chemises to wear under stays, lace-edged petticoats, new nightgowns and stays. The needlework was exquisite. The finished garments were packed in tissue paper and sent off to Gracechurch Street, each garment package labelled Jane or Elizabeth. They would have such pleasure in the unwrapping of all the clothes when they got back to Longbourn.

The next visit was to a haberdasher, where Mrs. Gardiner insisted that all the purchases were to be charged to her, as part of their wedding gift to Jane and Elizabeth. Kid gloves, long for evening and short for day wear, silk stockings, fine woollen stockings, reticules, lace, embroidery threads, needlework cotton for lacework, lengths of ribbon and lace, new workboxes, needles, hooks, etc., were selected for both of her nieces, and Mrs. Gardiner felt very satisfied as she directed the parcels to be sent to Gracechurch Street.

The milliner was next; the indoor caps were done, as were the wedding bonnets. Lizzy could hardly believe the rapidity of their readiness, since the milliner had had to work with the modiste to ensure that the bonnets complemented the gowns, but ready they were, and they looked ravishing. The evening headdresses were well underway, the milliner simply waiting to see the finished ball gowns, before finishing them. The cerise coloured bonnet was still a source of amazement for Lizzy, a wide straw brim, the inside of which was lined with pleated red satin edged with soft lace framing the face, soft red velvet for the crown, lace and braid edging the whole bonnet, black velvet ties and a magnificent black ostrich feather curving across the outside of the straw brim, sewn on but to be completed by the ruby brooch she had selected from the Darcy collection she had seen at Storr's.

It was truly the most magnificent bonnet she had ever owned! It suddenly brought to Lizzy's mind the day, still only a few months ago, that she, Jane, and Maria Lucas had met the Bennet family carriage at Hatfield on their return from visiting the Collinses in Kent, and London, in the spring, and Lydia and Kitty had met them at the inn, treating them to luncheon, for which she and Jane had had to pay for because the girls had just spent all their money at the milliner across the street, and they had bought the ugliest hat that she had ever seen! Lydia had made the remark that there were two or three much uglier ones in the shop, that she would trim it afresh with prettier coloured ribbon when she got home, besides which, it would not much signify what one wore in the coming summer because the militia were moving to Brighton in a fortnight. How far away that luncheon seemed today, and how many heart-stopping emotions had she and Jane not suffered since that day, and how Lydia seemed to have been the cause of most of the unhappy emotions. Still, Lydia was now happily married, according to her letters, and Jane and herself were going to be married to the most wonderful men of their acquaintance, whom they each loved unreservedly. Lizzy put away any reproachful thoughts and chose to think of her future with her dearest Mr. Darcy, wearing this splendidly beautiful bonnet.

When they got home to Gracechurch Street, Dorothy was waiting for them and informed them that her cousin was present, waiting in the kitchen, and if it was convenient to the ladies, she was at their disposal.

"Let us have some tea first Dorothy, and if you care to bring your cousin with you to serve it, we can talk to her then" said Mrs. Gardiner, before turning to Lizzy saying "if that is agreeable to you my dear?"

"Certainly, Aunt Marianne, an excellent idea" replied Lizzy, removing her gloves and pelisse, which she passed to Dorothy.

Tea was served, with seedcake, and Lizzy and her aunt settled to talk to Madeleine. She was a striking woman, dark hair, brown eyes and a demure look to her. She was wearing black, being still in mourning for her late husband.

"Please sit down, Madeleine, and take some tea with us" said Lizzy pleasantly "your cousin has spoken to me of your wish to become a lady's maid, can you tell us more of your experience and why you think that you could be what I require?"

Keeping her eyes down, feeling very out of place sitting with proper ladies taking tea, Madeleine crossed her hands on her lap and then raised her eyes to Elizabeth.

"I believe my cousin has told you something of my circumstances. I am the daughter of a French refugee and an English mother. My grandfather and his family fled from France during the revolution, because my grandfather was a minor nobleman in the Hainault region. The family came to England, as did many of their countrymen; England being the only safe refuge for them. Their children, my father and his three sisters, came with their parents. My father met my mother, a governess with a family in London. They married, and I am their eldest daughter. My mother educated me to the best of her ability, my aunts taught me their skills in sewing and dressing hair, and then I was very fortunate to be noticed by some French ladies of my father's acquaintance. They paid for my further education in a seminary here in London. When I was twenty, I met and married my late husband, he was a non-commissioned officer in the _____ regiment and very well thought of by his superiors. We were very happy together, but with the 'Upstart', peace was never permanent. When he, Bonaparte that is, escaped from his internment and raised yet another army to over-throw the new king, my husband was sent off with his regiment to somewhere south of Brussels, under the direct command of the Duke of Wellington. He was killed in action, and I have been mourning his loss ever since. He left me with no income; his being only a non-commissioned-officer, I receive no pension, so I must seek employment again. His commanding officer, Colonel C _____ can vouch for my husband's character, and hopefully thereby, my own." By now both the ladies had tears in their eyes, as did Madeleine and Dorothy.

Lizzy was very moved at her story and took her hand: "Such unhappiness indeed. My youngest sister is married to a military man, so I can comprehend something of your feelings. You say you can sew with some degree of competence; do you have anything you can show me?"

Madeleine opened her reticule and pulled out a small garment. It was a baby's gown, made of fine white lawn and beautifully embroidered in white thread. The craftsmanship was exquisite. It was edged in a finely worked lace, of a web-like consistency.

"I made this for the child I was carrying, but I unfortunately lost my baby when I heard the news of my husband's death. I also made the dress I am now wearing, from a pattern I found from fashion magazines sent to my aunts, from Paris" as she stood up to show them all aspects of her gown, which was worthy of the best of London's modistes.

Lizzy and her aunt were now openly dabbing their eyes with their handkerchiefs. How could fate be so cruel to one person? Lizzy rose and took Madeleine into her arms; not the behaviour of a mistress, but Lizzy could not help herself. Through her tears, Lizzy told Madeleine "If you would be happy working for me as my personal maid, I will be more than happy to have you. Your story is so moving, I feel you deserve some happiness. If we can agree on terms, I will take you with me when I return to Longbourn, unless you wish to spend time with your family, then you can come to me with my aunt and uncle when they come to my wedding."

"But you have asked nothing about my skills at dressing hair, Madame!"

"Oh! That is true! Perhaps you can stay with us here in my aunt's home, until I return to Hertfordshire and you can dress my hair and my aunt's until then? Would that suit you?"

A deep curtsey on her part, Madeleine gratefully accepted the offer, and a new friendship was made, the depth and length of which neither of them realised at the time.

The ladies turned up for dinner in such elegant hairstyles, far too elaborate for a family dinner, as made Mr. Gardiner and Darcy stare in amazement at the ladies. Even Mr. Bennet was at a loss for words.

"Not that I am much in the habit of observing of ladies' hairstyles, my dear Elizabeth, but your hair is dressed in a way that even the Ton would be envious enough to want to copy, how did you achieve such a result?" were Darcy's words.

"I believe, my dear Darcy, that I have found my new lady's maid. Thanks to my aunt's maid, Dorothy; Madeleine is her cousin, skilled in sewing and hair-dressing, as you can observe, and if you are agreeable, she is to start with us from today."

"Anybody you feel is the right person for the position, is acceptable to me, my dear; do not forget that you are the mistress of Pemberley, or will very soon be, and you make any choices you deem fit, in all household matters."

"Thank you" was all that Lizzy could say, overwhelmed for a moment at his total confidence in her.

Mr. Bennet noted the exchange and felt even more content that his daughter had indeed chosen a man she could respect, and by whom she was equally loved and respected.

Chapter 7

After a few more days of fittings, and allowing for the alterations to jewels etc., almost everything was settled in Town. The new landau would be driven to Longbourn before the wedding by staff from Darcy House, bringing down any belated articles and also the flowers from Mr. Betts' hot and cold-houses.

After affectionate farewells to the Gardiners, Darcy, Lizzy, and Mr. Bennet set off for Hertfordshire, well satisfied at the progress of their purchases, and each harbouring a secret satisfaction of having purchased a surprise or two for people they held in esteem, but making no mention of it to their travelling companions.

They were welcomed at Longbourn in time for dinner, by Mrs. Bennet, Jane, Bingley, Mary, and Kitty. It was a small party; Lizzy was somewhat surprised, but Jane told her that she had managed to convince her mother that perhaps Mr. Darcy would prefer a small party for his return, and that Mrs. Bennet, still in awe of him, had deferred to Jane's advice, and the Lucases, Mrs. Long and her nieces, the Gouldings, and the Phillips had *not* been invited to dine with them on the day of their return to Longbourn. They must wait a day longer.

Dinner passed very pleasantly; Jane having taken the precaution of placing Darcy next to her father, the opposite end to Mrs. Bennet, and next to herself and Bingley. Lizzy sat next to her mother, with

Mary and Kitty, where she could better manage her mother's conversation. She spent most of dinner regaling them with stories of her shopping, current fashions, hints as to the wedding gowns and ballgowns, a description of her travelling clothes, the hat etc., with promises to show them later.

Leaving the gentlemen to their port and cigars, the ladies withdrew to the drawing room where some of the packages she had brought back with her were on a sideboard, each labelled with a name.

"T'is like Christmas!" squealed Kitty, who had just seen her name on one of the parcels.

"Oh Kitty, you are still such a child at times!" laughed Lizzy "Go ahead, open it! And Mary, this one is for you" handing another parcel to the most studious of her sisters.

"Far be it for me to indulge in childish pastimes, but a gift from you Lizzy, will always be received with pleasure" replied Mary, "even if it does not feel like a book"

"Oh Mary, just open it please, I had a great deal of pleasure in procuring it for you"

Kitty was silent: she had ripped open the package and was stunned into silence. She was holding up a white gown of spotted sarcenet, with a peacock green velvet spencer with silver buttons, a pair of white kid gloves and a pair of peacock blue dancing slippers still lying in the paper.

"Oh Lizzy! Thank you! It is the most beautiful gown I have ever had! And the spencer! And the gloves and shoes!" as she leapt up hug her sister.

"No Kitty, you must thank Papa, I chose them but he insisted that it is a gift from him to you. It is your outfit for the wedding, as my maid of honour."

"Oh! how generous my father is! I will thank him presently, I had thought that he was still angry with me, for hiding Lydia's attachment to Wickham before she ran away" replied Kitty, almost sobbing with emotion.

Mary had opened her package, containing an identical sarcenet spotted dress, a pale blue spencer, gloves, and pale blue dancing slippers. Not in the habit of being effusive, she still however seemed to struggle to hold back some tears of delight.

"Indeed Kitty, we must both thank our father for his kindness. Jane, thank you for the honour of asking me to be your bride's maid. I shall endeavour to do my utmost to justify your faith in me." She even found the necessity of going to her three sisters and giving them all an emotional hug.

Another parcel was labelled in her mother's name and duly handed to Mrs. Bennet. Opening it with as much delight as Kitty, Mrs. Bennet was in raptures over the beautiful lace and ribbon trimmed caps it contained.

"Oh Lizzy, these are beautiful! The milliner in Meryton has nothing like these! Lady Lucas will be green with envy when she sees them! As will my sister Philipps and Mrs. Long! I shall put one on right away! Jane, can you help me remove this old thing and put this one on," holding up a lacy lavender beribboned cap. Jane acceded to Mrs. Bennet's request, glancing at Lizzy bemusedly. She had received no gifts, but she knew that packages had been deposited in her room. Almost like Christmas indeed!

The tea and coffee things had been set out and presently the hot water was brought up from the kitchen. Jane and Lizzy took over the preparations and managed to have a few quiet words together whilst Kitty and Mrs. Bennet were still in ecstasies over their gifts, whereas Mary just sat quietly, stroking her dress and spencer, which seemed to be as ecstatic as Mary could achieve.

"Lizzy, the dresses are beautiful! Are the spencers an indication of our gowns?"

"Yes, I decided it would look most elegant if our maids of honour were dressed in the colours of the brides. They haven't seen their bonnets yet; they are in their rooms so perhaps we might hear a few more cries of delight from Kitty"

"And my father paid for all this? How generous he is!"

"Wait till you see your wedding and ballgowns Jane, and then you will know just how generous he has been! Our bonnets and headdresses are a wedding gift from my dear aunt and uncle Gardiner, along with several other gifts. I have been overwhelmed with everybody's generosity!"

At this point the gentlemen came into the room and pandemonium broke loose.

"Oh Papa! Papa! Thank you, thank you, thank you!" squealed Kitty as she leapt at her unsuspecting father, almost bowling him over.

"Ah, I see you have received a parcel" he replied "and I see you are quite happy with the contents thereof, my dear."

"Oh Papa, I have never had such beautiful clothes in my life!"

Mary's more moderate "Yes Papa, I too am happy with the clothes you have most kindly gifted me." was for her as exuberant as she had ever been, and considered by her family as being at the same level of contentment as Kitty's noisier, more effusive thanks.

"And what do you think of my new cap, Mr. Bennet?" cried his wife, cupping her hands around the lace edging to show it off to its best effect.

"No, no, do not bore me with effusions on ribbons and lace, my dear! However, I am pleased that you are pleased, Mrs. Bennet."

Darcy and Bingley had managed to avoid the first of the noisy thanks, since they had gone straight to the tea and coffee table to be with their betrothed.

"I am so glad that you are back Lizzy, we missed both you and Darcy, and also Mr. Bennet. I know that you have not yet had time to talk to Jane, but I am sure that you will find that she has been doing splendidly in the arrangements, both here and at Netherfield" said Bingley, shaking Lizzy's hand with warmth.

"Come Mr. Bingley," cried Lizzy, "surely as *almost* brother and sister, we can give each other a little more than a handshake? A kiss or a hug would seem more appropriate for me" as she went up to him and gave him a hug on his shoulders and a demure kiss on his cheek.

He blushed but returned her hug and also a kiss on her cheek. Darcy looked on, but said nothing, he just smiled, feeling that his family was becoming larger than it had been, just himself and his sister Georgiana, and was very happy about it. Whatever had been his original thoughts about the Bennet family, he had always acknowledged to himself that in spite of their previously considered overwhelming shortcomings, they were a close and loving family, something he had missed since the passing of his parents. He now realised just how much he had missed the warmth of such a family group, and felt pleased that Elizabeth had brought this to him.

The evening passed with pleasant conversation between them all, cards not being necessary to pass the time before supper. After supper, Mr. Bingley's carriage was ordered, conveying himself and his friend to Netherfield, Mr. Darcy's to remain at Longbourn to allow his horses to rest till the following day.

The ladies all retired to their rooms, Lizzy and Jane to the room they still shared, where packages and hatboxes were piled up in a corner.

"Come Jane, your turn to be, I hope, as ecstatic as Kitty" as Lizzy gave her several large parcels. "open this one first if you please, it is the gown I felt you would like to be married in."

Subdued by the moment, Jane slowly and carefully opened the paper and was silent for a few minutes as she took in the beauty of her dress. "Oh Lizzy! It is even more than I had hoped for! I knew I could trust you with selecting the perfect gown for my wedding! Oh! And the spencer! And these boots! Lizzy! If I had never loved you before, I could not help myself from loving you now! What is this?" she asked as her sister handed her a hatbox. "Oh! Oh! It is absolutely the most beautiful bonnet! Thank you, Lizzy!" as she hugged her sister warmly.

The noise emanating from their room brought in their mother and Kitty, who was holding a new bonnet in her hands.

"Have you seen my bonnet Jane? It is so beautiful, oh lord! look at yours! and your gown! and the spencer! Oh! the boots! Mama have you ever seen anything so elegant?! See Mama, her gown is the same colour as Mary's spencer!" exclaimed Kitty with delight. "Where is your gown Lizzy? I am guessing that it is in the colour of my spencer, how elegant, how fashionable! We will be the talk of Meryton for months! Show us your gown, please Lizzy!"

Lizzy proceeded to unwrap her gown, spencer, and bonnet, she had the advantage of knowing what they looked like, so did not *appear* as excited as the others were.

"This is my gown" as she held it up against herself, "I know that the black lace might seem inappropriate for a wedding gown, but I preferred it to silver lace. And this is my spencer, oh my goodness! these are not the buttons I chose! How? Who? These are silver gilt with, I think, emeralds! It must have been Darcy who arranged this! What a wonderful gesture! I am truly blessed! Mama, see these buttons!"

"Lizzy! These *are* emeralds! Gracious me! Did not I tell you that your marrying Mr. Darcy was as good as a lord? Get your bonnet! Get your bonnet! I need to see your bonnet! Jane's is so beautiful; I cannot bear to wait to see yours! Oh my! Lizzy, it is the most elegant bonnet I have ever seen and look Lizzy! see the pins! They are surely diamonds and sapphires! Jane's is nothing to this! Such jewels already and you are not yet even married! I shall go distracted! Three daughters married! Ten thousand a year and probably more! Lizzy I am so sorry that I did not like him before, but I am most determined to make it up to him"

Lizzy was most thankful that neither Darcy nor Bingley were present to witness to these effusions, but still felt content that her mother was so happy with her choice of husband. Whatever her mother's failings might be in the domain of decorum and respectability, she made up in her absolute devotion to the material well-being of her daughters.

After all the emotions sustained from the wedding outfits, Jane and Lizzy felt that the rest might wait till the morrow, Lizzy was tired from her travelling and really wished to retire to her bed.

Kitty and Mrs. Bennet left under sufferance, but they were looking forward to the morning when they could examine the rest of the clothes at their leisure, since the gentlemen were engaged to hunt with Mr. Bennet.

Chapter 8

"Lizzy! Jane! Wake up, wake up!"

"What is it Kitty? Is there a fire? Is someone dead or dying? It is not even daybreak!" murmured Lizzy, arousing from her slumber

"No, but I want to see your ball gowns!"

"Go away Kitty! You are still in your nightgown, the maid has not yet replenished the fire, dawn has not broken, and I am not awake enough to even throw my pillow at you!" cried Lizzy. "We shall look at everything else after breakfast, when I am awake, so go away and let me slumber on!"

Through this Jane slept on. Lizzy wondered at her ability to sleep through anything and everything. Thunderstorms never disturbed her; she would awake in the morning and be surprised at the rest of her family talking about their disturbed night, over breakfast. This was another gift of Jane's that Lizzy wished she possessed., along with her patience and sanguine temperament.

Three hours later, once the fire had been refurbished and she had had a dish of tea, Lizzy felt a little more benevolent with the world. She turned towards Jane, who was just awakening from the arms of Morpheus, stretching and announcing how well she had slept. "Were you not awoken by the ructions Kitty created at, I believe, five of the clock this morning?" Lizzy enquired of her, knowing full well that she had not.

"Kitty? Was Kitty here earlier? I did not notice a thing." For which response she was hit with a pillow thrown at her by Lizzy.

"How can you sleep so soundly Jane?! I swear that the house could fall down about us and you would sleep through it! Kitty came asking to look at the rest of the clothes I brought back with me, but it was before the maid had even stoked up the fire, so early in fact that even the cockerels hadn't crowed! I told her that we would finish looking at everything after breakfast, when Bingley and Darcy have left to shoot with my father; we will have the whole morning at our leisure."

"That is an excellent idea Lizzy, I own that I am quite excited at the prospect of seeing everything else you have procured for us, my ball gown not being the least in my anticipation of delight. By the by Lizzy, I suggest that we keep everything here in our room, because I suspect that we will probably have several visitors in the course of the morning, everyone wishes to greet you on your return from Town."

"I think that is very sensible Jane, I would like to keep some element of surprise for the good ladies of the neighbourhood, otherwise they will be all gossiped out by the time of our wedding, and that would never do!" laughed Lizzy, rising to dress.

Jane and Elizabeth went down for breakfast at nine, surprised to find both Mary and Kitty already there, along with Mrs. Bennet, none of whom were normally to be seen before ten. They were all dressed and even their hair done, so obviously something was afoot.

"Good morning girls!" cried Mrs. Bennet "Kitty has told us that we were to see the rest of your clothes after breakfast, so we thought it would be easier if we had breakfast earlier than normal, since I am sure we will have several visitors in the course of the morning."

"An excellent idea Ma'am, it is exactly what we thought too" replied Jane "we also felt that, so that we could be uninterrupted, we could unpack everything in my room, so if that is agreeable to you, we shall break our fast and then go up directly."

At that moment Darcy and Bingley entered, accompanied by Mr. Bennet, who was equally surprised at the number of ladies present so early in the morning, for he was fully aware of their late habits of rising for the day.

"My word girls, I had thought that your dinner yesterday would have been substantial enough but it seems that it was not. Mrs. Bennet you must see to a more copious dinner today. I would not like to see any of my family pass away through lack of sustenance."

Darcy and Bingley sat down next to Lizzy and Jane, who just happened to have empty chairs beside them. Both girls smiled with delight, bringing a becoming glow to their cheeks.

"You must not pay attention to my father's words, Darcy, we simply have plans for the day whilst you are out with my father," said Lizzy "my mother's dinners have never yet left anyone hungry, unable to last until the morning."

"I am well aware of that, Mrs. Bennet, all of the dinners I have had the honour of sitting down to in this house, have left nobody in any doubt of your generous portions and numerous dishes." replied Darcy, addressing Mrs. Bennet directly, perhaps for the very first time.

Mrs. Bennet, wearing one of her new bonnets that Lizzy had brought back from Town, positively beamed with pleasure.

"Why thank you Mr. Darcy, such a compliment from you indeed warms my heart. In spite of my asking, Lizzy has never told me of any dishes that you would like, so if you care to let me know, I would be only too happy to oblige you." she replied. Lizzy cringed at her mother's obsequiousness but saw that Darcy had not even mildly flinched. Was he becoming inured to it or was it for her sake? Watching him, she then noticed him unclench his jaw as he turned to smile at her.

"Well gentlemen, it seems you have an excellent day for your sport" she said, feeling happy that Darcy was making such an effort to be pleasant to her mother.

The gentlemen looked very dashing in their buckskin breeches, hunting jackets, and hessian and leather boots. Something was to be said for the fashion, which was so different from the usual day or evening attire of a gentleman. Blushing at the idea, Lizzy thought that they looked very manly. Perhaps it was the primitiveness of actually hunting, to provide food for their mates and families that made her feel very warm, causing her cheeks to turn pink.

Pork chops, bacon, kidneys, eggs, mushrooms, freshly baked bread, butter and tea and coffee made up their breakfast, which the gentlemen addressed with appetite and the ladies in more gentile portions.

As Mr. Bennet, Darcy and Bingley rose from the table, the ladies wished them a good day's sport, whilst withholding their own excitement of going upstairs, to see the rest of the garments that Lizzy had brought back from Town.

"Jane! Lizzy!" cried Kitty as soon as the gentlemen had left the breakfast parlour, "please *now* may we go upstairs?" her enthusiasm only slightly exceeding Mrs. Bennet's

"Oh yes! Let us now retire upstairs, I was sorely disappointed that I missed advising you on the trip to town to buy your wedding clothes, but I was so needed here to help Jane, so I know nothing of what you have bought! Did you attend to the list I gave you Lizzy?"

"Yes, my dear mother, I did heed your list but I also took advice from my aunt, and also Mr. Darcy"

"Mr. Darcy? Why Mr. Darcy? What would he know of wedding clothes?"

"More than you would think" replied Lizzy, and as they ascended the stairs, she explained about his years of providing for Miss Darcy, as her guardian, and about their visit to Storr's and the carriage-maker.

"Oh lordy! Lizzy, what a match you have made! Jewels, plate, a new carriage and as many clothes as you want! I am starting to have such palpitations, such a fluttering of my heart!"

"If you could leave the palpitations until we have seen the rest of what I have brought back from town, I would be well pleased Mama."

Jane opened the door to their room and was immediately struck by a crystal vase of the most stunning flowers on the mantlepiece. There was a note attached and she read it aloud: 'To our beautiful brides-to-be, Jane and Elizabeth, from your devoted fiancés, Charles and Fitzwilliam'

"Oh, how considerate they are! I would wish that when I become engaged, my beau will be as romantic," cried Kitty, 'but now to the purpose of the morning, I have been aching since so early this morning to see your ball gowns!"

"I know you have Kitty; I was the one you awoke before even the cock had crowed," replied Lizzy, "so if you will all sit down, I will proceed. First of all, I will show you the undergarments," as she brought out the parcels. Chemises of fine lawn, the bodices edged with narrow lace were brought out, followed by petticoats, hemmed in broader lace, stays, stockings of silk and the finest wool were spread out on the bed for all to admire and feel. Even Mary was drawn into the ambiance.

Next, she brought out the ball gowns, first of all, Jane's. Unwrapping it, in totally enthralled silence from her audience, Mrs. Bennet was the first to find her tongue.

"Lizzy!" she gasped, "that is the most splendid gown I have seen in my life! The pearl white damask! the finest lace, which I know must be from Brussels, and the train! diaphanous silver silk! Oh! and the scalloped hem! Those ribbons! Are those seed pearls along the bodice? Oh Jane! You will be the most beautiful woman at the ball!" she cried, totally forgetting that Lizzy would also be present. This did not disturb Lizzy, since she was not vain enough to consider herself as handsome as Jane, and had never felt any jealousy of her sister's beauty, however much it had been talked up by her mother, since as long as she could remember.

"Let us not forget the dancing slippers my dear mother." replied Lizzy, as she brought out slippers of matching white damask, embroidered with seed pearls, with a small heel.

"And your father paid for all this?" cried Mrs. Bennet, "yet he would not give a penny to Lydia!"

"Lydia's wedding was not quite the same as ours, my dear mother" said Jane, "he was very angry with her at the time, for all the stress and worry she had caused by running away, and the shame of it being public knowledge that she had lived with Wickham for two weeks before their marriage took place." But Mrs. Bennet was deaf to such arguments and she would have continued in the same tone had Lizzy not opened another parcel.

"This, Ma'am, is *my* ball gown" as she drew up to her shoulders another creation of white damask and silver silk. Inspired by Grecian gowns of old, it had a fine silver sheath of ultra-fine silver silk as an over-tunic, gathered under the bust, and pinned to the dress at the gathers by a pearl and diamond brooch, and a train in the same silk, pinned to the shoulders by diamond clasps.

"And the pearls on Jane's gown and shoes are a gift from Mr. Bingley, the brooch and clasps on my gown are what I selected from the Darcy family collection, which I told you I had seen at Storr's, so please be at ease, Ma'am, my dear father did *not* spend his entire fortune on our gowns." explained Lizzy, who did not wish for her father's kindness to herself and Jane, to be held as a reproach against him, by his wife.

Mary and Kitty were still silent: Kitty by amazement and Mary by habit. Mrs. Bennet however, was still able to articulate.

'My word you have done well for yourselves girls, Jane, I always knew you would do well, I thought that you could not be so beautiful for nothing, but *you*, Lizzy! I had thought that Mr. Collins would be as good as you could get, but you have surpassed even Jane! I sincerely apologise for doubting your abilities to capture the attentions of a man such as Mr. Darcy! With you and Jane so well married, who knows who Mary and Kitty could obtain! With both of you being so rich, there is no knowing what other rich men they might meet!"

"I thank you for my share in your wishes for our future, Madam, but unless the gentleman in question has an excellent library, his relative wealth will be of no interest to me." was Mary's dour response to her mother's hopes for her future.

"Mary!" exclaimed Jane, in a fit of anger that totally surprised them all, "my mother has only your best interests at heart, as she has always done, so please do not offend her, or me, by your sanctimonious quibbles!"

Everyone stared at Jane in amazement, they had never heard her speak so harshly to anybody in her life, let alone one of her sisters.

"I am sorry for my outburst Mary, I did not mean to be so harsh, but my mother meant nothing but kindness by you and it hurt me to hear you seemingly spurn her wishes for your well-being." was Jane's very contrite apology to Mary.

Lizzy thought this was a very good time to bring out her cerise-coloured travelling clothes and hat, to distract everyone from Jane's most uncharacteristic outburst.

"See here, all of you, have you ever seen a bonnet as wonderful as this?" as she brought out the said headwear with a flourish from the confines of its' box. It had the desired effect: Mrs. Bennet and Kitty were in raptures, stroking the ostrich feather, admiring the ruby brooch that anchored the feather in place, Kitty trying it on herself, and Mary quietly wiping away a tear, for she felt that she had indeed been unkind to her mother, if even her sister Jane could find reason to reprimand her. She might be serious and studious, but she never wished to be unkind; she simply did not always know the best way to speak her thoughts, so over-shadowed as she had always felt, by her more handsome, loquacious and exuberant sisters.

The bonnet was followed by the gown and redingote. Cerise red velvet, an underskirt straight-hemmed with black velvet, exposed by a scalloped hem of the red, held up by dove grey satin ribbons, the bodice with military-styled grey braid made up the gown. The redingote was also of red velvet, hemmed with black fur which went up the front opening, and around the neck. The bodice was also decorated in braid, but in black, and gold buttons. Combined with the bonnet it was indeed a most striking outfit.

Before their emotions, from one reason or another, could overwhelm them, a maid knocked on the door, announcing that Mrs. Phillips and Lady Lucy were arrived, and were the ladies "at home"?

"Lady Lucas! My dear sister Phillips!" gushed Mrs. Bennet as she arrived in the parlour, where the visitors were waiting. She was followed by her four daughters, who greeted their aunt and Lady Lucas with affection.

The conversation was lively; Mrs. Bennet and Kitty full of the clothes they had seen upstairs, and it was only because Jane and Lizzy had specifically begged them not to divulge too much about the wedding and ball gowns, that they refrained from divulging all, though not without considerable effort. The bridal attendant's dresses were described, as was Lizzy's travelling outfit, and a direct request for details about the other clothes was politely refused with the reply from Jane that they wished to keep those details a secret until later. Such an explanation brooked no argument, so the visitors had to, albeit reluctantly, content themselves with that.

Refreshments were ordered, but before they arrived, Mrs. Long and Mrs. Goulding were announced. They too were told only so much as the two other ladies had been told, but it was sufficient for them to have something to regale their friends with as soon as they returned home. When the refreshments finally arrived, Mrs. Bennet was showing off her new bonnets, and Lizzy, thinking of her mother's indirect boasting rights, thought it was an ideal moment to explain her acquisition of a lady's maid.

"French, you say Lizzy?" enquired Lady Lucas "she must know so much about the fashions in Paris! What an acquisition! And her skills, you say, are up to the best of our modistes in Town? What gowns you shall have! You will be the envy of the neighbourhood!"

"For my daughter, the future Mrs. Darcy, of course only the best is good enough!" exclaimed Mrs. Bennet with great pride. "He has an income of ten thousand a year, as you know, and very possibly more! He has also told Lizzy that she was to open accounts with whomsoever she wished in Town, that money was no object, she is to order whatever she feels she needs! And have I mentioned the landau he has commissioned? She had the choosing of the colours, the fittings, everything, so Mr. Bennet tells me"

Embarrassed by their mother's excessive boasting, Jane and Elizabeth tried to turn the conversation to other subjects, but this would not do; Mrs. Bennet was so full of pride she could not help herself. Kitty, understanding her sisters' discomfort, perhaps for the first time in her life, diverted the conversation by mentioning the vase of flowers her sisters had received from their fiancés.

"Such a romantic gesture, I feel, lilies, dahlias, roses, carnations and gypsophila, all sent down from Darcy House! I had no notion that such flowers could be obtained at this time of year" added Kitty, surprising her sisters at her knowledge of the blooms.

"Mary, why do you not go upstairs and fetch them down, for I am sure our visitors would appreciate them." suggested Jane, who had noticed Mary sitting in silence, looking most unhappy, probably because of her own outburst, which she herself sincerely regretted.

"And ask Sarah to help you Mary, and bring down my red bonnet" added Lizzy, turning to the others, "I think you will all agree with me, that it is the most splendid bonnet I have ever possessed!"

"I will go with Mary' said Kitty, "because if I may, I would like to show the ladies my bride attendant's gown with the spencer, may I Lizzy?"

"Of course you may Kitty, and if Mary wishes it, she can bring her own gown down too."

Lady Lucas, and the Mrs. Phillips, Long, and Goulding had not hoped for so much after the initial refusal to describe the wedding and ball gowns. Here indeed was a source of felicity, for they knew that Lizzy had only returned from town the day before, and although they were expected for dinner later in the day, here was subject enough to spread around the neighbourhood, between their leaving, and their dressing for dinner, before returning to Longbourn later for the aforementioned dinner. Their husbands, except for Mrs. Long who had sadly lost hers, did not seem to understand this need for knowledge of whatever was going on at their neighbours or acquaintance, but the ladies smiled inwardly with indulgence, for they believed that their husbands were, in fact, the biggest purveyors of gossip in the country!

Mary and Kitty returned with the flowers, Lizzy's red bonnet, and their gowns, spencers, and shoes. The next fifteen minutes was spent in exclamations of wonder and delight as the flowers were admired summarily, before the more important gowns were passed around and were unanimously considered as the finest gowns that they had seen in many a day. Kitty smiled with delight, and even Mary wore an expression of pleasure, at the admiration that was inspired. The bonnet was equally much admired, and the ruby brooch was considered as the most fitting attachment for the feather that they could possibly think of, and how fortunate Lizzy was to have attracted the attentions of such a wealthy man, whom they had always thought of as more handsome than anybody else. It was therefore with great reluctance that the visitors rose to take their leave, after rather more than the thirty minutes of visit that etiquette and convention required.

The rest of the morning was passed more quietly, the only new subject of wonder was the number of letters received in the post, most of them addressed to Mr. Bennet, therefore they knew that they would have to wait until he chose to divulge their contents and authors, something they did not feel very sanguine about, since they knew their father liked to sport their curiosity.

They spent the rest of the day looking at everything again, and discussing maids, balls, and weddings, until it was time for them to dress for dinner, which was also when the gentlemen were expected back from the day's sport.

Lizzy and Jane were the first downstairs, so eager were they to greet their respective fiancé after being apart for most of the day.

As the gentlemen entered, they were still the only ladies downstairs, so they had some privacy for their greetings, if Mr. Bennet's speed at leaving them to themselves, as he maintained he had to go to his library, to see what the day's post had brought, could be seen as tact on his part.

"And how did you all fare today?" asked Jane and Bingley at the same time. "My dear, you must have the first question, I am sorry I was so precipitous in mine" apologized Bingley, giving Jane's hand a warm kiss. Jane laughed and repeated her question to Darcy.

"It was a very pleasant day; we found the fine covies that your mother had promised that Mr. Bennet would keep for us, and I believe that much pheasant, grouse, hares, and rabbit will be on the dining tables at both Longbourn and Netherfield for some time to come. We also had some infinite luck, in spotting a deer on your father's manor, so after some considerable effort on our part, venison will also be on the menu. Therefore, if you please ladies, could Bingley and I be excused for a while, we shall endeavour to refresh our persons and garments before we are fit to accompany you both to dinner."

"We guessed as much" replied Lizzy, "so my mother has arranged for a room for each of you, and we sent for your valets, who have brought you your fresh clothes. I will ring for the butler so that he may guide you. Do you require anything else?"

"No, thank you, we shall certainly thank Mrs. Bennet for her consideration, but *only* when we are fit to be seen in the company of ladies" replied Bingley. The butler arrived and escorted the gentlemen off to the rooms where their own 'gentlemen' awaited them, to transform them from intrepid, but dirty, sportsmen, into clean, well-dressed, and freshly shaved, civilised gentlemen who might be deemed worthy of accompanying their elected ladies in to dinner.

Chapter 9

And so, the days passed; dinner parties at Longbourn, Netherfield, or at the homes of other acquaintance, filling in the time between shooting parties, morning visits, and finalizing details for the wedding, the breakfast, and the ball. The days rapidly turned into weeks, and the week before the wedding was upon them. Mr. Bennet had divulged some of the contents and authors of his super-numerous correspondence over the past weeks: friends, distant relatives who had not written in many years, suddenly found that it had long been their most earnest desire to renew the acquaintance, friendship, or relationship, which had slipped over time through one reason or another. Word had got out about the Bennet family's forthcoming elevation into apparently higher circles, and many people wished to be part of the journey. Mr. Bennet had been entertained by the letters, and had in turn entertained the others, with some of the more outrageous pretentions to claiming kinship to them and their excuses for having earlier dropped their acquaintance.

On a more immediate note, the new landau had arrived from London, carrying Madeleine and several parcels for various people, which of course provided some excitement in the front parlour, before they went to dress for dinner.

First of all, two very large, well-wrapped packages were given to Mrs. Bennet by Darcy and Bingley.

"Mrs. Bennet, please allow us to offer you these paltry gifts, as a token of our esteem for you, for having raised two such wonderful women as Jane and Elizabeth." announced Bingley, who being engaged to the eldest daughter, was the spokesman for himself and Darcy. Lizzy had not mentioned this gift to anyone except Jane, and even to her, only sparingly, so the others were completely surprised by the gesture, none more so than Mrs. Bennet, as she unwrapped her packages. The paper removed, she was looking with speechless astonishment at two matching table centrepieces comprising vases, incorporating six candle holders, standing on clawed feet, all made of silver gilt, elaborately decorated, the latest thing in silverware.

"Mr. Bennet! Have you ever seen anything so handsome?! Jane! Lizzy! My dear Bingley, my dear Mr. Darcy, how can I thank you?! I have never had such a gift in my life! How envious … but lordy! they are perfect! How impressed everyone will be when they see them! So perfect for my dining table!" was Mrs. Bennet's sincere attempt of thanking them without being too effusive, which was seriously out of character for her, but she was still somewhat intimidated by Mr. Darcy. Before Mr. Bennet could collect his thoughts enough to reply to her, without saying something that might be thought of as derogatory, Darcy turned to him.

"Mr. Bennet, sir, we have also thought of you. We recall some remarks you have made over time, of the wish that you could have your horses on the farm more often than you could get them, when they were required for the carriage," said Darcy, with a strange smile, akin to a laconic grin, on his face, "so we took the liberty, sir, of acquiring two new horses for you, since we believe Mrs. Bennet will be requiring the carriage most days, for her visits to Netherfield. The horses can be used on the farm or in harness for the carriage. We calculated that since we were relieving you of the expense of two daughters, you would perhaps, in the future, be better able to support the costs involved of two extra horses; we sincerely have your interests at heart." he finished with a theatrical bow to Mr. Bennet.

Lizzy burst into laughter, as did Jane and Bingley. "Darcy!" she gasped, "you have become as bad as my father in your remarks and delivery!" before being overcome by hysterical giggles which lasted some time, Darcy having to assist her with some watered wine before she could compose herself. Once composed, she heard some of her father's thanks, but sank into her own memory, asking herself how she had ever thought that Darcy was insensitive to the feelings of others. The thought sobered her more than the wine had done and she was able to pay more attention to the others.

Mary and Kitty were each holding a jeweller's box in their hands, and were proceeding to open them. They each contained a short pearl necklace, with perfectly matching bracelet and earrings. Perfect for maids of honour, who were going to attend a ball the following day.

"But who are these from?" cried Mrs. Bennet.

"From their father, Mrs. Bennet, and before you have one of your nervous turns and its consequences, I must inform you that I also had a set sent down to your daughter, Mrs. Wickham. I will not have it said that I do not treat my daughters equally, and as you know well, I did not have the opportunity of providing her with anything for her own wedding" replied her husband. His words had such an effect as to put a dampener on the previous merriment and a few moments passed before anyone could say anything positive. Lizzy recovered first.

"Jane, Mary, Kitty, my new maid, Madeleine, came down with the carriage, as you know, looking after these gifts, and if you wish, she will be happy to dress your hair whilst she is here. Would any of you like her help before dinner today?" To her surprise, Mary responded first.

"If you please Lizzy, I would like to accept your kind offer, I have been wearing my hair the same way since I was thirteen. My father has provided me with a beautiful gown and pearls for the wedding, and it is such an important occasion, so I think it is only proper and suitable that I try something more fashionable with my hair." which was more words that she had uttered together, that were not related to her studies, or moralising over each morning visit, since she had first started wearing her hair in braids down the side of her head, coiled into a severe bun at the nape of her neck.

"Of course, Mary! You must talk to her, let her know what you want to achieve, she is very clever and if you give her an indication, she will transform your wishes into something very stylish. My Aunt Gardiner and I were both amazed at her skills with our hair" replied Lizzy, thinking at the same time, that she herself had not spoken so many words at once to her more studious sister, for a long time. "If you go up to her before the rest of us go to dress, you will have her full attention. She can also advise you on any vestimentary queries you might have."

In the period between Lizzy finding Madeleine, and her arrival at Longbourn, Darcy had made extensive enquiries into her references, having learned through his bitter experience with Miss Darcy's previous attendant, Mrs. Younge, that no matter how amiable they might appear, thorough inquiry into their past was a necessary step to take before engaging somebody in whom one must put so much trust. Madeleine Londot had obviously passed this strict inquiry, otherwise she would never have been entrusted with so many valuable packages, on her way to Longbourn, in the newest Darcy carriage, to look after his beloved Elizabeth.

Unbeknownst to Lizzy, and all the Bennet family, the carriage had not come straight to Longbourn, as was supposed, it had gone first to Netherfield, where numerous packages and trunks were unloaded, before continuing to Longbourn. The coachman and footmen were Darcy staff and knew better than to gossip with their fellow servants from either Netherfield or Longbourn, and Madeleine seemed to already possess an innate sense of loyalty to her new mistress, enough to know to keep silent when a surprise was intended for her mistress.

As they were dressing for dinner, Lizzy chose a favourite blue sapphire gown, which she had frequently worn before. As Madeleine assisted her, dressing her hair in a new style, she pinned a blue necklace in amongst the elaborate tresses.

"Where did you get this from? I do not recognise it," asked Lizzy as she looked at herself afterwards in the small mirror she shared with Jane.

"It is a gift from Mr. Darcy ma'am, he asked me to use it if I thought it would fit with your choice of gown. The sapphires, entwined in your hair, reflect the sheen of your gown madame." Her manner of speaking was a subtle mixture of the educated English of her mother, and her father's French, which had been perfected at the academy she had been sent to thanks to the generosity of some French aristocratic lady refugees. Whilst assimilating the information passed to her, Lizzy also thought that she should improve her own mind, and was considering asking her maid to teach her French, but not at the moment; after the wedding perhaps.

"How kind of him!" was what she actually said, whilst thinking that she was so blessed by such a thoughtful man.

As she left her room, she met Mary, about to go down to dinner, and although her gown was as staid as Mary's gowns always were, her hair looked astonishing. Lizzy was momentarily at a loss for words. Madeleine had worked her tresses out of the plaits and into a crown of soft curls, swept upwards by a sequence of tiny braids, interlaced with pale blue ribbons, the whole held together by a bandeau of gold lace. Lizzy recognised the lace and the ribbons, as being the excess from Jane's wedding gown. Mary did not ask her sister for her opinion; Lizzy's facial expression said so much, and she was still too shy to ask, being so unused to caring about her appearance, when her more handsome sisters were obviously so much prettier than she. It was one of the reasons she buried her head in books; she felt she needed to become more accomplished than her sisters, so that people would overlook her plainness. She had in fact, not even looked in the mirror after her hair had been dressed, so adverse was she at looking at herself with a critical eye.

Her appearance to the others brought quiet, admiring commendation from the gentlemen, a quiet compliment from Jane, but Kitty and her mother could not refrain from their exclamations of surprise.

"Why Mary! What a transformation! You appear as pretty as your sisters, I always maintained that your hairstyling did not do your face justice, but you would not listen, just as no-one listens to me, so this is the work of Lizzy's new maid, is it? I must ask her to help with my hair for the ball, or perhaps for dinner tomorrow" was Mrs. Bennet's remarks to her daughter.

Kitty was surprised at the transformation too, but feeling closer to Mary now, since Lydia had gone away, gave a warm, sisterly response, "Mary, you look lovely, the style brings out the soft curves of your face, if Madeleine could show me how, I will try to do it for you, after she leaves with Lizzy, if Sarah cannot."

Highly embarrassed by this sort of attention, something she was not at all used to, Mary blushed, another thing she had not been in the habit of, which gave a becoming glow to her normally pallid features.

Seeing her discomfort, Lizzy changed the subject by asking the gentlemen about their plans for the morrow, leaving Mary to recover her composure, and dinner passed in a most pleasant manner for all.

Chapter 10

The final week before the wedding was a flurry of activity, with so much to see to. Flowers arrived from Pemberley and Darcy House, bouquets and garlands were made to decorate the church, Longbourn, and Netherfield. Jane and Lizzy spent time at Netherfield, assisting the housekeeper to supervise the ballroom decorations and finalising the menu for the supper. Miss Bingley arrived with Mr. and Mrs. Hurst, whom Jane greeted warmly, Lizzy less so, still seeing some degree of sneering insolence in their attitude to Jane.

Her welcoming of Miss Darcy, to Netherfield, who arrived with Mrs. Annesley and Colonel Fitzwilliam was all that was sincere, hugging Georgiana as a sister, greeting Mrs. Annesley kindly, and Colonel Fitzwilliam as a friend. Darcy looked on with satisfaction, pleased to see that the two most important ladies in his life seemed to be becoming friends as well as sisters. Georgiana could hardly contain her delight at gaining a sister.

Mrs. Bennet remained at Longbourn, to ensure that the wedding breakfast would be as splendid an affair as she could contrive, with the assistance of her cook and Mrs. Hill. Kitty, with Mary's help, was charged with the flowers for the church. Only Mr. Bennet seemed to continue with his normal activities, seeing to the farm when required, but mainly retreating to his library, allegedly to attend to business, but mainly perusing some of the more entertaining letters from people trying to reclaim his family's acquaintance, for some were almost as good as Mr. Collins' correspondence.

The Collinses had arrived, staying at Lucas Lodge, and of course the Gardiners arrived at Longbourn, two days beforehand, so they were regaled with all Mrs. Bennet's trials, tribulations, and moments of glory, none of them more splendid than the two silver-gilt centrepieces, which were on display, filled with late autumn flowers and foliage, with the best wax candles in the holders.

The day before the wedding, a dinner was held at Netherfield, uniting all the guests for the first time. Everyone was on their best behaviour, though for some, the effort involved was greater than for others. Miss Bingley seemed to require more such inner strength, having to concede defeat in her attempts to capture Mr. Darcy's heart and fortune. However, since she wished to retain visiting rights to Pemberley, she tried hard to make up in her arrears of civility to Elizabeth, was fonder than ever of Georgiana and transferred her attentions from Darcy to Colonel Fitzwilliam, who was, after all, the son of an earl, no mean conquest if she could get him, and his uniform certainly did him no disservice.

After tea and coffee, over which Miss Bingley presided for the last time as the hostess in her brother's house, the group separated, the Bennets and Gardiners to Longbourn, the Bingleys, Hursts, Darcys, and the colonel remaining at Netherfield. They would all next meet at the church.

Jane and Lizzy retired for the night, sharing their room for the very last time. Lizzy was certain she would not be able to sleep, but her attempts to talk to Jane were met with silence after five minutes, for she had fallen asleep.

Chapter 11

The next day dawned bright but chilly, the clear skies overnight leaving a hoar frost that left icy patterns on their bedroom window. Lizzy was grateful for the warm fire in her room, and even more so for the tea her new maid had brought her. She had a second cup as she sat down at her dressing table, and Madeleine proceeded to style her hair. When she was done, Lizzy was feeling very bride-like indeed, and asked to try the bonnet on to ensure that it fitted correctly, without disturbing the wonderful coiffure atop her head. She then returned to warmth of her bed, sitting up as she watched Madeleine dress Jane's hair. It had been agreed, after seeing her stunning styles over the past week, on their sisters and mother, that she would also do Jane's hair for the wedding.

For dressing on this all-important day, Sarah assisted Jane, and Lizzy was half dressed by Madeleine, but this was only after the other ladies of the house had been coiffed by Madeleine and dressed by Sarah and another maid.

Lizzy, feeling very hungry, asked Sarah to procure her some food, any food, from the kitchen. The kitchen staff had been hard at work since before dawn, finishing the preparations of the wedding breakfast, but Lizzy could not wait until after church, since she usually broke her fast around nine o'clock, and they would not be back from church until after noon. The maid came back with a tray of food for them all; the rejected cakes, pies, and biscuits, deemed unworthy of being served at the breakfast. Jane and Lizzy ate hungrily, still in their petticoats and dressing robes, before putting on their gowns. Kitty and Mary carefully protected their gowns as they ate.

Looking in the mirror and then at each other, they embraced each other, the momentousness of the day coming home to them. Mrs. Bennet, finally dressed, came into the room at this moment and was overwhelmed at the sight of two of her daughters, on the morning of their wedding, bringing tears of joy to her eyes.

"Oh Jane! You have never looked so handsome! I have waited for this day for such a long time, and look at you! A duchess could not look better! And you Lizzy! I had my doubts about your choice of colour for your gown but it looks splendid! I have never seen you in better looks! What do you think of my hair? Your maid dressed it for me Lizzy."

"I am sure it is beautiful Mama, from the little we can see with your cap on. And have you seen how handsome Mary and Kitty look?"

"Why yes, you both look splendid, but will those flowers on your heads not get squashed by your bonnets? I am glad you have those warm spencers to wear on top of your gowns, or you would freeze to death in them in the church; how came you to choose white sarcenet for the gowns Lizzy?"

Declining to respond to the last question, Lizzy said "As you will recall, ma'am, Mr. Powell has allowed us to have small braziers in the church, to take the edge off the chill, so with their warm petticoats, spencers, gloves, and shoes, Mary and Kitty should both survive the ceremony without freezing to death, in spite of not wearing bonnets. There are also heated bricks and blankets in the carriages, to keep them warm, to and from the church, ma'am"

Mrs. Gardiner knocked on the door, to remind them all of the time, and smiling her approbation of everybody's looks.

"Mr. Bennet is suggesting that you should be down by now, if you wish to arrive at the church before the brides. The ceremony is at eleven, as you know, and it is now thirty minutes to the hour. As Mrs. Bennet, and Mary, and Kitty are to come with us, and our carriage is at the door, I would advise you to come down with me."

"So late already!" cried Kitty "Come Mary, come Mama, we must leave now if we are to perform our duties for Jane and Lizzy as they arrive." So, with a flurry of activity, the party started for the church.

Lizzy and Jane, both feeling very emotional, descended the staircase together, to greet their father, waiting for them in the spacious lobby.

"My dearest girls, I know I feign to ignore everything about gowns, bonnets, and other female paraphernalia, but I feel bound to say that the pair of you look beautiful; *nobody* shall be as proud as myself, walking his daughters down the aisle. And by you getting married together, I have saved a small fortune by paying for only the one wedding breakfast" he added with a wink. Their father was incorrigible, but they would not have changed him for the world.

Sarah and Madeleine curtsied to them as they handed their bouquets to Jane and Lizzy: bouquets of lilies, orange blossom, gypsophila and carnations, with green foliage interspersed with strings of seed pearls, cascading down to form an upside-down teardrop effect. Kitty had been the author of these creations, showing a skill that even she did not know she had.

A footman opened the door to the awaiting Bennet carriage, where their maids assisted the girls in, taking care not to crush their gowns, handing them their flowers again, once they were settled. Lizzy was grateful that their comfort had been considered, with their feet on hot bricks and warm fur coverlets, for the morning was still very cold, the frost holding, in spite of the sun.

The short journey to church was made in almost total silence; each of them thinking of the changes about to be made to their lives by the ceremony ahead. The sisters would lose the close proximity of a beloved sister, and Mr. Bennet hid how forlorn he would be, at losing all sense of conversation at the dinner table by his handing over of his two most deserving daughters to Mr. Bingley and Mr. Darcy. He however kept smiling, knowing he was giving them to men who truly loved, appreciated, and respected them, and whom his daughters looked up to and equally respected. He most sincerely did not want them to go through life *not* respecting their partner, as his own youthful infatuation with a pretty, vivacious, but foolish woman had led him into marrying.

As they arrived, five minutes before eleven, they found Mary and Kitty waiting for them at the entrance of the church, to assist them with their gowns and flowers: their duties as maids of honour to the brides.

Chapter 12

The wedding breakfast was enjoyed by all, Mrs. Bennet serene at her table, certain that even Miss Bingley was impressed by it. Her daughters looked as handsome as anyone had ever looked, her table was spread with every delicacy possible, and in her new silver-gilt centrepieces, the candles and flowers were as splendid as any fashionable table in town, servants aplenty, her own and some from Netherfield to assist, and she had the supreme satisfaction that she had found not *one* but *two* wealthy men to join her family. Mr. Bennet, in a more sombre fashion, was equally happy with disposing two of his daughters to two such kind, respectable gentlemen, albeit not as entertaining as Wickham and Mr. Collins.

Mary was still in surprise at all the compliments she had received from the large congregation, which the grooms, brides and their maids had greeted at the end of the ceremony. Was it possible that she was not as plain as she felt? Had it simply been a question of her previous choice of dress and hair? She had much to ponder on, but in the meantime, she applied her stilted conversational skills to making polite wedding conversation with some of the other guests present at the table. She was fortunately placed between Jane and her Aunt Gardiner, both of them realising that she was making a great effort to be congenial, and assisting her whenever possible, happy to help her out of her self-imposed shell.

Kitty was in her element, having always been gregarious by following Lydia's lead, but also having learned some valuable lessons on decorum from Jane and Lizzy; how much a young lady may say, and to refrain some vulgarisms of expression which had marked her previous behaviour. She was sitting next to Georgiana Darcy, on her right, whose impeccable, though somewhat shy manners, she decided was the lead she should now follow. Mr. Gardiner was on her left, between herself and her mother. Next to her mother sat Mr. Phillips, who had Mrs. Gardiner to his left. Mary was at the end of that side of the table, with Jane and Bingley at the head of the table end. To their left, on the opposite side, sat Mrs. Hurst, Mr. Hurst, then Miss Bingley. Mr. Powell, the clergyman, had been invited to make up the numbers to eighteen, and to assure him of the family's esteem for his services. He was also useful because Mr. Bennet, sitting to his left, had determinedly refused to sit next to Miss Bingley, the woman who had been the source of such unhappiness to his dear Jane. To compensate this favour, he had to suffer sitting next to his sister by marriage, Mrs. Phillips, who was as invariably silly and ignorant as his wife, but fortunately she was rendered almost silent, enough to be considered as sensible, by her proximity to Colonel Fitzwilliam, sitting to her left. At the other end of the table, sat Lizzy and Darcy.

As the meal tended towards its end, Colonel Fitzwilliam and Mr. Hurst rose together.

"Ladies and gentlemen, with the servants' assistance, may we look to raising our glasses" proclaimed the colonel, as the said servants handed everyone a glass of champagne. Mr. Hurst, who still never spoke much in the present company, asked for everyone's attention once the glasses were distributed. "To the brides and grooms, Mr. and Mrs. Bingley, and Mr. and Mrs. Darcy" bowing to each couple as he proposed the toast.

"To the brides and grooms!' responded the whole company.

After the meal, most of the guests returned to their respective homes: Miss Bingley and the Hursts hoped to cleanse their memories of having sat down to a table with such people as the Bennets,

Phillips' and Gardiners, whilst Miss Darcy and Colonel Fitzwilliam returned to Netherfield for Georgiana to regale Mrs. Annesley with all the details of the wedding. Mr. and Mrs. Phillips returned to Meryton to relay the latest gossip, having been of the very select few who had been invited to the wedding breakfast, due to their relationship to the brides. Mr. Powell, a widower, wondered if the idea of inviting the officiating clergyman to the wedding breakfast would catch on, for he was not often invited to dinners, which he could not reciprocate, but he had enjoyed the occasion immensely.

At Longbourn, the much-reduced party talked over tea and coffee, then the newly wed couples went for a walk together in the grounds, to take the air, whilst the others went for a rest or an escape into the library, whichever suited them best. Mr. Bennet was even prepared to share his sanctuary with Mr. Gardiner, for the occasion.

It had been agreed that both couples would spend the wedding night at Netherfield, since the ball would be taking place there the following evening, so as the shadows began to fall on Longbourn, both carriages were ordered to take them home. Mrs. Bingley's and Mrs. Darcy's trunks had been taken over earlier, accompanied by their maids. Mrs. Bennet had agreed to Jane's request that she might have Sarah in her service, so that she would not feel totally estranged in her new home.

Mrs. Bennet wept as she waved them goodbye, turning to her husband, "I have often thought, that there is nothing so bad as parting with one's friends. One seems so forlorn without them" wiping her eyes.

"This is the consequence, you see, Mrs. Bennet, of marrying your daughters," replied Mr. Bennet, "it should make you thankful that you still have two who are single."

"It is no such thing! Jane will be at Netherfield, but Lizzy will be moving so far away. Derbyshire is at least three days' journey from here, so far off, that I cannot visit her as much as I should wish!"

"However, Madam, you will thankfully not have to wait three days before you see them again, if you recall, there is a ball to be held at Netherfield tomorrow, which even I shall attend, and if you promise not to bore me with details of gowns, lace, fortunes, beaux, and such, I shall even sit with you" was her spouse's response. Lizzy's sharp wit and ironic humour could not have come from her father, thought Mrs. Bennet in an enlightened moment, because he had lost none of his!

Chapter 13

The following evening, the Bingleys, the Darcys and the remaining Bennets stood at the entrance of the ballroom at Netherfield to greet their guests. Mrs. Bennet could not remember ever feeling so gratified and proud: welcoming guests to a ball in her daughters' honour! Who would ever have guessed such a thing! She was wearing a new gown for the occasion; burgundy silk with a profusion of pale gold lace trimmings, exactly to her taste, and a golden train; she felt positively majestic!

"I am sure even Lady Catherine De Bourgh has never had a gown as splendid as this one" was her exclamation to her four daughters, when she received the gown from town, totally unexpectedly, the week before. It was a gift from Mr. Bennet, who still cared for his wife, albeit in his own eccentric way. Having provided gowns for all of his daughters, it was only fitting that Mrs. Bennet should also receive a mark of his consideration on the occasion of their daughters' nuptials. However silly, ignorant and illiberal as she was, she had still managed to produce such daughters as Jane and Elizabeth, of whom any father could be proud. Mary seemed to have improved in looks, and Kitty was becoming less frivolous, so perhaps Lydia would be the only disappointment to his paternal feelings. A gratifying thought indeed.

Everyone who had been present at the wedding in church, but not invited to the wedding breakfast at Longbourn the day before, now had their opportunity to be part of the occasion, and to have something to regale the lesser people of their acquaintance with, in the following days and weeks. The whole Lucas family had arrived, been announced and moved on towards the brilliantly lit ballroom. Only Mr. Collins lingered, trying to do his obsequious best to gain favour from both Mr. Bingley and Mr. Darcy, but he was taken away by Sir Lucas, on his daughter Charlotte's instructions, to meet people that he, Sir Lucas, felt that his son by marriage, heir to the Longbourn estate, should meet. Elizabeth observed the stratagem and intended privately thanking her friend at some moment when they should not be under such scrutiny. The Gouldings passed through, as did Mrs. Long and her nieces, Mr. Powell, the Philips's, the Gardiners, and most of the local gossips of Longbourn, Meryton and the neighbourhood, who had pretensions enough of gentility, to be invited to what was considered as the social event of the season.

Who would have thought of such an event, after the infamous affair of Miss Lydia Bennet, with the now equally frowned upon Mr. Wickham, who had left the town with so many debts, having seduced most of the daughters of the tradesmen, and whose said debts had been paid by the generosity of Mr. Bennet? He certainly deserved some good luck after *that* particular incident, but they noted that he was a gentleman, he always had been, and good breeding will come to the fore, as they had always said.

The ballroom was ablaze with the best wax candles, and masses of blooms decorated the niches, sideboards and occasional tables. The card room was equally well decorated, with new packs of cards on each table. The company, in general, all agreed that everything had been done in a superlative style, and apparently, it was the new Mrs. Bingley who had had the organising of it all, before she was even mistress of the house!

The orchestra was now ready to start the proceedings, having entertained the early arrivals with their warming up exercises. Protocol decreed that the bride would open the ball, but here there were two brides! Protocol had the solution. The eldest bride would open the ball, seconded by her younger sister, and then they would alternate through the evening. Protocol certainly had its place in such delicate affairs.

Both newly married couples were still in a state of euphoria, having met the loves of their lives, in spite of a few minor impediments, and here they were, opening a ball at Netherfield, with Jane as its new mistress. But then, did the rules of etiquette have an answer to the following conundrum? Jane, as the elder of the two brides, had precedence over Elizabeth, but now, being the hostess of the ball, Elizabeth, as a guest and new bride, had precedence over her. Fortunately, the sisters did not attend to what etiquette might have to say on the matter, and decided to do as they pleased: Jane and Bingley would open the ball as the hosts, newlyweds, and the elder sister to Elizabeth, and Lizzy and Darcy would lead the next dances, alternating through the evening, which would give each couple time to mingle with the guests, whilst the other couple danced.

Lizzy and Darcy walked to the front of the assembling couples, second to Jane and Bingley. Overwhelmingly impressed as he had been, watching Lizzy walk down the aisle yesterday on her father's left arm, he had been almost speechless when he first saw her come out of her dressing room, seeing how beautifully his now wife was dressed. She was stunning in a creation of pearl-white damask and silver silk. It was like an old Grecian gown, consisting of a damask silk under-gown, with a fine sheath as an over-tunic, of ultra-fine silver silk, gathered under the bust and pinned to the under gown at the gathers, by a pearl and diamond brooch, which he recognised as having belonged to his mother, and an elegant train in the same silver silk, pinned to the shoulders by diamond clasps. Her headdress was a circlet of diamonds, with drop pearls, a white ostrich feather passing diagonally over the crown of her head, encircling her curled hair, which cascaded and looped down to her shoulders, held in place by diamond and pearl pins. The ensemble was finished with elbow length white kid gloves, held over the elbow by silk ribbon garters with pearls knotted at the end.

"Elizabeth, my dearest, you look like a faery queen from one of Shakespeare's tales, I knew you would look amazing, but even I could not imagine how much. Yes, Mrs. Darcy, you are most certainly handsome enough for me to dance with" as he took her hand to start the dance.

"My dear Mr. Darcy, you make me *feel* like a faery queen, and I am glad I finally meet with your approval, for I know how you hate to give consequence to young ladies who have been slighted by other men."

"Elizabeth, I doubt any man could slight you, looking as you do tonight, unless he was a blind fool, in which case he had better not dance. Speaking of such; I noticed your friend, Mrs. Collins, sent her father to rescue Bingley and myself from her husband's assiduous attentions, I shall find a way to thank her later."

"No Darcy, *I* shall do so, because she would be highly embarrassed if she thought you had noticed her stratagem. It is embarrassing enough being married to such a man, but she chose him with her eyes open, and so far, appears satisfied with her lot. Now *there* is the man who, if he was the last man in the world, I could not be prevailed upon to accept. Fortunately, thanks to your infinite kindness, I shall never be put to the test, again." laughed Lizzy.

Cotillons, quadrilles, and even the new dance, the waltz were danced, along with the country dances which were still popular. The sets were full, the older ladies sitting together, comparing opinions on the dancing ladies, their gowns, and had anybody noticed how like her sister Elizabeth, the new Mrs. Darcy, Miss Mary Bennet looked in her white gown? and did not she look almost handsome with the way she had done her hair? They must of course remember that she was now 'Miss Bennet', being the eldest unmarried daughter of the Bennet household, and had they heard that Mrs. Darcy had a French maid now?

Mrs. Bennet sat with Lady Lucas, Mrs. Phillips and Mrs. Collins, Charlotte, using her condition as an excuse *not* to dance with her husband, who had therefore retired to the card room, was enjoying herself immensely. Mrs. Bennet was unstoppable in her felicity of having two daughters so well married. Lydia and Wickham were forgotten, Jane and Elizabeth were her favourite daughters. Having Jane settled at Netherfield was such a comfort to her, for she would miss Lizzy terribly, Pemberley being so far away, and did they know that the grounds of Pemberley were a full ten miles round? Her sister Gardiner had told her so and she had had it from Mr. Darcy himself when they were there with Lizzy in the summer. Lady Lucas bore with it all in good grace, recalling the previous ball at Netherfield, twelve months previously, when Mrs. Bennet had gone on and on about her hopes, at her joy of having Jane well settled, which at the time had turned into nothing, whilst she herself had had no hope of such happiness, but that was before Charlotte had surprised them all and married Mr. Collins. Even now, Lady Lucas was still one step ahead of Mrs. Bennet, because her dear Charlotte was with child.

Kitty was never without a partner, so therefore was happy, and Mary was not sure of how she felt: she had received many compliments on her appearance, she was addressed as 'Miss Bennet', a title she had always known Jane to carry, and so many gentlemen asked her to dance, that she could not accept them all! She tried to seek refuge with Mrs. Bennet, but hearing her in full flow of her felicity, she looked about her to see if her Aunt Gardiner was free and not too surrounded by the local gossips. She found her sitting with Miss Darcy, who was also feeling a little lost among all the unknown faces, and had sought refuge with the kindly person whose acquaintance she had made in the summer. They willingly made room for Mary and they settled down for a cosy talk, though Mary herself did not say much.

Mr. Bennet and Mr. Gardiner had retreated to the cardroom, Mrs. Bennet's constant talk of gowns, lace and jewels having released her husband of his promise to sit with her. By playing with Mr. Goulding and Mr. Phillips, they managed to avoid playing with Mr. Collins, so even the gentlemen were having a very pleasant time.

The call to supper was made, the two bridal pairs leading the way. A slight rearrangement of groups occurred, bringing Kitty into Mrs. Gardiner's, Mrs. Long and her nieces joined Mrs. Bennet, and Charlotte escaped and sat with Lizzy and Jane. The cards players, oblivious to their surroundings, would have played on had Darcy and Bingley not gone themselves to fetch them. Whilst they were gone, Lizzy took the opportunity to thank Charlotte for her astuteness earlier in the evening.

"I know, Charlotte, that Mr. Collins meant well, but we appreciated you sending Sir Lucas to fetch him away. As we were still welcoming our guests, Darcy and Bingley could not attend to his conversation as well as they felt they ought."

"Make no apology for their behaviour to Mr. Collins, Lizzy, I know how he can rattle on, and it is not always to the taste of his listeners. Not everyone has Lady Catherine's forbearance with him" was Charlotte's laughing reply "but hush, here come your husbands. I am so happy for you, I am sure you both will be very happy, though I will miss you terribly Eliza. Please write to me when you can, I shall look forward to your news. It will be refreshing to hear of things that are not told me by Lady Catherine, and repeated by Mr. Collins. Being at Pemberley or town, you will be able to tell me news that my family will not know of."

"Mrs. Collins" said Darcy as he kissed her hand, "I am sure Elizabeth has expressed her great pleasure that you were able to come into Hertfordshire for our wedding, I know she set great store by you being present."

"Thank you for your kind words, sir, I would not have missed Eliza's wedding for the world, and I have just been telling her and Jane, of mine and Mr. Collins' wishes for your happiness. Ah, I see him now, he is with Mr. Powell but he is looking for me, so I will leave you to your supper and I will join them."

"Now there goes a very tactful lady, my dear Jane, I can understand why she is yours and Lizzy's particular friend" said Bingley.

Supper over, the dancing continued, though with fewer couples. The waltz was played again, still considered quite scandalous. Lizzy did not know the dance, but Darcy and Georgiana did, so they lead the way and everyone looked on. Opinions were divided: some thought the close proximity of the couple was outrageous, others felt that the speed and movements would prevent any impropriety, besides which, a lady would need to be supported as they spun around and around. And if Mr. Darcy could dance the waltz with his sister, at a private ball, then surely it could not be as bad as the talk from town had made it out to be.

The ball started to draw to a close, people were departing, impatient to tell all that which they had seen and heard. Miss Bingley was relieved that she did not have to stand and bid farewell to the guests, that was now Jane's task. Mrs. Bennet again managed to manoeuvre it so that their carriage was the last to arrive, though this time, the hosts managed to hide their fatigue somewhat better than some of the hosts of twelve months ago.

"My dearest Jane, it was a wonderful ball, everybody said so, the flowers were splendid, nobody had ever seen such a display, or could have done better, and the supper was delightful. With my assistance, you did very well with your first duty as mistress of Netherfield! Now Lizzy" added Mrs. Bennet, "remember that you are all invited to the Lucases for dinner tomorrow. It will be the last dinner we have together for a long while, for you leave for town the next day."

Mr. Bennet hugged both of his daughters and shook his sons' hands "It was a very pleasant evening, you did extremely well my dear Jane, in spite of your mother's assistance. You both looked so handsome in your gowns, I almost felt I could describe them to the people in the card room, but fortunately, I refrained from disturbing them, keeping my descriptions to myself, however I am sure Mrs. Bennet will remind me of the gowns, lace, and jewels worn by every female in the room for days, weeks, even *months* to come."

Chapter 14

Dinner at the Lucases was a noisy affair, everyone determined to further discuss yesterday's ball, anything they might have missed from the wedding, catch the latest news, gossip, and Mr. and Mrs. Darcy's travel plans. The Collinses were to leave the following day also, to face Lady Catherine's wrath, if required, but Charlotte's feelings were bolstered by seeing her friends happily married, and Mr. Collins must fend for himself, her own condition being an excuse for not accompanying him to Rosings *quite* as often as he would wish. Her affectionate goodbyes to Lizzy occurred in the privacy of the breakfast room.

The following morning, the Bennet family, along with the Gardiners, came to breakfast at Netherfield, for Lizzy and Darcy were to set off from there afterwards. There were two Darcy coaches to travel to town; the family coach which had brought Georgiana and Colonel Fitzwilliam down for the wedding, and the new landau. Because the weather was so cold, it was decided that they would all travel in the coach, with warm blankets and hot bricks, and their servants would travel in the landau, equally equipped against the cold, but not as spacious as the carriage. They were only travelling to Darcy House, so it would not be too arduous.

Elizabeth looked splendid in her travelling outfit, and she certainly appreciated the layer of flannel petticoats under the velvet gown and redingote. Her gloved hands also had the additional warmth of a black fur muff.

"Lizzy, take care, and be sure to write when you can,' cried Jane, "and tell me all about Pemberley when you get there. We are so looking forward to joining you for Christmas!"

"Yes Lizzy" repeated her mother, "be sure to write and tell us all about town"

Kitty and Mary farewelled their sister in quieter tones, promising to write on Kitty's part and promising to spend more time with her mother than she was wont to do, on Mary's. They also said goodbye to Georgiana, whom they had befriended during her time in Hertfordshire, and her guardian, Colonel Fitzwilliam.

Mr. Bennet was very emotional, farewelling his favourite daughter and her husband, who he had learned to sincerely esteem and respect.

"I know you will take good care of her, Darcy" was all he could bring himself to say as he shook his hand warmly.

The Gardiners hugged them all and promised to visit them when they themselves returned to town in three days' time.

"Let us be off or else we shall be obliged to remain for dinner, and Mrs. Clayton shall be somewhat displeased with us missing the excellent dinner she and the cook will have undoubtedly contrived" said Darcy, trying to curb the emotions everyone was feeling.

"Just let me hug Jane one last time" begged Lizzy, putting the action to her words, before rushing on to hug her father. "You must come to Pemberley for Christmas, Papa, I shall be sorely disappointed if you do not" and then turned back to Darcy so he could help her into the carriage.

Everyone was assembled on the steps of Netherfield to wave them off, even Miss Bingley and the Hursts; Miss Bingley, because she wanted to make a good impression on the Colonel, and the Hursts because Bingley had made it quite clear that he wanted them all to be assembled to send the party off.

The journey was uneventful, the heated bricks still retaining much of their warmth as they arrived at Darcy House. The landau had travelled on ahead, so had already arrived, thereby giving Madeleine time to unpack her mistress's trunks, some of which had been sent off before the wedding.

The senior servants aligned in front of the house, to welcome their new mistress. Mr. Parsons and Mrs. Clayton, Lizzy had already met, and they did the honours of introducing the first and second footmen, the parlour maids and Mrs. Appleby, the cook, before following the Darcy's indoors, where it was considerably warmer.

A meal was declined, but light refreshments with tea was acceptable to the travellers, before retiring to their rooms to rest and change for dinner. Not at all sure as to where her room was to be found, Lizzy looked somewhat lost, until Darcy took her hand on his arm and said "Come my dearest, I shall show you your London accommodation, well, at least the resting and changing for dinner part, for the moment. Your rooms are next to mine."

He showed her a handsomely fitted room, blue and cream with gold accessories and fittings. Through an archway, was her dressing room, where Madeleine was preparing the water and towels for her ablutions, before a gown and jewels were selected for the evening. The space for gowns was enormous, by Lizzy's experience, her clothes looking insignificant in the space allocated. There was a tall, vertical row of narrow drawers, where her jewels were to be kept, and she wondered whether she would ever have enough of anything to fill the space. Rest was out of the question, so eager was she to explore her new chambers, but after an hour, Madeleine reminded her that she should now dress for dinner. Not wishing to keep everyone waiting, she hastened to dress, still unused to the assistance of Madeleine, who facilitated the process enough for her to have time to re-dress her hair, which had been somewhat crushed by the wearing of her splendid bonnet during the journey.

Dinner was even better than the previous one she had had at Darcy House, in the company of her father and Mr. and Mrs.

Gardiner. As the gentlemen remained behind for their port, Georgiana led her to the same drawing room as before, saying that her brother had had it decorated to her taste because she had taken a liking to the room during the previous winter, but of course if her sister Elizabeth liked it for herself, then of course she would remove her possessions.

"You will do no such thing, Georgiana, the room is perfect as it is, and I am hoping you will indulge us with some music when the gentlemen return" was Lizzy's response, "and I am also hoping you will instruct me into being as nearly proficient as yourself on the piano, if it can be achieved *without* spending all day practicing that is, in which case you will have to suffer my continuous requests to hear you play, for you play so well my dear sister."

Georgiana blushed with pleasure, feeling that life was going to be a lot more agreeable with a sister such as Lizzy to talk to and confide in. She had never before realised what she had missed: she had always had her brother to talk to, but with him being ten years older than herself, and also her guardian, her awe of him had not really encouraged the sort of intimacy she was now already beginning to enjoy with Elizabeth.

The gentlemen soon joined them; Darcy because he was still euphoric at being actually married to Elizabeth and the Colonel because Darcy had stood up after just one glass of port, and announced that he was going to join the ladies. The evening passed very pleasantly, with Georgiana's playing, some songs from all concerned, including a beautiful duet from Georgiana and her brother.

If this was to be her daily fare; elegant, intelligent conversation, talented piano playing by her new sister, and pleasant singing, and Darcy, Elizabeth felt she would adapt very well to her new life.

Chapter 15

———•———

The next few days passed very pleasantly, with mornings spent finding her way around the house and meeting with the housekeeper, Mrs. Clayton, and Mrs. Appleby, the cook, to discuss how they would manage things. Lizzy, being the mistress, could of course do what she wanted, but since she felt a little shy at taking on such a seemly well-run household, thinking that she would perhaps offend, she simply asked the two ladies to carry on as before, and to bear with her as she learned her new duties, and to answer her honestly if she asked them for their opinions.

Darcy delighted in accompanying her to many of the points of interest in town, knowing that most of them would be a novelty to her, so they spent many a happy hour together, even finding time to drive along Rotten Row and in Hyde Park, when the weather was fine. Everybody seemed to know Darcy, or seemed to want to know him, and they were all very curious to catch a sight of the country girl who had walked away with the most eligible bachelor of the past few seasons. Lizzy soon learned the meaning behind some of her husband's reactions: a curt nod in the direction of whatever salutations were directed at them, meant the person was not to be encouraged. A nod and a touch of his hat meant he was willing to make an effort, whilst if there was a smile included, Lizzy would pay attention as to the name of the person thus favoured. If he smiled and actually introduced her to them, then she felt confident that she was meeting one of his friends.

One such couple were a naval gentleman and his wife, Admiral and Lady Wentworth. The admiral had been knighted, about ten years previously, and now recently made a baronet. Lady Wentworth was herself the daughter of a baronet, albeit an impoverished one, but had been happy and prosperous since her marriage to her husband, whose suit, Lizzy found out later, had been refused initially, due to the persuasion of her family, who thought him unworthy to become the husband of a baronet's daughter. After several years of mutual unhappiness, they had met again and come to a better understanding, and since Anne Elliot was then of age, she did not need her father's approval, had he sought to withhold it, but Sir Walter had not approved with the best of grace.

The Gardiners arrived back in town and visited Elizabeth in her new home, seeing her for the first time as mistress of her own house in town. Elizabeth positively glowed with happiness, and once again Mrs. Gardiner secretly felt very self-satisfied, in having been of real assistance in bringing the couple back together, with their travels and residence in Derbyshire during the summer. It was indeed a happy marriage when the couple were so well matched in temperament and tastes. Mr. Bennet could not have disposed of his dearest daughter to a better man.

The Gardiners and the Wentworths were invited for dinner that evening, and with the Colonel expected too, it promised to be a very pleasant affair. Elizabeth dressed with care, choosing yet another new gown, for which Madeleine had selected the appropriate jewels and dressed her hair with ribbons and jewelled pins. Lizzy felt like a queen and her husband's smile, as he joined her to take her down to await their guests, was silently eloquent in his admiration.

True to military punctuality, the Wentworths arrived precisely at the designated hour, closely followed by the Gardiners, who were punctual as a natural courtesy to their hosts. It had been agreed between themselves that Darcy would make the introductions between the invited guests, so it was done without too much ado and without many of the embellishments that seemed to be the fashion of the day. Colonel Fitzwilliam and Georgiana had met the Wentworths before, so were quite at ease with everyone. They were in the more formal drawing room, preferring to keep the smaller one for private, family use.

Without it being intended, the ladies and gentlemen settled into two groups, one with the gentlemen talking of the latest news in the country and the ladies, of fashions, people, and admiring each other's' gowns and hair. Through this informal channel, they got onto more intimate subjects such as weddings and how they themselves came into the married state. All of this was new to Georgiana so she listened in relative silence, as Lady Wentworth modestly divulged some of the trials and tribulations of her courtship with the first of all Lieutenant, and then later, Captain Wentworth. That was now over ten years ago and she felt even happier now than at the time, having been blessed with three children, a son and two daughters. Before anyone else could start on their own journeys to the wedded state, Mr. Parsons announced that dinner was served, so whispering to each other, the ladies promised to continue the conversation whilst the gentlemen took their port after dinner.

Again, dinner was superb. Even though accustomed to her mother's excellent table, Elizabeth was surprised at the talent Mrs. Appleby had for contriving victuals into dishes that would not make a French chef blush; the woman was amazing! Mrs. Appleby had admitted that when there was a big dinner to be prepared for, she did have the assistance of two chefs from one of the top hotels in town, because try as she may, she could not get her staff comfortable in preparing for large dinner parties for five-and-twenty or thirty people, incorporating up to forty different dishes. Elizabeth fully understood the staff's trepidation.

As dinner was finished, Lizzy rose from the table and invited the ladies to join her for tea and coffee, leaving the men to their port and cigars. Darcy was somewhat surprised at the alacrity of the ladies as they quickly followed Lizzy.

"Now," said Mrs. Gardiner, after being helped to tea, "since Lady Wentworth was so kind as to assuage our curiosity as to how she came to be married, I supposed it is up to you, Elizabeth, or myself to tell the next tale, which would you prefer, Lizzy?"

"Oh! you, please my dear aunt, my tale is still too new and perhaps, apart from Lady Wentworth, you are fully aware of my journey, so your story will be new to all of us, and I admit to a great curiosity myself, never having dared to ask till this moment, for fear of seeming impertinent or unduly curious."

"So be it then, settle down ladies, because this is how my journey to matrimony began: I was raised as the only daughter, in fact the only child of a very respectable merchant. At first, we lived in Derbyshire, only five miles from Pemberley in fact, but as his business prospered, my father moved to London. He was able to give me a good education, sending me to one of the better ladies' seminaries here in town, but so that I did not get too many airs and graces, he also insisted that I learned how to run a household, from the kitchen hand upwards, so I was made to replace the scullery maid for a day, and then all of the other servants, a day at a time. It might seem unjust, even cruel, but I am glad I was made to do it, because I now fully appreciate what each of my servants does, and I hope that I am never unjustly short with them, or condescending. When I was old enough, my father also took me to his warehouse, two days a week, and taught me how he made his money, how to keep the accounts, and how to see if someone is cheating. Again, a valuable lesson that I learned, which later was to stand me in good stead.

When I was two and twenty, my father unexpectedly died, leaving the business to me, on the understanding that I was to take care of my mother, which I thought was only natural. He recommended a friend of his, an older merchant, resolutely unmarried, to go to if I needed advice on any business matter. I occasionally went to him for advice, but only on small matters, for I was able to manage the warehouse, thanks to my father's judicious instructions and forethought. Things were going quite well until my mother decided to remarry.

The man, and I call him just a 'man', for he certainly was not a gentleman, who had somehow won her affections, had persuaded himself, and then my mother, that she should have inherited my father's business, instead of me, his daughter. He persuaded her that, as her husband, he could act for her, to get the business back, under her name, quite omitting to mention to her that, as her husband, all her property would belong to him, to do with as he pleased. So, totally under his influence, they were married. From that moment on my life became quite uncomfortable. We were all living in the same house, the one my father had built, and my step-father then started and then kept on demanding money, insisting that since it was stipulated in my father's will that I was to look after my mother, as my mother's husband, he should be looked after as well.

I felt this was not right, neither for my mother nor myself, so I went to see my father's friend, to whom I explained all that had occurred, including the continuous demands for money. He just sat there, looking at me gravely. I thought that either he didn't believe me, or that I was some foolish young woman who had gotten herself into a scrape. Then he stood up, leaned towards me and said "There is only one thing to do then"

"What? sir?"

"You must consent to be my wife, and then I can act for you in all good conscience"

"But Mr. Gardiner! you barely know me, nor I you! I cannot and will not marry a person simply for the sake of convenience, no matter how grave my situation is!"

He then took my hand and told me that my response was exactly what he was hoping for, proving to him I had integrity, and would I give him permission to attempt to win my heart. Well! As you can imagine I was quite shocked and had to sit down!

It appeared he did not relish the thought of marriage to someone of weak intelligence, having seen his own two very ignorant and giddy sisters captivate normally quite intelligent gentlemen, whose only failing was to have succumbed to the beauty and charm of youth, and then each had had time to repent over the years. He admitted he had long admired me, but felt himself too old for me, so had said nothing. I was in such a state, as you can possibly imagine, that I completely forgot why I had gone to him in the first place, until he reminded me.

"Miss Gaze, I will make enquiries for you and act for you, independent of whether you accept or not to be my wife. I promised your father I would do so if you needed help, and I am a man of my word. I know some men of law, and my own solicitor can help me find the right people, he is a very talented attorney."

And so, he enquired and found that my father's will stood firm and in fact, there was a codicil which mentioned that in the event of her remarriage, my mother was to receive an allowance which would amount to a total of one hundred and twenty pounds per year, since her new husband would be supposedly supporting her, and therefore she would not require more.

You can imagine how relieved I was, that that man could not take everything that my father had worked for, and squander it, for that was why he married my mother, he initially thought that she had inherited the business, and when he found that it was not the case, he sought to manipulate her into coercing me to give her everything.

Well, girls, Lady Wentworth, I can hear the gentlemen about to join us, so, as you can guess, Mr. Gardiner did indeed win my heart and we married, at about the same time as yourself, Lady Wentworth."

After such a tale, Lizzy, Georgiana, and Lady Wentworth ("please, call me Anne,") could hardly say a word, indeed they had to force themselves to appear their normal selves as the gentlemen came into the room. Who would have thought that Mr. Gardiner was in fact a terribly gallant romantic? Lizzy herself had only heard that her uncle had met her aunt, as an older man, in a later period of his life. Aunt Marianne was in fact twenty years younger than Uncle Edward!

The rest of the evening passed as pleasantly as an evening could, with company so equally suited in manners and like minds, as Lizzy took care to mention to Darcy as they retired to their dressing rooms, where their maid and valet awaited them.

Chapter 16

The days passed, each as new and fascinating to Elizabeth as the previous one, but after a week, she was quietly pleased when the day arrived for their departure for Pemberley.

Georgiana was to remain in London with Mrs. Annesley, for another two weeks, to have the advantage of tutors and dancing lessons, returning to Pemberley with Colonel Fitzwilliam, in time for the yuletide festivities. This also gave Fitzwilliam and Lizzy time alone together. London, society, and the constant activity was pleasant as a novelty to Lizzy, but they both felt they needed more private time together, to enjoy each other's company and learn to know each other better.

Heading off to join the Great North road, which followed the ancient roman road, they spent two days on the journey, stopping off overnight in the town of Peterborough, which, at Lizzy's request, they visited the cathedral the following morning, before continuing their journey. This allowed the landau, carrying their servants, plus much of their luggage, to go on ahead and be ready to assist them when they arrived at Pemberley in the early evening, dusk coming down very early thus far north, being but three weeks away from the winter solstice.

Torches lit the wide approach to the house, and as at Darcy House, the senior servants awaited their master and new mistress on the front steps. Some, such as Mrs. Reynolds, the housekeeper, and Mr. Robson, the butler, Lizzy had met during the summer, so the introduction was not as intimidating as her first meeting with the staff at Darcy House. Formal bows and curtsies were executed rather rapidly, as everyone was wishing to return to the warmth of the house, a clear sky filled with stars announcing a very cold, frosty night, and the early evening air was already very chill. Tea and refreshments were ready in one of the drawing rooms to warm the travellers up.

Mrs. Reynolds had asked her, once the tea had been poured and handed to her, at what time she would like dinner to be served. Although she knew she was now the mistress of Pemberley, Lizzy realised that she would need time for the role to come naturally to her. She therefore asked Mrs. Reynolds at what time would the cook think it the best, since she did not wish to spoil what she knew would be an excellent dinner. Coming back to her, the housekeeper suggested that seven o'clock would be ideal, if that suited Mrs. Darcy. It did, so Mr. Robson was informed and the household reacted accordingly, each knowing their role and place. From the morrow, Elizabeth would settle meals and times for the day, with the housekeeper, during their daily morning meeting.

"Thank goodness for flannel petticoats and a warm, velvet travelling dress!" exclaimed Lizzy to Madeleine as she was shown to her new rooms. "I hope you were not chilled to the bone travelling up today, I was certainly most glad of the heated bricks, and the fur blankets kept us warm and snug as well."

"No madame, we were quite warm, thank you" as Madeleine showed her to rooms in a part of the house that Lizzy had not previously seen during her visit in the summer. Again, she was pleased with the taste of the man she had married: nothing was ostentatious, the furniture and ornaments were quietly elegant and of the best quality, no awkward taste had marred the beauty of the fine rooms. The walls were lined with pale primrose yellow silk damask and some very fine paintings. The large windows were draped by matching yellow brocade curtains, thickly lined, trimmed with green, blue and gold. A large cream-coloured marble fireplace housed a fine fire which had warmed the room in spite of the cold outside, and the oak floors were covered with thick carpets of blues, greens, pinks and golden yellow. It gave the rooms an impression of Spring! Her heart was starting to swell up with pride, it was certainly quite something to be married to such a man as Fitzwilliam Darcy, and to be mistress of such a fine home.

At six, Madeleine came to assist Lizzy with her ablutions and selection of her evening attire for dinner. The dressing room contained more gowns, and shawls, and shoes, and boots, than she had ever possessed in her life. All of them new, most of them acquired in Town and sent up ahead. A relatively simple green and yellow gown was her choice, perhaps inspired by her room's spring-like decoration, finished with a magnificent cashmere shawl in coordinating colours. It being her very first dinner actually alone with her husband, she decided on a simple hairstyle and a plain gold neck chain and cross, and earrings.

Darcy obviously approved as he met her at the top of the staircase, to escort her down to dinner. "You look beautiful my dearest" he said, "I can see that you share my taste for less finery when we are alone at home."

"I am glad of it, my dear Fitzwilliam, for I would like to keep our private family time quite simple, saving the finery for the grander occasions, and tonight is our very first dinner with just you and I." she replied, "And my first as mistress of Pemberley. You cannot imagine how the feeling is, you who have always lived here; my heart is swelling almost to bursting, at my good fortune in having found and attracted such a man as yourself, who also happens to possess a very nice house!" she added mischievously, her natural spirit starting to come back to the fore, after the long days of novelty and travel, and the slight intimidation she had felt when she had first arrived earlier in the evening.

Dinner was served in the small family dining room and was as excellent as Lizzy had anticipated: Mrs. Bruton, the cook at

Pemberley, was obviously every bit as accomplished in her art as Mrs. Appleby in Darcy House. Having been accustomed to a good table at Longbourn, she was very pleased to have such skilled staff of her own; she could recall some dinners she had attended at families in Hertfordshire, which had left herself somewhat hungry and had often over-strained Mrs. Bennet's ability to remain tactfully silent. Lizzy smiled at the remembrance and shared her feelings with Darcy.

"Had I known, my dear Elizabeth, that you were in danger of fading away from lack of food, I would have made my offer of marriage so much sooner!" he answered, replying to her sense of humour with his own, which suited them both. They never seemed to lack subjects for conversation, which would have surprised most of his early acquaintance in Hertfordshire, who had judged him as a somewhat proud, taciturn man, above being pleased. Lizzy herself had been one of his earliest and most severe critics, but here they now were, a year later, husband and wife, and both very happy to be so.

Dinner finished, they both returned to the small drawing room, there being no gentlemen present to require Darcy's presence over port and cigars. Lizzy offered to play for him, but he declined, preferring for them just to sit together with her head on his shoulder, talking quietly about everything and nothing, the wedding, the ball, their time in Town, Peterborough cathedral, the staff, the estate, which he would show her over the next week if she cared to do so, and the weather was fine, how did she like her rooms, was there anything he could do, did she want any alterations made, because she just had to say so and her wishes would be attended to, and perhaps tomorrow they could go to Lambton, and next week to Matlock.

And thus passed their first evening together at Pemberley, before retiring for the night, to their adjacent rooms, having been assisted by Thomas Giles, his valet, and Madeleine, her maid. It is nobody's business but their own of how the nights were passed and it is not the intention of this work to pry the doors open.

Chapter 17

Whatever plans they may have made the evening before, were to be put on hold for several days, for word had got out of their return and everyone wished to come and pay their respects, and meet the new bride who had made off with the most eligible bachelor in the country, of the last eight years! For some she was all that they had heard about her, beautiful, talented and charming, for others she had little fashion, was too provincial in her manners and she must have entrapped him with charms a lady would not stoop to use, for she had possessed no fortune worthy of mention, as far as they had heard, and for still more she was judged as a lady, who had yet to make her mark in society, rather pretty or quite handsome, and if she gave balls and good dinners, would most certainly do well. However, no-one voiced their opinion whilst at Pemberley, Mr. Darcy's position in society was far too high to allow such liberty of expression in his own house.

The most interesting to Elizabeth of this influx of visitors were Lord and Lady Matlock, Darcy's uncle and aunt. His mother had been Lady Anne Fitzwilliam, sister to Lord Matlock and to Lady Catherine De Bourgh. She had married the Mr. Darcy of the time, for love, which had caused eyebrows to be raised, for surely no successful marriage should be based on love; that was something the lowest classes possibly did, or heroines in novels. However, the marriage had proved to be very happy and it was only cut short by her untimely death some dozen or so years ago.

Darcy made the introductions, proud of his wife, and proud of himself for having made her his wife, and he said as much to his aunt and uncle. As Lizzy curtsied to them, she blushed from embarrassment at his effusion, it was so unlike him! Apparently, his relations thought likewise, for they just looked at him in surprise, before smiles wreathed their countenances.

"My dear boy" said Lord Matlock as he took Darcy's hand between both his own and shook it warmly, "we are all so happy for you! Richard told us all about Elizabeth and the wedding, but we did not dare hope that the half of it was true! Your mother and father would be equally, if not more delighted for you Fitzwilliam!" Lady Matlock had turned to Lizzy and embraced her, welcoming her into the family, and commenting that she had not seen her nephew look happier since he was a child.

"He is so changed! Not in fundamentals, but he was not a very outgoing child, from the moment his mother died, and having been sought after, so avidly and for so long, as a highly desirable and suitable match for many a daughter, all over the country, he withdrew further into his shell. I was beginning to despair of him ever being tempted into matrimony! You have changed all that, Elizabeth, and we could not be happier for you both."

"Indeed," added Lord Matlock, "Lady Catherine *did* write to us to voice her opinion on what she considers a disgraceful connection, but having heard Richard speaking of Elizabeth so positively, we decided to withhold *our* judgement until we had seen you both together, and we can certainly say that my sister Catherine has got her opinion wrong, yet again. You may have noticed, my dear Elizabeth" turning to her, "that Lady Catherine can be quite vociferous in her opinions on most things. This intimidates many people, but I believe you are not one of them, from something Richard said in one of his recent letters to his mother. He writes mainly to his mother, only writing to me to request the occasional funds, but since I recall doing exactly the same myself, when younger, I cannot be too harsh on him." he chuckled.

The morning visits were now over, and the Matlocks were about to leave, when Darcy asked them if they cared to accompany himself and Elizabeth to Lambton, and perhaps stay for dinner. The dinner invitation was declined, for they had other arrangements for the evening, but they were happy to go into Lambton and further their acquaintance with Elizabeth. The ladies strolled arm in arm along the well-paved streets, looking at the displays in the shop windows and making the occasional purchase, the gentlemen were happy to walk behind them, watching with pleasure as their wives become better acquainted.

During their absence, more calling cards had been left, which boded ill if they wanted to spend quiet time together over the next few days. They came up with a plan over dinner: by rising relatively early, having breakfast by nine, they could leave and go around the estate for an hour or two in the landeau or curricle, before returning to dress for visitors by noon. Anybody who called before noon deserved to be disappointed, was their united opinion. By allowing two and a half hours for visitors, they themselves could return any visits they wished to make between three and half past four, by which time the sun would be setting on the horizon and it would be time for them to return to Pemberley. This would give them ample time to rest and to prepare for another intimate dinner for two, unless by some barbaric abuse of etiquette, they had been invited to dinner by persons they felt they could not refuse. Fortunately, Mr. Darcy's status was such, that there was actually nobody that he felt he could not refuse.

So passed the first few days at Pemberley, and it was only when Darcy caught up with his steward after five days, that Lizzy actually had time to sit and speak with Mrs. Reynolds about plans for Christmas. The housekeeper already knew that there was to be a large party of visitors over the Christmas period, but did not know the details until Elizabeth discussed it with her. Another meeting was arranged for the following day with the other senior staff, Mr. Robson and Mrs. Bruton, to discuss the menus, the bedrooms, the decorations, and any activities that would involve the outdoor staff, such as hunting, clearing paths of snow or ice, for the ladies to walk over etc. If the weather was cold enough, a small, shallow pond by the house could be made into a skating rink for the more adventurous guests.

One afternoon, Darcy took Lizzy into the conservatory to show her the splendid array of plants and flowers that she could use for decorative purposes, accompanied by Mr. Colin Betts, the Pemberley head-gardener, who incidentally was the twin brother of Mr. John Betts at Darcy House. There were ferns, lilies, still some late flowering chrysanthemums, orange blossoms, early spring flowers such as hyacinths, tulips, daffodils, crocus, snowdrops, all on the verge of flowering in time for Christmas. There were also more exotic plants such as poinsettias, with bright red or white leaves at their tips that looked like flowers. The array was stunning, Lizzy had never seen such an impressive display. They then went into the gardens, to see the holly, the ivy and the mistletoe growing in the old apple trees in the orchard. There was certainly enough to decorate the entire house for the whole of the twelve nights of Christmas. Lizzy was looking forward to receiving her family in her new home, and felt a great deal of pride in her husband, in having managed the estate so well: he knew the first name of almost every single member of the staff. She would have to work hard to achieve the same ability.

On the 20th, Georgiana arrived from Town, escorted by her cousin and guardian, Colonel Fitzwilliam, or Richard as he was called when he was with the family. He only stayed overnight, travelling on to Matlock to spend time with his parents, who were also invited to Pemberley for dinner on the day after Christmas, Boxing Day, so called because it was when the contents of the charity boxes in churches were distributed amongst the poor of the parish. In the same charitable spirit, Pemberley was accustomed to distributing gifts of food and clothing to the poorer members of the estate and parish. The parcels had been made up under the housekeeper's supervision, and Lizzy and Georgiana spent two days visiting all the families and handing them their parcels. Georgiana knew all of them; Lizzy was yet to learn, and remember their names and circumstances. She took the precaution of taking a notebook with her, filling in any details she obtained from Georgiana, and from talking to the family during their visit, as the coachman drove them on to the next family.

The Bennets and Gardiners were expected on the 23rd, allowing time for delays due to the state of the roads, depending on the weather. Lizzy awoke early in the morning, too excited to sleep any longer. She had really nothing to actually do, for all the rooms were ready, flowers in all the ladies' rooms, fires lit, bedding aired, and servants assigned to assist everyone settle in. The nursery was made ready for the Gardiner children, toys brought down from the attics, washed and awaiting somebody to play with them. Before breakfast, she went down to the library, to see that all was ready for her beloved father, whom she was sure would spend as much time as possible in there, social duties permitting. A display of red and white poinsettias was the only concession made to the festive period, respecting her father's taste for simple things.

She then returned to her room to dress for breakfast, which she shared with Darcy and Georgiana in the small breakfast room, for the last time until the festive period was over, and all the visitors returned to their respective homes. The larger breakfast room would be in use from now on.

Chapter 18

In spite of time standing still, or so it seemed to Lizzy, everybody arrived. The Gardiners arrived first, with their four children and servants, and they were all settled in their respective rooms and apartments as the Bingley's and Bennets arrived in two carriages, having travelled up from Hertfordshire together.

Lizzy and Darcy greeted them on the front steps of the house as they descended from the carriages. Lizzy hardly knew who to hug first, but since Jane reached her first, she started with her favourite sister, followed by everybody else as they arrived. She sensibly saved her effusions of delight until they were all inside, servants having removed bonnets, hats, gloves, scarves, cloaks, and pelisses with an efficiency that made her proud of her staff. They went into the drawing room where tea and coffee had been prepared, with cakes and an array of various foods for those who felt hungry. Mr. and Mrs. Gardiner and Georgiana were there to greet everybody too, so noisy conversation was heard all over the room, everyone wishing to greet and talk to those whom they had not seen since the weddings in November. The four gentlemen took refuge near the table bearing sandwiches and wine, discussing more mundane things such as the weather and the latest news from town, whilst the ladies could not keep to one subject at a time.

"How well you look Lizzy," cried Jane, embracing her warmly yet again "married life obviously suits you."

"As it does you my dear Jane!"

"It suits both of you, my dear girls," enjoined Mrs. Bennet, "what an enormous house you have Lizzy, you must be worn out trying to supervise everything, oh, but I am sure your housekeeper will look after all that side of things for you; with ten thousand a year, possibly more, you do not need to worry about exceeding your income!"

"Lizzy!" exclaimed Kitty, "you must have a wonderful gardener to produce all of these flowers! Do you think I may speak with him one day, to ask how he can get these spring flowers to bloom so early?"

"Lizzy, do you think I might be allowed to look into the library tomorrow?" asked Mary somewhat shyly. "Georgiana has already kindly permitted me the use of the pianoforte in her sitting room, whenever I wish."

"Oh Mary, ever the scholar I see, of course you can use the library, in fact before dinner, I will take both you and my father to see it. It is so large you could both spend your whole visit there and not disturb each other, though I do suggest that you join us for breakfast and dinner."

Georgiana and Mrs. Gardiner were talking together by the piano, almost as old friends, having met again more recently in London. They were discussing music and piano lessons, since Mrs. Gardiner was considering having her two little girls taught, having herself never learned.

After half an hour, Lizzy rang for the butler, and asked him to bring in the servants allocated to her guests, to show them to their rooms, where their trunks had been unpacked whilst the travellers were warming themselves in the drawing room and catching up on news.

Lizzy introduced each guest to the servant who was to tend to their needs whilst they were at Pemberley, and it was with secret pride that she remembered each of their names. She must remember to thank Mrs. Reynolds later, for giving her the list of names of which servant was to look after which guest.

Dinner was served later in the formal dining room, which was to be used for the duration of the visitors' stay. Mrs. Bennet was very impressed with the settings, reflecting with satisfaction that she too had similar gilt candlesticks and vases, and that the flowers were indeed very pretty. Lizzy had taken care to keep her mother at an unsubtle distance from Darcy, and placing her father at the opposite end to Mrs. Bennet, next to Darcy.

Mary was positively radiant with happiness, having visited the library with Lizzy and Mr. Bennet, and in the short stay there had found several books that she had long wished to read. She had also continued to take more care with her appearance, since the wedding, and with Kitty's help, to whom she had become closer since Jane and Lizzy had gone away, her plain gowns had been retrimmed with brighter ribbon and the addition of narrow lace, along with gowns that Lizzy had left behind, since she and Lizzy were of a similar build and colouring. In fact, she could hardly be called plain any more, something Mrs. Bennet mentioned to Mrs. Gardiner with great pride.

"I may not have produced a son for Mr. Bennet, my dear sister Gardiner, but you will have to admit that all my girls are very handsome, even Mary. I have high hopes of finding both her and Kitty husbands, every bit as good as Mr. Bingley and Mr. Darcy" which made Lizzy, who could not help but hear, very glad that her husband could *not*.

As dinner concluded, Lizzy rose and took the ladies back into the drawing room, whilst the gentlemen retired to the sanctuary that was the library, for their port and cigars, to allow the servants to clear the dining room and start setting it ready for the morrow, which was apparently to be a grand affair, in spite of it only being the day before Christmas.

The Gardiner children were in the drawing room, being allowed to stay downstairs an extra thirty minutes to meet and greet their relatives. Being extremely well-behaved children, all the ladies cooed over them, except Mary, who was not yet ready to pretend any attraction to such little people, though she did greet them as warmly as she could, because they were her cousins after all. The nursery maids soon bore them all off before the gentlemen returned from the library, although Mr. Gardiner did digress as far as the nursery to bid them goodnight, before coming to the drawing room.

Tea and coffee were served and music was spoken of. After speaking with Georgiana, Lizzy invited Mary to play the piano for them, with Georgiana and Kitty to sing. It was a solution to please everybody; Mary, at being the first to be asked to play, and the Bennets, current and former, in avoiding listening to Mary sing. Although she assiduously applied herself to her accomplishments, singing was not one of her finer talents, having a weak voice, which did not lend itself to public display, prolonged or otherwise.

The plans for the following day were divulged to the visitors: the company was to put up the greenery in the drawing room, dining room and hallway, the servants were doing the stairways and servants quarters. The children were to help dress the Yule log and place it in the hallway. The afternoon was for them to do as they pleased, though the cold, frosty weather promised the possibility of the small pond being frozen deep enough to allow skating.

"Oh, that would be wonderful!" exclaimed Mrs. Gardiner, "None of the children have ever skated before, though I wish I had thought of it before we came, for we have no skates for them!"

"That is not a problem my dear aunt," answered Lizzy, "we have unearthed the Darcy family collection of ice skates from the attics, accumulated over several generations, so although perhaps not the most fashionable, I am sure we can fit everyone out with skates."

With such a long, two days of travel behind them, and a busy day in front of them, all the guests were happy to retire at an early hour to the warm, well-lit, elegant rooms they had been allocated for their stay.

Chapter 19

———————•———————

After a bitterly cold night, the sun slowly extracted itself from the frozen horizon and greeted the earlier risers as they gathered in front of the roaring fire in the breakfast room. The room was filled with the aroma of breakfast, tea, and coffee tantalizing their senses.

"Well, I think the skating idea is going to happen." announced Darcy, with both Mr. Bennet and Bingley agreeing with him.

"The children will be so pleasantly surprised," added Mr. Gardiner, "I hope!"

"I am sure they will discover the pleasure with delight, Uncle" replied Lizzy, who as the hostess, had risen early to greet her guests for breakfast. "In fact, I took the liberty of sending up a parcel to the nursery, for each of them, containing warm knitted hats, scarves, and mittens. Now please, help yourselves to breakfast, there are chops, sausages, bacon, eggs, kidneys, toast, bread and butter of course, and should you require anything further, you just need to ask John, the footman, or Harriet, the maid."

She was feeling rather hungry herself, so as Darcy helped her to her chair, she instructed Harriet as to what she wished to eat, but could she have a dish of tea first? She was glad that her dressing gown was lined with fine wool, for even with the roaring fire, the cold outside was so bitter that it penetrated through the window panes. She chatted happily to those present as they broke their fast, and everyone had finished when the rest of the ladies arrived. Lizzy left the gentlemen to their own wives, daughters, or devices, and returned to her rooms to dress for the day.

Flannel petticoats over her chemise, and warm woollen stockings, were the foundation for a cream, finely woven woollen gown, and green leather boots. Her outer garments were a pine green velvet pelisse, a finely knitted woollen lace scarf for her throat, leather gloves, and a fur muff, with the addition of a hooded fur-lined cloak should she still feel the cold.

As she went down the stairs, she caught up with her young cousins, with their nursemaids and a Pemberley footman. The children were in a high state of excitement for they knew that they were going down to try skating on the small pond. They had never skated before and were delighted at having the opportunity. Lizzy decided to accompany them, for the other ladies, having broken their fast later than herself, had only just gone to their rooms to dress, so sending a message to her husband via a passing maid as to her whereabouts, she joined the happy party of apprentice skaters.

The young footman, James, had been sent to accompany them to ensure that the ice was safe, and to help the children with their skates, and teach them their first steps on the ice. The nursemaids stood by the side of the pond, happy for their charges, but also apprehending falls, cuts, and bruises. After half an hour however, they were less nervous because in spite of some initial falls, the children were skating around the pond, without a broken bone between them. It was at this point that Mr. and Mrs. Gardiner appeared, naturally curious to see their children's enjoyment.

"Oh, how they are enjoying themselves Lizzy!" exclaimed Mrs. Gardiner, "and how thoughtful of you to provide them with the scarves and mittens. The bonnets are similar to those worn by the village children when I was a girl!"

"The village children still do, I believe," replied Lizzy, "for it was one of the village ladies who made them for me."

"There you are my dear!" a masculine voice intoned, and Lizzy was grasped around the waist by Darcy. "I thought you would not be able to resist the skating party; I am only surprised that you are not skating yourself!"

"I did consider it, Fitzwilliam, but since I haven't skated in many a year, I had no wish to lose my dignity by falling head over heels in front of my more intrepid cousins."

"Well, your dignity may remain intact for a while longer, for everyone is now ready to gather greenery for the decoration of the house. The servants have already gathered pine branches and mistletoe, our task is to cut the holly and the ivy. The maids have started making the garlands and sprigs of mistletoe seem to be sprouting under every doorway through the house!"

Leaving the happy children to their play, the Darcys and Gardiners returned to the house where the others were waiting in the front hall.

"How festive you look Lizzy!" cried Jane, who was equally warmly dressed in pale blue.

"I think we all look rather festive; do you not think?" was Kitty's response. She was standing next to Georgiana, who was dressed in scarlet, whilst Kitty was wearing a golden yellow pelisse over her russet-coloured gown.

"Indeed, we do" answered Bingley. "By the bye, Elizabeth, Darcy, Mr. Bennet has asked to be excused from our excursion, for he has taken up residence in the library, as has Mary. And Mrs. Bennet has decided to stay indoors too, for she is hoping that Mrs. Reynolds will show her around the house."

"Very well then, let us be off!" cried Georgiana. She adored Christmas, and this was going to be the best yet, with so many friends and family around her with whom she could share her joy.

After much walking and cutting, the cart was filled with greenery and was taken back to the house by the groom who had accompanied them. He was instructed to send the landeau back to them when he got to the stables, for those amongst the ladies who were tired. Mrs. Gardiner, not being a regular walker, was among them, along with Jane, so Lizzy and Georgiana went back to the house with them, in the landeau. Once back in the house, tea and refreshments had been prepared, and the ladies began to realise how very cold the weather was, now that they were warmed up by the blazing fire, mince pies and hot tea.

The gentlemen returned to the house on foot, having diverted via one of the fine fishing spots pointed out to Mr. Gardiner by Darcy during the summer. They took mulled wine and sandwiches to refresh themselves, the wine filling the room with a spicy aroma of cloves, cinnamon, nutmeg, and oranges.

The aroma lingered on, permeating the rooms and hall, adding to the festive smells as garlands of pine were attached to the stairs and archways, after being decorated with ribbons, holly, ivy and mistletoe. Plants of hellebore, with rich cream blooms, were scattered on side tables, as well as pots of red tulips, white snowdrops, yellow, purple and white crocus added even more bright colours.

Satisfied with their efforts, it was realised that the daylight had almost ended, the sun was already low in the sky, so the ladies retired to their rooms for a rest before dressing for dinner, which they had been informed was to be somewhat grand.

Dinner had been ordered an hour earlier for a very practical reason. The whole family was expected to attend the church service on Christmas morning, so the servants would not have much time to prepare everything for the meals on the actual day. The idea was Lizzy's, which had occurred when she was discussing meals and decorations with Mrs. Reynolds. She felt that it was unkind to expect the servants to arise extra early on Christmas morning to carry out their duties, because they were expected to attend the service during the morning as well. The maids and footmen were extremely happy when they were informed of the arrangement, to allow them time to complete their tasks before retiring for the night.

Retreating to her room, Lizzy felt very exultant; hosting her family for her first Christmas as mistress of her new home, and in such a beautiful home as Pemberley was something she had never imagined in her younger years. Not feeling at all tired, she sat down in an armchair and just gazed around, noting the elegant furnishings and the tasteful decorations. Glancing down at the little round table by her chair, she noticed a prettily wrapped parcel addressed to herself. Curious, she wondered if she should open it, and then scolded herself; it was addressed to her in her husband's hand, so obviously, he meant for her to open it in the privacy of her chambers. Satisfied with her own reasoning, she excitedly took off the wrapping, keeping the silk ribbon which bound the paper because it was so pretty, and found herself with a jewellers' box on her lap. Opening it, she was astounded to find a parure of blue and green set in a pale gold setting. The necklace resembled an Egyptian style collar, the earrings cut in the same stones, a matching bracelet and even shoe buckles for her slippers. The green stones were jade, but she was not sure what the blue stones were, lapis perhaps? She must ask Darcy or her father. Beneath the circlet she found a little note from Darcy

"My dearest wife, Elizabeth,

I shall never tire of addressing you as 'my dearest wife'; you have made me the happiest of men since you accepted me to be your husband.

I know you do not wish for me to spoil you, but when I saw this, I could not help myself. The colours are so utterly right for you, so I indulged myself by purchasing the parure for you. I continued my extravagance and ordered a gown and slippers to complete the outfit, and your maid is instructed to dress you in it this evening, as I wish to show your entire family how much I admire and love you. Please forgive me this small vanity. It is a fault I have acquired since the day we overcame our previous misconceptions of each other, and has been blossoming ever since the day you became my wife.

I love you my darling Lizzy.
Fitzwilliam"

"Oh Fitzwilliam, if only you realised how happy you have made me, not by gifts, although you are *not* getting this back! but by simply being your own beloved self" murmured Lizzy out loud, not realising that her husband had crept up to the doorway, intent on witnessing if the gift pleased her, but he was now somewhat overcome himself, by her simple, loving words, uttered when she thought herself alone.

They were both still in each other's arms when Madeleine knocked discreetly on the door sometime later, suggesting that she would get her mistress some tea, and then dress her for dinner.

Chapter 20

———•———

Madeleine had done a superlative job on Lizzy's hair, soft curls framing her face, the bulk of her hair scooped up at the top of the back of her head, the ribbon from her gift entwined around her head, holding, or sometimes *not* holding, stray curls. It was a relatively simple style, but it certainly showed off her new parure and gown. The gown was of jade green silk with a scalloped hem, with a tunic of pale green-gold lace, studded here and there with tiny diamonds and lapis. Her shawl was in peacock blue with green and gold flowers and pale gold shoe buckles adorned her slippers. She was a vision of loveliness in both Madeleine's and Fitzwilliam's eyes as he escorted her down the stairs to meet up with the family before dinner. Lizzy herself felt as though she was gliding down the stairs on a cloud.

"Oh Lizzy! You look absolutely stunning!" gasped Mrs. Bennet, "I had always thought Jane the handsomest of my daughters but you surpass her in that gown! How fortunate it is that you do not have to worry about money to buy gowns! And the parure! I have read about them but yours is the first that I have seen! Where did you get it from? How much did it cost?"

As soon as she could get a word in, Jane tried to halt her mother's dialogue, "Mama, Lizzy has always been handsome and you know full well that we should not say such things when we are guests in her home. Have you not got a new gown yourself? I do not recall seeing it before. It certainly enhances your fine features."

"Oh, this you mean? It is quite a handsome gown indeed, your father kindly allowed me to order it from Town. He is grown quite generous since you and Lizzy got married; the expense of raising and keeping you must have been more than I had previously thought! Now that he has only Mary and Kitty to pay for, he might permit me a more liberal allowance. Lady Lucas says …"

This was going down another dangerous path, and neither Jane nor Lizzy wanted her querulousness to come to the fore over what had been planned to be a fine family dinner. Mrs. Gardiner helped by taking Mrs. Bennet by the arm and leading her away from where the gentlemen were, asking "Indeed, my dear sister, it is a splendid gown, who did you go to? And your cap is certainly most becoming to your face, I can only hope to be nearly half as handsome as you, when my daughters are married."

"Oh! my dear sister Gardiner, do not flatter me so. When a woman has five grown up daughters, three of them well married, as I do, she should give up thinking of her own beauty."

Mr. Bennet, unable to avoid overhearing, and determined to keep to the spirit of the season, said "In such cases Madam, such women usually have little beauty left of which to boast, but since you are still as handsome as you were, you should feel flattered, since it is well deserved."

Mrs. Bennet was surprised into almost silence, which had been the aim of their conjoined efforts, and sat down, stroking away imaginary creases in her gown with a great deal of complacency. She herself felt as handsome as ever, but it was not in Mr. Bennet's nature to compliment her in any regular way.

Mr. Darcy had fortunately missed the exchanges, having gone upstairs to escort Georgiana down for dinner. He now came down the staircase with his sister and Kitty by his side. Georgiana and Kitty were becoming firm friends, one having never had a sister before and the other seeking to replace the sister who had been her best friend, even though her influence had not been the best, now that Lydia was in the north with her husband.

Mary emerged from the direction of the library, she was dressed for dinner, having gone up to dress before the others so that she could escape back to the library before dinner. She was truly trying to become more sociable, but books still had the strongest hold on her, and with such a splendid library, and so little time before she went home again, she really did not want to waste such an opportunity to indulge whenever she could. Madeleine had dressed her hair and she did feel quite pretty; she would never compare herself to Lizzy, whom she most resembled when she took care of her appearance, because Lizzy looked like an Egyptian queen in that gown and jewels!

The only stranger to the family group was the Pemberley clergyman, Mr. Edwards, invited every year, as Darcy put it, to sustain his strength before the enormous task before him on Christmas Day

Everybody now assembled, Darcy lead Lizzy into the dining room, followed by Mr. and Mrs. Bennet, Mr. and Mrs. Gardiner, the Bingleys, Mr. Edwards and Mary, who, as Miss Bennet took precedence over Kitty, and then the girls, Georgiana and Kitty, Georgiana preferring to stay with Kitty.

Everyone, excepting Lizzy and Darcy, were struck into awed stares as they surveyed the formal dining room. The servants had turned it into something that resembled the great banquet halls of yore, festooned with holly, ivy, mistletoe, red velvet, and gold tapestries and swags. There was even a yule log in one of the fireplaces. The table stood out in its simple, dazzling white linen tablecloth, but the candelabras, the vases of flowers, platters of silver gilt, laden with a beautiful porcelain dinner service by the factory in Worcester, white with green and gold rims, the centres decorated with flowers etched in ivy green underglaze, made it into something quite magical. Gold cutlery, crystal glasses and carafes, perfectly pressed white linen, and the finishing touch was the fact that there were wrapped gifts on each of the guest's plates. Names had been set so that everyone knew where to sit. Unbeknownst to their guests, the Darcy's had wanted to start the Twelve Days of Christmas with the distribution of their gifts to the family, on the night before Christmas.

The hosts invited their guests to be seated and to open their gift whilst the wine was served. The exclamations of delight and pleasure was music to their ears. They had together selected the gifts for each of their guests, when they were in Town. Signet rings, earrings, bracelets, shawls, music sheets, books, had all been selected according to the tastes of each of them. It was such a warm feeling, being able to give pleasure to their loved ones.

Needless to say, that after such a start to the festivities, the dinner was splendid and was the forerunner of the best Twelve Nights most of them had ever had. Gifts continued to be exchanged over the following days, spreading the joy throughout, to the satisfaction of all.

Chapter 21

Mrs. Bennet was thoroughly satisfied with herself. She had married three of her daughters to men of fortune, well, that is, excepting her dearest Lydia, but she was sure Wickham would do well, eventually, all he needed was a little help from his friends, but here she returned her thoughts to Lizzy. How well she had done for herself! She was married to a man of large fortune, who possessed a great estate, ten miles around, and a house in Town, Grosvenor Square no less, and she was being showered with gifts of value, the cost of which Mrs. Bennet could only guess, but what stories she would be able to tell her friends and acquaintance when she returned to Longbourn! Now if only Jane or Lizzy could get with child, her triumph would be complete. Lady Lucas was becoming quite unbearable with her 'dearest Charlotte's condition', and there was always the possibility that Mr. and Mrs. Collins would have a son, and that would be even worse! However, the awfulness of them inheriting the estate after the demise of poor Mr. Bennet was now somewhat less fraught with worry, with the comforting thought that she would be looked after by some one or other of her sons by marriage. She was confident that her eldest daughters would look after her and any remaining unmarried daughters, when the unhappy event occurred. She had spoken to Mr. Bennet, about mentioning this to Jane and Elizabeth, but Mr. Bennet had absolutely forbidden her to speak to them about it.

"Who knows, Mrs. Bennet, I might even survive you and then all this discussion of it would have been unnecessary. Do not spoil the festivities with talk of my demise and your need to be supported."

"But Mr. Bennet! I must be prepared for the future! How will I be able to support Mary and Kitty once you are gone? The Collinses will like as not turn us out of the house before you are even cold in the ground!"

"Madam, I repeat, you are not to raise the subject under any circumstances!" was his final response, which left no illusions as to his meaning, and therefore must be abided by.

Mrs. Bennet had consoled herself with the thought that, once Mr. Bennet *was* gone, there would still be time to talk to the girls and come to some arrangement. A little estate, with perhaps one thousand a year would do quite nicely, and if she was economical, and she was sure she could be, she would be able to send some money to Lydia, for Lydia never seemed to have quite enough and was frequently requesting some assistance.

All in all, she was having a very pleasant time at Pemberley; Mrs. Reynolds had showed her around the house, as had Lizzy, the servants were very deferential to her, Mr. Bennet spent most of his time in the library or in the grounds with the other gentlemen, the ladies were all well dressed in gowns of the latest fashion, she herself was very satisfied with her own gowns, all of which were to be the envy of the neighbourhood when they returned home to the usual winter season of balls, albeit somewhat sparser this year, due to the departure of the militia, dinners and dances, interspersed with visits, and since they now had a second pair of horses, she could go visiting in the carriage every day. How very clever of Bingley and Darcy to gift the horses to Mr. Bennet! And no-one in the neighbourhood had such handsome table centres as she had! She must take them with her when the Collinses turned them out of Longbourn, for they were her very own, not part of the estate! How anyone could see fit to entail an estate away from a family of daughters was beyond her patience and comprehension, and she was sure that if she had had anything to do with it, she would have done something about it long ago. Jane and Elizabeth had explained several times something about entails to her, but she was sure that they were not as well-informed as herself on the subject, for her brothers Philipps and Gardiner had both explained something of the matter to her years ago, but she had quite forgot what it was. Hopefully 'dearest Charlotte' would only have girls, though more like as not, Charlotte would not be able to produce daughters as handsome as her own, for Charlotte was quite plain, and Mr. Collins would never be called a handsome man, and even Mr. Bennet said something of his not being as bright as their own girls, though he had also at some point said that Lydia and Kitty were the silliest girls in the kingdom, but she had scolded him about that, saying that he should not slight his own children, for things were difficult enough for them, things being settled as they were. She could not clearly remember his response, something about hopefully being sensible of his children's silliness, but she could not recall his mentioning it again, so perhaps he had taken heed of her upbraiding.

She could boast of having had dinner with a true lord and lady, since Mr. Darcy's uncle, aunt and cousin had come to dinner on the day after Christmas, along with other local notables, and Lady Matlock had made much about the lace on her new gown, and the dressing of her hair. They had also been invited to dinner at Matlock and she had been awed into silence at the size of the rooms, and the number of servants waiting at table, although Lizzy's home was quite equal to it in size and splendour, she felt. Yes, she had done well in finding Mr. Darcy for Elizabeth.

The sheer size and elegance of Pemberley was not lost on her either, and she tried to remember some of the details about the size and history, which Mrs. Reynolds had been at pains to explain to her. Fortunately, the housekeeper had also given her some notes, so she would be able to regale her acquaintance at home with the details, once they got back to Longbourn. Lady Lucas and Mrs. Goulding, and even her sister Phillips would be so envious!

Such were the gentle musings of Mrs. Bennet, sitting in her dressing room, having her hair set in rags, as the evening closed in on the end of the year. Tomorrow was a new year, and after her success during the old one, she was certain she would do as well for her family in the next.

Chapter 22

As the dawn proceeded and the sun crept over the horizon on this new day of a new year, Lizzy cuddled up to her husband's body, revelling in the warmth of a husband, not quite comprehending her mother's words of disdain of the alleged duties of a woman sharing a bed with her husband.

It was required of them, Mrs. Bennett had explained to Jane and Lizzy, before their wedding, but as soon as they became with child, they could refuse any further distasteful intimacy until after the child was born, retiring to the sanctuary of their own chambers. Monthly courses could also be used to the same effect, and of course after the child was born, any decent man would not bother his wife until at least the child was old enough to walk. Lizzy began to feel somewhat sad that her parents had not seemed to have known the love, warmth and intimacy that she now had with Fitzwilliam. Her own delicacy, as well as Jane's, meant she could not even discuss such things with her, to see if Jane knew of such happiness, but she was very grateful that her husband loved her as much as he did, which could only be equalled by her own love of him. She also began to realise why her father had spoken so earnestly to her, the night that Fitzwilliam had asked him for her hand in marriage.

"Lizzy" he had said' I have given him my consent. He is the kind of man, indeed, to whom I should never dare to refuse anything which he condescended to ask. I now give it to *you*, if you are resolved on having him. But let me advise you to think better of it. I know your disposition Lizzy. I know that you could neither be happy nor respectable unless you truly esteemed your husband – unless you looked up to him as your superior. Your lively talents would place you in the greatest danger in an unequal marriage. You could scarcely escape discredit and misery. My child, let me not have the grief of seeing *you* unable to respect your partner in life. You know not what you are about"

She had been earnest and solemn in her reply to her father, and at length, by repeated reassurances of her choice, by explaining the gradual change which her estimation of him had undergone, relating her absolute certainty that his affection was not the work of a day, but had stood the test of many months suspense, and enumerating with energy all his good qualities, she conquered her father's fears and reconciled him to the match. Now of course, he could see for himself how much she was esteemed by her husband, and how worthy he was of her love and respect for him. Mr. Bennett could return to Longbourn tranquil in the knowledge that she had chosen her partner well.

A fire in the hearth was blazing, taking the edge off the early morning chill, and Madeleine had brought her a dish of tea. So far, the festivities had gone well and her family were still on their best behaviour. It had taken several combined family efforts to contain Mrs. Bennet when she was feeling querulous but thus far, she had not yet had any attacks of her poor nerves. Mary was becoming more sociable, and Kitty less fretful, since she spent much of her time with Georgiana. Even Georgiana, Lizzy reflected, was less shy, now that she had girls of her own age with whom she could converse. Sipping her tea, Lizzy thought of suggesting that Kitty could be asked to stay on at Pemberley when the rest of the family left to return to Longbourn after Twelfth Night. Kitty and Georgiana seemed to have found an affinity with each other, making the one less shy and the other less silly. She was sure that her mother would have no objections, and it would enlarge Kitty's knowledge of the world and the social niceties of which Georgiana was the better mistress.

Kitty could return to London with them in March, and from there to Longbourn, when the Darcy family returned to Derbyshire in May. An excellent idea, thought Lizzy to herself.

At breakfast, after having discussed the possibility with Fitzwilliam, she made the suggestion to Kitty and her parents.

"Oh, how wonderful, Lizzy, I would like that more than anything!" was Kitty's response, and Mrs. Bennet's was hardly less enthusiastic.

"She will have such opportunities in London, perhaps she will even find a husband!"

"That is *not* the reason why I am asking her to stay with us, Mama, I merely thought that she would enjoy Georgiana's company. I know Georgiana enjoys hers."

"Perhaps, that well may be, but you will be going out in society and going to balls, and who knows who she might meet! Four daughters married!"

"With two young ladies under my care, ma'am, I shall be a severe chaperone. My father would never forgive me if anything happened to Kitty, as it did to Lydia."

"Exactly so Lizzy," replied Mr. Bennet "however, under your care I will entrust her. I have not forgotten the wise words of warning you gave me last year, which I unfortunately, to my eternal regret, did not heed at the time, and we know of the consequences. Mind you Kitty, should Lizzy and Darcy have *any* cause to doubt your behaviour and regret their offer, they are to send you home immediately!"

Disregarding the last part of her father's speech, Kitty was ecstatic, Georgiana hardly less so.

Georgiana knew the story of Lydia's behaviour, but would not judge, having so very nearly done the same thing herself, with the very same man, the previous summer. She was but only *now* learning to get over the blaming of herself, with Lizzy's help, who had pointed out to her that, at the time, she was but fifteen and barely more than a child, and that her guardians did not blame her at all, especially as she herself had told her brother of their intentions, before the planned elopement took place. Having Kitty as a friend made her realise that she was in fact much like most young ladies of her age: in love with the idea of being in love.

The knowledge that they would spend the next few months together made her as happy as Kitty; she had never had a friend of her own before and was enjoying the sensations it created since she became acquainted with Lizzy and her sisters, more especially Kitty, who was nearer to her in age. Having breakfasted, the pair of them went off to dress, happy that they would be together for the next few months.

Once gone, the breakfast room would have appeared empty, for Mr. and Mrs. Bennet had withdrawn to dress, leaving just Lizzy and Darcy alone.

"My dear Lizzy, seeing how happy our sisters are, I concur that you had indeed an excellent idea in asking Kitty to stay on with us. Georgiana is less shy since first you, and then your family, have been here. Having many acquaintances of my own, and also being ten years older than Georgiana, I think I did not realise how lonely she could be, having no-one but servants to talk to."

"Seeing them together gave me the idea, dearest, and I thought it would do them both good. Kitty has missed having someone to talk to over things, the way girls do, since last summer. She and Lydia were always very close, not always to Kitty's advantage, I concede, but she has a truly affectionate heart and I think under our supervision, she will improve considerably, especially with Georgiana as an example, and Georgiana comes more out of her shell since Kitty has been here"

At this point the Bingley's arrived, followed by the Gardiners, already dressed, for they had broken their fast earlier than the Bennets. The Gardiners were to set off for home the following day, business requiring Mr. Gardiner's presence by the end of the week, and Mrs. Gardiner did not like to travel without her husband, so today was the last day of them all together, and neither Lizzy nor Jane wanted to miss the opportunity to spend as much time with them as possible.

Chapter 23

———•———

The Twelfth Night Ball in Derby finished off the festive season. The Darcy's attended, of course, with Miss Darcy and Mrs. Darcy's younger sister, Miss Catherine Bennet, Mr. and Mrs. Bingley, and Mrs. Bennet. Mr. Bennet did not wish to attend, and Mary did not want to lose time from the library. Her quest for knowledge would nearly always take precedence over a ball, and with all the various dinners, banquets, and dances that had taken place since her arrival, surely nobody could accuse her of ignoring her social duties. One more evening in the Pemberley library and she would be content to submit to the social niceties required of her at Longbourn, for with Kitty remaining at Pemberley, she would be the only daughter remaining at home, and she knew her mother was quite unable to sit or visit alone, so she would have to withdraw from her pursuit of accomplishments until Kitty returned in the spring.

Two days after the ball, the Bennets, albeit reduced to three, and the Bingley's, returned to Hertfordshire. Lizzy was sad to see them go, but also pleased that she and Darcy would have more time for each other, since Kitty and Georgiana had become inseparable, spending all their time together. Georgiana was teaching Kitty skills on the piano and in embroidery, Kitty teaching Georgiana about flowers and the arranging of them, when they were not walking about the estate when the weather permitted, or riding. Kitty had the use of a lady's horse during her stay, for there were several, and only Georgiana made use of them, Lizzy was not a competent horsewoman and not really willing to overcome her lack of equestrian skills.

"Perhaps in the spring" replied Lizzy to Darcy's question, some days later, as to whether she would like to improve her riding. Knowing that her husband loved to ride, she wanted to be able to join him sometimes, but not just now, not in the middle of winter. He promised that he would teach her himself, and that she would have the gentlest mare in his stable.

Feeling that she was behaving somewhat childishly, she explained her fears. As a child, she had learned to ride, but one day, she had mischievously decided to ride her father's horse, against his strict instructions never to do so, and she had been thrown from the horse, so from that day forth she never wished to ride again. However, she had grown up since then, and yes, she would learn to ride under Darcy's instruction, for as she said to him, "I want to spend as much time as possible with you, and if you are riding, I would lose precious moments with you. Besides, when we are in town, I am sure you would prefer riding in Hyde Park, rather than sitting with me in the landeau." Darcy positively beamed at the thought of being able to ride with his beautiful wife by his side.

"Thank you, Elizabeth, I shall be very careful with you, now that I understand the source of your apprehension, and of course you must have a riding habit. We will go into Lambton to see if the seamstress is able to make you one. Would this afternoon suit you?"

"With an offer of new clothes! my dear husband, how can a lady refuse?"

The trip to Lambton fulfilled the need for a riding habit, for the seamstress served most of the ladies of the neighbourhood, and nearly all of them rode. Having taken measurements, selected the pattern, fabrics and trimmings, chosen the correct headwear, Lizzy felt proud of herself for agreeing to learning to ride again, though not without some lingering trepidation. But her efforts would please her husband, and that was worth any effort on her part.

Over dinner, the party now reduced to the four of them, Kitty exclaimed when told of her sister's intention to ride again. "But Lizzy! you always said that you would never ride again!"

"True, but resolutions taken as a child should not be considered as binding when one is an adult, and besides, I am getting a new riding habit from it!"

Georgiana was delighted, "It means that I will always have someone to ride with me, once Kitty goes home, not that I am not very happy to ride with you, Kitty."

"Well this means I must become proficient before we get to town. Husband, we will start tomorrow morning, if I can borrow a habit from either of the girls, that is."

"I have several habits, one of my old ones would fit you I am sure, for you are slighter than I, and if you don't mind, it would do until yours is ready" offered Georgiana.

"Well, it seems I now have no excuses, so Fitzwilliam, arm yourself with all of your patience tomorrow, and ignore my attempts of procrastination, should any arise."

The following morning appeared bright and fine, so after breakfast, Lizzy, dressed in one of Georgiana's old riding habits, accompanied Darcy to the stables, where he introduced her to a placid roan mare, Stella.

"Just let her nuzzle your hand Lizzy, here, take an apple, she loves apples. See? She is very gentle. You are not going to actually ride today, although you do look very handsome in a riding habit; we are just going to get you and Stella acquainted. Talk to her like you would a dog or kitten, she likes being talked to."

Complying, Lizzy felt some of her fears evaporating, for Stella was so gentle and nuzzled her face when the apple was finished. After a quarter of an hour, she asked if she could sit on her, so a ladies' saddle was produced and strapped to the mare. A step was brought and Darcy's strong arms assisted her up into the saddle. Sitting high up, Lizzy felt a little queasy, and would have willingly got off, but she silently scolded herself for her foolishness; nothing could happen whilst Darcy was holding the reins, and the mare was as gentle as he had promised.

"Do you think we could walk around the stable yard?" asked Lizzy, determined to overcome her angst. "Just a little, so I can get used to the movement again" Surprised, but proud of her determination, Darcy lead the horse around the stable yard. Lizzy started to relax, remembering her early years of riding: it was all returning to her!

"Can you let me have the reins Fitzwilliam? I think I can handle her around the yard"

"Are you sure?" he replied, hoping she wasn't forcing herself to do more than she wished, just to please him.

"Yes dearest, do not look so concerned, it is all coming back to me and I promise I will not go off at a gallop, or at least not today."

After ten minutes of riding around the yard, Lizzy suggested that Darcy get his own horse and perhaps they could have a little ride around the paddocks at the back of the stables. With alacrity he complied, delighted with her progress. He had been prepared to take weeks, if required, to get Elizabeth comfortable on a horse again, and here was she, suggesting that they ride together, after barely an hour!

They returned to the stables an hour later. Lizzy, as promised, had not gone off at a gallop, but certainly had remastered the trot and the cantering part of the equestrian sport. She was in fact, a natural horsewoman: only her childhood incident and subsequent self-recriminations for her disobedience had held her back, as she realised, when handing Stella back to a stable hand.

Darcy congratulated her on her efforts, even the head stableman said she sat well on a horse. Lizzy was feeling elated; she could ride again! Perhaps not ready to join in the hunt, but she could certainly ride by her husband's side along Rotten Row, with a little more practice of course.

Georgiana and Kitty had meanwhile slipped down to the stables, keeping out of sight, to watch Lizzy's efforts. They were equally delighted with her re-found skills and bounded out to greet her when she had dismounted, with Darcy's assistance.

"Papa will be amazed when I write to Longbourn about this, it is almost a shame to waste the news in a letter to Mama!"

"Then why do you not write to Papa? He likes to get letters from us"

"Because I have never written to him before, but then again, I have never been away before either. I will do so Lizzy, so you must promise not to tell him yourself, or my letter to him will have no purpose."

"Well I promise not to mention it then, and now at least, I do not have to draw lines for you to follow when you write your letters. Do you remember how I used to do that for you when you were learning to write? It seems so long ago now" laughed Lizzy.

Over the following days, her skills improved so rapidly that she and Darcy were able to ride out over the estate. It was exhilarating! Lizzy could scarcely believe that it was her own stubbornness which had deprived her of such pleasures for all these years. Yet another instance where her prejudices had influenced her life in a negative way, though fortunately, like her initial opinion of Darcy, this one too, had finally been overcome, with Darcy's help.

Chapter 24

January and February passed, Georgiana and Kitty becoming as close to being sisters as they could be, Lizzy was improving her riding skills and Darcy could not be happier as to how his family was progressing.

In March, they were to go back to Town, to enjoy the remainder of The Season, before everyone went back to the country to avoid the summer heat and smells of London. Mrs. Bennet had intimated several times as to how Lizzy should project Kitty onto the marriage market, but Lizzy refused to take heed. In agreement with Darcy, Georgiana would be 'out' but not yet on the search for a husband. They both agreed that Kitty and Georgiana should enjoy the season as it was; there was no hurry to find them husbands, there would be time enough, no matter what Mrs. Bennett's thoughts were on the matter. Lizzy also had private intelligence from her father that he was in no hurry to marry Kitty or Mary off for the time being. Jane and Elizabeth, having waited until they were past twenty, meant that they were more mature and certain of what kind of man they required to be their partner in life, and Mr. Bennet felt that girls should be over the silliness of their teens, before making such an important decision, with regards to their future.

Mr. Darcy agreed with him wholeheartedly; he was in no haste to be rid of his sister, and he was growing quite fond of Kitty as well;

she was not as silly and fretful as he had at first thought, and she was very good as a companion to Georgiana. He was looking forward to Town, the remainder of the season being now so short, there was little danger of her throwing herself at the first simpering, loquacious fool who flattered her. This was another advantage of having Kitty with her: she was no longer so lonely that she would *need* the attention of an admirer quite so much. He reflected with much satisfaction on how much he had gained with his marriage to Elizabeth, and if his private source of information was to be believed, he was to have even more joy bestowed on him, according to Thomas, his valet, who had it from her maid, but since Lizzy herself had not yet told him, he preferred to contain his delight. So many things could go wrong in the first few weeks, and he understood her need to be certain before letting him and the rest of the family know.

"Well ladies," he said over breakfast "I hope you are fitfully bored of living such a retired life in the country, for we shall proceed to town at the end of the week. I have sent word to Darcy House to expect us on Saturday"

For Georgiana, this was nothing exceptional, for they went to town every spring, but for Kitty it was the place she had always dreamed of going to, but thus far, had never reached. She was ecstatic, it was something she had aspired to since coming out. She had never even been to her aunt and uncle's house in Cheapside!

"Oh Mr. Darcy! How splendid! I have never actually been to town, so it will all be so new to me. Lizzy, will my gowns be sufficient? Should I get more? I will trust you to guide me in my choices, of course. Do you think my father would let me have some more money?"

"Catherine, make no such request of your father: as my sister, you are entitled to my care, as much as Georgiana is," interposed Darcy, "you and Georgiana are under our care, Elizabeth will be your chaperone, and if possible, we will arrange for all three of you to be introduced at Court."

All three, Lizzy, Georgiana and Kitty were so stunned his words, that for several moments they were speechless. Being presented at court, would mean they were part of the Ton.

"But how?" enquired Lizzy, "I fear we know nobody who could sponsor us. For the ladies of the Almanack to accept us, we must be sponsored, I believe"

"You will be sponsored, rest assured" replied Darcy "I have made enquiries, and Lady Spencer and Lady Wentworth have both replied that they would be most happy to sponsor you all, as would my aunt, Lady Matlock. Indeed, you could all have your own sponsor, should you so wish. In fact, I think that is an excellent idea; three separate sponsors. How my aunt De Bourgh will fume when she finds out!"

"Oh Fitzwilliam!" exclaimed Georgiana "I had no idea that you were intending to do so. How exciting it will be, will it not Kitty? Lizzy?"

"And of course, ladies, this will mean new gowns, for the Ton has its' exigences, and you must wear white court gowns, white ostrich feathers and learn to walk backwards. I realise, that this will be a most difficult, challenging prospect, but I am confident that you will all be up for the task. You, Elizabeth, as a married woman, will have to wear a tiara, but I am sure you will find something suitable, lurking in the family collection"

"Oh Lizzy! exclaimed Kitty, "think how proud my mother will be! We will be able to talk about it for many a dinner, though hopefully, I will not be as repetitive as Sir William. I regret to admit, that after so many years of hearing him tell of his presentation at court, I find him a little boring."

"Well, I tend to agree with you Kitty" replied Lizzy, "his presentation at court has been his dinner conversation for these fifteen years at least, so perhaps it is time for you to take over the glory. You, hopefully, will be able to give full credit to the gowns, jewels and grand persons present, which Sir William no longer can."

Georgiana, somewhat pensive, said "Lizzy, Kitty, we are going to have to learn walking backwards, whilst wearing a court dress, with a train! I will start practicing this very day. And court dances, Kitty we must practice them, I would die of embarrassment if I tripped over my gown in front of the queen and all those people!"

Kitty, now starting to feel more alarmed rather than thrilled, totally agreed with her, and the two of them left the breakfast parlour to put their words into action.

"Thank you my dearest" said Lizzy, putting her hand into Darcy's, "I know how you hate the Ton and all of its' superciliousness, I recall you once saying to Sir William that you would not compliment the place by dancing at St James'"

"You recall correctly, my dear, but that was before I met, and had the great good fortune to marry *you*. Now however, I am quite happy to grace the court with my presence, because I will have you on my arm."

"Your flattery is very touching, my love, but you will possibly have more than just me on your arm. I believe that I am with child, so, there will be two of us requiring the strength of your support"

"Oh! my dearest Elizabeth, that is wonderful news! Are you quite well? We can remain here at Pemberley if you are at all unwell, I am sure our sisters would understand, we can go to Court next winter."

"My love, I am with child; I am not ill, and in fact, I would like to consult a physician when we get to town, precisely to ensure that all *is* well. I would prefer to wait until I have seen him, before we announce our good news to the rest of the family, so please do not cancel our trip to town on my account."

"Whatever you wish Lizzy, you only have to say, and whatever it is, it will be done. We are to blessed with a child! I thought I could not be happier than the day we married, but now I am feeling such palpitations, of joy mind you, that I begin to understand your mother's concern about *her* palpitations! Oh! my dearest Mrs. Darcy, you continue to make me the happiest and proudest of men"

Chapter 25

Three weeks later, attired in white court gowns, the requisite white ostrich feathers, accompanied by the Ladies Matlock, Spencer, and Wentworth, Lizzy, Georgiana, and Kitty withdrew from their presentation, *'reculant'* with an elegance they had initially thought impossible. As soon as the doors were closed behind them, the six ladies hugged each other in delight and relief.

The ladies of the Almanack had had no problem with accepting Miss Darcy, for she was, after all, *Miss Darcy* and she could not be refused. Mrs. Darcy and Miss Catherine Bennet however, required some consideration. Stories had reached them as such, that they were, perhaps, not the sort of ladies one could accept. Lady Matlock, Lizzy's sponsor, then went in, all sails deployed. She was herself a member of the club, and she insisted that Mrs. Darcy be accepted: she was the daughter of a gentleman and the wife of a gentleman, of Mr. Darcy no less! And as Mr. and Mrs. Darcy's sister, Miss Catherine Bennet could hardly be refused. Lady Wentworth, herself the daughter and the wife of baronets, highly recommended Kitty, whom she had very graciously accepted to sponsor. Such arguments could not be ignored, so with delayed grace, both Lizzy and Kitty were accepted for presentation at court.

"I thought I should have died if I had tripped over my train, which I was sure I would do" exclaimed Kitty, "I am so glad it is over. I now better understand Sir William's trepidation at his own presentation! I hope I shall be more understanding when he speaks of it again"

Darcy embraced them all, thanking the sponsors warmly. Their husbands had joined them and Kitty was congratulated and greeted by gentlemen she had never even dreamed of knowing, Lord Matlock, Sir Charles and Admiral Wentworth. How Lydia and her mother would gawp! But she then suddenly realised that Lydia's thoughts on the event did not now matter to her, as much as they might have done in the past.

Less than a year had passed since Lydia had gone off to Brighton, but how much had changed! She no longer felt any dependency on Lydia; in fact, she felt ashamed of how much she had let herself be led astray by her younger sister's ignorance. Now, she had Georgiana as her sister, leading her by a so much better example and she felt extremely grateful to Lizzy and Darcy for taking her under their care. Thankfully, they had been able to convince her father to entrust her to them. Lydia would never have been able to do so, and she certainly would not be wearing a court gown, about to go to a ball at the court of St James! 'Trepidation' she now realised, was a combination of great excitement and equally great anxiousness.

Nothing had prepared Lizzy for the sheer enormousness of Court; never had any of the three ladies seen so many people congregated together, but they felt relatively comfortable within their own group of friends, who, being well-known in town, made introductions between the girls and several personable young men who requested them to dance. Their having just been presented, both very handsome, and one of them being Miss Darcy, meant they were very much sought after. Darcy, with Elizabeth's assistance, managed to contain his feelings about Georgiana being led off, even if it *was* just for a dance. She managed it by dancing with him in the line next to where Georgiana and Kitty were, for neither of the girls would dance without the other next to her, an added satisfaction for Darcy, so he could watch her when he wasn't talking to Lizzy.

Darcy knew many of the people present and took great delight in introducing his wife to them. Lizzy's head was soon spinning trying to remember all of the names and asked to sit down for a while. Darcy was instantly all concern for her.

"Oh Elizabeth, how unthinking of me! Of course, you must sit down, I will find a footman to bring you some refreshment, what would you like? Tea? Wine? Here, sit yourself down here. You must not dance any more, you have over-tired yourself, I will sit with you, or would you prefer that we go home?"

"I think I can see our aunt Matlock over there; may we not sit with her? I do not wish to leave so early; the girls are enjoying themselves so much, it would be a shame to leave *now*. I shall be quite alright once I have had a rest. Merely a consequence, I believe, of carrying our child."

"I should have considered that, my love, how inconsiderate of me, please forgive me" entreated her concerned husband.

"How were either of us to know, dearest? This is, after all, the first time we have been with child!" laughed Lizzy, "I am feeling somewhat refreshed already, so please do not fret yourself and let us enjoy the evening. It was indeed quite warm dancing down the lines."

Returning to Darcy House after the ball, everyone was tired but still excited about the events of the evening.

"Thank you so much, Mr. Darcy, for including me in this visit to Town" said Kitty, holding back a very inelegant yawn.

"Kitty, I was pleased to have you here, you are an invaluable and dear companion to Georgiana, and an even dearer sister to Lizzy, so how could I not include you? And please, call me Darcy or even Fitzwilliam; you are my sister by marriage and I am proud to be your brother"

Georgiana muttered words to intimate her happiness but was too tired to speak coherently. Lizzy, beyond tired, slept with her head on her husband's shoulder, her ostrich feather headdress coming a-wry from the diamond tiara and tickling his nose, and she had to be carried to her room by the said husband, where Madeleine took over and got her mistress to her bed, in appropriate night attire for a lady, and her hair curled in rags.

Chapter 26

Two days later, the fine spring weather tempted many a lady and gentleman into Hyde Park. Darcy was very proud of his wife as she rode beside him; she had overcome many years of her fear of riding in such a very short time. She was in fact a natural horsewoman, and a most handsome one at that, in one of her new riding habits.

"Who is that gentleman waving at us Fitzwilliam?" asked Lizzy, with some curiosity. Looking in the direction she indicated, Darcy turned his horse in the direction of the said rider, asking her to follow him.

"My dear, that is Sir William Gordon and his wife, formerly Miss Osborne, a very charming couple who, I am sure, you will enjoy making acquaintance with. Her brother, Lord Osborne is about as taciturn of feature and manner as you once thought me, but he is simply shy. He's married to a Spanish lady, very happily it seems, he dotes on her"

"Hello Sir William, Lady Gordon" doffing his hat to the lady, "Lady Gordon, may I have the pleasure of introducing my wife, Mrs. Darcy to you? Elizabeth, Lady Gordon, who by choosing to marry Sir William, caused quite some consternation at the time."

"The pleasure is all mine Mr. Darcy" as Lady Gordon bowed her head to Lizzy, who did likewise, since the ladies were both on horseback, "and I do not at all repent causing any of the said consternation, if I may say, as Sir William's humour suits me better than most gentlemen's attempts of flattering me" she replied, with a broad smile. Lizzy warmed to her immediately. This was a woman who would not be easily offended or shocked at Lizzy's own form of wit and humour.

"Lady Gordon, we are having a dinner party tomorrow evening, we would be honoured if you and Sir William could attend. It is a small gathering, but I believe you may enjoy the company. Perhaps you already know some of them, but being myself somewhat new to the social rounds of Town, I know not yet exactly who knows whom" requested Lizzy.

"We would be delighted to attend, Mrs. Darcy" replied Lady Gordon "Who else will be there? We might know them indeed."

"Admiral and Lady Wentworth, Lord and Lady Matlock, - Mr. Darcy's uncle and aunt - and his cousins, Henry and Adele Fitzwilliam, Mr. and Mrs. Churchill, and I believe, Mr. and Mrs. Parker."

"Yes, we do know them all, Lord and Lady Matlock to a lesser degree, but I know the ladies from the social rounds of balls, card parties and dinners"

"Then you will be amongst acquaintance, Lady Gordon!" exclaimed Lizzy "the ladies have been most kind to me, introducing me to their friends and guiding me through the intricacies of the Ton. In fact, Lady Matlock sponsored me for my court presentation."

"Yes, I read about it in the paper only this morning! Many ladies were in raptures about your gown and headwear, and of course Miss Darcy has been expected to be presented for this past twelve months at least. I believe your sister was also presented?"

"Yes, my sister Catherine; she and Miss Darcy have become firm friends, so we thought it would be less intimidating for them to be presented together."

"Indeed, you were right; it is frightening enough to be presented, but when you are by yourself, amongst so many strangers, it is enough to make you trip over your gown whilst attempting to curtsey to the correct level! I was terrified I would do everything wrong! In the end I only caught my heel in my train *after* the door was closed."

"Oh! the walking backwards! I was convinced I would end up sprawled on the floor in front of the whole Court!" laughed Lizzy.

Her laughter drew the attention of the gentlemen, who inquired as to the cause of their mirth.

"We were comparing our Court Presentation experiences, my dear Mr. Darcy"

"Yes, Mr. Darcy, the indignity of tripping over one's train seems to be a common fear for most of us ladies" added Lady Gordon, who then, addressing Sir William, "We are invited to Darcy House for dinner tomorrow, William; I have accepted, since I believe that it will be more pleasurable than the card party you were thinking of attending at the Dashwood's. You had only accepted conditionally because Mr. Dashwood was so insistent, but I would prefer to accept Mrs. Darcy's invitation, and we know all the other guests, except perhaps Miss Bennet, Mrs. Darcy's sister."

"An excellent idea, Henrietta dear, I will send our apologies to Dashwood, muttering something about a prior engagement made by you, of which I was not aware at the time. Only a little stretching of the truth, I know, but I am sure you will forgive me Mrs. Darcy" smiled Sir William.

Lizzy laughed and said, "I am learning of the arts and skills one needs to survive the social rounds of Town, and it appears you are very talented in the art."

"That he is, my dear, but I am afraid we must move on and wait till tomorrow to continue the conversation" interposed Darcy "We must return to dress for the theatre. I am pleased you were able to accept our request Sir William, Lady Gordon" bowing to the lady.

The ladies parted with good impressions of each other, each looking forward to furthering their acquaintance, for they were both of an equal sense of humour and wit, not common in the parading giddiness of the Ton.

Chapter 27

In May, after a whirlwind of balls, dinners, visits to the theatres, rides in the park, shopping at the best shops and warehouses, meeting Darcy's London friends and acquaintances, and most importantly, a visit to a well-respected physician to confirm that all was well with Lizzy, the return of Kitty to Longbourn was being prepared.

The Darcy's would be accompanying her, planning to stay at Netherfield for a fortnight, Lizzy still not confident of inflicting Mrs. Bennet onto her husband for any long period. Dinner and social events at least had the advantage of coming to an end after a certain time, whereas staying at Longbourn, there would be no escaping her attentions.

The trip was uneventful, being very comfortable in the family carriage which carried four with ease. Lizzy reflected on the blessing of having money enough to allow such luxuries. Not that she had ever been deprived as a Miss Bennet, but the Darcy fortune certainly helped make life so much easier for travelling. They arrived at Netherfield at the end of the morning, where the Bennets were waiting for them, along with Jane and Charles.

With so much having happened since Christmas, the ladies could not talk enough, Kitty merrily regaling Jane, Mary and Mrs. Bennet, with Georgiana joining in, whilst Jane and Lizzy talked more quietly together. In spite of them both being very happily married, they missed the companionship they had shared for over twenty years, and letter-writing was not quite the same as talking to each other. The three gentlemen were discussing home farms and Bingley's wish to purchase an estate, now that he was married. He had looked at some properties in the neighbouring counties, but had not yet found one to his taste. Darcy did mention one that he knew of in Leicestershire, and promised to give him the details of the agent later.

Dinner was at Netherfield, with just the Bingleys, Darcys and Bennets, at Lizzy's request. Having all congregated in the drawing room before dinner, after returning from dressing, Lizzy smiling broadly, Darcy made the all-important announcement.

"I am especially glad that we are just the family for dinner today, for we have news which we want to share with you before the rest of the neighbourhood learns of it."

"Oh! what news? What news?" cried Mrs. Bennet

Smiling at her enthusiasm, Darcy continued, "It is our joy to announce that my beloved wife is with child, we will have the delight of becoming parents in November... "as pandemonium broke loose.

"Oh Lizzy! Well done of you, so quickly too! I am sure it will be a boy! Just wait till I tell Lady Lucas! "was Mrs. Bennet's reaction.

"How wonderful! Congratulations to you both!" was the reaction of Georgiana, Kitty and Mary, whilst Jane hugged her sister warmly and whispered, "I too am with child Lizzy, I can understand your delight"

Bingley and Mr. Bennet shook Darcy's hand and the smiles of happiness were truly genuine, though Mr. Bennet could not refrain from adding "Make sure the nursery is at the opposite end of the house, or you will never pass a comfortable night again! Well done my son"

Looking at his wife across the room, Bingley understood her nod and in the mood of the moment, told the rest of the family of their own happy prospects.

"Two grandchildren! Oh my! No! That will be *three* grandchildren! I forgot to mention it to anyone, but I got a letter from Lydia today, and she and Wickham expect their first child in September. I shall go distracted! Mr. Bennet, would you send some more money to Lydia? She will need to buy clothes for the child."

Choosing to ignore her last request, Mr. Bennet shook Bingley's hand and told him that the same advice applied; nursery at the other end of the house!

He then went over to the ladies, handing Lizzy a letter, written in the hand of her friend, Charlotte Collins, addressed to her at Longbourn. "I am guessing she will be telling you something that I learned from Mr. Collins in another of his inimitable pieces of correspondence, but I will let you read it first. This has been quite a day for good news!"

"I think I can guess the news, for Charlotte is due to be delivered any time now, so pray do tell me Papa, is she well? Is the child well?"

"As you wish my dear" then raising his voice slightly, "It is also my pleasure in announcing yet another birth; the heir to the Longbourn estate, the worthy Mr. Collins, has informed me that his lady has been safely delivered of a child, who is healthy and well."

"Oh! Mr. Bennet! How can it be a pleasure to you, knowing that he is depriving our girls of their rightful inheritance! If I had been in your place, I would have done something about the entail many years ago! I have no patience with the man! And to think that he thought himself worthy of our Elizabeth! And so, I suppose Charlotte has given him a son? She always seems to do whatever is required that is to her advantage" cried Mrs. Bennet.

"Well, in this instance, Mrs. Bennet, she has very kindly taken into account your frequent lamentations on the subject, and given Mr. Collins a daughter, Catherine, after Lady Catherine, of course, Charlotte, after the child's mother, and apparently, the said mother, Charlotte, has insisted on Elizabeth being added, much to Mr. Collins discomfort, until Charlotte reminded him that it was the name of his own late mother, so all is again well in his world. A very clever woman is Charlotte, she is rising again in my esteem."

"A girl! I have always thought Charlotte a very practical woman, not at all handsome, raised quite well enough for *her* situation in life, so I am surprised she gave him a daughter!"

"If you recall, Mrs. Bennet, neither husbands nor wives seem to have a choice in the matter of the gender of their off-spring, they take what they get. You gave me five daughters, in spite of your insistence that each one would be a boy, so if *you* could not, I hardly think anyone else could determine on the sex of their future child"

Not wishing to spoil the previous joyous mood, Bingley intervened in the conversation, "Whether or not one can decide on the sex of their unborn child, let us drink to the good health of Charlotte and baby Catherine Charlotte Elizabeth, and to the continuing health of our expectant ladies, Jane, Lizzy and Lydia"

"To their health!" as everyone raised their glasses, "and now to dinner, we have much to celebrate today" finished Bingley.

Chapter 28

———•———

After two weeks of visiting their Longbourn relations, with the seemingly never-ending visits, dinners and dances with the Lucases and other Meryton notables, Lizzy and Darcy left, to return to Pemberley, via the Lake District, leaving Georgiana with the Bingleys, so that she could remain close to Kitty.

The Darcys had decided to go to the Lake District because Lizzy had not been able to go the previous year, with the Gardiners, as her uncle had had to curtail their travels in order to be back in London, but since the ensuing happy understanding had occurred precisely *because* of the curtailment, neither Lizzy nor Darcy thought it had been quite the disappointment that Lizzy had initially felt when she had first learned the news, so both of them felt it would be pleasant to extend her knowledge of places she had only read about before, especially now, in just each other's company. They took a leisurely route, so as not to tire Lizzy, and returned to Pemberley by the end of June.

"It has been delightful, visiting so many places," remarked Lizzy to Darcy as they drove up to the house, "but nothing compares to coming home again. I do so love Pemberley, my dearest Fitzwilliam"

"As do I, my love. For several years, before you came into my life, I had tended to avoid Pemberley, because of the continuing sadness I felt since the loss of my parents, but since you graced me with your love, Pemberley is once again the happy place I knew as a child and I love it again. And we will also hear the laughter of children in the corridors and gardens. I will show you some more of my favourite haunts, now that the weather is somewhat better. I would spend most of my summers playing in places, pretending to be a pirate, or Robin Hood, or Sir Walter Raleigh, with Wickham and a couple of other boys. I trust our child will have as many happy years here as I did."

"I am certain he or she *will*, my dearest, for if we have a daughter, I would like her to be able to run as freely as we would allow a son. It will be time enough for her to conform, when she nears her leaving of the schoolroom. My father allowed me to run free as a child, even though it *did* lead to my incident with his horse, but I think I would have been a very difficult child had my mother had her way, and kept me indoors, sitting nicely, being seen but not heard, during the morning visits, listening to all the local gossip, but no real intellectual stimulation, for we did not even have the benefit of a governess. I actually agree with Lady Catherine now, that nothing is to be done in education without steady and regular instruction, and nobody but a governess can give it. Do you think I ought to ask her to recommend someone when the time comes?" added Lizzy cheekily, knowing full well that her husband had not, as yet, forgiven his aunt for her loudly voiced opposition to his marriage.

She herself had been at pains to persuade his forgiveness of his aunt, pointing out that it was too late for her to change things, and that it was simply because he had not married his cousin, Anne, as Lady Catherine had hoped for so many years. It had been her dearest wish, to join the two great estates, and her disappointment had been as great as her former aspirations. Darcy could have understood her disappointment, but he would not forgive her active efforts in trying to thwart his marital intentions, even though her account to him of her visit to Longbourn, to force Lizzy to promise *not* to marry him, had actually given him the hope of possible future success in his suit. All of this had been discussed several times between himself and Elizabeth, and he had always been adamant that he could not forgive her, so it was a surprise to himself that Lizzy's cheeky remark now brought a smile to his face. Could the prospect of being a father do this to a man? Could parental love become so overpowering that one could do *anything* for the love of their child?

"As you see fit, my love," he replied, "but I will *not* allow my daughter to be called Catherine!"

"So be it Fitzwilliam, therefore we will discuss all of the names you will *not* allow, in order to come to an understanding of what you *will* accept" replied Lizzy smiling, knowing that deep inside, her husband was starting to forgive his belligerent aunt.

Chapter 29

After several days spent at home, going into the attics to find nursery items and linen for the coming child, Fitzwilliam and Lizzy set off again. This time to the seaside, for Lizzy had never seen the sea. After some deliberation, they had decided to avoid the more frequented places, and opted for a small village on the south coast, recommended by the Parkers, Sidney and Charlotte, who as acquaintances of Darcy's, Lizzy had met several times in Town. She liked them; Sidney Parker had a sense of humour similar to Mr. Bennet's and Charlotte Parker was very pragmatic, much like Charlotte Collins, and Lizzy had warmed to them immediately, so their recommendation of Sanditon was heeded.

The Parkers themselves were to meet them there, since they were to go down for the summer, allegedly to meet the rest of the Parker family, but more because it was the place where they had met and it held a special place in their hearts. Although the Darcy's had been warmly pressed to stay with them, they declined the Parker's invitation, preferring to take a house near the seafront. From what Sidney and Charlotte had told them of the rest of the family, they could be quite invasive, especially the Miss Parkers, so Lizzy and Fitzwilliam preferred to have a place to retreat to, if required, and in fact Sidney Parker thought it such an excellent idea, he inquired as to whether he might himself escape with them. On his recommendations, the Darcy's took the best house in Waterloo Crescent, a newly constructed, handsome affair, built in the shape implied by the name, nearby to Trafalgar House and Heywood Cottage, Sidney and Charlotte's seaside abode.

Having arrived some hours after Madeleine and Thomas, who as usual, travelled ahead in order to have everything ready for them when their master and mistress arrived, they found everything unpacked and set out, their bed made up with their own linen, servants hired, and a cook, recommended by the Parkers, ensconced in the kitchen. Not that dinner would be required that day, for they were to dine at Trafalgar House, the home of Sidney's elder brother, where the whole Parker family were to be assembled.

"From what Sidney was saying, my dear Elizabeth," as Darcy watched her hair being dressed by her maid's skilled hands, "you will have much to divert you in meeting with the rest of his family. He did however give me a word of warning, with regards to his sisters, not to mention one's health: they take great interest in anything in that regard and will talk at great length about it, whether you are paying attention or not."

"Thank you for the warning, but Charlotte has also told me about them. Some natural delicacy of constitution, with an unfortunate turn for medicine, especially quack medicine, had given them an early tendency at various times to various disorders; combined with charitable hearts and many amiable feelings, but also a spirit of restless activity. They take everybody's health very much to heart and are most generous in their suggestions of treatment, be it from an ear-ache, a sprained ankle or how to prevent being poisoned by the scullery maid, who doesn't rince the dishes!"

"My word, it sounds as though there is some vanity in their afflictions and benevolence! I am glad we were forewarned, dearest."

"And what did Sidney say of his brothers? I understand he has two brothers, the younger, Mr. Arthur Parker, just lately married to a West Indian lady of very large fortune, and of course his older

brother, Thomas, or Tom, and his wife Mary, who have a fine family
of three or four children" enquired Lizzie.

"Well, I believe the gentlemen are quite loquacious in their
fields of interest, but the ladies are somewhat quieter, especially
Mrs. Arthur Parker. But we shall find out in due course. Madeleine,
you have, as usual, done a splendid job with Mrs. Darcy's hair, and
you, my dear wife, look very becoming in that primrose gown, it
sets off the necklace and earrings to perfection. You always look so
handsome with emeralds."

The weather being relatively fine, albeit not exactly what one
would expect during summer, the Darcy's decided to walk to
Heyward Cottage, to join their friends, and then together in a
landeau to Trafalgar House, to meet the united Parker family.

Sidney performed the introductions, first to Mr. and Mrs.
Parker, then Mr. and Mrs. Arthur Parker, followed by Miss Parker
and Miss Diana Parker. Charlotte stood by Lizzy, to assist. The
formal introductions made, nearly all of the Parkers started to talk
at once to Sidney. Noticing that Mrs. Arthur Parker, standing a
little behind, seemed to look somewhat intimidated or shy, Lizzy
approached her with a smile, Charlotte at her elbow to smooth the
way, knowing how timid her sister-in-law really was.

"Adela my dear, you are looking so well! Sanditon is certainly
agreeing with you since you came last summer. Elizabeth, my sister
is a very talented artist, more as a naturalist would draw and paint,
her work is very detailed, if you care to look at these paintings beside
the fireplace, they are a set she painted for our sister Mary."

Lizzy bent forward to admire them and found them exquisite
indeed, "Why, I feel I could almost touch the shells you have depicted
Mrs. Parker; you are so talented! I have never seen such beautiful
shells, are they found here? I have never seen the sea until today, and
we have not as yet walked down to the beach."

Sensing a genuine admiration of her work, Adela got over her
shyness, to talk about her shells, so she pointed out to Lizzy that the
paintings were of shells found in her collection, which she had always

had with her, even when travelling, though now she was settled in Sanditon since her marriage to Arthur, her prize shells were now displayed in specially constructed cabinets, for all to admire.

Mr. Arthur Parker joined them at this point, not liking to be long away from his wife, whom he looked after with a great deal of tender affection. "Yes Mrs. Darcy, it was thanks to her illustration skills that we became so well acquainted. I developed an interest in seaweed, but I lacked illustrated reference material to identify the fresh specimens that I found, so Miss Lambe very kindly offered to paint them for me as soon as I had collected them. We fell in love over an interest in seaweed, did we not my dear Adela?"

Noting a deep blush on her cheeks, Lizzy refrained from laughing at such an explanation, sensing that it would make Mrs. Arthur Parker somewhat uncomfortable. At this point they were called to dinner, so she joined Darcy, for they were to lead the way, being the guests of honour.

During dinner Lizzy was placed so that she could listen to everybody's conversation, and had to refrain from many a quip and laugh as the two Miss Parkers regaled all, with their various ailments, solutions, and the importance of all the particular herbal teas required to digest whatever they had managed to eat, as though it had not been an excellent dinner. The three Mr. Parkers had tried to introduce other topics into the conversation: Mr. Parker lauded the benefits of visits to the sea, Sanditon in particular, in order to be in optimal health, Arthur talked of nothing other than seaweed, and Sidney tried, with some degree of success, to suggest an Assembly at the hotel, similar to the one organised the previous year. This caught his elder brother's attention, because it would bring all the Sanditon notables and visitors together and would add to the prestige of the place to be able to boast of "occasional Assemblies *every* summer" in the annual *Guide to Watering Places*.

What Lizzy could not comprehend however, was why Charlotte Parker was trying to stifle a broad grin, as she glanced at her husband, into a more ladylike smile. She would have to wait until later however, to inquire as to the reason, as Miss Diana Parker had taken over the conversation, boasting with no small vanity, that she knew how to organize large-scale entertainment of this kind and how to supervise people successfully, everyone was always ready to work under her direction. Lizzy noticed Sidney slip a sly wink to his wife, whilst stroking the back of his hand, and Charlotte's swift raising of her hand to her mouth, to hide and suppress a laugh.

Lizzy found it difficult to wait until the ladies withdrew to the drawing room and the arrival of the tea and coffee, before she could talk to her friend. The Miss Parkers had commandeered the tea urn, concocting their various herbal teas to assist their digestion and were totally absorbed in their labours. Mary Parker was seeing to the comfort of Adela, so Lizzy and Charlotte had the opportunity to talk between themselves.

"Charlotte," began Lizzy, "I could not help but notice that the idea of an assembly and Miss Diana's mentioning of her organisational skills, seemed to cause yourself and Sidney some hilarity. If it is not indiscreet, could you tell me the source of your humour? My curiosity has, I admit, got the better of my good manners."

"Oh dear, I should not have laughed when I did Elizabeth, but it was Sidney's look and gesture that broke my resolve and I could not help myself. You may have noticed that Diana *does* like to organise everything. What you may not realise, is that she is not as skilled as she likes to think she is. Normally, I would not say such a thing, but since being married to Sidney, he has managed to disrupt much of my normally considerate forbearance to people's foibles.

Last summer, after a visit to Brinshore, a neighbouring resort further along the coast, Mr. Parker organised an assembly, or rather, he suggested, without knowing he had been manipulated into the suggestion by Sidney, that an assembly should be organised. His wife felt a little unsure as to whether such a thing could be organised in such a short time, for she only had a week to do so. Diana very kindly offered to take over the organising, for which Mary was very grateful. To Diana's credit, the assembly *did* get organised, although not quite to her own satisfaction. The crowning glory of the evening supper was to be a blackberry syllabub. The freshness of the fruit being the key to her special recipe, she had expected all the ladies of our circle to spend the morning of the assembly, picking the berries. Needless to say, none of them wished to ruin their complexions, stooping in the hot sun on the very day of a ball, so I offered to collect all the blackberries in the morning. I wasn't expecting to enjoy the ball much myself, because I did not think Sidney would be there; he had gone back to London, so I did not mind. I had picked the berries, taken them to the hotel for the cook to deal with and then joined the rest of the party, congregated at the tea rooms, where, to my great surprise, Sidney was too. He had come down from Town, specifically to dance with *me* at the assembly, he told me, but I did not believe him. Anyway, I had thought the assembly had been a success, but Sidney told me, at the end of the evening, that the syllabub had been a disaster: Duckworth, the cook, had used a glass bowl, not the earthenware pot Diana had decreed must be used, he hadn't been able to find Diana's recipe, so he used sack instead of Rhenish, he had not used lemons to bring out the flavour, it was deplorable, according to Diana, and then Sidney had run a finger lightly across a scratch on the back of my arm, from the brambles, with the most engaging smile possible. That gesture, he repeated over dinner and that is why I had to stifle my laughter, because I would not like to hurt Diana's feelings; she is a very well-meaning person and it would have been quite unkind to laugh."

"Oh! Lord! I do not think I could have contained myself as well as you did Charlotte!" exclaimed Lizzy, as she resolved to have more forbearance to the weaknesses of others, their follies and nonsense, whims, and inconsistencies, in the future, for as she freely admitted, she liked to laugh at such things in general, but it would be more generous of her to refrain from doing so when people's feelings might be hurt, something, she reflected to herself, Jane had always practiced, which is why she was so well beloved by all who knew her.

Chapter 30

———•———

Having survived her first encounter with the rest of the Parker family, Lizzy felt confident she could handle any of the other notables of the neighbourhood. The next few days were spent taking walks along the beach, picnics with Sidney and Charlotte Parker during the day, and dinner with various acquaintance they had made during their daily perambulations about the place.

Sunday brought them to the church in old Sanditon, for modern Sanditon did not possess a church. The procession on leaving the church was led by Lady Denham, the local person of rank, who lived at Sanditon House. She was a widow, a very wealthy widow, and a co-investor, with Mr. Parker, in the building up of modern Sanditon into a seaside village of increasing popularity and renown. She was accompanied at two steps behind by a niece, Miss Brereton, who was herself followed by another of her ladyship's nieces, by marriage, Miss Denham. She walked alone behind her aunt and her companion, which surprised Lizzy, and she was most curious to know the reason, but she must of course wait till she could ask Charlotte, for Charlotte was following Lady Denham and Miss Brereton as they were handed up to Sidney's carriage with an alacrity that left his brother Tom surprised.

"My word, Sidney has deprived me of my weekly good deed! "as he turned to the Darcys, "Lady Denham prides herself on walking to church every Sunday, but that is because it is downhill from Sanditon House, I usually offer to drive her back after the service, for I know that she does not like to walk *up* the hill. However, she is coming to dinner at Trafalgar House this afternoon, so if you would do me the honour of joining us, I will be able to make the introductions, for I believe you have not met Lady Denham and Miss Brereton as yet, although I am certain that you have seen them walking about, for her ladyship is still very agile for a woman of her years, though I am convinced that it is due to the finest sea air that we have in Sanditon; nobody wants for health when they stay here, nobody lacks spirits, if the sea air is not sufficient, then the sea water is the cure, to all ills of the mind, body and spirit."

Lizzy and Darcy smiled at each other; Mr. Parker was overly enthusiastic on the healing properties of the sea, Sanditon in particular, which Sidney had warned them about. Something in the very air of Sanditon seemed to encourage people into hobbies and causes with the greatest of enthusiasm; even the very placid Mrs. Parker was an avid gardener, pottering around in her greenhouse at every opportunity, Mr. Arthur Parker was a fervent collector of seaweed, and the Miss Parkers were always alert to any problems, or even a suspicion or hint of a problem, of health in *anybody*. Only Sidney and Charlotte Parker seemed unaffected, but then, they did not actually live in Sanditon, although Sidney *had* been born and raised there, until he got sent off to school with his brother Tom.

The Darcy's left the church, going home to change for a walk along the beach. Lizzy had never seen the sea before arriving in Sanditon, and her first walk on the sand had been exhilarating. The sound of the crashing of the waves on the beach, the smell and the freshness of the air, the sunshine, the combination was a delight to her. Since then, she felt the urge to walk along the beach every day, then retire to the tea-rooms for a cup of tea, before walking back to Waterloo Crescent.

Today their walk was kept purposely shorter, as the Parkers, or rather, Lady Denham, kept early hours and dinner had been arranged for an earlier than usual time, more in keeping with her habits, so they returned to rest and then dress for dinner. Wishing to respect Lady Denham's position, Lizzy chose a gown more formal than she would have normally worn for a dinner with friends in a seaside town, a crimson damask creation trimmed with pewter coloured braid, a finely knitted lace shawl from the Shetlands and a ruby necklace and earrings. She kept her hair quite simple, for an elaborate town style would be out of place, but Madeleine's hands still created a stunning effect with the weaving of ribbons into her hair and curls cascading to her shoulders.

Thinking that they had arrived in good time, they were surprised to note that Lady Denham, Miss Brereton and Miss Denham had already arrived before them, and the great lady settled in the best seat in the drawing room, which permitted Lady Denham to rise in a somewhat majestic manner, as she allowed the introductions to be made by Mr. Parker, which had been her intention from the start. Miss Brereton seemed a very amiable lady, some few years older than Lizzy, who was Lady Denham's companion, looking after her needs, and managing very well, respectfully without being subservient, a lot like Charlotte Collins. Miss Denham was totally different in manner, reminding Lizzy of Mr. Collins in her assiduous attempts of flattering Lady Denham, feeling put out by her aunt's obvious preference of her other niece and unable to hide her sentiments as well as she might have. Lizzy wondered at her discontentedness, but chose to ignore the rudeness.

Lady Denham was of middle height, stout, upright and alert in her motions, with a shrewd eye and self-satisfied air but not an unagreeable countenance; and as her manner was rather forthright and abrupt, as of a person who valued herself on being free-spoken, Lady Catherine sprang to Lizzy's mind, however there was a good humour and cordiality about her, a civility and a readiness to be acquainted with friends of her old friends, that inspired a degree of goodwill which Lady Catherine had never managed to achieve.

During dinner Lizzy had time to observe the interactions of the *grand dame* and her nieces. Miss Brereton chatted with ease and confidence with everyone, whilst attending to anything her aunt might require, whereas Miss Denham was obviously doing penance, speaking very little, except to her aunt, and then only to agree with whatever she said, pointedly ignoring Miss Brereton and only managing small, stilted conversations with Mrs. Parker or Lizzy, being seated between the two of them and therefore unable to totally ignore them. A very disgruntled lady, thought Lizzy.

It was only after dinner however, once Lady Denham and Miss Brereton had left, taking Miss Denham with them to drop her off at Denham House, that Lizzy's curiosity could be assuaged.

"I know you are most curious Elizabeth" started Charlotte "as to the mystery about Miss Denham, I could see your eyes during dinner, querying as to her motives for such apparently strange behaviour."

"Was my curiosity so obvious? I am sorry that it was so." apologised Lizzy.

"No Elizabeth, it was certainly not obvious, but my own mind is similar to your own, I think, and *I* would have been most curious myself, if I did not know the cause."

"So hopefully, Charlotte, you are now about to enlighten me?"

"Do you read novels Elizabeth? For if you do, you will be able to enjoy, and possibly comprehend the story."

"Yes, I do enjoy novels; Pemberley processes an excellent library, to which my husband is adding to assiduously; he acquires all the latest literature, be it serious, learned, or not."

"Well then, you are well prepared for something that you will think you could only read of in a novel!

Last summer, Mr. and Mrs. Parker were driving their carriage along the road in front of my home, on an errand to hire a physician, who most certainly was *not* living in our parish. They mistook my village of Willingdon to be *Great* Willingdon, where the said physician was actually to be found. Because of the state of the road, their carriage overturned and Mr. Parker badly sprained his ankle, so they were obliged to stay with my family for a fortnight, whilst his ankle healed.

After the fortnight, they persuaded me to return to Sanditon with them, as thanks for my family's hospitality. During my stay with them I met Sir Edward, Miss Denham's brother, who considered himself as quite a Lovelace, convinced that any fair lady was his to flatter and woo. With such personal advantages as he felt himself to possess, and such talents as he gave himself credit for, he regarded it as his duty to be as seductive as possible. At first, I thought him quite an agreeable gentleman, but then, through continued acquaintance with him, I thought him quite odd, in fact a very muddled and silly young man, who had read far too many novels and who considered himself quite worthy of any villain in any novel, in the pursuit of woman, in spite of all convention. The very name of Sir Edward, he thought, carried some degree of fascination with it"

"What an odd character he seems to have!" exclaimed Lizzy

"That is but the start of it, Elizabeth. To be generally gallant and assiduous about the fair, to make fine speeches to every pretty girl, was but the inferior part of the character he had to play. Myself or any other young woman with any pretensions to beauty, he was entitled, according to his own views of society, to approach with high compliment and rhapsody on the slightest acquaintance. His references to poetry, from our best poets, was in fact, quite erratic. His aim, at the time, was to seduce and marry Miss Clara Brereton, Miss Elizabeth's cousin, who was companion to Lady Denham last summer, for he suspected that Lady Denham was going to leave her fortune to Clara, and he did not want to miss the opportunity of marrying a very beautiful heiress. Whether Lady Denham had even considered Clara as a beneficiary to her estate, did not enter Sir Edward's head.

To cut a long story short, Elizabeth, Sir Edward had decided to abduct Miss Clara when she was on her way to meet Miss Elizabeth, in Hailsham, who had finally been invited to Sanditon House, but what he did *not* know at the time, was that Miss Clara had on the *same day* eloped with her cousin, to whom she had been betrothed since *before* Lady Denham had selected her as a companion, and *I* had taken her place to meet her cousin, Miss Elizabeth. Am I quite clear so far?"

"Perfectly clear Charlotte, but I now understand what you meant by it sounding as though it was from a novel! How incredulous it sounds! So, what happened next?"

"Well Sir Edward had gone to Hailsham the day before, in his one-horse gig, for he could not afford anything bigger, in order to abduct Miss Clara before she met Miss Elizabeth. I had arrived a good hour before the mail coach from London was due, so I went for a walk along the streets that brought me to the road that leads to Willingdon, my home, where I was due to return to myself, two days hence. I was quietly reflecting on my own homecoming, when I was suddenly assailed from behind, accosted by Sir Edward, who had mistaken me for Miss Clara, even though we were totally different in height, build and dress. He forced me into his gig, even though he had finally realised who I was, and continued his planned abduction with a totally different woman! I tried to calm him down, to no avail, but since I realised which road we were on, the actual road to my home, I decided to let him carry on. He had mentioned, in previous conversations, that he had a friend, currently away abroad, who had a hunting lodge 'down Willingdon way', so I assumed that that was where he was planning to abduct me to, since he could not afford anything grander. I was quite uncharitable with him. I told him what I thought of him, and his sister, telling him that I thought him quite childish in his behaviour. This angered him and he whipped his poor horse into speeds that it could not keep up, in his efforts to frighten me. What he did not know, was that he was in fact, driving me home. So, when his horse could walk no more, it simply stopped, in front of a field not far from my house, where one of my father's labourers greeted me. I simply jumped out of the gig, thanked him for bringing me thus far and walked home from there, surprising my family at tea.

The following morning, I had written a letter to the Parkers to try and explain what had happened, but on the same day, Sidney turned up at my parents' home, desperate for news of me. Fortunately, with his then declaring his love for me, which *I* had till then thought impossible, we came to an agreement, Sidney and I, and all turned out as well as you have found us, but Sir Edward was more or less banished from Sanditon.

Miss Denham has lost so much favour with Lady Denham, who as you may have noticed, is quite forthright with her opinions, so poor Miss Denham is paying for the sins of her brother, a situation which you may comprehend is not a happy one, hence her difficult position and strange demeanour."

"You are quite correct, Charlotte, in saying that it is a most incredible tale! Poor Miss Denham, I pity her indeed, hers is a most difficult situation. I will try and pay her more attention during our stay here, or do you thing that would be wrong of me?"

"I do not think that it would be wrong of you, Elizabeth; as visitors to Sanditon, with your status, you may do as you wish. *I* cannot make overtures to her company, because I was, inadvertently, the injured party, and therefore the whole Parker family tend to refrain from too much contact. But it is quite unfair that she should continue to suffer for the faults of her brother, Sir Edward"

"Then I will talk to Darcy about inviting her to dinner whilst we remain here. My cook is determined to prove her worth and is quite disappointed at our lack of large dinner parties. Will you be able to attend? I am thinking of in three days' time"

"We would be delighted to attend Elizabeth, but may I suggest that you do not invite Lady Denham to the same dinner? Miss Denham would feel as uncomfortable as she was tonight, in her presence. This of course means you would have to invite her ladyship to a separate dinner. I am sorry to have to mention that."

"That is quite alright, I am sure my cook would be more than delighted to prepare a dinner for Lady Denham and Miss Brereton the day before. Would you be able to attend both days? I do not feel quite up to handling Lady Denham on my own. I shall ask Mr. and Mrs. Parker too. I think a small circle of her friends would be more agreeable to her ladyship."

"We will be very happy to help you, and if you and Darcy could attend tea with us and Arthur and Adela tomorrow, I think you will find her a lot more interesting and knowledgeable than her natural shyness would give one at first the impression of. She is more comfortable in smaller parties and she mentioned to me that she was flattered by your admiration of her work."

Chapter 31

———•———

Dinners, teas and the 'occasional ball' were dealt with, with great success: Miss Denham was much less unsociable without the company of Lady Denham, and Lizzy's ball gown and hair had upped the tone of the ball, enough to be mentioned in the newspapers in Town, and simply their presence in Sanditon, added to the upcoming fame of Sanditon, so Mr. Parker was extremely satisfied with the season thus far, even though the fine weather one would expect during the summer, was but in very short supply.

Lizzy's increasing girth becoming somewhat cumbersome, the Darcy's resisted Mr. Parker's insistence that a six-week stay was absolutely necessary to their health, and left at the end of the month, heading back to Pemberley, with a slight detour to Gaddesley House, the Bingley's new estate in Leicestershire, only thirty miles from Pemberley.

The Bingley's had taken advice from Darcy and had looked at an estate in Leicestershire. Just as with Netherfield, Charles Bingley had looked at it for half an hour, and decided to purchase the estate, though this time, with the knowledge that his friend, Mr. Darcy, had recommended it.

After three days of travelling, at a slow pace, the Darcy's approached the house at the end of a cloudy afternoon. Passing through the village, Lizzy noticed the local church, St Luke's which was a fine building, placed next to the local inn, The Cheney Arms, which sent her into irrepressible giggles; the thought of men leaving the sanctity of the church, after the Sunday service, straight into the inn. On past the well-tended farms, which she supposed were part of the estate, they arrived at Underwood Lodge, where the Park Hill drive lead up to the house, which had previously been called Gaddesley Park. The reason why the Bingley's had changed the name was simply due to their wish to not appear as pompous new arrivals, for it was known that Mr. Bingley had acquired his fortune through trade. A 'Gaddesley House' sounded less pretentious than 'Gaddesley Park', even though the approach to the house was indeed a well laid out park, apparently designed by Repton at the end of the last century, so the trees were well grown and the whole effect was very tasteful, almost as good as the Pemberley grounds, though Lizzy thought that nothing could equal the beauty of Pemberley.

Arriving finally at the house, Lizzy, helped out of the carriage by the ever-thoughtful Darcy, fell into her sister's arms, though both were somewhat encumbered by their stomachs.

"Goodness! how big we are! Are you quite well Jane?" exclaimed Lizzy as they greeted each other.

"As well as you seem to be my dear Lizzy, though I am relieved that we have settled into this new house without too much effort, on my part at least. I am grateful that the servants have done such an excellent job in making the move as seamless as possible for me. Mrs. Nicholls, the housekeeper at Netherfield, agreed to come with us, as did Mr. Bruce, the butler, and even Mrs. Duce the cook, so everything was done without any real effort on my part at all, for which I am exceedingly grateful. Having never moved an entire household before, for we had always lived in Longbourn, I had no concept of the almost military precision required in uplifting an entire household to a new country!"

"That is something I have been spared, Pemberley being the family home for so many generations! I am so happy that you are now closer to me, we may visit each other more often, or we may do so, once our babies are born!"

"Then we must spend Christmas here," pronounced Jane, "if you and your child are able to travel. I will have recovered enough to organise everything by then, since the baby is due in early October, though by the size of my stomach, it may come earlier. I feel as big as a whale!"

"Lizzy! Darcy! You have arrived!" Kitty exclaimed as she ran into the room, closely followed by Georgiana, who was equally delighted to see them

"Fitzwilliam! Lizzy! My word! How big you have grown, Lizzy!'

"Indeed girls, Jane and I were just reflecting on our ever-expanding girth!" laughed Lizzy, who was very pleased to see them both, having left them with the Bingley's at Netherfield in May.

"Come," said Jane, "let us go into the parlour and have some tea, I am sure Lizzy must be in need of some refreshment and some rest."

"Tea would be most welcome Jane, but for rest; we have been travelling for three days and after all that sitting, I really must walk around a little, it is so refreshing after remaining in the same posture for so long, although Fitzwilliam ordered the carriage to stop every so often, so that I *could* exercise a little, for I suffer from discomfort in my legs if I sit too long." as she followed Jane into a good sized room off the main entrance hall.

"What a lovely room Jane! And well is it set up! Since Netherfield had been rented furnished, you must have had quite a business to furnish Gaddesley House."

"Not as bad as you make it sound Lizzy, for when we purchased the estate, we were able to acquire some of the furnishings and the furniture that we liked, so with the help of catalogues and only one or two trips to town, the main rooms were furnished at remarkably little expense. There are still rooms to be addressed, but for our small family, it is currently sufficient. In the spring, when we have lived here for a few months, we will be better able to choose furniture to suit our taste. My mother was most insistent that I furnish the house from top to bottom before we arrived, but I felt it would be foolish, even imprudent, to do so, until I could decide which rooms I preferred, their aspect and to which use they were to be intended."

"This room seems to be very tastefully done Jane, I like the way you have combined older, well cared-for furniture, with the newer pieces, it works well together and makes the room look as though you have been here for many years, it reminds me of Pemberley."

"That is very kind of you Lizzy, I admit that I have taken your home as a standard I hope to achieve, in time. Kitty, my dear, would you be so kind as to bring us some tea please?"

Chapter 32

The next few days were spent with Jane showing Lizzy around the house, obviously very proud and pleased to be able to do so. The afternoons were spent driving around the estate in a landeau, neither herself nor Lizzy able to walk so far in their condition. The gentlemen explored the estate and home farms, Firs and Bell Bush, on horseback, Darcy thoroughly approving everything and making some suggestions for minor improvements, which Bingley intended to implement, such was his admiration for his friend, who had many years' experience in running a large estate.

After spending a quiet week together, the Darcy's set off for Pemberley, leaving Georgiana and Kitty with the Bingley's. As they finally entered the grounds, Lizzy, although she was now mistress of Pemberley, never ceased to be delighted at the approach to her home, a place for which nature had done much, and where natural beauty had been so little counteracted by an awkward taste. After a gradual ascent of half a mile, they found themselves at the top of a considerable eminence, where the wood ceased, and the eye was instantly caught by Pemberley House, situated on the opposite side of a valley into which the road wound with some abruptness. The handsome stone house, standing well on rising ground, was backed by a ridge of high woody hills; and in front, a stream of some natural importance was swelled into greater, but without any artificial appearance. She recalled her thoughts on approaching Pemberley for the very first time, a year ago now, with her uncle and aunt Gardiner, that it would indeed be something to be mistress of Pemberley! How much had happened since then!

After so much travelling over the past months, it was a relief to Lizzy to be in her own home, settling down to the quiet routine of daily life at Pemberley. The weather was still unseasonably cold, but she could walk in the grounds, either by herself or with Fitzwilliam. Occasional rain made the earth smell so rich, the grass so green, refreshing the trees, that she did not mind being occasionally confined to the conservatory or the picture gallery for her daily exercise.

The nursery was ready, a nurse engaged, a reputable midwife hired from Derby, all Lizzy had to do, was wait. However, news arrived from Newcastle in the first week of September: Lydia was safely delivered of a daughter, Jane Elizabeth, and would Darcy contemplate becoming the child's sponsor?

"My love," started Lizzy during dinner, "Lydia and Wickham have had a daughter, Jane Elizabeth, and they are wondering whether you would be agreeable to become the child's godfather. Jane, after my mother and also my sister, who has agreed to be the godmother, and Elizabeth, apparently after myself. What do you think?" as she passed the letter over to her husband.

"I admit to being surprised, yet *not* surprised at their application. What are your thoughts on the matter, my dear?" as he read the letter, written by Lydia. "And what does she mean when she asks you to send her *more* money?"

"I periodically send her some monies, saved from my pin money, when she needs some assistance. I was sure you would not mind."

"I suspected as much, and do not worry, I do *not* mind at all, but perhaps you are not aware that they frequently apply to the Bingley's for funds as well. From what I know of Wickham, and from you have learned of him, he is an opportunist, and it appears that your sister writes in the same vein; she asks me to sponsor their child, in the most basic sense of the verb, hoping that I will pay for its upkeep, which should be the poor child's father's responsibility. I hope I do not offend you dearest, by speaking this way."

"No, Fitzwilliam, I think we are of the same mind on the matter. As much as I am sure I will love my niece, I feel it was very impertinent of Wickham to ask you, albeit through my sister, who is too ignorant to see the manipulations of her husband, or at least I hope she is, for otherwise she has become the same as him."

"Then you will not be surprised or offended if I decline the invitation, Elizabeth?"

"Certainly not, the contrary would have surprised me, but as you can read in her letter, if you refuse, then their friend Mr. Denny will do, even if, as Lydia writes, 'he is not as rich as Darcy', how could she be so base?"

"I am sorry that you have been hurt by her remark, I am sure she did not mean any malice by it, but being married to Wickham cannot always be easy. I will send some funds down to Newcastle, specifically to Lydia, to assist them"

"And I will send down baby linen, for she cannot spend them"

"As you wish, my dear. Have you considered how the news will be received in Longbourn?" enquired Darcy

"Goodness! No! I was so concerned about your feelings, I quite forgot about my mother and father! My mother will of course be delighted! Lydia will be her favourite child again, and she will probably be attempting to persuade my father that they should all go down to Newcastle to meet their first grandchild."

"I can imagine his response to that, my dear!" chuckled Darcy, which instantly lifted Lizzy's mood.

Chapter 33

However, they were both surprised, for although he refused to go down to Newcastle himself, or allow either Mary or Kitty to go, Mr. Bennet *did* allow Mrs. Bennet to travel to see her daughter, to her great delight.

"Oh, Mr. Bennet! I knew I should persuade you in the end! I shall see my dearest Lydia and dear Wickham, and my first grandchild, named after me, as you know, little Jane Wickham, how well it sounds! I am sure she is the most beautiful child."

"Whether the most beautiful child or not, I feel it is right that Lydia should be noticed on the occasion; since the debacle of her marriage was such, that you were not able to do anything for her, and I was too angry with her myself, at the time. I will arrange for the carriage to take you to Hatfield to meet the mail coach, with your maid and a manservant of course."

"I knew you loved you daughter too well, Mr. Bennet, to remain angry with her for too long, for she is a good girl, at heart." Mr. Bennet refrained from replying.

Within days, Mrs. Bennet was on her way, laden with more baby linen, the good wishes proffered by the neighbourhood, and all the latest gossip: she had so much to catch up on with Lydia, once she got to Newcastle. So, it was a shock for her when, arriving at the coaching inn, there was nobody to meet her! Fortunately, her maid,

Susan Hills, the housekeeper's daughter, had the directions of the Wickham's home, so the manservant hired a hackney coach and they proceeded to the given address.

The coach rattled down a narrow street, and drew up in front of a small house, the Wickham's current abode. The door was opened by a trollopy-looking maid servant, who rudely asked what they wanted.

"We are here to visit Mrs. Wickham" replied the manservant, Hamilton, for Mrs. Bennet was too shocked to reply.

"And who are you?" the maid enquired, "does the missus know you? Is she expecting you?"

Stunned at the girl's rudeness, Mrs. Bennet found her voice, "I am Mrs. Wickham's mother, and I insist you let us in, and announce our arrival to your mistress!" Reluctantly, the servant led them into a small, badly lit room, filled with shabby, dirty, ill-kempt furniture and told them to wait whilst she informed Mrs. Wickham of their arrival.

Absolutely shocked at the conditions her daughter was living in, Mrs. Bennet did not even have the energy or inclination to feel palpitations or to allow her susceptible nerves get the better of her. The sound of someone running down the narrow stairs caught her attention and Lydia flew into the room, embracing her mother with warmth.

"Oh Mama! I quite forgot you were coming today! I have got nothing ready for you, and I am sure there is not a bit of meat to be had! Would you care for some tea? I will call back the servant."

"Lydia!" cried Mrs. Bennet, "how is it you are living in such a shabby house? The furniture is atrocious! And how came you by such a servant? She would be refused work as the scullery-maid at Longbourn!"

"She is not as bad as the previous one we had; *she* was truly awful and she kept making eyes at my dear Wickham. His being such a handsome man, he cannot help attracting women, but I would not tolerate it happening under my own roof, especially as I was so large and fat at the time. I sent her on her way, and I have heard since that she is now with child! A slattern of a girl if ever there was, I suppose she does not even know who the father is!"

"But Lydia, my dear child, I have been sending you money, so why such a house? I am sure you could afford better lodgings with what I have been sending you, as well as the allowance your father gives you. Your father cannot be aware of the situation! How can Wickham keep his family thus?"

"Oh! my dear Wickham would do so much more for us, were it not for his bill at the officer's mess. He is expected to spend every evening there, till very late, and I am sure the other officers are taking advantage of his generosity, for most of his money goes on paying for their drinks, he says, which although unfortunate, he cannot avoid, if he wishes for any promotion. It has to be done; he says. He is trying to improve our fortunes by playing at cards, but without much success, I am sure that they cheat, so we are here until he has better luck."

"My poor, dear girl, how bravely you bear it! But you are looking well; you have recovered quickly, but a woman often does, after her first child. It gets more difficult with ensuing births"

"There will be no ensuing births! It is such a disgusting process that I refuse to go through it again, getting so fat I could barely waddle, and the birthing! I have got a wet-nurse to look after the infant, so I don't have to do anything with it. If I could only get the woman to heed my instructions; that I don't wish to see or hear the squalling thing, then it would be so much the better." Mrs. Bennet could not believe what she had just heard, how could Lydia speak of her own child in such a way?

"I am sure you exaggerate, Lydia, I am sure that baby Jane does not cry all the time. May I see her? She is my first grandchild and I long to see her. Please send for her."

"As you wish" replied Lydia, turning into the hallway and bellowing up the stairs, "Nurse! Bring it down, my mother wishes to see it!"

Mrs. Bennet, shocked as much as she had been since arriving, had to sit down on a none too clean sofa. She looked at her daughter in open-mouthed silence, and waited for the nurse to bring the baby in to her. For all her faults, Mrs. Bennet had always been a loving mother, sometimes one daughter would have her favour over another, but she loved all her girls. She was appalled at Lydia's comportment with regards to her new-born child. Her maid, still with her, for neither of Mrs. Bennet's servants had received any indication as to where they were to go and so had remained in the room, tried to assist her obviously distressed mistress.

"No, I shall be well, Susan, for I am not the sort of woman who easily allows her nerves to get the better of her, fortitude will carry me through, so put away your salts, I shall be well in a moment."

At that point, a clean, but shabbily dressed young woman, came into the room, lovingly carrying a tiny, swaddled infant. She pointedly ignored Lydia, who equally took no notice of her or the child. The nurse dropped a small curtsey to Mrs. Bennet and handed the baby to her.

Mrs. Bennet immediately had eyes for nobody else. Such a beautiful child! Why, little Jane could even surpass her aunt Jane in beauty! She was totally overwhelmed with love for her first grandchild, forgetting even Lydia's shocking behaviour; grandmama would be there for her, come what may, even if Mr. Bennet opposed her. As she crooned over the infant, Lydia's vociferous voice came through her euphoric haze of emotion.

"Mama! you have said nothing about my new gown, do not you think it very becoming?"

Raising her eyes to look at her daughter's gown, Mrs. Bennet felt anger rising, something she had not felt since Elizabeth had refused Mr. Collins' offer of marriage. Tenderly handing the child back to her nurse, who appeared to love the infant, Mrs. Bennet answered in a shaking voice.

"I had not noticed the newness of your gown, Lydia, because you claimed to be so short of money, so it did not occur to me that you would spend money that you do not have, on a gown, when you are now a mother, who should do anything for her child. How came you by the money to afford such a gown?"

"Oh," answered Lydia carelessly, "The baby linen that you, Jane and Lizzy sent down, caught the attention of an officers' wife, so she bought it all, allowing *me* to buy a new gown."

"Lydia! How could you do such a thing? So, are telling me that your child has nothing, but that you have a new gown?"

"Why yes Mama, I thought that *you* would understand; as a married woman, I must always look my best, especially after having being so fat and going through the dreadful birthing of a child. Wickham hardly notices me now!"

"Lydia, oh Lydia!" cried Mrs. Bennet, "You were always my favourite child! How could you have become so unfeeling? Do you feel nothing for anyone but yourself? Have I raised you to be so selfish? You could not even remember that I was coming today: you sent no-one to meet me! I had to find my own way here, even though I sent you word! It took me a great deal of persuasion with your father, to come down to Newcastle at all, and I find you in this situation! You have no compassion for my poor nerves, I must sit down!"

"Well if Jane and Lizzy would only send me more money, we would not be in this position! They are so mean! *They* have plenty of money and they should send more to me, I *am* their sister after all. What can I do with the measly five pounds they each send me every month?"

If ever Mrs. Bennet had thought she had suffered with nerves and palpitations in the past, it was absolutely *nothing* to what she felt now. If she had been physically able to move, she would have struck her daughter. Her maid was so alarmed, she rushed to her side to try and assist her.

"Lydia, I am aghast to think that you could behave this way. I am beginning to think as your father does; nay, he just called you silly and ignorant, I think you are callous and selfish and am only ashamed that I may have made you thus, with my possible over-indulgence of you in the past. I alone defended you when you ran away, I tried to assist you with every means possible, I too have been sending you money, because I did not know that your sisters were doing as much, in fact more; economy may not be within my understanding, but even *I* cannot comprehend how, with the income bestowed on you by your father, of one hundred pounds per year, the ten pounds a month your sisters are sending you, plus what I have been sending, that you cannot survive in better circumstances than this! It is a husband's duty to provide for his family, so why is not Wickham doing so?"

"Mama, you are making such a fuss! Why should not my sisters, and mother and father look after me? You have the means and I have the need. I will need more now, now that I am a mother; that nurse needs to be paid and fed and clothed, and I cannot afford to do so"

Mrs. Bennet's maid was convinced that her mistress was on the point of apoplexy and so was applying the salts and trying to rub her temples, anything to relieve her. She nodded to Hamilton, with whom she had been quietly talking during the previous discussions, and he immediately left the house, returning some ten minutes later.

"Ma'am, come, Hamilton has procured a hackney cab and loaded our trunks into it, you cannot stay here Ma'am."

During the time her manservant had been away, Mrs. Bennet had become more and more quiet and subdued, listening to Lydia justifying her own behaviour, by blaming everybody but herself, not even noticing the pallor of her mother.

"Thank you, Hills," replied her mistress, in a surprisingly even tone, "send Hamilton to fetch my grandchild and her nurse, and whatever of her belongings my daughter has *not* yet managed to sell; they are coming with me"

Somewhat startled, Susan Hills did as she was bid, and within a very short time, Mrs. Bennet, her servants, her grandchild and the child's nurse were transported away from the house, to a respectable inn in town, from where the mail coach would leave the following day.

Lydia, finally realising that her mother was not supporting her behaviour, cried and begged her mother to stay, but to no avail, because perhaps for the first time in her life, Mrs. Bennet had thought upon a serious matter, made a decision, and acted upon it. There was no way in the world she was going to leave this poor, innocent child behind with such a selfish, uncaring, neglectful, mother. She would have to find a way of persuading Mr. Bennet that she had done the right thing, but now, all she wanted, all she cared about, was to get away from Lydia and to care for her granddaughter.

Chapter 34

———•———

Three days after Mrs. Bennet's supposed arrival in Newcastle, the surprise of everybody can be imagined when she drove up to Gaddesley House, in a hired post chaise, totally unannounced, and accompanied by a tiny infant and its' nurse.

Rushing out to greet Mrs. Bennet as soon as she had been notified, Jane was astonished by her mother. She seemed to be a changed person, no longer concerned about her own comforts, discomforts, imagined or real; Mrs. Bennet appeared very clear and coherent.

"Jane, my love, this is your god-daughter and namesake, little Jane. I am aware how surprised you must be, but if you will organise some tea for me, and show the nurse to the nursery, I will explain."

After hearing her story, as much as Mrs. Bennet recalled of the events, Jane was at once all concern for her mother.

"What a dreadful experience you have had, Mama, not being met, in a strange town, with no other acquaintance to assist you, having to find your own way and then to be treated in such a fashion! How your heart must have grieved! My poor dear mother! However, the worst is Lydia's behaviour to her child! Referring to the babe as 'it', how cruel and unfeeling! I do not care at all about her selling the baby linen, to buy herself a gown, but to treat her own child in such a way! You did the right thing, I think, in getting the child away from there, but does my father know what you have done?"

"That is part of my concerns, Jane; when I left with the child, it seemed to be the only thing to be done, but now, I am not so sure, what if your father disapproves? He has nearly always disapproved any of my decisions, and this, even *I* now realise, is going to have some serious consequences. I have not told him yet, and I know not how to go about it. Should I take the child straight down to Longbourn or should I write? Or will he insist that I take the child back to Lydia? Oh Jane! What must I do?" as she started to weep, emotionally overcome by the events of the past few days.

Jane consoled her as best she could, and suggested that Mrs. Bennet go to her room for a rest, as she was obviously too tired and distressed to think of what to do for the best, they would discuss it with Bingley before dinner, he would advise them as to the best course of action to take. Mrs. Bennet, feeling a little better, having explained the events, took the advice so kindly given and retired to her room, leaving Jane to tell Mr. Bingley.

When he heard what had happened, Bingley was as horrified as Jane had been, at Lydia's behaviour to her child, but as he pointed out, Mrs. Bennet's taking of the child was tantamount to kidnapping, for nowhere in the account had Mrs. Bennet been able to say that she had had permission to take little Jane. The fact that Lydia had made no attempt to stop her, would probably not hold up in a court of law, should, heaven forbid, the Wickhams wish to complain to the courts.

"We must inform Mr. Bennet and Darcy immediately, my dear, but in the meantime, the child must stay with us, until something is sorted. I will write by express to Longbourn, and I will send a rider to Pemberley. This must be untangled as expeditiously as possible, to the best benefit to the child."

"I knew you would understand, Charles, and between the three of you, I know this will be arranged to the benefit of all. If Lydia really does not love her child, then it would be for the best for the child to be raised elsewhere. I shall now go to the nursery to see that the nurse and child are settled."

After several hours rest, Mrs. Bennet came down to dinner, still somewhat discomposed, but in a happier frame of mind.

"I am so sorry, my dear Bingley, to bring this upon you, but I really did not know what else to do! Kitty! my love! "interrupting her apology as Kitty and Georgiana came into the parlour. The account of her unexpected arrival was gone through again, with much of the tale being told by Jane, for Mrs. Bennet, after her stalwart exertions of the past days, was returning to her more usual state of incapability and nervousness. The knowledge that the gentlemen were to take care of it all, had set her mind at rest from the responsibility.

During dinner, Jane mentioned that she had been to the nursery, and had talked for some time with the nurse, who seemed very honest and took great care of the baby. She had been hired the day after the child's birth, as a wet nurse, for Mrs. Wickham had taken a dislike to the child from the beginning, and refused to touch her. The nurse had only just lost her own child, also a little girl, and took to the baby immediately, giving her everything that was required, including affection. She fully approved Mrs. Bennet's actions, saying that Mrs. Wickham had already threatened to put the child out to a family in the country, where she would not have to see it, so when Mrs. Bennet sent for her and the child, to take them away, she had had no hesitation in leaving with her.

"The woman, Sarah, will need some clothes, for she left Newcastle with just the clothes she stood in, but I am sure we can find something suitable; I have day dresses that I no longer wear, so perhaps they can be made over to suit her." added Jane, as kind and benevolent as ever.

"And we will make some more linen for the child" added Kitty "for we are her aunts after all, are we not, Georgiana?"

Chapter 35

The following day, at around noon, Darcy rode up to the house, gave his horse to the groom and went in to greet the Bingley's and Bennets, giving a big hug to Georgiana first.

"I received your message last night Bingley, your rider certainly made good time! I left at first light this morning, and Elizabeth is following in the carriage. She should be here this evening, I do not wish her to rush, in her condition."

"Thank you, Darcy," replied Bingley, "I knew you would come. We need your clear-headed thinking to sort the situation out. We sent an express to Mr. Bennet, and I have no doubt we shall see him late tomorrow afternoon, or the day after."

After taking some refreshment after his thirty-mile ride, Darcy retired to his room to change into fresh clothes, before meeting Bingley in the library. The nurse was summoned and Darcy heard her side of the story, having heard Mrs. Bennet's version of events already.

"Well," said Darcy, as soon as Sarah left them, "we certainly have a delicate situation on our hands. We cannot do much until Mr. Bennet arrives, but I think we must let the Wickhams know that their daughter is safe, with you. I will send an express to them now. How very sad that the poor child, in less than four weeks of existence, should have become such a hindrance to her mother. I did not hear any mention of her father however. Does he even know that his child is gone?"

"I do not know," replied Bingley, "but if he cared at all, he surely must have tried to contact one or other of us by now, and we have heard nothing! Perhaps he thinks Mrs. Bennet went straight to Longbourn, which means he would have written to Mr. Bennet."

Having sent the express, the gentlemen returned to the ladies, where Mrs. Bennet was ensconced in the best chair, being plied with refreshments, and consoled for the onset of nerves and palpitations that had returned to her with an added vengeance, now that the gentlemen had taken over the situation that she had caused. Her valiance throughout the whole unfortunate incident had now left her, returning her to her normal, indecisive, querulous self.

"If I had been able to carry my point, to go to Lydia before the birth, as I requested, this would never have happened, for she is not the sort of girl to behave in such a manner, but I was over-ruled, as I always am! What is to become of the poor child? I did what I thought was best for the child, so how could I be accused of kidnapping her? She is my grand-daughter, so how can it be thought that I did wrong?"

"You did not do wrong ma'am," replied Jane, "but Lydia may be frantic with worry about her child, and we do not know what Wickham thinks of the whole affair. It is to be hoped that they understand your motive for doing so; that you had the child's best interests at heart. As soon as my father arrives, I am sure that the gentlemen will find a satisfactory solution for all parties, so do not fret so much my dear mother, for it pains my heart to see you so, and I am so near term …"

"Oh! my poor dear Jane! How thoughtless of me! And I brought the worry to your home! Mr. Bennet will be most cross with me for doing so, but I knew not where else to go!" wailed Mrs. Bennet, who was interrupted mid-speech by the arrival of her second daughter Elizabeth.

"Lizzy!" cried Jane, "you must have travelled much too fast for a woman in your condition; we were not expecting you for another two hours at least! Are you quite well? Pray, sit down on this chair and I will call for more tea and refreshments"

"Indeed Lizzy," added Darcy as he embraced her, "I shall have words with the coachman, I specifically told him not to travel too fast, I would not wish for you to suffer any avoidable discomfort!"

"You worry too much my dear, the coach is so comfortable, and there were so many cushions and blankets I could not come to any harm, even if the carriage had overturned!" she replied laughingly, before turning back to Jane.

"Jane! We look like two galleons in full sail! If we get any bigger, we shall surely burst! I think *you* should be sitting down yourself and taking some tea. How are you dear Jane?"

"As you surmised, about ready to burst. The babe is due anytime soon, so the midwife has taken up abode and the child's nursery maids too. It is just as well they *are* here, for I have put my niece there for the moment, with her wet-nurse, until we can sort out this current situation"

"Lizzy! let me embrace you my dear child," cried out Mrs. Bennet, who was truly happy to see her, but also somewhat contrite at being the cause of her travelling so far in her advanced state of gravidity.

"You should not have travelled so far in your condition!"

Mr. Darcy smiled and said, "Exactly my words to her, Mrs. Bennet, but she would not heed me and insisted on coming."

"Oh, Mr. Darcy! She was always a stubborn, wilful child, and try as I would, I could not get her to heed me, when she had an idea in her head, contrary to mine; she brought on many a nervous spasm! Indeed, I am sure that she is the child that caused my nerves to be so susceptible as they are!"

'Come, Mrs. Bennet, let us allow these two 'galleons' rest, would you like a glass of Madeira, ma'am?" asked Bingley, leading her back to her chair, "and I will get you two ladies some tea and cake."

"I wonder that this commotion has not reached Georgiana and Kitty, are they about the grounds, Bingley?' enquired Darcy, "I have not seen them since my arrival."

Answering in her husband's stead, Jane said, "No, Darcy, our sisters are up in my nursery, cooing over their very first niece, under the pretext of sewing baby linen, and chatting quite merrily to Sarah, the child's nurse."

"Well Darcy, it seems that *our* children will have very devoted aunts, once they make their appearance" chuckled Bingley.

Chapter 36

After a good night's sleep for all, followed by a hearty breakfast, the ladies all went up to the nursery, to greet their niece and granddaughter. Sarah, now properly dressed in one of Jane's former gowns, had just finished feeding her charge and was changing her into clean linen.

"Good morning ladies, you are just in time to see her at her best; well fed and dry."

"Let me hold her!" cried Mrs. Bennet, "oh what a beautiful baby you are, my *dear* little Jane! I do not understand what your mother meant, when she said that you cried all the time, for I have heard barely a whimper from you since we left Newcastle!"

"She *is* a good child ma'am," replied Sarah, somewhat nervously, for it was not her position to speak up, "but perhaps she feels more loved here, which she was not when we were up there, bairns feel that you know."

"Oh Mama, you are quite right, she is a beautiful child!" cooed Lizzy, who took her into her arms, "and she smells of lavender, I love lavender, do you use lavender soap?" addressing the child's nurse.

"Yes Ma'am, Mrs. Bingley has very kindly let me use everything she had already prepared for her own child, including the nursery maids, so I have been able to wash all the bairn's linen, which sadly needed it, what little she had."

"Well she has more linen now, Sarah, for Georgiana and I have been most industrious, look Mama, Jane" said Kitty, holding up three little dresses made of fine lawn, trimmed with narrow lace, with matching bonnets and the appropriate round cockades.

"Industrious indeed!" answered Jane, "you both must have worked all night to finish all that!"

"Not quite, Jane," laughed Georgiana, "for we had made the bonnets and cockades for *you*, three of each, for a boy or a girl, so we will just make some more, for a girl, should you have a daughter!"

"How remiss of me!" exclaimed Jane, "I have a fine woollen shawl that I knitted for this little one, but I quite forgot to send it up to Lydia with the rest of the linen! Kitty, could you look in my workbox in the parlour and find it for me? It is folded up in the bottom, pale yellow wool. It was most fortunate that my mother brought back the linen we sent up with her, for the poor child would have had nothing otherwise."

Whilst the ladies were thus engaged, Bingley and Darcy were in the library, coming up with various possible solutions. Bingley thought that perhaps he and Jane could take the child, should the Wickhams choose not to raise her themselves, until his friend pointed out that it would be difficult to bring up their niece with their own child, being almost the same age, for little Jane could not have the same future expectations as their own child. It would possibly be even unkind to do so, for there would always have to be small differences, and the child must be adequately provided for, as in either a marriage portion, or a provision, enough for a gentlewoman, should she not have the means or inclination to marry. He refrained from mentioning what had occurred with himself and George Wickham, the child's father, but Bingley understood his meaning.

"So, by the same arguments, Darcy, you and Elizabeth cannot take her either. What is to become of her? Do you think Mr. and Mrs. Bennet could raise her?"

"I think that is perhaps the best solution so far, but we must wait to see Mr. Bennet first. He should arrive this evening, or tomorrow morning. He has over a hundred miles to travel. We must consult with him, before going any further. Wickham should have received my express by now, so if he answers promptly, we should know more by tomorrow, as to *their* intentions."

In the middle of the afternoon, a carriage was heard approaching, which drew everybody's attention: could it be Mr. Bennet arriving already? or the Wickhams, coming to claim their child? It was almost with universal relief that Mr. Bennet stepped out of the carriage, followed by Mary.

"Welcome Mr. Bennet!" cried Bingley, moving forward to greet him, followed by Darcy, "You must have travelled during the night to get here so early. And welcome to you Mary, you must be worn out by the exertion, but we thank you for making such haste."

"Yes, Mr. Bennet, we are relieved to see you, for nothing can be decided without you" added Darcy as he shook hands warmly with the weary travellers.

"Your surmise is correct, gentlemen, we travelled overnight, for the situation, as I understand it, requires a rapid conclusion!" replied Mr. Bennet, "Mary, go to your sisters and mother, they will take care of you, whilst we sort yet *another* situation caused by Lydia! I am beginning to believe that I should have perhaps heeded the advice of my esteemed cousin, the inimitable Mr. Collins, when he advised me to throw her off, to reap the fruit of her actions, last year! It would have saved me a great deal of trouble and economy, and I would have been able to continue supervising the harvests, what little we have, after such a miserable summer! The price of grain is a concern, is it not?"

Upon which, the gentlemen retired directly to the library to discuss what could or should be done, leaving the ladies to their own devices and to wonder what the gentlemen could possibly find as a solution. They could themselves talk of nothing else, so Mary was told of all that had happened, and fatigued as she was, she had to endure everybody's thoughts on all sorts of possibilities for the future of the child. Once she was herself a little recovered from her journey, and that there was gap of a moment or two of the incessant talking by everybody, Mary spoke up, "It seems to me that there are but two possibilities: either Lydia claims her child, or she does not. From what I have observed of her behaviour in the past and apparently the present, she is too self-centred to care for anyone but herself, or possibly for people who can help her to achieve what she wants, and the child does not fulfil any of her criteria, so she will leave the child. The question that needs to be asked is, with whom?"

"I would take her gladly, she could be raised with my own child, she would be no trouble" said Jane, "but Bingley has said that we may not, for it would create difficulties as to her place within the family."

"Darcy said as much to me also, and considering how the child's father has turned out, after having been raised almost as a son in the Darcy family, I tend to agree with him" added Lizzy, not wishing to pronounce Wickham's name in front of Georgiana.

Mrs. Bennet looked from one daughter to the other, wondering at what seemed to her, were flimsy excuses at best, but secretly, not being as upset as she thought she might be, because if Jane and Lizzy could not take the child, then that just left herself and Mr. Bennet to have the care of little Jane, so instead of arguing and remonstrating with her daughters, as they had fully expected her to do, she just smiled inwardly and hoped that Lydia would not create a scene.

After what seemed like an eternity, although it had been but an hour, the gentlemen joined the ladies, where Mr. Bennet, having quieted the bevy of women asking incessant questions, made the following announcement, "Although the wretched girl is hardly worth the trouble of our exertions, yet again, we have decided on the following: should the Wickhams come for their daughter, then she must go back with them, but on the following terms: the nurse is to have the total care of the child, Darcy and Bingley paying her wages, which will be quite generous, for the woman can write and she is to use that skill should she have any concerns about the child's welfare. In fact, she is to write to Darcy, because Pemberley is the closest to Newcastle, every month. Should no letter arrive, then one of Darcy's agents in the north will make discreet inquiries, and he will be authorised to take the child and her nurse away again, should either he or the nurse consider the situation requires such drastic action." Turning to his wife, "Mrs. Bennet, I gather you have had some concerns on my possible judgement on your actions, so let me now say, in front of the whole family, that I thoroughly *approve* of what you did. I am only astounded that you managed to make such a momentous decision by yourself, and carry it through."

"Oh, Mr. Bennet! I am so relieved! I was so sure you would be angry, that you would think I was wrong, but what if Lydia does not come for the child? What will become of the poor mite?"

"If you would allow me to finish, Mrs. Bennet, I will tell you. Should they not come for her, and they let us know of their intentions regarding the child, we will offer to take her off their hands and raise her amongst us,"

"But with whom, Mr. Bennet? For we have discussed it also and can come to no happy conclusion … "wailed Mrs. Bennet.

"*If* you would allow me to finish, Mrs. Bennet, I will tell you. Jane Wickham will come to Longbourn, with her nurse, to be raised as our grand-daughter, only *this* time, I will take a more active part in the raising of the child. I do not want the same mistakes made, as occurred with the upbringing of her mother! Mary, if you are agreeable to the idea, you will see to the child's education, should you still be with us when the time comes, otherwise a governess will be engaged." finished Mr. Bennet.

"Oh! Mr. Bennet! Oh Papa!" were the main sounds heard after the announcement, and they would have plied him with more questions had he not waved his hand, shooing them away saying "Any questions that you may have, address them to Bingley or Darcy, I will say no more on the matter until we have heard from Newcastle" and withdrew, taking refuge in the library.

Chapter 37

Everyone waited for some news from the Wickhams, any news, for several days, but none came.

Her time being due, Jane was delivered of a healthy girl, named Elizabeth Louise. Mother and child doing well, the whole family was elated, all the more so for being at Gaddesley at the time. Bingley was over the moon, Mrs. Bennet was delighted, for now she had two grandchildren, whereas Lady Lucas had only one, Mr. Bennet was pleased too, though in his own quiet way; he warmly congratulated the new parents and said little more. The Darcy's and the Hurst's were the child's sponsors, so Caroline Bingley was apparently slightly put out, but her sister Louisa made claim to her seniority and nothing more could be said, and Kitty and Georgiana were simply delighted to have another baby to coo over.

Mary, having been asked to possibly teach her eldest niece, little Jane, spent more time with *her*, as her sisters crowded around Jane and the new baby. Having suffered as a child, watching her younger sisters seemingly receive all of their mother's favour, she felt a growing sympathy for her niece, much to her own surprise. "Yes, my sweet little Jane, *I* will love you, and no-one will usurp your place in my heart. Oh, I do so hope your mother lets us keep you" she whispered to the sleeping child. She was sitting by the crib, watching the child sleep, whilst Sarah, her nurse, was supervising the nursery maids set up a second crib for the new baby. A nurse had been hired for the new baby, but she had not yet arrived, so Sarah was setting everything ready for when she *did* come.

Sarah noticed Mary's presence, noting that in her own quiet way, she was connecting to the child, and Sarah was very pleased. Having lost her own newborn, she had been happy to be able to look after a new child, but had been horrified at the way things had gone on in Newcastle. Although the move away had been very sudden, she had had no qualms in leaving with Mrs. Bennet that day. She knew that Mrs. Bennet truly had the child's best interest at heart, and now, here she was, head of a nursery with two children, well at least until the other nurse turned up, and she had received several dresses, finer than any she had ever owned, and she smelled of lavender. If only her poor mother had lived to see it!

She was still a little worried though, for the Wickhams had still given no news of their wishes or intentions. She would of course return to them with Jane, if that was the choice they made, but she was secretly hoping that she and the bairn would go down to the Bennet estate, in Hertfordshire, which was apparently somewhere near London, Longbourn it was called. She liked Mrs. Bennet; she had more feeling than sense, but that is what grandmothers were supposed to be like. She would be very busy until the Bingley's nurse arrived, but she herself, only had to nurse her charge, for Mrs. Bingley intended nursing her own child, and one of the nurse-maids could take the child to her and bring her back. Now *she* was a proper mother, not like that Mrs. Wickham.

Having waited a full week for the Wickhams to react to Mrs. Bennet's taking of their daughter, there was still nothing heard from them, so in agreement with Mr. Bennet and Bingley, Darcy wrote to his agent in Newcastle, asking him to make inquiries about them, and to send the news to him at Pemberley, and also a copy to Bingley and Mr. Bennet. The Bennets were to stay with the Bingleys until Jane was fully recovered, and then they would go up to Pemberley in November, once the Darcy baby came into the world, but the

Darcys had to return to Pemberley, for Lizzy's advanced state would not allow her to travel far, and Darcy, being very protective of her, insisted that they return home the following day.

By the Bennets remaining in Leicestershire, this also meant that should the Wickhams wish to retrieve their child, then they would not have so far to travel. Their continuing silence was of concern, for surely, if they had wanted her, they would have sent word by now? Mrs. Bennet and Mary were more hopeful than concerned; they could already picture themselves at Longbourn with the tiny child, Mrs. Bennet was imagining herself during morning visits, in having her grand-daughter to show, as opposed to simply talk of, and Mary was looking forward to having somebody to love and to guide.

The following morning, after the breaking of their fast, the Darcy's left for Pemberley, leaving Georgiana at Gaddesley House. Darcy had initially intended for her to return with them, but upon reflection, he realised that he would be too preoccupied with Elizabeth's continuing well-being, so thought it wiser to leave Georgiana with the Bingley's and Bennets, where she had the company of Kitty, Mary and Jane.

"Are you sure you are comfortable, my dear?" fussed Darcy, "would you be more at ease with another pillow behind your back? It is quite cold this morning, let me put a blanket on your knees"

Lizzy bit back the retort that she did not like being so fussed over, and instead, sweetly answered, "Fitzwilliam, do not worry so, I am warmly dressed, I have more pillows and cushions around me than in a harem, and the coachman is driving so slowly, no possible harm can come to me. You will be of more use to me by sitting by my side so that I can lean on your shoulder, should the need come over me."

Darcy complied, though it was with some difficulty that he refrained from continually trying to see to her comfort, but he was assisted, or rather hindered in his attempts, by Lizzy putting her arm through his and leaning her head on his shoulder, effectively pinioning him down.

"So, my love, what are your thoughts on the situation with little Jane? Is not it strange that her parents have given no indication of their wishes?"

"My thoughts," replied Darcy, "are that the child is better off away from them. From what I understood from your mother, even she was shocked, and from what I learned from the nurse, your sister has taken no notice of the child since the day she was born. I have not been idle, whilst we waited for news from them, I have already had my agent make discreet inquiries, which I chose not to share whilst we were at Gaddesley."

"How terrible can it be that you could not tell Bingley and my father?"

"Not as bad as you seem to think, Lizzy, I am sorry for worrying you, my dear, I did not intend to do so. No, I chose not to mention it because I did not wish to spoil the joy of the new baby's safe arrival and Jane's safe delivery and recovery."

"Then what did your man discover?"

"Simply that the Wickhams continue with their daily lives, going to dinners and dances, without a care in the world, and no thought for their daughter. They received the express, for I had it delivered to my agent, who was instructed to deliver it to them himself."

"How dreadful! How could she behave so? I am glad you did not mention it before, Fitzwilliam, it would have upset Jane immensely."

"Well, my dear, I *did* inform Mr. Bennet, with a copy of my agent's report, just before we left, and I leave it to his discretion to decide if, or when, he feels the rest of the family are to be informed, but I would have no secrets from you, my dearest Lizzy"

"I am pleased to hear that, Fitzwilliam, I would feel very hurt if you did."

"I am glad you understand my reason for keeping silent about it, Lizzy, now, can I get you some refreshment, my dear wife?" before having to duck from a cushion thrown at him by the said dear wife.

Chapter 38

⁂

The weeks passed, and still nothing was heard from Newcastle, so Jane Wickham and her nurse settled down in Gaddesley, where both the baby cousins thrived, surrounded by love, care and attention.

Lizzy, Mrs. Darcy, the mother of the future heir of Pemberley, was supervised, mollycoddled and looked after by the staff in a way that Lizzy was most uncomfortable with, but suffered, because she knew that it was her husband who was behind the instructions, and his instructions, having been so long adhered to, would of course out-rank her own, so newly come to the household.

After what seemed an eternity, during which Lizzy was very thankful that she did not have to go into confinement, as ladies of her status had had to do until relatively recently, she was safely delivered of a healthy son, James Charles Alexander. Darcy was of course relieved that the delivery had gone so well, so much so, he wanted to name the child James, after Mr. Bennet, although she did point out to him that the late Mr. Darcy's name was also James, so *that* name was relatively easy. Charles, was Mr. Bingley's first name, he was godfather to the child, and Alexander, because not only it was an ancestral Darcy name, Lizzy simply just liked it.

Letters were written, word got out, and congratulations flew in from around the country, as did the Bennet family, who arrived three days after the birth, being only thirty miles away at Gaddesley

House, at the time of Mrs. Darcy's delivery. The Bingley's remained at home, to give Jane time to recover from her own delivery, only some weeks before, but she sent her best love to her sister, along with some baby linen that she had made herself, and a letter, to keep Lizzy informed with the news of their mutual niece, little Jane Wickham, who was doing very well under the care of her nurse, whom Mrs. Bingley was not looking forward to losing, when the time came for her to leave, for Sarah had become the pivot upon which Mrs. Bingley's nursery turned, in spite of the arrival of her own nurse, Rebecca, whom she had herself hired.

The arrival of the Bennets also brought Georgiana back to Pemberley, and she could hardly bear to wait to see her nephew; from the moment the butler opened the front door, she rushed past him with barely an acknowledgement, running to greet her brother and asking to see Elizabeth and the child.

"Is Lizzy able to receive visitors, Fitzwilliam? Can I perhaps see the baby?"

"Georgiana, you are hardly a 'visitor', and yes, Lizzy is able to see you, but perhaps you could possibly remove your travelling attire before doing so, and tidy yourself up? You came into the house in such a rush, your bonnet is askew, so I am assuming your hair is in need of a few stray curls being brought back into order" laughed Darcy, before turning to greet the Bennets.

"Welcome Mr. Bennet, Mrs. Bennet, Mary and Kitty. Elizabeth is well and will be ready to see you shortly, I have just left her as you arrived, she was devouring scrambled eggs with some smoked salmon. If you wish to go to your rooms to refresh yourselves after your journey, I will order some tea for you before we go up to see them both."

"Oh Mr. Darcy!" cried Mrs. Bennet "that would be delightful, I can hardly wait to see my darling girl, and my first grandson, but I will admit that some tea will do me the world of good just now."

"And you, Mr. Bennet, would something more substantial than tea be more to your liking?"

"Congratulations Darcy, you must be a very happy man with the safe delivery of your son, and a glass of something more substantial would be welcome, to whet the head of young James" he beamed, secretly flattered that the child had been named for him, even if the late Mr. Darcy *had* shared his name.

Twenty minutes later, Lizzy, sitting up in her bed, hair carefully dressed under a very becoming lace cap, wearing a beautifully trimmed short cape over her nightgown, received her family with great pleasure, delighted to see them and boasting of her son, sleeping in his crib near her bed.

'Is he not the most beautiful child, Mama? He has thick black hair under his bonnet and is very sturdy already!"

"Oh! dear Lizzy, you have done very well indeed, how clever of you, to produce a son so quickly! Mr. Darcy will be very pleased with you, I am sure; men always seem to prefer sons to daughters, for some reason, though I infinitely prefer girls, for I know how to raise girls."

"As you have proved, Mrs. Bennet," harrumphed her husband "with only one small exception, but four out of five is not at all bad. Congratulations Lizzy, you do indeed have a fine child, you did very well" as he kissed her paternally on the forehead.

The girls were crowded around the crib, in doting adoration, as aunts are supposed to, trying to find likenesses with their nieces, whom they had left that morning, or to decide which of his crumpled traits were Darcy or Bennet.

Half an hour later, the family left Lizzy's room, to allow her to rest, for Lizzy wished to join them for dinner, to which request both her mother and husband agreed should not be allowed, but she pleaded with them, pointing out that she was strong enough and that she would rest beforehand. She would not dress for dinner, but since they were just family, she could be allowed to dine in her dressing robe or some other comfortable gown. Although Mrs. Bennet exclaimed at the possible damage it could do to her health, Darcy could not refuse her.

Dinner was a happy affair. Lizzy had dressed in an older, comfortable gown of primrose muslin, her hair dressed and garlanded with green ribbons, a paisley shawl around her shoulders, glowing with health. She had to endure everybody's attention to her slightest wish: was she comfortable, would she not be better on a different chair, would she like another feather cushion, is the fire too hot, is she too far from the fire, which dish would she prefer, would not this dish or that dish be more to her liking? Normally Lizzy would have detested such attentions, but she was in a very happy frame of mind, still euphoric after the safe delivery of her beautiful son, glad to have her body back, for the last weeks had been somewhat difficult, being slenderly built and unused to being so cumbersome.

She did not prolong her stay after dinner; she had some tea, and then was notified by a servant that her son was requiring her presence, for she was nursing him herself. She would nurse him until he was two or three months old, and then engage a wet nurse. She already had a nurse in charge, a niece of Mrs. Reynolds, Gwen, with three nursery maids under her. The midwife was also still in residence, to ensure there were no post-delivery complications and that Mrs. Darcy rested enough.

Chapter 39

The following week passed very happily, Lizzy gaining strength rapidly and the child doing very well. She was delighted that her family were with her, so they could see for themselves what a beautiful child she had produced. She sometimes had to remind *herself* that the child in her arms was the result of the love between her and the wonderful man she had married.

Mrs. Bennet spent much of her time with her, advising her on how to raise a child, what to be attentive to, colic and wayward nursery maids, and when to allow her husband back to her bed.

"My dear mother, please, give Darcy the credit of being a gentleman; he would never force himself upon me and will only come to me when I am ready."

"But gentlemen have needs, Lizzy, and I have heard that some gentlemen go back to their wives far too early!"

"Mama, I know you mean well, however I am certain my father would never have forced himself upon you, but pray do recall that there is barely thirteen months between myself and Jane, so I assume that once I have healed, I will know when to allow my husband's attentions again. What do you think of this blanket I have made for James' walking carriage?" she replied, in an effort to change the subject.

"You may think I am being meddlesome Elizabeth, but I gave Jane the same advice also. Some men just see their wives as brood mares, though I am sure that neither Bingley nor Darcy see either of you as such!" added Mrs. Bennet, seeing Lizzy's face grow stern at the mere suggestion that her husband could ever consider her that way. "and yes, you have worked it very well, however do not send the child out in a baby carriage until the spring, for you do not want him catching a chill, or worse!" Before anything further could be said, Darcy joined them.

"I thought I might find you both here. I wished to speak to you of some matter of importance, it being the future of little Jane. What I have to communicate will be possibly both pleasant and unpleasant."

"What do you mean my love?" queried Lizzy.

"Since we have had no word from the Wickhams, regarding their child, and after consultation with Mr. Bennet, I sent my agent to see them, to offer to take the baby and raise her in Longbourn with her grandparents."

"And what had they to say?"

"This is the unpleasant part, ladies: they said that they did not really care where the child was brought up, or by whom, so long as *they* did not. They were quite happy to leave her in our care, to be brought up as we saw fit, and that we should understand that they expected monetary 'compensation' for their 'loss'."

"Is that all they care about? Money?" exclaimed Lizzy, absolutely disgusted, whilst Mrs. Bennet, although saddened by what her once favourite daughter had become, was smiling inwardly, for she knew now that her granddaughter would be returning to Longbourn with her.

"So, Mrs. Bennet, it appears you will be opening your nursery again, and I am certain the child will be well loved and nurtured under your care. Mr. Bennet has agreed to this and has sent word to Longbourn for Mrs. Hills to engage a nursery maid, to assist Sarah, who is perhaps the only thing Lydia has done right, when she hired her to take care of her daughter."

"Oh Mr. Darcy! Thank you! I knew you were too generous to leave the poor mite in such an uncertain situation!" gushed Mrs. Bennet, "and although it saddens me to realise how my Lydia has behaved to her own child, I believe it is for the best. I will certainly not be sending *her* any more money!"

"Yes, my love, thank you for arranging this, for as my mother says, it is for the best. I would have worried and fretted about her if we had sent her back to Newcastle" added Lizzy.

During dinner, the subject was thoroughly canvassed by all, Mary looking forward to being of some comfort and value to her little niece, Mrs. Bennet was imagining Lady Lucas being very jealous of *not* having a grandchild to show off during morning visits, Kitty and Georgiana planning to make as many pretty dresses as the child could possibly wear, and even Mr. Bennet was pleased, for he had been seriously concerned about the child's welfare, if she was to be returned to her parents.

"Have you informed Jane and Bingley of what has been agreed?" asked Lizzy, "I am sure Jane will miss the child, but she will perhaps be happier with a smaller nursery, knowing that her namesake is in a safe and good home, thoroughly loved."

"Yes, I wrote to them as soon as we had settled matters."

"I am still cross with them" she replied, "for their impudence in asking for more money! I hope you did not accede to their demands, for they in fact, should be sending money to my father and my mother, for the upkeep of *their* child!"

"I did not accede, my dear, pointing out the same to them as you have just mentioned, so they will have to manage on their income. It is not for my wife, or *anybody's* wife, to keep on supporting them, especially when they seem to take it for granted that we will continue to do so. By this I do not mean that you are not to send them *anything*, but please do not feel obliged to regularly do so."

"I concur, sir," said Mr. Bennet, "though *I* will go so far as to forbid *my* wife to send them any more money. Before you get upset, Mrs. Bennet, I said 'no more money', but should you wish to send your daughter a gown, you may do so, once a year!"

"Mr. Bennet, I have no inclination to send her anything, especially *not* a gown, for it is still a sore point with me, that she sold the baby linen we had all sent her, to buy herself a gown" was his wife's remarkably calm response. Lydia had definitely fallen out of her favour, and her place was now taken by her granddaughter. Mrs. Bennet would never become a sensible, amiable, well-informed woman, but her grandmaternal feelings could not be faulted towards the defenceless child.

Since everything had finally been settled with the Wickhams, regarding their daughter, and Lizzy and the baby continuing to do well, it was agreed that the Bennets would return to Longbourn, via Gaddesley, to take little Jane and her nurse, and everyone would stay quietly at home for the Christmas season, to allow the new mothers to recuperate and the infants to continue well and strong,

Chapter 40

Christmas came and went; the weather had been so bitterly cold and inclement that travelling was best avoided if at all possible, so any thoughts that had been had of travelling, were deemed quite unnecessary, staying safe and warm in a comfortable home seemed be the only sensible thing to do.

Spring finally came, and it was time to consider going to Town again. Through their regular correspondence, the Darcys and Bingleys decided they would all go together, along with Kitty, who had stayed on at Gaddesley the previous November, for as she had pointed out, "James will have his aunt Georgiana, Jane will have her aunt Mary, but poor Elizabeth will have no aunt present if I go back to Longbourn!"

It was quite a cavalcade of carriages that arrived at Darcy House, for of course the two babies travelled with their nurses, the valets and ladies' maids had travelled with them, in separate carriages, two hours ahead, with wardrobes and jewels, Kitty and Georgiana travelled in the Bingley coach with Mrs. Annesley, for they had so much to catch up on, that the two-day journey from Gaddesley House was hardly sufficient to go through all that they wished to speak about, plus all the attending footmen, coachmen and outriders. Jane and Bingley travelled with Lizzy and Darcy, also discussing as many matters as possible, even though it had all been canvassed in their correspondence over the past five months. The two sisters had never been apart for so long before, so it was a delightful prospect of being together for the remainder of the Season.

The two gentlemen were more concerned about the tenants on their respective estates, for the previous summer had been disastrous for crops, the ensuing winter had been extremely harsh, many people had died from hunger or the cold in the country, according to The Times, and they themselves had had to help their tenants with supplies of food and wood to get them through the winter. Hopefully this year would be better, but they had had to put guards up to protect their stored seeds for the coming season's crops, for the poor had had to eat their own meagre supplies they had harvested from the preceding summer. Both Bingley and Darcy had ordered their stewards to distribute provisions to the needy, including firewood, fish, game and venison, anything in fact, to help feed the families and keep them from freezing to death.

The ladies, apart from with regards to the babies, were more engaged in what was to be done in Town. Lizzy, Georgiana and Kitty having been presented at Court last Season; the idea was canvassed as to whether Jane wished to do so.

"Jane, you must wish to be presented, for think, neither Miss Bingley or Mrs. Hurst have been allowed to go to Court, imagine how they will feel if you are permitted to do so!" argued Kitty.

"It is exactly for that reason that I would rather not, thank you Kitty, for imagine how they would feel, as you say?" replied Jane.

"Perhaps so, Jane," said Georgiana, "but by your successfully being presented, as Mrs. Darcy's sister, and mine and Kitty's, it will be easier for *them,* next Season, to possibly succeed themselves, for you will have created the precedent"

"Oh! Imagine how that would make them feel! To be beholden to you for their possible presentation!" squealed Kitty gleefully, "I have not forgotten how spitefully they treated you when you were in Town, the year before last, and how they tried to keep dear Bingley from ever learning that you were in town."

Lizzy, inwardly blushing from the knowledge that her own husband had had a part in the subterfuge, preferred to deviate the subject to a less embarrassing train of thought.

"That is not the way to persuade Jane of *anything,* Kitty, you know full well that she is incapable of gloating over *anybody,* but you, Georgie, *do* have a valid point. Jane, I know you have said that you now better understand Mrs. Hurst and Miss Bingley, although you could not trust them as much as you initially did, but this is a case where you might be able to truly assist them. If *you,* as Mrs. Bingley, succeed to be presented at Court, and therefore the Ton, then it will not be beyond the realms of possibility that *they* could aspire to the same spheres, to which *you,* as a gentlewoman-born, will have opened the doors. So yes, as Kitty says, they would be beholden to you, but I think that you would perceive it more as a gratification that you were able to procure them, and feel genuine pleasure in being able to do so."

"Since you put it so Lizzy, then I am beginning to think it may be worth the trouble. How do I go about it? I know you explained it to me in our letters last year, but if I am to do so, then I will first discuss it with Charles and then come back to you girls. It is only now, that I am myself back in Town, that I fully realise the social enormity you achieved last Season!" responded Jane.

"Yes, discuss it with Bingley and I will discuss it with Fitzwilliam, and you, Georgiana and Kitty, and if we come to an agreement, then we will proceed further for your sponsors, for of course Bingley will have to be presented also."

A *family* party of six was quite a large family assembly, as such, for Darcy House, but Mrs. Appleby, had everything under control and a superb dinner was provided, with the panache to which the Darcy's were accustomed. The current Mrs. Darcy had risen even further in the esteem of the staff, for having provided a healthy male heir within a year of marriage, which said male heir was now ensconced in the nursery above. It had been nearly twenty years since the nursery had been in such use. Of course, the next few weeks would be very busy, with dinners, dances and supper evenings, but the staff, from the butler, cook, housekeeper and head-gardener down, were fully competent in their roles, so no real concerns were felt. Superb meals would be provided, with impeccable service, in rooms furnished in the best possible taste, with fresh floral displays that could rival any house in Town.

The conversation over dinner was mainly over the possibility of the Bingley's future Court presentation; the advantages, the disadvantages, the hurdles to be overcome, and whether it was deemed worthy of the effort.

"I own," said Bingley, "that our natural inclination is to decline the offer, for Jane and I both prefer a quiet life in the country, but we have discussed the possible benefits to the family, the Bingley family that is, and the future Bingleys-to-be, including our dearest little Bessy. To put it simply: if the efforts required to get myself and Jane presented, are not too overpowering, then we shall agree to do so. If, however, they prove to be so, then we are quite happy to continue as we are, leaving the next generation, and my sisters, to make their own opportunities in the future."

"We cannot argue with such sound logic" replied Darcy, "so I will make enquiries as to the steps we would need to take. I have no hesitation in sponsoring you myself, Bingley, and I think it would be advisable for my aunt Matlock to sponsor Jane, for she sponsored Lizzy last year. I am sorry, my love," turning to Lizzy, "that I do not propose *you* to sponsor your sister, but you now know how supercilious the Ton can be; you were only presented last Season, so someone of my *aunt's* vintage should overcome any querulous society complaints or queries."

"I totally agree with you my dear, for I have not totally recovered from my own fears and trepidations of last year myself, so I am indeed very happy to pass the responsibility to our Aunt Matlock" was Lizzy's response, "though we will help you, Jane, with the walking-backwards-whilst-curtseying part, won't we Kitty, Georgiana?" she added, laughing.

Chapter 41

After discussion between themselves, Mr. and Mrs. Bingley agreed to subject themselves to the procedures required to be presented at Court; not for their own gratification, let it be perfectly understood, but for the greater good it could bring to the family as a whole.

Again, Lady Matlock's assistance paved the way to a successful application for Mrs. Bingley, and Mr. Darcy, who had never even *hinted* that he would ever sponsor *anyone,* was so well known and respected enough for it to be succinctly understood that he would *never* propose a man unworthy of the honour, so Mr. and Mrs. Bingley became the first members of a former merchant's family, albeit that the lady *was* a gentleman's daughter, to be presented at Court, since many a day, causing general excitement amongst those who aspired to gentility, currently denied them, in spite of their sizeable fortunes, because still tainted with connotations of 'Trade'.

The consequences of this social elevation were to be expected; everybody wished to make their acquaintance. The Hursts and Miss Bingley had only been withheld, by social obligations and natural shyness, and fearing to intrude, from seeking their company more frequently, and how were the children? The Matlocks, the Wentworths, Parkers, Knightleys, Churchills, and others of the Darcy's acquaintance, happily included the Bingley's into their social rounds, introducing them into circles beyond the reach of his sisters, so when the Bingley's and Darcys gave a dinner, card evening, supper, or musical evening, the Hursts and Miss Bingley were most eager to attend, to mingle with members of Society, of whom they had only been able to dream about meeting, prior to Jane Bennet ensnaring Charles. It is said that every cloud has a silver lining, and if Jane could get herself and Charles presented to Court, who knows what else she could achieve under that apparently very meek and docile exterior?

Others, of the wishing-to-be-acquainted set, such as the Dashwoods, Crawfords, Ferrars, Willoughbys and other such people were carefully kept away from the Bingleys, for they were both too soft-hearted, and their friends did not wish to see them taken advantage of, by such mercenary social climbers.

The Bingley's having been presented at Court, meant that there were no obstacles for both families to be invited to all of the major social events of the remaining Season, allowing Georgiana and Kitty as full an agenda of balls, dances, dinners, theatre outings, suppers and music evenings as any young lady could possibly wish for, and because they had each other for company, they felt protected from any insidious attentions, for which Fitzwilliam Darcy was again, very grateful.

Not that the girls did not attract attention, they had several admirers, none of them good enough for Georgiana, according to her brother, but one gentleman stood out with regards to Kitty; a Mr. Edmund Bartram, younger son of a baronet in Northamptonshire and apparently destined for the cloth. He seemed a very personable young man of about five and twenty, had been to Oxford, and had been ordained at Michaelmas. His family not wishing him to rush into a career as important as the Church, had insisted on the current Season in Town, to perhaps test his chosen vocation.

Being so much in the company of Georgiana, with so many social engagements, Kitty had not found the time to write to her mother as much as she would have done in the past, and Lizzy felt that *no* interference from her mother, would allow the relationship to develop naturally, either as a success or a decision that they were perhaps, not compatible. Lizzy had not forgotten the uncomfortable time of her own courtship and engagement, with her mother's assiduous, but ill-judged attempts of making herself conciliatory to Darcy, and she still blushed at the memory of Mrs. Bennet's efforts to get Bingley and Jane together. If she could spare Kitty the same embarrassing experiences, then she would feel that she had done well by her sister. So, although Mr. Bartram was invited to several of the evenings hosted at Darcy House, no overt attempts were made to get Mr. Bartram and Catherine onto a more intimate footing. Having discussed the matter with Jane, they both felt that this was the right way to proceed, so no mention of him was made in any letters sent to Longbourn.

Kitty did confide in her two eldest sisters, admitting to admiring him very much. "I find him very handsome, of course, and he has as kind a heart, I believe, as either Darcy or Bingley, and he speaks very well of his future as a clergyman. Who would have thought, that after having met our own Mr. Collins, that I would ever consider a clergyman as a husband?" she added, which made both Jane and Lizzy laugh.

"I am sure that Mr. Collins does mean well, Kitty, but I agree that he would not be what *I* would consider to be a very charitable, albeit devout, man of the cloth" was Jane's reply, which caused Lizzy to exclaim "My goodness! Jane! That is as bad an opinion of anybody that I have ever heard you utter!"

Chapter 42

─────●─────

Jane and Bingley had not been idle during their time in town, Charles had felt that although he knew that they would always be welcome at Darcy House, it was time to consider a house in town for themselves. Enquiries were made, a few houses were visited, and a house near Wimpole Street was chosen. It was not as large as Darcy House, but in a very respectable part of town, and they felt it would be large enough for their needs. The ladies, under the guidance of Mrs. Gardiner, spent many a happy morning browsing through shops and warehouses, selecting furniture and furnishings for the new house.

Mrs. Gardiner was also able to assist the Bingleys in finding suitable staff, for once they returned to Gaddesley House, the town house could not be left unattended. A very respectable housekeeper was found, none other than Madame Eliane Georges, Madeleine's mother, a sensible, well-educated woman, who could not be grateful enough to the family who had helped many of her own relations find employment. Her daughter, Madeleine, wrote to her frequently about how happy she was as Mrs. Darcy's maid, for she was treated more as a trusted companion than as a servant, and her niece, Dotty, or Dorothy, had been in Mrs. Gardiner's employment for several years. Even some of the boys had been engaged as grooms, footmen and clerks by the Gardiners, more of them employed by the Darcy's and now, by the Bingley's.

If the nieces, Mrs. Bingley and Mrs. Darcy, were anything like their aunt, Mrs. Gardiner, thought Madame Georges, then their servants were sure of being appreciated, if they worked to the best of their ability. She had heard it said that Mrs. Gardiner's own father had made her work in every servant's position, so that she could better comprehend what their tasks consisted of, under what conditions, and therefore be able to better understand any future servants she might have. The stratagem certainly seemed to have been successful, for Mrs. Gardiner was considered a very just mistress, for whom any honest servant was willing to work.

Mrs. Bingley had asked her several pertinent questions, regarding keeping a house, within a set amount, how she would treat servants who did not do their work, how she would treat the lower servants, how was her book-keeping, for Mrs. Bingley expected her to be able to show her the accounts at any time, and surprisingly, whether she would actually like to be employed by her! Nobody had ever asked her such a question! After settling matters to their mutual satisfaction, her new mistress then gave her full permission to hire a nephew and two nieces to work under her, saying that since she was their aunt, they might be happier to work in the same household. Never had a mistress been so kind and considerate! She suddenly felt very protective of her, for with such a mild, complying, and generous temper, Mrs. Bingley could easily be cheated or taken advantage of, by unscrupulous servants. She would make it her task that it should not be so.

The housekeeper settled in the following day, to supervise the decorating and setting up of the parlours, the drawing rooms, the dining room, the breakfast room, the bedrooms, the nursery, in fact every room in the house, except the kitchen and scullery, over which the cook would reign.

The cook was a very competent, younger woman, Miss Maude Bolton, who had been apprenticed to and trained by Mrs. Appleby, the cook at Darcy House. Mrs. Appleby herself had recommended her, so with such a reference, she was promptly engaged. She would henceforth be addressed as "Mrs. Bolton" as a courtesy to her position, and if her talents were anywhere near as good as Mrs. Appleby maintained, then the family was assured of excellent dinners!

Chapter 43

In a surprisingly short space of time, the house was ready for the Bingley family to take up residence, and Jane was very proud to invite the Darcy's to the very first dinner held in her new London home, as well as the Gardiners and Bennets, for Mr. and Mrs. Bennet had of course been invited for such a momentous occasion: *two* daughters with a house in Town! Mrs. Bennet could not have been more delighted, though perhaps having *three* daughters presented at Court, could distract her attention from the proportions and furnishings of the houses, of which she would regale her friends and acquaintance during many a social call when back in Longbourn. And let it not be forgotten that she also had three grandchildren, whilst Lady Lucas had only one, albeit that Charlotte Collins was again with child.

"My dear Jane! How well you look" cried Mrs. Bennet as she and Jane came down the staircase together. "and how magnificent is the house! I knew that Bingley had a good income, as soon as he came into the country, I said so at the time, four or five thousand a year and possibly more! You certainly did well for yourself Jane, I knew you could not be so handsome for nothing and that you could not do anything but well."

Jane gave a soft sigh, Mrs. Bennet would never change, finding a wealthy husband for her single daughters seemed to be her only purpose in life, although she had become a little less silly since the incident involving the taking of her granddaughter, little Jane Wickham, who appeared to be thriving at Longbourn, under the loving care of her nurse and relations. In fact, Mary had chosen to remain behind in Longbourn, allegedly so that little Jane would not be alone, but in reality, because in spite of her best efforts to be more sociable, she preferred to be left to the peace and tranquillity of her studies and piano practice, and now her niece, on whom she doated.

"As do you ma'am, that gown always make you appear at your best, and is that a new cap?"

"Why yes, I am glad you noticed it, the ribbons match those on my dress. You look exceedingly handsome in your white gown, is it the one you wore to Court? Oh, how I would have liked to have seen your presentation, I am sure you were the most handsome woman in the room. I said as much to Lady Lucas when I read your letter to her and your Aunt Phillips, and your aunt, and Lady Lucas entirely agreed with me."

"Yes, I thought to celebrate the first dinner here with my most recent dress, and I know you like us to wear white" replied Jane, glad to have distracted her mother from speaking of money, and hoping that the other guests would arrive soon, for she was feeling quite hungry. Therefore, she was pleased to find the Darcy's, Kitty and the Gardiners already assembled in the drawing room, which was very handsomely decorated in cream and blue, with some beautiful Persian rugs and handsome pieces of furniture, the inspiration for which she had taken from her sister's private apartments at Darcy House.

"Lizzy, how pleased I am to see you! As I am for you all" cried Jane, addressing everyone, "I have been so looking forward to receiving you in our new home, I was afraid it would not be ready before we left Town, but the work was done at an amazing pace, I am quite astonished at it!"

"It is most tastefully done, my dear Jane," replied Mrs. Gardiner, "we were quite fortunate when we went to some of the warehouses."

"Indeed Jane, I like it very much," added Lizzy quickly, who sensed that Mrs. Bennet was about to launch into the cost of everything, which would have been embarrassing to most of the present company, "and ma'am, how does little Jane? She must be much grown now, is she as well grown as Bessy? Tomorrow you must come and see James. He is trying to sit by himself, but keeps rolling over."

"Oh yes, Mrs. Bennet, you must see him, he is grown so sturdy, you will hardly recognise him!" exclaimed Georgiana, who was a very proud young aunt to her little nephew.

"And he has got his first tooth Mama!" added Kitty, who pointedly ignored the theatrical rolling of Mr. Bennet's eyes, who followed it up by a wink at Darcy, who now understood most of Mr. Bennet's idiosyncrasies and wit.

For their first formal dinner, Mr. and Mrs. Bingley proudly escorted Mr. and Mrs. Bennet into the dining room, where a splendid table, large enough for four and twenty guests filled the centre of the room, with sideboards and tables and some beautiful pieces of silverware around the sides of the room. Dinner itself was a credit to Mrs. Bolton's skills, quite justifying Mrs. Appleby's faith in her, and doing great credit to Jane's taste and economy.

After dinner, the gentlemen remained for their port and to discuss the now probable likelihood of a second, consecutive summer of terrible crops, the possibility of buying grain and seed for sowing the following year, from the Americas, and how to get their tenants through another winter: these were definitely not subjects to be discussed in the presence of ladies.

The ladies were more pleasantly engaged in the drawing room, discussing fashions, children and their various friends. The Collinses came up, and mention was made of Charlotte's condition. Jane then shyly announced that she too was expecting another child. "Oh, dearest Jane! How well done of you!" exclaimed her mother, who was now going to be able to lord it even more over poor Lady Lucas, for in spite of the Lucas family being so large, only Charlotte had as yet produced any children, the two eldest Lucas boys only recently having got married, having been unable to afford to do so until they could marry young ladies with some fortune, something that was not as prevalent as one would wish, but Mr. Lucas and his brother Henry both seemed to be happily married to young women who had each brought ten thousand apiece to their respective marriage settlements; very good matches for the boys was the general consensus in the neighbourhood, for not everyone could expect the exceptional good fortune that the two eldest Bennet girls had enjoyed. Their weddings of course did not meet the standard that the Bennets had set.

Chapter 44

The Bennets were to stay only a few days, for Mr. Bennet did not like to leave the farm whilst the elements seemed so temperamental and he felt he ought to be present to supervise whatever hay they could get in, and the general planting for summer, which had been delayed by several weeks due to the cold weather. His discussions with his two sons by marriage had at least born some fruit, for they had agreed to charter a ship together, to bring grain and seeds over from the old colony of America, more than they would require, but they would then be able to assist less fortunate friends and neighbours, should the crops be as bad as the previous year's, which they seriously feared would be the case.

Dinners at Darcy House alternated with those with the Bingleys and Gardiners and visits to the theatres, which Mrs. Bennet enjoyed immensely, for she had never really been permitted to spend much time in town in the past, for Mr. Bennet had always maintained that they could not afford to do so, but now, with Jane and Lizzy so well settled, there was no longer any impediment to coming to town more frequently. How she would be able to regale the morning visits in Longbourn, Lucas Lodge and Meryton, for her own experiences would be so much better to relate than just repeating what one or other of her daughters had written to her! What a pity she had not been able to see any of the girls being presented at Court, but a woman of her capabilities will always make do with what she has.

To the dinners, Mr. Bartram had been a regular visitor, and it did not take Mrs. Bennet long at all to see his eligibility as a husband for Kitty. She was even more delighted with him being the son of a baronet and was discussing the possibilities of their marriage, with Kitty, in great detail. Kitty, now being more sensible of the damage her mother could inflict on any budding relationship, did her best to underplay the real state of affairs, stating that they were still just getting to know each other and that he was to be given his living before any permanent relationship could be contemplated.

"But that is no obstacle Kitty, I am certain that his own father has a living put aside for him, and if it is not large enough, I am sure that Bingley or Darcy would be delighted to help."

"Indeed ma'am, you are too precipitous in your ideas, we have only just ascertained that we both like gardens and plants, that he does not like his beef too well done and that his mother is in no hurry to have him marry" replied Kitty "and having seen that a longer courtship has worked so well for Jane and Lizzy, I would rather not rush into such an important relationship as quickly as Lydia did, for we know how *that* has turned out."

"Have it as you will, but I am certain that it will be a match. You must invite him to Longbourn, for you come back with us, and if I have anything to do with it, you will be wed by the autumn."

"Ma'am," intervened Lizzy, "I know you mean well by Kitty, but I do agree with her; let them find their own way, and if it is meant to be, it will be."

"But what if she misses her opportunity?" responded Mrs. Bennet, "then she will have to start all over again!"

"Then she will start all over again, it was successful with me: I refused Mr. Collins and you thought I would never have another opportunity, and you see that I in fact met someone even better than Mr. Collins. Marriage is not a situation one should rush into on the first acquaintance."

"Yes, my dearest mother," added Jane, "even Charles and I feel that, although we might have been wed earlier, the obstacles and misconceptions we had to get over, drew us closer together and we understand each other all the better for having been through them, and of course Lizzy and Darcy had even more to overcome, for it having begun with their own pride and prejudices."

Reluctantly, Mrs. Bennet had to agree to refrain from trying to promote the match, against her own better judgement, she felt, but with all three of her daughters insisting on it, she could not carry her point, as she complained to Mr. Bennet later.

"And quite rightly so, Mrs. Bennet, interfering does not always bring a happy outcome, and Jane and Lizzy have managed to do quite well for themselves, in spite of your assistance, so let Kitty go at her own pace. And besides, if Kitty is in such a hurry to marry, I must consider some serious and immediate, retrenching in order to pay for her marriage settlement and wedding clothes, so perhaps, with this in mind, you will prefer *not* to go to the warehouses tomorrow, since you plan an autumn wedding, which is only a few, short months away."

It did not take Mrs. Bennet long to reflect and concede that perhaps, she was being a little forward in the wedding plans, for she sincerely did not wish to forgo her visit to the shops and warehouses on the morrow, for they were to return to Longbourn the following day.

Chapter 45

The London season finished and the Bingleys and Darcys returned to their respective estates. The summer proved to be as bad as they feared it would be, so the plan implemented by the gentlemen was executed. Grain and seeds were purchased from the Americas, wood was cut in great quantities and tons of coal were ordered and stored, to help the tenants survive what would probably be another harsh winter of food shortages and bitterly cold weather. Again, it was decided that the tenants would be allowed to snare rabbits and hares on their estates in order to provide food for their families. Fishing, in moderation, would also be permitted, but only after application to the head-keeper and at his discretion. More gamekeepers were hired to ensure that nobody took more than what they needed, so that hopefully, they would all survive until the next spring.

Michaelmas came, Mr. Bartram obtained a living, and nothing more was said of Kitty's reluctance to admit that they had come to an understanding. Permission was sought from both fathers and very kindly given. Mr. Bartram had the possession of a small living, but it was not enough to allow him to marry early, for the incumbent of the best living at his father's disposal was of apparently indomitable health and not likely to retire soon. After consulting with Mr. Bennet, who had again turned up at Pemberley when not expected, Darcy proposed to Mr. Bartram, the living of Kympton, the best in his gift, which had been held until Darcy found the right person for it. It was the same living that had been promised to Wickham, had he taken orders, which he had declined, been compensated accordingly, and then had tried to reclaim it when his circumstances were again bad. Darcy had no qualms in offering it to Bartram and Kitty, but stipulated that he did not want them to marry until the following year.

In spite of all the respect he felt was due to his benefactor, Mr. Bartram felt obliged to ask the reason for the stipulation. "I thank you for the honour, Mr. Darcy, but I am curious, even troubled, sir, as to why you would propose such a clause, asking us to wait until next year to marry."

"I doubt not that you wonder, sir, but I am sure you will agree, that with the hardships our people are suffering, due to another year of poor harvests, the prospect of another cold and hungry winter ahead, it would not be charitable to have the wedding of their clergyman, a baronet's son, and Mrs. Darcy's sister, which would be, rightly so, a splendid affair, whilst they go uncertain as to whether they and theirs will even survive till the spring. Should you not agree to this, I would be most surprised, but since I have already made the gift to you, I cannot stop you doing as you please, with regards to the date of your wedding to Catherine."

"Sir, I am humbled and shamed by my own thoughtlessness, compared to your noble feelings. I am ashamed to say that I had not thought of the people of my new parish, of their suffering, as they try to survive another winter of near famine, when I thought of being able to marry soon. I am sure that Catherine will agree with your terms, when I point out to her, what should have been quite obvious to *me*" answered Bartram contritely.

"Do not be so harsh on yourself Bartram," laughed Darcy, to Bartram's amazement, "a man in love does not think as coherently as a sensible man normally would, I have learned this myself; it is no reflection on your own intelligence and charitable feelings to your parishioners. Enough said on the matter, let us join the ladies to inform them of our mutual good fortune."

"Our *mutual* good fortune, Mr. Darcy? I believe the good fortune is all mine, thanks to your generosity."

"*Our* good fortune because I have waited quite some time before finding the gentleman, whom I believe to be the right person for this living, and you are he, unless I am very much mistaken, and I will have you know, sir, that I do not take well to being mistaken in my judgement."

They found Lizzy, Georgiana and Kitty in the drawing room, along with Mrs. Reynolds, who was teaching them to knit sturdy garments for the tenants' children. The ladies had decided that it was all very well sewing linen to make shirts for the poor; thick, knitted, woollen garments would be far more useful to them, in what was generally conceded, going to be a harsh winter ahead.

Kitty had spent the summer in Longbourn, but had come up with Mr. Bennet, when he had decided that the Pemberley library fireplace was so much better for his aching limbs, than the one at Longbourn. The fact that she knew that Mr. Darcy had asked Bartram to see him at Pemberley, after his obtaining a living, had nothing to do with her decision to travel with her father, but neither Lizzy nor Georgiana truly believed her.

Looking up from their endeavours, the ladies were pleased to see all three gentlemen smiling and settling down in comfortable chairs. Mrs. Reynolds rose, bobbed a curtsey to her mistress and offered to send up refreshments, to which Lizzy agreed. "Thank you, Mrs. Reynolds, we will resume our efforts tomorrow, if you do not mind."

Turning to her husband and father, "And you, gentlemen, look like the cat that got the cream. Good news, I take it?"

"Good news indeed, my dear. Mr. Bartram has kindly accepted my offer of the living of Kympton, and will take up residence as of next month, giving him time to settle his affairs in Northamptonshire."

"Oh, that is wonderful news, is it not, Kitty?"

"Wonderful indeed! It means that we can marry sooner than we thought we might be able to!" she replied delightedly, turning to Bartram.

"I have been thinking a great deal about that, my dear Catherine, and I, Mr. Bennet, and Mr. Darcy agree that we should set our wedding date for next year, in the spring, once the winter is over."

Seeing his daughter's face quiver with the initial disappointment, Mr. Bennet intervened, "My dear child, if you recall, winter can be a bitterly cold experience for a wedding, and, would you *want* to be celebrating merrily, whilst your husband's parishioners are shivering with cold and hunger? And more to the point, your mother will never forgive me, if I do not allow her to organise your wedding; she seems to have cruelly missed out on three opportunities to do so, first with your younger sister, who gave nobody even the possibility to do anything, and then of course Lizzy and Jane, who would not let your mother do all that she wished; she still has not forgiven your sister for *not* being married by special licence, nor that Lizzy went to town, *without* her, to buy the wedding clothes, so it would be most kind of you, for all our benefits, to give your mother the occasion to finally organise a daughter's wedding. In fact, if you do not, I shall be obliged to leave the country and live abroad, for there will be no peace in the house if you deny her this pleasure, so, my dear Catherine, the fate of the entire family is in your hands; marry in haste and all is lost, or marry next year, giving your mother several months to enjoy the glory of marrying yet another daughter, with all the ribbons, lace, bows, bells and such things as you can tolerate, and I can remain in England" he finished, with a laughable attempt to beg her, on his knees.

Realising that her father was attempting to lighten the disappointment for her, Kitty was somewhat mollified, but was only completely satisfied after a lengthy conversation with her betrothed.

Important things, like dates, were to be decided, who was to attend, which also influenced where the wedding would take place, etc, and it was agreed that these things were better discussed with

Mrs. Bennet, but Lizzy still felt the need to guide Kitty as much as possible, so that she would be able to make choices for her own wedding, without offending her mother. Kitty herself, having spent so much time with both Lizzy and Jane, now knew better what was acceptable behaviour, and having spent two seasons in London, with the cream of society, felt much more confident in being able to curtail any of her mother's probable excesses, than Lizzy gave her credit for, for Elizabeth, obviously, still saw her as that flighty, petulant girl who had followed wherever Lydia had led. She was much changed from that girl.

Chapter 46

The winter was as dismal and cold as had been expected. So many of the poor suffered greatly, but, thanks to their forward planning, none of the tenants on the Bennet, Darcy, and Bingley estates starved or died of the extreme conditions. Even the woollen garments and blankets, knitted by the ladies of the three houses, were of assistance. Kitty, who had thought that *nothing* could be of more importance than her marriage, was forced to concede that a wedding in such conditions would have been an insult to their suffering. She had remained at Pemberley with Lizzy, and had seen firsthand, the impact of the winter on her fiancé's poorer parishioners.

March came, and Spring made a feeble attempt to overcome winter. None of the Darcy's, Bingley's or Bennets had wanted to spend the winter season in Town, whilst the people dependant on them, were wondering whether the benevolence of their landlords would hold out till the seasons finally came back into their proper pattern.

The sun finally came out in mid-March, warming the frozen soil enough to give hope to all, so after instructions to their stewards, who, being honourable men, were to be trusted, the Darcy and Bingley families set off to spend the remaining months of the Season in town.

After much discussion between them, Kitty and Bartram agreed that she would go to town with her sisters and he would join them after Easter.

The winter may have been bitterly cold, but the postmasters had not been idle. Those who chose not to travel, wrote, and the correspondence between Pemberley, Gaddesley, and Longbourn had kept many a rider employed.

Mrs. Bennet had been overjoyed with the knowledge that her daughter, Catherine, for she could not possibly be called Kitty anymore, was to marry the son, albeit a younger son, of a baronet. She could talk of little else. Lady Lucas tried to revel in the pride of having another grandchild, for Charlotte had been safely delivered of another daughter, Harriet, but still Mrs. Bennet retained the boasting rights, for she had just received news that Jane was expecting another child in November, who would be her fifth grandchild. Mrs. Phillips, being a member of the family, could bask in pride by deflection, being Mrs. Bennet's sister, but it was a testimony to their true friendship, developed over five and twenty years, that Lady Lucas, Mrs. Long and other acquaintances could bear to listen to Mrs. Bennet prattling on and on about her daughters and their offspring, and still dance little Jane on their laps with genuine affection, when they called at Longbourn.

Now that Jane and Lizzy were both in Town, Mrs. Bennet joined them, staying with the Bingley's, where she could coo over the cradle of baby Charles, born the previous November, play with Bessy, and talk with Kitty about the wedding. It had been decided, through their regular correspondence over the winter, for the marriage to take place in Town, which was the most convenient venue for most of the guests, the only thing to be decided was, from which of her sisters' houses she would she marry from.

During a visit to Darcy House, with Jane, sipping tea and eating cake, Mrs. Bennet turned to her favourite topic of conversation.

"Catherine, my dear, it is of importance to know from where you marry, for you must marry in the parish where you reside."

"Yes Mama, which is why we would like to marry from Darcy House, if Lizzy does not mind, for we are quite fond of St George's church."

"But that is in the parish of Westminster, why do you not marry at the Abbey? You are marrying into a baronet's family, it would be most fitting for you to marry in such an imposing place of worship, it is certainly not too good for you, my love" was Mrs. Bennet's response. Kitty glanced at her sisters, who refrained from saying anything, for this was Kitty's wedding and it was not their place to make decisions for her, and then back to her mother.

"I understand your reasoning ma'am, but like Jane and Lizzy, we do not wish for a grand wedding, so we would prefer St George's, where the organist is said to be one of the best in the country. The music will be wonderful, for the acoustics in the church swell the sounds of the music and singing beautifully."

"Never mind acoustics, child! Think of how your friends will be impressed in the setting of the abbey!"

"I am not marrying Mr. Bartram in order to impress my friends and acquaintance, Mama, and true friends will understand our choice, so we will marry at St George' s church, next month, and perhaps we could have the wedding breakfast at Jane's home, and although not a ball, but a soiree in the evening, at Darcy House?" Kitty replied confidently, for she had discussed the possibilities with her sisters at great length, and they thought it was an excellent plan. Mrs. Bennet reluctantly conceded defeat on her wish for Westminster, but cheered up rapidly, when Lizzy rose and announced that it was time for their trip to the warehouses, to select the linen for the wedding clothes. In a flurry of happy activity, the ladies were soon in the carriage and heading for the shops.

Several hours later, Mrs. Bennet was the happiest woman in the world, for she had finally achieved her dream of shopping for wedding clothes for a daughter, and although they had not bought as much as she felt was required, the quality was of the best and she could not quibble with the design of the wedding gown. They had gone to Lizzy's modiste, who had made hers and Jane's wedding and ball gowns, and a very handsome creation was being made up in a beautiful primrose yellow, with sufficient lace to impress, flounces, ribbons; any woman would be proud to wear such a gown. An evening gown was also being made, in the white that Mrs. Bennet was so fond of, for it implied wealth, enough to employ a laundry maid at least, and the Bartram family were giving her a tiara for a wedding gift, so Catherine would truly look beautiful on her wedding day.

Just as with the previous weddings, the Gardiners were buying the accessories for their niece, who had grown much in their love and esteem since Kitty had spent so much time with her elder sisters. Jane and Lizzy were providing the table and bed linen for Kitty's new home at Kympton, buying the best quality linen and having it made up with the young couple's monograms embroidered on the centre and corners, which impressed Mrs. Bennet immensely. Seeing her mother's pleasure, Lizzy also had some bed linen made for her, with her own monograms.

Chapter 47

Easter was over, and as promised, Mr. Bartram joined them in town, staying in his father's house. As with any man, wildly in love, he spent as much time as possible with his fiancée as he could. He could only stay for a week, for his duties meant he could not leave his parish for too long, since he would be coming down again, in May, for the wedding, fixed on Thursday, the fifteenth of the month. So, during the week, in between dinners, the theatre, balls and such, the days were spent organising the big event. The organising was left to the ladies, whilst the three gentlemen attended more to getting to know each other, since they were to become brothers. Mr. Bennet had remained in Longbourn, along with Mary and little Jane, but they were to come to town before the wedding.

A problem which had caused some heartache was the attendance of Lydia and Wickham. As her sister, Kitty wanted her with her, but the previous year's issues with little Jane had caused a rift in their formerly close friendship, and although she wanted Lydia to attend, she rejected her mother's suggestion that Lydia be her bridal attendant. She cleverly put it to Mrs. Bennet that, as a married woman, Lydia could not be her bride's *maid*, so this left just Mary or Georgiana. After first consulting with Mary, who had preferred not to be in the limelight again, it was agreed that Georgiana, as her sister-by-marriage and best friend, would attend Kitty on her wedding day.

The wedding breakfast and the soiree were in Jane and Lizzy's hands, whilst consulting Kitty for her wishes, since they were the mistresses in their homes, so Mrs. Bennet was unable to do more than give them the benefit of her opinion, which she duly did, suggesting bigger, richer, grander, more opulent, for everything. She was not entirely unhappy however, for there was the continuous distraction of fittings for the gowns, the delivery of parcels and gifts, the making of a gown for herself; an azure blue satin, with silver trims and lace, with a detachable, wired, stiffened, wide collar of very fine lace, quite Elizabethan in style, and it had the advantage of framing her face and shoulders very becomingly.

The bans were read, the invitations sent, the wedding clothes were delivered, as were the new gowns and bonnets, Mrs. Bennet was delighted: a wedding in Town, to the son of a baronet, it was justifiably a moment of triumph to her maternal feelings for many a day. Three of her daughters were part of the Ton, something she had never even dared *dream* about before, two of them had very handsome houses in the best parts of Town; she felt very satisfied with the way she had brought them up. The only worry she had, was the arrival of the Wickhams; what if they decided that they wanted their daughter back? To avoid any temptation, she and Mr. Bennet had agreed to leave the child at Longbourn, only himself and Mary would be coming to the wedding, although bringing Mr. and Mrs. Phillips with them. The Phillips were to stay with the Gardiners, the Bennets with the Darcys and the Wickhams with the Bingleys.

The Wickhams arrived from the north, Lydia as fearless, carefree and noisy as ever, Wickham as easy of manner, as though they had not a care in the world. They were to stay with the Bingleys, for neither Lizzy nor Mrs. Gardiner felt that they would be able to adequately control their feelings and tempers, when constantly confronted with their impudent manner. Jane and Bingley would manage so much better. Even Mrs. Bennet did not greet her daughter as warmly as she would have done in the past.

Mr. Bennet and Mary arrived at Darcy House, with Kitty's Aunt and Uncle Phillips, where the Bingleys and Gardiners awaited them. The Wickhams were not present, for in spite of having been invited, Lydia had preferred to go to the theatre and her husband retired somewhere else to enjoy himself. The rest of the family were quite relieved at the reprieve. Mary, true to form, immediately found the library, whilst the gentlemen retired to the billiards room for something more substantial than tea, leaving Mrs. Phillips with the ladies, to be suitably impressed with her surroundings, for Mrs. Bennet insisted in showing her as many of the rooms as possible, whilst waiting for the tea to be made.

Having not had children of her own, Mrs. Phillips was quite content to be happy with the achievements of her sister's daughters, so she was as impressed as Mrs. Bennet herself could wish, in admiring the noble aspect of the rooms, the fine, tasteful furniture, handsome rugs, and magnificent curtains in Darcy House, all the while thinking of how she could obtain a similar effect at home in Meryton. Perhaps, when Lizzy next decided to refurbish any of her rooms, she could be prevailed upon to send the old furniture, rugs or curtains to her. She would not mind at all, taking her niece's old effects, when they were of such excellent quality, for they would still be far more impressive than the furnishings of her friends and neighbours. Looking at the fine pieces of china on the mantelpiece of the main drawing room, Mrs. Phillips felt acutely how indifferent her own imitations were. She had always been attributed with the same lack of taste as her sister Bennet, but Mary Phillips had only been curtailed in her taste, by the lack of sufficient income. Since the likelihood of her obtaining sufficient income for her taste was now very unlikely, she would have to adapt, by becoming a more regular correspondent with her nieces, as well as a more regular visitor when they were in town. Meryton was such a convenient distance from London for such things.

An hour later, the Gardiners left, taking the Phillips' with them, the Bingleys returned home and the Bennets and Darcys retired to their afternoon activities, before dressing for dinner, which was to be held at Gracechurch Street. Never before had the entire Bennet family, former and present, been in Town at the same time, and it had also been nearly two years since they had all sat down to dinner together

Chapter 48

The last of the guests were leaving Darcy House. The wedding had been magnificent, the bride in great beauty, the church filled with the cream of society, the wedding breakfast was stupendous, and the soiree was considered as one of the highlights of the end of the London Season. What more could a mother ask for? were Mrs. Bennet's thoughts.

There had been a slight incident with Lydia, who had slipped when descending from the carriage when she arrived for the evening, badly spraining her ankle. Considering how much unwatered wine she had drunk at the wedding breakfast; this was hardly a surprise. She was sent back with the carriage to the Bingley's house, and a physician called. Her husband had returned with her, and it was supposed he had stayed with her, for he was not seen again that evening.

The soiree was as grandiose an affair as even she herself had imagined, the magnificent drawing rooms opened up to accommodate so many more people, flowers, candles, the mingling of guests, the bride looking as a bride should, the tiara literally her crowning glory, made of silver with pearls and diamonds, a gift from the groom's parents. Sir Thomas and Lady Bartram were very quiet, dignified people: Sir Thomas from natural, decorous habit, his lady, from being a person of very tranquil feelings and a temper remarkably easy and indolent.

With such dignified and placid manners, it was therefore quite incomprehensible that they could possibly have produced a daughter such as the infamous Mrs. Rushworth. Sometime previously, according to the newspapers of the time, and then improved with gossip, it was said that within only a few months of her name being enrolled in the lists of hymen, and who had promised to become a brilliant leader in the fashionable world, the beautiful Mrs. R. had quit her husband's roof, in company with the well-known and captivating Mr. C, a friend and associate of her husband, who was himself, apparently, engaged at the time, with a cousin of Mrs. R's. Once she had been retrieved from her scandalous situation, she had been settled very quietly and secluded in the country, with her aunt to keep her company, in total disgrace, because her father had adamantly refused to condone her actions, so far as to not wishing to insult his neighbours, by expecting the country to notice her, which could have been understood to be the case, if she was living under his roof.

Their younger daughter, Mrs. Yates, had attended the wedding, with her husband, and seemed very chatty and fashionable, although it was also said that she had eloped with Mr. Yates at the same time as her sister had gone off with Mr. C, the difference being, that *she* was free to marry the man she had run off with, whereas her sister, most certainly, was *not*. In spite of his initial fears, Mr. Yate's situation was not quite as desperate a business as Sir Thomas had initially thought; his estate rather more and his debts much less, than rumour had led him to believe, and he was willing to learn from and be guided by someone he could look up to, such as Sir Thomas himself. So, from a somewhat scurrilous and dubious beginning, the marriage had turned out better than expected.

Kitty, now Mrs. Bartram, had returned to the Bartram's town house with her new husband. They were all invited for dinner on the morrow, at the Bartram's request, and Mrs. Bennet was looking forward to it immensely. She had already decided to wear her burgundy silk ball gown, made at the time of Jane and Lizzy's wedding, for Lady Bartram will not have seen it before, and with the train removed, it was perfectly suitable as an evening gown.

Mrs. Bennet's musings then brought her to the thought that she only had one daughter left at home, Mary. Who could she think of as a suitable partner for Mary? Fortunately, Mary had been taking more pains with her appearance, in fact several people had noticed that she looked quite similar to Mrs. Darcy, so perhaps, considering Lizzy's luck in finding a very wealthy husband, Mary would have some success after all. But then, if Mary married, there would be nobody left at home for her to talk to! What was it that Mr. Bennet had mentioned to her when Jane and Lizzy got married? Something about being thankful that she still had two daughters at home? Perhaps there was some wisdom in that. Perhaps she should not be in such a hurry to find a husband for Mary after all. And besides, after the success of today's wedding, it would be quite difficult to do better, when Mary's turn came.

Yes, the burgundy silk gown will be perfect for tomorrow.

Chapter 49

———•———

Summer finally came, and everyone returned to their country homes, to escape the city in the heat. Everyone that is, except the Darcy's. Totally unexpectedly, they had received an invitation from Lady Catherine, to visit her at Rosings. Darcy's initial reaction was to refuse, but with a little persuasion from his wife, he finally agreed.

"I know that you said that you would not forgive her, my love" Lizzy was saying as they left London for Kent, "but the fact that she invited us, is as much of an apology as I am ever going to get from her ladyship, and besides, I would like to see Charlotte again, and much as I know that you love me, I would not inflict a visit on you, that required us staying in my cousin Mr. Collins house, when Rosings is just across the park."

"That is a dire thought indeed, dearest, to be avoided at all cost, but I will still be observant, and if my aunt shows any of her unpleasant side to you, we will leave within the hour!" announced Darcy. "It is perhaps also because Rosings reminds me of the first time I asked for your hand; it will ever bring to my mind my objectionable behaviour to you."

"We are both heartily ashamed of our behaviour that night, but I have learned to see that visit as the end of our former prejudices, not immediately, but it led to your letter to me, then to my realisation that I had judged you so unfairly, without knowing you at all. It was, I feel, the *beginning* of our coming to an understanding."

"Well, dearest, I will be on my best behaviour, and if Lady Catherine starts anything, I will send in our son to distract her. Either he will be as good as gold, and utterly charm her, or as grumpy as the devil, and it will serve her right, but he will make *me* appear so much the better. An excellent idea, if I may say so" said Darcy with a smug smile.

Georgiana, observing her brother's banter, was very happy. She was not looking forward to the visit, but with her brother and her sister Elizabeth by her side, she felt she could face her ladyship, and it had been years since she had seen her cousin Anne. Much too long in fact, but she had grown up since then, had been through two London seasons, been presented at Court, yes, she certainly felt grown up enough to face her aunt.

"Before we arrive at Rosings, there is something I wish to share with you both" started Lizzy, with a smile, "young James, as charming as he can be, is not going to be an only child for much longer."

"Oh! my dearest Elizabeth" exclaimed Darcy "how wonderful! When is the child due?"

"Yes Lizzy, that is wonderful news, do you intend to let my aunt know during our visit?" asked Georgiana

"To answer you both, in January, and yes, we will let her ladyship know, for it will irritate her exceedingly if she has not truly forgiven your brother and I for marrying, and if she has, she will be pleased to be amongst the first to know. Either way, you will be prevailed upon to provide the music during our visit, Georgiana, for my playing is not up to her Ladyship's standard, and I quite agree with her on that."

They were now approaching Rosings, driving along the Hunsford lane where the rectory was situated, and as had been expected, Mr. Collins had been on the lookout for their arrival, so he could pay his respects with a low bow.

"Could we stop the coach, my love?" asked Lizzy, "for I would like to see Charlotte for just a few minutes. I will not be long, but unless he escorts me into the house, you will have to tolerate my cousin in the meantime, for I will not be long enough to justify us all getting out of the carriage"

Darcy pulled the cord leading to the coachman, indicating the request to stop.

"Whatever you wish my dearest. Ah! Mr. Collins is coming, he is gesticulating to the house, so I suspect Mrs. Collins has been notified. Mr. Collins! How good it is to see you again!" as Darcy got out of the carriage, to assist his wife down the steps. "Please forgive us the intrusion Mr. Collins, but Mrs. Darcy could not help asking to stop and see the parsonage, where she spent so many happy weeks with you and Mrs. Collins."

"There is no intrusion, sir, it is indeed all honour on our part that my noble cousin recalls her visit to us in our humble abode with such fondness" as he bowed low and kissed his cousin's hand.

"Mr. Collins, you are as full of benevolence as ever, I just wished to see Charlotte quickly, before we go to Rosings, I will not detain you long" as Lizzy walked quickly up the garden path where Charlotte had just reached the front door. "Oh Charlotte! It is so good to see you again" as the friends embraced each other warmly. "I have an ulterior motive for seeing you Charlotte, before we see her ladyship" whispered Lizzy, "I just wish to know whether she has truly forgiven me for marrying her nephew, or is this another ploy on her part?"

Holding the embrace, Charlotte replied quietly "Yes, she has forgiven you, but I think also that she is not in good health, and perhaps wishes to make peace with her nephew, but I have not said this to you Eliza" then in a louder voice, "It is so good of you, Mrs. Darcy, to think of calling in to see me on your way to Rosings. Please come and visit, if you would be so kind, when you have settled in."

"Of course I will Charlotte, it has been such a long time, we have much to catch up upon" as Lizzy turned back to the carriage, where Mr. Darcy handed her back in. Slightly bowing his head to Mr. Collins, he thanked the gentleman for his kindness and as he got in the coach, told the coachman to drive on.

"So, what was that about my dear? Was it really as you said, a wish to see your friend before going to Rosings?' inquired her husband.

"Well my love, it *was* a stratagem: I wanted to know whether we are truly forgiven, or does Lady Catherine have another motive, and only Charlotte could tell me. You will be happy to learn that she *has* forgiven us" said Lizzy, who did not wish to mention her friend's suspicions of the great lady's possibly declining health at that moment.

"Well that is good to know, I shall be able to greet my aunt with a happier frame of mind" acquiesced Darcy "and here we are, approaching the house" as they entered the park.

Chapter 50

———•———

He was still startled however, when they arrived at the main entrance, for both his aunt and cousin were waiting for them at the top of the steps.

"Fitzwilliam! How delighted I am to see you my dear boy! And you, Elizabeth. Georgiana! How you have changed! Come in, come in!" exclaimed Lady Catherine, astonishing her visitors with her gregariousness, so exceedingly different from her normal, unconciliatory manner, which had marked her previous behaviour to Lizzy. By comparison to her mother, Miss de Bourgh, cousin Anne, appeared almost sullen with her much quieter greeting and slight curtsey.

Escorting Lizzy into the entrance hall, Darcy quietly asked her if Charlotte had mentioned his aunt's health, but she could not discreetly reply, so just slightly nodded her head.

Leading the way through the ante-chamber to the drawing room, where Elizabeth had first met her ladyship, Lady Catherine was still as talkative as she had ever been, but her voice seemed to have lost some of its' authoritative tone and volume, and could it be that she was not as large as Lizzy remembered?

"Yes, Fitzwilliam, I have already met your son, a sturdy, handsome boy, your mother, my sister, Lady Anne, would have doated on him. Very sensible of you, to send him on ahead with your servants, I have always done so, it means that your own servants can set up your apartment for you, just the way you like it. I have put you in your usual rooms, and Georgiana as well, though it has been such a while since you have been here, Georgiana, you might not recall. Elizabeth, I have put you in the room my sister used; as Mrs. Darcy, I must show you every courtesy."

"That is very kind of you, Aunt" replied Darcy, "but if Elizabeth is in my mother's former rooms, I will then move to the rooms my father used, for my current rooms are some distance away from there."

Lady Catherine made as if she was biting back a retort, with some difficulty, but modified the response to a dignified "Certainly, as you wish Fitzwilliam, I forgot that your usual rooms were purposely kept some distance from your parents' rooms. Mrs. Jenkinson, let the housekeeper know."

As Mrs. Jenkinson left the room, Miss de Bourgh finally spoke, "I am so pleased you accepted my mother's invitation to visit us at Rosings, Fitzwilliam, it has been too long since I have seen you or my cousin Georgiana, and it is a pleasure to welcome you again, Elizabeth."

Lizzy was astounded: she had never heard Miss de Bourgh put so many words together in one sentence, in fact she had never heard so many words from her at all!

"The pleasure, I believe, Miss de Bourgh, is entirely ours" she responded graciously, whereupon Lady Catherine intervened with "Of course it is a pleasure for you, but your pleasure cannot equal ours in seeing you all here. Nobody enjoys the company of family or appreciates it more than I do. I am sure, with young James, you are starting to realise the true value of family"

This was the Lady Catherine of the past, that Lizzy knew and could understand, the new, subdued Lady Catherine was going to take a little time to unravel in her mind. Charlotte must know more than she had had time to say in their brief encounter, so at the first opportunity, Lizzy would visit the parsonage, but she would have to engage Fitzwilliam in distracting her cousin, Mr. Collins, or there would be no possibility to talk freely with her friend, or perhaps she, like Miss de Bourgh, could drive past in a little phaeton and simply invite Charlotte for a drive; yes, that was a much better idea, being Mrs. Darcy, her cousin Mr. Collins, could not refuse her request, and her dearest Fitzwilliam would not have to suffer his company.

Such were Lizzy's wandering thoughts as she sat beside Darcy, and when she attended the conversation again, Lady Catherine was giving her opinion as to the optimal size of a gentleman's family, oblivious to the fact that she herself had produced but one child.

"The ideal size is four children, preferably two boys, an heir and a spare, and two girls, who can enhance the family's repute with judiciously and carefully arranged marriages" she decreed. Hiding a smile, Lizzy nudged her husband, and squeezed his hand; he understood the hint and interrupted his aunt's dialogue.

"We heartily agree with you, Aunt, which is why we are *particularly* happy to let you be the *first* to know that we are expecting another child, either the spare or a daughter."

"Oh Darcy! That is delightful news! And you say that I am the first to be told?"

"Yes, Elizabeth only told *us* as we were coming up the Hunsford road to Rosings, not half an hour ago, and she only mentioned it *then*, because she thought that you would appreciate such news, knowing how much you set by family."

"And two years between the children: a ladylike space between them; for I do not approve of the practice of some, mainly the poor, who cannot afford to feed the ones they already have, but even some of the more well-off, seem to breed like rabbits! I heartily disapprove of such behaviour, treating their wives like brood mares!"

"Ma'am, please remember that you are talking to my cousins, I am sure that my cousin Georgiana would rather not hear such talk" interposed Miss de Bourgh, to everyone's surprise, but none more so than her mother's.

"Well! Well I never! You have finally found your tongue, young lady! You are so like your father that I had despaired of making anything of you, no matter what flattery Mr. Collins continuously comes up with!" exclaimed Lady Catherine.

Seeing her poor cousin's discomfort under the stern gaze and reprimand of her mother, even Georgiana found the strength to speak.

"Thank you, cousin Anne, I *was* starting to feel a little uncomfortable, listening to the breeding practices of rabbits, especially when applied to people whom I hold dear, such as the Bingley's, who have recently welcomed their second child and already expecting a third."

"Ladies, ladies!" intervened Darcy, who did not wish for such happy news to cause such ructions between them "Let others do as they deem fit, and let us return to our joy. The baby is due early next year, so we will have another quiet Christmas at home, unless of course, you and our cousin would care to join us, Lady Catherine. You have not been to Pemberley in a long time, and my cousin even longer."

"An excellent idea, my love. We would be honoured by your presence, your ladyship, as we would be by yours, Miss de Bourgh" added Lizzy, very relieved that Darcy had hopefully diffused what looked as though it could cause a breach in the peace only so recently obtained.

After a moment's thought, Lady Catherine graciously accepted the invitation, and called for refreshments. The conversation then turned to less dangerous subjects, such as the terrible past two winters and the promise of a better summer's harvest.

An hour later, the visitors and their hosts retired to their rooms to prepare for dinner. Lizzy was led to rooms in a part of the house she had not seen before, tastefully decorated in a style more in keeping with Pemberley, than with the rest of Rosings. She recalled, however, that these had been the late Mrs. Darcy's rooms, so obviously, in her taste. Madeleine had been busy since her arrival, unpacking her mistress's trunks, so everything was ready for when Lizzy got there.

Unlike the previous dinners that she had attended at Rosings, as the guest of the Collinses, there was no cousin hurriedly knocking at her door, telling her to make haste, and to not worry about her attire, for now, as Darcy's wife, she could dress as grandly as her ladyship herself. Madeleine had selected an emerald green evening gown, trimmed in Mrs. Darcy's now favourite black lace, diamond and emerald jewels, and having dressed her hair in an almost courtly style, finished it off with a diamond circlet across the middle of her forehead. Madeleine was satisfied with the result, Lizzy equally so, and Darcy beamed his approval as he led her down the stairs.

Chapter 51

The following morning, after a good night's rest, Lizzy met with the ladies of the house in the summer breakfast room. Georgiana had joined them shortly before Lizzy's arrival. Seating herself between her sister and Miss de Bourgh, opposite Lady Catherine, Lizzy said little, just asking the servant to bring her a dish of tea and some toast with a little butter, to settle her stomach.

"And what are your plans for today, Georgiana? Elizabeth?" asked her ladyship directly, pointedly ignoring Anne.

"I thought to walk around the grounds with Anne, if she would care to accompany me," answered Georgiana, "and then to the music room, for my daily practice."

"Well, if Miss de Bourgh joins Georgiana in her walk, then perhaps I may have the use her little phaeton, to call on Mrs. Collins and perhaps persuade her to come for a drive with me. I am sure she does not often get the opportunity, with two small children, and the weather seems quite perfect for such an exercise" said Lizzy quickly, before Lady Catherine could say anything.

Following Lizzy's lead, and before her mother could reply in her stead, Anne eagerly accepted Georgiana's invitation, and did not hesitate in offering Elizabeth the use of her phaeton, adding "I know that I should offer to take Mrs. Collins for a drive, when I go past her house, but I fear intruding upon her, for she cannot really refuse me, should I ask, and it may not be to her liking, or at her convenience to sit with me."

Lizzy could *sense* that Lady Catherine was on the point of saying that Mrs. Collins should feel honoured for the notice, and so she smiled when, in her attempt at being less authoritive in her behaviour, her ladyship brought it down to, "I am sure Mrs. Collins would appreciate the offer, Elizabeth, and it is our duty, after all, to offer benevolent attentions to those less fortunate than ourselves. Mrs. Collins is a very sensible woman; she always heeds my advice, whenever I choose to give it."

"I am sure that my friend will appreciate the offer in the spirit in which it is given, your ladyship, Mrs. Collins is, as you say Lady Catherine, a very sensible woman. Thank you, Miss de Bourgh, for the offer of the phaeton" responded Lizzy.

"Please, Mrs. Darcy, as we are now cousins, would you consider calling me Anne?"

"Only if you will call *me* Elizabeth: I think that within a family, one should not keep up the same distance one would with strangers or simple acquaintance, and you are a dearly loved cousin to both my husband and Georgiana."

"Humph! I agree with you, Elizabeth; we are family indeed" said Lady Catherine, with a mere hint of grumpiness, just as Darcy walked into the room, after an early morning ride.

"I am very glad to hear you say so, Aunt Catherine, for my children will welcome all the relations they have, and my wife has shown me the benefits and joy of having an extended family. Families are made of different people with very different characters, and I have learned to live with their differences, to my own advantage and happiness" replied Darcy.

"Fitzwilliam! I did not know you had already been out, have you had breakfast?" cried Lizzy eagerly, making room at the table so that he could sit next to her.

"I have broken my fast, my dear, but it was so early that I will willingly eat again. Have you eaten yourself? I can only see crumbs of toast on your plate. You must keep your strength up in your condition, dearest."

"I will have some of the scrambled eggs, my love, with some more toast."

Once breakfast was done, everyone proceeded to their activities for the day, and Lizzy was driven in the phaeton to the Collins's house. The coachman assisted her down and she was welcomed at the door by Mr. Collins and Charlotte.

"Mrs. Darcy, welcome to our humble abode, we are indeed most honoured by your presence!" began Mr. Collins.

"I have many happy memories of my previous visit to you, Mr. Collins, but today I am wishing to enquire whether Charlotte would care to accompany me for a drive around the grounds of Rosings. You have previously mentioned how fine they are, so I thought that I would request Charlotte's company, for she will be able to point out the finer points to me" replied Lizzy.

"She would be delighted to do so, fair cousin, Charlotte, you of course would wish to do so, would you not?" said Mr. Collins in his usual pompous, obsequious manner. "You would not wish to disappoint Mrs. Darcy, when she has been so kind to invite you."

"I would be very happy to accompany Mrs. Darcy, my dear, but please allow me to fetch my shawl, and see to the children. Their nurse has just gone down to the laundry" answered his long-suffering wife. How her friend could bear his company was quite beyond Lizzy's comprehension, but she had to admit that Charlotte was possibly the only woman who could make the best of the situation that she herself had created by accepting to be his wife. She had married him without affection or respect, knowing that his company was irksome and that his attachment to her was imaginary, but she had been prepared to tolerate much in order to obtain an establishment by marriage; the only honourable provision for a well-educated woman of small fortune, such as herself.

Once Charlotte had joined her, Lizzy asked the coachman to drive along the open grove which edged the side of the park, where Lizzy had often walked by herself, during her first visit.

"Now Charlotte," began Lizzy, "please tell me your news, and then explain to me the change of heart with her ladyship. It is so unlike her! You mentioned that she was suffering from a decline in health, and she does not appear to me to be as strong as she was."

"My news is quite usual, I am with child again, as you can see; Mr. Collins is determined to have a male heir, so as not to repeat the situation your father has found himself in, with an entailed estate and a family of daughters. This one is due in a month's time."

"Oh Charlotte! So soon after your last! Hopefully this time it will be a boy and he will leave you in peace for a while afterwards."

"And as to the rest of your question, Eliza, you are correct, her ladyship has suffered a set-back in her health, which scared her immensely. I think she had felt herself to be above such things, that her constitution would continue to obey her wishes, but about six months after your marriage, she seemed to be unable to exert herself as before, almost as though her mind was tired. Physicians were consulted and she was diagnosed with melancholy. She of course would be mortified if anyone found this out, but I believe that it is the base of her wish to reunite with her nephew and niece, and if that means accepting you as his wife, then she is now prepared to do so. I do think that your presentation at Court gave her an excuse, for if the Ton could accept you, then she would not appear to have lowered her own high standards by accepting you also" explained Charlotte, "*and* you have provided Mr. Darcy with an heir."

"And I am about to provide him with either a daughter or a spare heir, Charlotte, for I too am with child again. We let Lady Catherine be the first to know, only yesterday, so please do not mention it yet in your correspondence with your family, for I would like to let my own family learn of it from myself first."

Having discussed the points that were troubling them both, the two friends settled into easy conversation and Lizzy mentioned Miss de Bourgh's trepidation of inviting Charlotte to accompany her for a drive when she called on her at the parsonage, for fear of imposing on her, knowing that she could not very well refuse. Charlotte laughed and said that she had realised that it was the case, for Miss de Bourgh was a very shy, timid person, but if Lizzy could let her know that she would be delighted, at any time, to accompany her, and that Mr. Collins would not object at all.

Chapter 52

Two weeks passed, with very little altercation from Lady Catherine. Anne seemed less intimidated and spent much time with her cousin Georgiana, Lizzy and Darcy visited and dined with the local notables, and the Collinses were invited several times for tea and once for dinner. Lizzy had also gone down to the Hunsford rectory with her son, James, and he played happily with Charlotte's eldest child, Catherine, or Cathy, much to Mr. Collins' delight.

Mr. Collins had wanted to invite the Darcy family to a dinner, but Charlotte had objected, pointing out that if the Darcys were invited, then Lady Catherine and Miss de Bourgh must also be invited, and that it would put a strain on their income, for her ladyship would expect the same standard of dinner with *them*, as to which she was accustomed at Rosings, and they simply could not afford to do so, with their growing family. Such calm, logical arguments prevailed, and refreshments only, were provided whenever her ladyship, Miss de Bourgh or Lizzy and Georgiana called on Mrs. Collins. Miss de Bourgh had heeded Lizzy's counsel, and now felt more at ease in offering the occasional drive to her neighbour, since Lizzy and Georgiana were often with her too.

Lady Catherine still gave her opinion on any conversations that anybody had, on any subject, on which of course her own excellent, natural taste or experience made her feel she had the authority to inform others what she felt was the final opinion, which was still irritating to her listeners, but since it was delivered in a tone somewhat *quieter* than in the past, was not quite as grating to the ear and mind. Lizzy had also spoken to both her husband and Georgiana on their aunt's health, telling them what she had learned from Charlotte, so they felt pleased that they had accepted the invitation to visit Rosings, and had offered the invitation to Pemberley, before they had been aware of her decline in mental strength.

Little James was another source of delight: he was strong, healthy, and both Lady Catherine and Anne took great pleasure in his company before dinner, when he was brought down by his nurse, after being fed and cleaned, dressed in fresh linen, and at his best and most charming. Lady Catherine, of course, had her opinion on this too, warning the proud parents that the next child would be much more difficult, though how she could possibly know this, having had only one child herself, caused Lizzy and Darcy to glance at each other and just smile. It could possibly be true, but they would still love the child as much as they loved James.

They had intended to stay for a fortnight, but at her ladyship's request, they stayed another week, Darcy writing to his steward to inform him of the change of plan. This also gave Lizzy more time with Charlotte, but since it was summer, Mr. Collins was more often to be found working in his garden, Charlotte actively advocating the benefits of the exercise to his health, making her friend smile into her teacup as he was sent out of the house again.

Darcy spent time with his aunt's steward, talking about the crops and plans for the future, in his aunt's stead. He could see for himself that she was no longer as sharp of mind as she had been before, and wanted to assist her as much as he could, by simple actions, such as talking to the steward, the gamekeeper, overseeing and visiting tenants, ensuring that everything was running as smoothly as possible before he left for Pemberley. He also felt a little guilty at the time that had lapsed since he had last seen her and his cousin, which was entirely his own doing, for had not Elizabeth been suggesting for two years, that he ought to forgive his aunt for her interference prior to his marriage?

Although Lady Catherine asked for them to stay yet another week, Darcy declined, saying that he had to be in Pemberley to see to the estate, to which argument she could not criticize, knowing herself how large estates like Rosings and Pemberley needed the presence of the landowner at this time of year. Darcy had not mentioned his actions and discussions with her steward and the head-gamekeeper, but Lady Catherine knew of it; her steward knowing better than to try and hide such a thing from his employer.

Their visit to Pemberley for Christmas was much canvassed over dinner; Anne almost glowing with anticipation at being somewhere else than Rosings. Her poor health had been the excuse for not doing anything, or going anywhere, for far too long. In fact, she sometimes wondered whether her constitution was actually as bad as her mother made it out to be. She was feeling so well and strong at present; perhaps it was the time of year, but she herself thought that it was the presence of her cousins, the novelty and variety in her life, that made her feel thus.

Chapter 53

———•———

Stopping only two nights in town, the family arrived home to Pemberley with a sense of relief. It was certainly agreeable, going to town and visiting friends and family, but it was so pleasant to come home and spend the summer in relative peace and quiet, spending their days walking or riding around the gardens and grounds, morning visits, afternoon visits, picnics, dinners and the occasional dance.

The summer was fine, with sufficient sunshine, warm days and rain to ensure, at last, good crops. The previous two years' disastrous summers were a thing of the past; the farmworkers and their families all working happily together to bring in the hay, the corn and the wheat, the potatoes and vegetables, which were at last in sufficient quantities, enough to last through the winter. The harvest feast in September was a joyous occasion for all, the Darcy family even joining in the dancing in the evening.

Autumn was golden, the first frosts coming only in the beginning of November, and Lizzy was glowing with health as her child grew within her. Christmas arrived, along with Lady Catherine and Anne. The Bingley's were to spend the festive period with them, as were Kitty and her husband, but the Bennets preferred to stay in Longbourn, so it was a surprise when Mr. Bennet arrived the night before Christmas; yet another of one of his impromptu visits.

Lady Catherine seemed to have lost more weight, just as her daughter seemed to have gained enough to not look as sickly as she had done before. In private, Lizzy and Darcy discussed her ladyship's health, wondering whether they should talk to her about it.

"You know your aunt better than I do Fitzwilliam, perhaps you should speak to her" said Lizzy.

"I might know her better, my love, but I think it would sound better if any questions came from you, because it could be women's problems and she would feel most uncomfortable if *I* broached the subject, and she seems to have taken quite a liking to you since we went down to Rosings last May. She is more likely to speak to *you* about her health."

"You are right, dearest, so I will try to find an opportunity at some point. Perhaps if I took her up to the nursery, to show her the preparations for the new child, she might be in a frame of mind to speak of health; I could start by talking about my own health."

The following day, as Georgiana, Jane and Anne went into Kympton to visit Kitty, the gentlemen went shooting, leaving Lizzy alone with Lady Catherine. Lizzy offered to show Lady Catherine the nursery, and as she lumbered up the stairs, she could not help but notice that the dowager was struggling to keep up with her. Resting on a bench in the hallway, Lizzy invited her ladyship to sit with her whilst she found her breath.

Deciding that this was her opportunity, Elizabeth started with "Your ladyship, are you quite well? You seem to be suffering, I could not help but notice that you have grown thin, even gaunt, and these stairs to the nursery, although causing me to require a rest, are not as arduous as the main staircase at Rosings" as she allowed herself to take the old lady's hand.

"You are a very observant young woman, Elizabeth, I noticed that, the first time I met you. I also noticed that you have a tendency of speaking from the heart; my visit to your home, before your marriage, which you know I was trying to stop, taught me that, so I am not surprised at the question" replied Lady Catherine, calmly.

"Yes, I am ill, I let it be known to Mrs. Collins that it was melancholy, for she is another such woman as yourself, and saw the change in my health, but it is unfortunately more serious than ill-humour or melancholy, much to my annoyance."

"Oh! Lady Catherine! I am sorry to hear that. Can the doctors help you? Is there anything we can help you with?"

"No, my dear, they can *not* help. I have a growth inside me that is slowly making me more and more ill, I think they call it a cancer, in my female organs, which will be the death of me in the end."

"Does anyone else know? Does Anne? How long do the doctors think you have? Can I tell Fitzwilliam and Georgiana? What can I do for you?" cried Lizzy, thoroughly and sincerely shocked.

"It is very strange, Elizabeth, but you are the first person I have told, with whom I have spoken of it, apart from my physicians. Perhaps I thought that if I did not speak of it, it would go away, which is utterly foolish, I know" replied her ladyship, in a voice as quiet and calm as Lizzy had ever heard her speak. "I have been greatly at fault, in not telling Anne, my own child, so I will address that as we return to Rosings, but if you would be so kind as to not mention this to my nephew and niece, until *after* my departure, I would much appreciate your discretion, for I do not wish to see their pity. I have perhaps another six months, if the physicians are to be believed."

Lizzy could think of nothing better to do than take Lady Catherine in her arms and hug her warmly, trying to keep her tears to herself. Heeding the request made of her, she took her ladyship's arm and walked with her to the nursery, talking of the baby and their hopes.

Lizzy was deeply saddened by what she had just heard. Just as the peace between the two families had finally occurred, they were to lose her. What would happen with Anne? She was of age, and of course would inherit the estate, for unlike Longbourn, it was not entailed, but was she capable of looking after it as her mother had done? She would be highly sought after as a wife, by every impoverished gentleman, and his family, in the country! Was she capable of seeing through the scoundrels and fortune seekers? Wickham came to mind; heaven forbid that poor Anne should marry such a person, but that could very likely be the case, for she had led such a very sheltered life, due mainly to her domineering mother insisting that her health did not allow her to join in society. Fitzwilliam and his cousin, Colonel Fitzwilliam, and her uncle and aunt, Lord and Lady Matlock will have to take care of her future, watch over her, to avoid such a catastrophe.

Chapter 54

Perhaps it was the shock of Lady Catherine's revelation, or possibly she was mistaken in her dates, or maybe the baby simply wished to be born, but two days later, on the eve of the new year, Lizzy was safely delivered of a baby daughter.

Darcy was delighted, as was everyone else, not least Lady Catherine. The naming of the child was discussed yet again. Darcy had once maintained that he would never call his daughter Catherine, because of his disagreement with his aunt, but now, things were different, for in spite of her ladyship's request that she *not* tell Fitzwilliam, Lizzy had spoken of her conversation with her to her husband, for she would have no secrets from him. He was equally shocked by the revelation. They had initially thought to name the child Anne, after the late Mrs. Darcy, and Catherine, after Kitty, who was to be the child's sponsor. They then considered reversing the names, to make her Catherine Anne, to honour Lady Catherine, but then decided against it for two reasons. The first was that it would perhaps betray Lizzy's telling Darcy of what she had learned of her ladyship's health, but secondly, there were Catherines enough in their circle of family and friends, and it would be confusing, to know of which Catherine they were speaking, so they decided to remain with their initial choice and the child was named Anne

Catherine, which still delighted both the de Bourgh ladies, as well as Kitty.

In spite of Lady Catherine's prediction, Anne Catherine proved to be a very placid child, sleeping through the night after only two weeks, causing very little concern to her family.

Lady Catherine returned to Rosings with her daughter, in the middle of January, and during a consultation with her physician, which Anne attended at her mother's request, she learned of her mother's illness. Her letter to Pemberley, initially started to thank them warmly and sincerely for her stay, ended with her obvious distress at the news, begging her cousins to stand by her, if they could find it in their heart to do so. Such a letter could not leave them unmoved and Darcy promptly replied that he would do anything for her and her mother that was required, all she had to do was ask. He proposed going down to Rosings at Easter, but if his aunt's health declined, at any time, they were to go to Darcy House immediately, in order to be in town to have on hand the best physicians available. Elizabeth would write to Mrs. Clayton the housekeeper, to this effect, immediately.

Anne's letter had a very sobering effect on the family; they had become closer to Anne, who seemed to have come out of the shell of her mother's overwhelming protection since their visit in the beginning of summer, and of course the news of her mother's health had a devastating effect on them all, not just Anne.

The Matlock's went down to Rosings, for her ladyship was, after all was said and done, Lord Matlock's sister, and any altercations they had ever had in the past now paled into insignificance with the learning of his sister's pending demise. They intended to stay with her, to teach Anne how to manage the estate, to ensure that the current staff were trustworthy, and to be of any assistance that they could to their sister and niece.

This allowed Darcy to remain at Pemberley, to look after his own family, for Lizzy had just given birth and was still recovering, so he did not wish to leave her at that moment in time. Georgiana was most helpful, distracting them with her playing and singing, and Kitty and her husband were regular visitors.

It was a strange situation, for they felt as though they were already mourning the loss of Lady Catherine, even though she was still clinging on to life. They somehow felt guilty if they laughed too much, and yet scolded themselves for being so mourn, when the lady herself was still very much alive. She might not have been able to talk to them, but she still had the strength to write and give her opinions on everything, except her health. They depended on Lord Matlock, Anne, and Charlotte Collins for any news on that count. From that correspondence they were able to learn that although declining, Lady Catherine was still fighting, convinced that her will could delay the doctors' verdict. One could not help but admire her tenacity.

Lizzy having recovered enough to allow travel, the Darcys went down to town in March, passing by Gaddesley and Longbourn on their way, to show off and admire the various babies and children. The Bingley's had decided not to go to town this season, and so had let the Hurst's and Miss Bingley use their town house for the Season, for they needed somewhere from where they could entertain, as the ladies were still trying to get themselves presented at court, and it was only by hosting splendid parties and dinners that they could achieve this aim, selecting guests to whom they had been introduced to the previous season. As Mr. Hurst maintained, it was not *what* you knew, but *whom*.

However, it had been a shock to both the Bingley's when Madame Georges wrote to them after a month of their taking up residence, to express her concern to her mistress that neither the Hursts or Miss Bingley were actually paying for the lavish entertainment; all was being charged to their brother Charles. The said brother immediately wrote to his sisters and set them straight as to how the arrangement was to be. They had the residence at no expense to themselves, but *they* were to pay for the housekeeping costs of their entertainment. It was one thing to stay with him and his family at no expense, but quite another to treat his benevolence to the extent of expecting *him* to pay for *their* social expenses when not in residence himself. This correspondence was followed by a decided chill in ensuing letters, especially to Jane, but it was not sufficient a chill for the sisters to take it upon themselves to search elsewhere for accommodation.

Chapter 55

When the Darcys had left Longbourn, they had brought Mary with them. It was not Mary's choice, more Mrs. Bennet's, who was lamenting on the decided lack of any gentlemen in the neighbourhood in the possession of any fortune, small or large. It was all very well for Mary to have improved in looks; if there was nobody to be captivated by them, it was all to no good.

Lizzy thought it would be beneficial to Mary for other reasons than her mother. Mary was so content to be her niece's doting aunt, that she seemed to want for nothing else; even her studies, formerly so important to her, were being left aside. Perhaps a stay in London, where she could visit the museums, libraries and galleries, attend concerts etc. would bring her back to enjoying her learning. However, it was still a reluctant Mary who came with them to Darcy House.

Once settled in her apartment, the sight of the magnificent pianoforte and the library brought Mary into a happier frame of mind. Lizzy and Darcy accompanied her and Georgiana to see some of the greatest collections of books, artwork and artefacts in the country. Mary's love of learning was reawakened: she could not learn enough of all that her inquiring mind requested. Lizzy was happy and Mary was happy.

The social rounds were made; they of course called on Gracechurch Street, where the Gardiners were delighted to see them, the Hursts and Miss Bingley, and all of their London acquaintance. Dinner invitations, card parties, concerts, the opera, plays etc. were a nightly occurrence, to which obligation Mary underwent in order to please her sister rather than herself, but with some new gowns, and Madeleine to dress her hair and select the right accessories, Mary was turning into quite a handsome young lady.

Darcy made a quick visit to Rosings, to visit Lady Catherine and his cousin, to assure himself that everything was being done for his aunt; but under Lord and Lady Matlock's care, of course nothing was remiss. They had been instructing their niece in the running of the estate, with some success, for Anne might be shy, but she was by no means short of intellect. Lady Catherine was so determined to prove the physicians wrong, that through sheer stubbornness, she appeared to have slowed the progression of her disease.

After many discussions with his uncle, Darcy felt reassured that everything was being done that could be: his cousin was proving to be more stalwart under the circumstances than anyone had thought she could be. Anne still had her companion, Mrs. Jenkinson, but she had also become friends with Mrs. Collins, whose calm, sensible, reassuring manner was in stark contrast with Mr. Collin's panicky, cloying attempts of trying to gain her favour, as the heiress to Rosings. Mrs. Collins could be relied upon to give Anne sensible advice, and Lord and Lady Matlock approved of the acquaintance.

Private conversations with Lady Catherine told him of her wishes, after her demise, and she had insisted that Anne should be mentored by Fitzwilliam and her uncle, Lord Matlock. Because Anne was of age, she did not require guardianship, but her mother wanted to be reassured that the male members of the family would look after her. Surprisingly, Lady Catherine's wishes for her funeral were very simple: she wanted a private service at Rosings, with Mr. Collins presiding, and only close family to attend. She wanted to be buried next to her late husband, Sir Lewis de Bourgh, in the family mausoleum on the estate. Darcy acquiesced to everything, knowing that his aunt had made him an executor of her will, along with Lord Matlock, who presumably, she had also made acquainted with her wishes.

Darcy left for town in early May, after more discussions with Anne and Lord and Lady Matlock, and insisting on being kept informed of any changes; he could ride to Rosings at a moment's notice.

Chapter 56

———•———

Upon his return to town, the Darcys were engaged to attend a ball, organised by the Bartrams, at the Mayfair Hotel. Mary of course was invited, as the Darcy's guest and as Catherine's sister, so it was a very well-dressed foursome that arrived to be greeted by Sir Thomas, Lady Bartram, Mr. Bartram, their eldest son, Mr. and Mrs. Edmund Bartram, and Mr. and Mrs. Yates: the whole family in fact.

Mr. Bartram was introduced to them, for he had been away in Antigua, attending to business to do with his father's estates at the time of Kitty's wedding, so they had not met him before. A very amiable young man, of about eight or nine and twenty, very courteous and attentive to the Darcys, knowing that Mrs. Darcy was Catherine's sister. The two young ladies were certainly handsome, one being Miss Darcy, the other being Miss Bennet, another of Catherine's sisters. As soon as the introductions were made, he requested the honour of the first dance with Miss Darcy, and equally gallantly requested Mary for the second dance. Both girls were very happy to accept, Mary fully understanding that a Miss Darcy would always take precedence over a Miss Bennet in any social event.

As the girls were dancing, Kitty found time to sit with Lizzy, both of them deciding to sit out the lively country dance.

"You look radiant, Kitty, being married has brought an extra glow to your complexion" began Lizzy.

"Happiness does that to a woman Lizzy, as you well know" replied her sister, "and being with child adds to the happiness, does it not?"

"Indeed, it does, Kitty, indeed it does. I am very happy for you both"

Smiling contentedly, Kitty abruptly changed the subject, "Now Lizzy, what do you think of Tom? Edmund's *brother* Thomas, that is, not his father, *Sir* Thomas."

"I do not know him, or of him, enough to form an opinion: why do you ask?"

"I am thinking that he would be an ideal match for Georgiana; he is the heir to the Bartram title and estates, he is very sensible, kind, and considerate, and already being part of our family, through my dearest Edmund, Darcy might not be so recalcitrant in approving such a match, should their acquaintance come to anything."

"Oh Kitty! Have you been talking to Mama? I am half surprised that she has not written to me to demand to know how many gentlemen are battling to win Mary's hand!"

"Mary's hand will be hard to win, but I think I know that she has always held your Mr. Edwards in high esteem, since that Christmas when he walked her into the dinner you held on Christmas Eve, do you recall? It was the first time, I believe, she had truly understood that she was *Miss* Bennet, as opposed to Miss *Mary* Bennet."

"Really? I had no idea!" replied Lizzy with some surprise "Perhaps we could help things along by inviting her back to Derbyshire with us. She could stay with either us or you at Kympton …. Oh, hark at us, Kitty! we sound just like Mama! But it would be good for her to have an opportunity of getting to know him better, if she does, as you say, hold him in esteem. However, getting back to Mr. Bartram, what do you know of him? As his sister by marriage, you would know more than the rest of us."

"He is a very steady young man, these days, but it was not always the case: he had been considered a rather wild young man in his younger years, until he fell ill, very seriously ill, after a neglected fall followed by excesses of drinking, during a trip to Newmarket, with some of his friends of the time. When the party broke up, they left him at the house of one of the young men, leaving him in just the care of the servants, until, as his disorder had increased considerately, in his very real distress, he requested his physicians to dispatch a letter to Mansfield to ask them to come for him and take him home.

It was Edmund, my own dear Edmund, who fetched him home, and nursed him for many a long day, reading to the invalid, feeding him when he was too weak to hold even a cup or a spoon; indeed, during the first week of his return home he suffered a relapse, perhaps due to the haste in getting him back to Mansfield; the whole family was terrified that he would die!"

"How dreadful for them!" exclaimed Lizzy, "and how noble and kind of Edmund!"

"Yes, so like Edmund, a very caring man, I am lucky to have found him Lizzy."

"As I am too, with Fitzwilliam, and Jane and Charles: yes, we three are so very fortunate. So, go on with your story, Kitty, for now I must know the rest of it!"

"Well he did of course recover, as you can see for yourself, but he was a changed man: he no longer lived merely for himself, he became most useful to his father, hence the trip to Antigua last year, and as quiet and steady, as you have found him. He is truly the better person for his near to death experience."

"Strangely, Kitty, I am thinking of how terrible it must have been for Sir Thomas and Lady Bartram, for as I understand it, Tom's illness occurred around the same time as the scandal involving their eldest daughter, Mrs. R, and the elopement of their other daughter, Julia, with Mr. Yates!"

"It was indeed a dreadful time for them Lizzy; of their four children, only Edmund seemed to have given them satisfaction, but apparently, even *he* was causing them concern, for he had been enamoured with the sister of Mr. C, everybody had thought it would be a match, but of course, after the discovery of her brother's part in the scandal of Mrs. R, that could no longer be the case. Edmund was heartbroken, not because of the then impossibility of the match, but by the subsequent attitude of Miss C, who was more concerned with the culprits being caught out, and how to patch it up, to make them presentable to society, rather than the actual sin of what they had done."

"Poor Edmund! I feel for him, but I cannot help being pleased that it turned out that way, for it means he was then free to find you, Kitty" replied Lizzy. "I know that sounds dreadful, but that is the way I think of it. The younger Thomas must have also suffered greatly, to be so near death, so young! Well, I shall observe him, even though I trust your judgement, but if he is not unworthy, I shall then certainly not stand in the way of any understanding that he may come to with Georgiana, but as you well know, Fitzwilliam will be more difficult to persuade of anybody's worthiness of his sister. We will let things take their own course."

Chapter 57

———•———

The day after the ball, the ladies at Darcy House were full of the previous evening's entertainment. Kitty had called by to visit her sisters, so it was a very loquacious foursome that discussed the evening's activities.

"You began the evening well, Georgiana," began Kitty, "I believe you enjoyed the dance with Thomas."

"He is a very personable young man, so much so that I did not hesitate to accept to dance with him again, and being quite handsome in his person, did not hurt his cause, Kitty" replied Georgiana with a smile.

"Yes, he is certainly a polite young man," added Mary, "for he talked to me of books that we have both read; I was surprised that he felt that he could talk of such subjects during a ball, for my mother has always told me that I should not talk of books with gentlemen, they might be intimidated … knowledge is something a lady should not display, apparently."

"That is praise indeed, Mary, coming from you" said Lizzy, "but you should feel free to discuss anything you wish; if the gentleman cannot accept that, he is not a true gentleman."

"I thought that he is just as a gentleman ought to be; able to converse on subjects that would interest a lady, without sounding condescending, I liked that about him," said Georgiana, "I shall not object to meeting with him again."

"I shall take that as an admission that you found him interesting enough to wish to further the acquaintance, my dear Georgiana, so I am sure you will not object to meeting him again during dinner, for I am also come to you with a request from Sir Thomas and Lady Bartram, for your presence for dinner in two days' time, all of you of course, before Edmund and I return to Kympton" announced Kitty.

"Are you to return so soon?" exclaimed Lizzy, "Forgive me Kitty, I forget myself, of course you must return; Edmund is not the sort of clergyman who would forget the duty of his presence for his parishioners. We are most fortunate to have him at Kympton"

"You are right, Lizzy, he does take his duties very seriously, but I would not have him any other way" replied Kitty.

Turning to Mary, Lizzy said "Mary, I know that you have been more than patient with our efforts to tempt you back into your studies, so perhaps you would enjoy a reprieve of our visits to museums, galleries, concerts etc., therefore you might like to go up to Kympton, with Kitty and Edmund. You would of course have full access to Pemberley, for books and practicing your music, should you feel shy of practicing in Kitty's home. I believe you have not yet seen Kympton, so it would be an opportunity for you to do so, should you wish to accept the opportunity, that is."

Mary was actually blushing as she replied, "Yes, Lizzy, I did realise your whole stratagem of getting me away from my little Jane, and I agreed to it, only because it was preferable to listening to my mother constantly telling me I would never find a husband by staying at home at Longbourn: it was beginning to be quite unbearable, so thank you for inviting me to town, but I do admit that it is not really what I enjoy, although I did truly like visiting the galleries and the concerts; it has inspired me to practice more and perhaps take singing lessons, should there be anyone near Kympton to instruct me, for I know that singing is *not* one of my better accomplishments."

"You are more than welcome, Mary, to stay with us" replied Kitty, "and I *do* in fact know of a singing tutor, a *very* good one: he was the choir master at York Minster for many years, before retiring to Kympton. He has very kindly undertaken to train our little choir at church, so I am sure that he would accept to help you, he is totally in admiration of my husband, and would do almost anything that he asked. You could not do better than to take instruction from him."

"I should think on it, Kitty, for I do not wish to be a burden on you, but I do believe I possibly *shall* accept your invitation." replied Mary, having somewhat recovered her colouring.

"Excellent Mary, I shall enjoy having your company, for we never did spend much time together at Longbourn: you were always studying and I, to my shame, was being silly and frivolous with Lydia."

Comfortably settled with refreshments and plenty of different subjects to talk about, the rest of the morning was spent in cosy conversation by the four sisters, discussing the ball, dinners, gowns, and Mary's singing lessons.

Chapter 58

Dressed in their finest evening gowns, the ladies from Darcy House were escorted from the carriage up the steps of a very fine-looking house; the London residence of the Bartram family, by a very proud Fitzwilliam Darcy. Vanity was not one of his failings, but he felt that sometimes he was approaching it, when accompanied by his beautiful wife and sister. Mary had turned into a surprisingly handsome woman too; amazing what a difference a well-cut gown and well-dressed hair could do, and he felt that it was in great part due to himself, or rather his very comfortable income, that she had thus blossomed. Yes, it was definitely a vanity problem, but he would deal with it later, he was enjoying the feeling much too much to keep it in check just now.

They were welcomed very warmly by Kitty and her husband, when compared to the natural gravity of deportment which marked Sir Thomas' welcome, and the equally natural languor of his lady wife's greeting. Tom was in the drawing room, speaking with his friend and brother, Mr. Yates, but interrupted the conversation when he saw the Darcys enter, to allegedly go over and greet them, as guests to his father's house, but more to ensure to himself the attention of Miss Darcy, whom he thought was the handsomest woman he had ever had the happiness of knowing. He had thought of little else since the ball, so he wanted to take every opportunity of getting know her better. He had even been to the dining room, to change the seating arrangements so that he could sit by her during dinner. Fortunately, his mother would not notice, and if she did, quite probably would care even less, and he was sure that Catherine would not object, in fact he thought that she was secretly promoting his case; an excellent sister-in-law indeed, Edmund was a most fortunate man to have found such a wife.

Georgiana looked like the most beautiful heroine in any novel he had ever read: her dark hair skilfully dressed, showing off her gracious neck and perfectly symmetrical features, he could not perceive an angel looking more beautiful. Perhaps it was her creamy white gown that brought the angelic look to the fore, but Tom could not take his eyes off her, to the point of ignoring the conversations of others, so intent was he to hear her voice, her opinion, her thoughts on anything and everything. This of course did not escape her brother's attention, and he was starting to look thunderously at Tom, until his wife, Mrs. Darcy, smiled at him and diverted her husband's attention away to other guests. Tom immediately liked Mrs. Darcy even more than he had before, but he also realised that he would have to tread very carefully if he was to make any good impression on Miss Darcy, because he would also have to impress her brother, the formidable Mr. Darcy.

The call came for dinner, and Tom had made sure that he was in the vicinity of Miss Darcy, to escort her in, and fortunately, etiquette was on his side, for he, as the eldest and single son of the hosts, must escort the highest ranking single lady, which just happened to be Miss Darcy, in to dinner. Tom was going to spend every opportunity to get to know Miss Darcy better, and sitting beside her at dinner was the best possible situation in which to do so.

Neither Tom nor Georgiana could remember what they had eaten or spoken about, all that they *did* recall was that the conversation had been scintillating; Mr. Bartram had been so very attentive and Miss Darcy was not only beautiful, she was also very knowledgeable on many subjects, and they both desired to know more of each other.

After dinner, the young ladies were called upon to provide music, Miss Bennet preferring to play on the magnificent pianoforte, whilst Miss Darcy sang. Lizzy and Kitty were silently grateful that Mary had had lessons since they had come to Town, from the piano teacher who had done such an excellent job with Georgiana, and within a few surprisingly short weeks, Mary's playing had vastly improved. She had had the knowledge, the technique, and the skills, but somehow had missed *something*, nobody knew what, which had given her playing a somewhat pedantic air, and although playing so much better than Lizzy, she was not listened to with as much pleasure. Now, her playing was as good as Georgiana's and vastly superior to Lizzy's, who still would not practice as often as she ought, if she seriously wished to improve her skills.

Mr. Bartram took it upon himself to turn the pages for Miss Bennet, which also gave him the occasion to be near Miss Darcy, gaze upon her person and listen to her beautiful voice without having to attend to the social niceties of conversation with the other guests. Once other guests offered to raise their voices in song, Tom decided that Miss Bennet was quite capable of turning the pages herself, and went to sit near Georgiana, who had gone to sit next to her friend Catherine, or Kitty, as she seemed to be called by family and close friends.

None of his behaviour had escaped Mr. Darcy or Sir Thomas. Mr. Darcy had Mrs. Darcy to keep him in check, and Sir Thomas had his own natural character to withhold any remarks he might have thought of making on his son's apparent neglect of the other guests.

"Fitzwilliam," began Lizzy, having taken him into the seclusion of a small conservatory, "you *must* let Georgiana get acquainted with gentlemen, without putting on your thunder-face: you will scare off anyone who tries to get to know her!"

"She is my sister, so I must look after her Elizabeth, you know that! There are so many scoundrels out there, and I do not wish for her to be hurt."

"I know that, my love, but she is now one and twenty years of age, many young women are married by then, as I was, so you must learn to trust her more. She is older and wiser, she has survived three Seasons in Town, without coming to grief, she has not given you any cause for concern since the unfortunate incident with Wickham, of which she herself informed you, before it actually took place."

"Do not remind me! I still have not forgiven myself for being so deceived by that woman, through my own carelessness!"

"It was six years ago, Fitzwilliam; have *you* not grown wiser since then? Of course you have, and so has Georgiana. If it sets your mind at ease, I have been making enquiries as to his character, and although he *was* a wild young man in his early years, he has totally and genuinely changed, since a dangerous illness that almost cost him his life, brought on by his own selfish and wild habits, woke him up to, or scared him enough to realise the error of his ways, and he has been a model son and brother ever since then, and if Edmund can vouch for him, as he does, then I think he can be trusted to tempt his luck with Georgiana. Come my dear, put that frown away and let us re-join the Bartrams, for they will start to wonder where we are"

Chapter 59

The following morning, Kitty and Edmund came to collect Mary and her trunk, to head back to Kympton. This just left the Darcys in town, but with their many engagements, with their large acquaintance, they did not feel the loss too keenly.

The journey back to Kympton was uneventful, but with three days of travelling, the three young people could not help but get better acquainted. Edmund did not really know Mary, for she had always been rather quiet, but it was one of his qualities that he could draw shy people out, and that is what he did with Mary. She was positively loquacious by the time they arrived at Kympton, which made even Kitty remark on it.

"Mary, I am astonished to admit that for the past hour, I have hardly been able to get a word into the conversation! I did not know that you were interested in astronomy or star gazing, for you never mentioned it at Longbourn."

"That is because my mother said that it was unladylike, Kitty, and I did not like to disturb my father, therefore I have had to learn from books. I recall seeing some very interesting books on the subject in the Pemberley library, and even a telescope, so with Edmund's offered assistance, I am certain to learn so much more. I am so very glad I decided to come to Kympton with you!"

"As are we, Mary" replied Edmund, "Kitty can get a little lonely at times, so your company is certainly most welcome, and here we are at last. Let me help you out Kitty, there, now you Mary"

They were in front of a very generously sized stone building; everything pronounced it to be a gentleman's residence. A portico, supported by stone pillars, in the centre of the front of the building added shelter to the front entrance, and there were three windows to each side of the door. The building was two stories high, topped by attic rooms in the Dutch-gabled roof. The front garden was formal, with clipped low hedges around a circular lawn containing a central bed of magnificent roses that were contained by a border of lavender, around which carriages could drive to the entrance. There was a row of well-established elms between the garden and the road, sheltering it from prying eyes, without the solidity of a garden wall, but still with a picket fence. The entrance itself was wide, with two broad stone steps up, with quite large yews in pots, clipped into a conical shape. Mary could see her sister's stamp on the arrangements.

Once shown to her apartments, Mary was preparing to unpack her trunk when someone knocked at her door. Calling for the person to enter, Mary was surprised to see a maid, who introduced herself as Abigail, saying that Mrs. Bartram had told her that she was to be Miss Bennet's maid for the duration of her stay.

"Thank you, Abigail, I was about to unpack my things, but since you are here, let me at least help you, for I wish to select my gown for dinner"

"As you wish ma'am, and I am also to help you dress and attend to your hair, for I am hoping to become a lady's maid and it will help me, to assist you in whatever manner I can" replied the maid.

Smiling, Mary replied, "Well consider yourself my lady's maid for my stay, Abigail, for I have never had one, I have always used my sisters', so it will be quite a novelty for me to have one of my own."

Having found the gown she wished to wear, Mary returned downstairs to join Kitty, who was going to show her around the house and gardens before dinner.

Having seen the spacious parlours and dining room, the breakfast room and the bedrooms, Kitty pointing out the views to be seen from the French- windows, they proceeded to well laid out gardens, including a large, sheltered kitchen garden. They walked to the southern side of the house, where Mary was quite in awe of a small conservatory attached to the house, "A new addition," said Kitty, "a wedding gift from Sir Thomas and Lady Bartram, and quite my pride and joy; I can sow seeds, transplant seedlings, propagate plants, force spring bulbs in the middle of winter, it is absolutely wonderful!"

"How generous of them, Kitty! You have been very fortunate in your choice of husband, as have Jane and Elizabeth, I hope to be as fortunate one day" replied Mary, blushing for no apparent reason.

"Come, Mary, do not be shy with me, if you cannot confide in a sister, then in whom can you? I am convinced that you have someone in mind, and *that* someone would not be too far from here. I know that you have silently admired Mr. Edwards ever since he escorted you into dinner, that first year that we spent Christmas at Pemberley. Well, let me tell you that you are often on his mind too. Each time I have visited Pemberley, he always asks after Miss Bennet, how she does, etc."

"Does he really ask after me?" exclaimed Mary incredulously, "you never mentioned it before!"

"Yes, he does, and I never mentioned it because I was not sure how you felt and did not wish to embarrass you, and you know how my mother would have picked up on it and plagued you mercilessly. It was entirely for your own benefit that I did not mention it, but I certainly *wished* to talk to you about it."

"Does Mr. Edwards know anything of this? I would be so mortified if he knew that I admired him!"

"I do not believe he does, but we can start with a new beginning from henceforth; I shall invite him for dinner tomorrow, to give you time to compose yourself and adjust to the idea of regarding a young man as something more than a person to be tolerated during enforced social engagements!" laughed Kitty, "and I will also invite Mr. Hemmings, our former choir master at York Minster, I mentioned him to you before, and his wife; that should make six for dinner, cosy enough even for you Mary"

"Thank you, Kitty, for not teasing me on the subject, and for giving me such an opportunity to meet with Mr. Edwards, I mean, I do not even know his Christian name!"

"It is George, Mary, Mr. George Edwards, it sounds very noble, does it not?"

"Now you *are* teasing me, so I shall retire to dress for dinner, and thank you for lending me Abigail, by the bye" responded Mary, who still smiled at her sister.

"Yes, please forgive me Mary, I did not mean to, but sometimes the words just slip out of my mouth, so I am glad that I haven't offended you. I must be more careful, I should think before I speak; I really should take Jane as my example, as Lizzy tries to. Let us return to the house to dress, as you suggest" as she companionably took her sister's arm and walked back to the entrance of the house.

Chapter 60

Somewhat nervously, Mary entered the drawing room, dressed in her finest gown, a creation in pale jade green silk edged with narrow ivory coloured lace around a modest neckline and the edges of the sleeves, a necklace of pearls, the one she had received for Lizzy and Jane's weddings, adorned her neck, her hair dressed to the best of hers and Abigail's abilities; Mary making suggestions to the maid, from what she had herself learned from Madeleine. She wanted to look her best, but felt that she could have looked better: if she only had the handsomeness of her sisters ... not realising how much like her sister Elizabeth she resembled, when well-dressed and smiling. Jane and Kitty kept telling her so, suggesting that it was not vanity to look at oneself in a mirror, when dressing, it was indeed a duty, to appear well-groomed. Perhaps she should start to use the very pretty mirror that she received that first Christmas at Pemberley, it was part of a set, with a hairbrush and comb, silver, with her initials. Yes, she recalled, Jane and Charles had given the set to her, whereas Lizzy and Fitzwilliam had given her a set of books that she had longed to read, and at the time, she was more impressed with those, rather than such frivolous things as a mirror and hairbrush. How things had changed since *that* Christmas.

Only Edmund was present, Kitty was still at her toilette, and in her fear of being late, Mary was in fact quite early. This was fortunate, for it gave her time to compose herself; for some incomprehensible reason, her heart was fluttering and seemed to be in her throat, her stomach seemed to be in knots, could this be what her mother meant when she referred to her palpitations and nerves? Somehow understanding her situation, Edmund kindly spoke to her of sundry things, anything to take her mind off the fact that she was about to meet Mr. Edwards again. A small glass of madeira helped as well, and she was quite composed when Kitty joined them.

"You look lovely Mary, that dress looks splendid on you, and your hair! Did Abigail do that? She is more clever than I had first thought!" exclaimed Kitty, just as the butler, Mr. Thorburn, introduced Mr. and Mrs. Hemmings to the room, effectively preventing Mary from making any response or apology.

Kitty stepped forward to make the introductions, "Mr. Hemmings, Mrs. Hemmings, we are so pleased you were able to come! May I have the pleasure of introducing my sister, Miss Bennet to you? Mary, this is Mr. Hemmings and his wife Mrs. Hemmings, formerly of York, and happily for us, now of Kympton."

The two ladies curtsied and the gentleman bowed and then hands were shook as all three of them spontaneously spoke of having heard so much of each other beforehand, immediately followed by simultaneous apologies for not letting the other speak first, and then laughter, as Mr. Edwards walked into the room, seeing four people charmingly grouped, which included Miss Bennet, laughing in an unaffected manner, and she had never looked so less self-conscious as she did at that moment; she was truly beautiful!

As no introductions were required, since everybody knew him, Mr. Edwards joined the merry group, delighted with the opportunity of standing next to Miss Bennet. Mary was not quite sure whether she was highly delighted or highly embarrassed, but since nobody seemed to be making any untoward observations or looking at *her* in particular, she recovered enough after several minutes, to re-join the conversation, which Kitty had kindly led onto mundane subjects as the weather and the progress of the choir.

"Mr. Hemmings," started Kitty, "my sister has expressed a wish of taking lessons in singing, and I was bold enough to suggest to her that you would be an ideal tutor for her. She is very knowledgeable in music, but has never had the opportunity to train her voice, and she feels that she would benefit from instruction. Would you be considerate enough to take on the role as her singing master? You would of course be remunerated accordingly, but it is a pleasure that I long to be able to give to my dear sister, should you be so accommodating as to oblige my whim."

"Mrs. Bartram, I will be very happy to oblige you in your request, but please, let us not talk of remuneration, it would be my pleasure to assist Miss Bennet." Mary did not know where or how to look as her more outspoken sister made the request, but when Mr. Hemmings so kindly and cordially accepted the task, her face broke into a smile of delight.

"Oh Mr. Hemmings, you do not know how much I appreciate your generosity," she said, "for it has been a standing joke in my family for many years, that I cannot sing, although I have tried, but I simply do not seem to have a natural ability to be listened to with as much pleasure as my sisters, I lack a natural modulation to my voice, so anything you can teach me would be most welcome, dear sir, not only for myself, but for the benefit of my audience even more!"

"Miss Bennet, your honesty in what you consider to be a failing is most disarming!" exclaimed Mr. Edwards, who could hardly believe that the lady he so admired, who was so talented in so many accomplishments, could so naturally and without false modesty, admit to failings in anything. She rose even more in his esteem, without even realising that she had done so.

"Yes, Miss Bennet," replied Mrs. Hemmings, "it does indeed take a fine mind and a natural modesty to accept, and understand one's weaker qualities, and an even finer mind to wish to do something about it. Many ladies would never admit to being less talented than hearsay would have them be."

Mary blushed at such praise, bringing colour to her cheeks. "I feel it my duty to deal with my shortcomings, Mrs. Hemmings; it has little to do with having a fine mind, though I do *try* to improve my mind with extensive reading, but alas, reading has not improved my vocal skills, so I will truly appreciate anything Mr. Hemmings can teach me!"

The conversation was then interrupted by Mr. Thorburn, calling them all in to dinner. The Bartrams escorted Mr. and Mrs. Hemmings into the dining room, followed by Mr. Edwards leading Mary, who both secretly blessed such social protocols.

Dinner was a very congenial affair; everybody well suited to each other and many topics were covered. Mary felt elated in being listened to with as much apparent interest as she was, on subjects Mrs. Bennet had strictly told her *not* to speak of in the presence of gentlemen, for fear of appearing too well-read. She was also thankful that Lizzy and Darcy had taken her to see the major museums and art exhibitions when she was in town, for she could now speak of them with some creditable degree of knowledge, and even voice her own opinion on the work of the different artists.

Chapter 61

———•———

Lizzy was at breakfast at Darcy House when the letters were brought in, several were for herself, including two from her sisters in Kympton. Mary wrote very seldomly, so her curiosity was aroused in receiving one from her *and* Kitty at the same time. She decided to read Mary's first:

"My dear Lizzy,

What an excellent idea of yours, to send me to stay with Kitty here in Kympton. Did you know that the choir master was previously the choir master for York Minster? Of course you did! how silly of me, you were present when Kitty mentioned it in town, and it being part of the Pemberley estate, you obviously would have been aware of Mr. Hemmings' antecedents.

Mr. Hemmings has very kindly accepted to help me with my singing, which we all have known for quite a long while, is not my finest accomplishment. Would you believe that I had been breathing the wrong way all these years? Mr. Hemmings started by first teaching me to breath properly, then to sing the notes using the different breathing techniques he has taught me. The difference is astounding Lizzy! I no longer sound like a weak-chested hen, squawking to be heard! I do not claim to have _vastly_ improved, but Kitty no longer visibly cringes when I raise my voice in song, and Mr. Hemmings seems pleased with my progress. He is a very kind and patient tutor to me.

Kitty is well, she is very happily settled here with Edmund, the picture of marital bliss, just as with yourself and Fitzwilliam, and Jane and Charles. I used to have a very sad opinion of marriage in general, seeing how my father and mother behave, and my aunt and uncle Phillips are not much better. I knew my aunt and uncle Gardiner had a better relationship, but to be honest, I did not know them very well, always escaping to my studies when they visited Longbourn and until you married and we came to town more often, I never really saw them enough to remark how happily matched they are. I have never heard my uncle Gardiner speak to my aunt in the disparaging way my father speaks to, and of, my mother, or my uncle Phillips to my aunt Phillips either, for that matter.

The summer weather is delightful, Kitty has been walking with me, showing me the many paths and views in this beautiful part of the country. No Lizzy, I did not suddenly decide to take more exercise, it was Mr. Hemmings who suggested that perhaps walking would improve my lungs and therefore my singing. I am so determined to improve my voice, for my own satisfaction, but also for those of you who have had to listen my caterwauling for so long. Yes, Lizzy, I have finally learned the difference between singing and squawking and I am _so_ relieved that I have been taught how to modulate my voice!

The current fine weather here in the north has also been very beneficial to Kitty's gardens. Who would have thought that she would be so talented with all things growing in the earth?

Her greenhouse provides her with ferns and flowers of the more exotic variety, whilst her garden beds are a delight to see. If she had been a boy, she would have been a very worthy heir to my father's estate. I cannot imagine, however hard I try, seeing Mr. Collins managing even half as well as my father. Fortunately, for him at least, he has Charlotte as his helpmeet.

I know not what else to tell you my dear sister, so I will bid you adieu until next time.

Your ever-loving sister Mary"

Lizzy smiled as she folded Mary's letter and proceeded to open Kitty's:

My dearest Lizzy,

All is well here in Kympton and Mary seems quite happy to be here. It has something to do with her lessons with Mr. Hemmings, I believe, but I suspect that the frequent meetings with Mr. Edwards has a little to do with matters too.

Lizzy, you will not believe how much better Mary sings now! It is now quite delightful to listen to her and we have had several evenings being entertained by her playing and singing. All these years we cringed when she took to the piano and sang; now we ask her, indeed, beg her to do so, for she is vastly improved, so much so that I believe she plays and sings better than you do!"

Lizzy inwardly blushed at this remark, for she knew that it was her own lack of practice that made it so.

"Mr. Edwards is a frequent visitor, either for dinner or tea, or to consult Edmund on some clerical matter, or just 'passing

by' as he says. He seems to much admire Mary, and I think she reciprocates the feelings, but there has been no declaration as yet. I have not mentioned anything to my mother, for you know how she would insist on meddling, in order to hurry things up. You would think that she would not be in such a hurry to get Mary married, for she is the only daughter left at home, well, except when her sisters make her leave Longbourn that is, and we know my mother cannot sit alone for long. Do not mention this to <u>anybody,</u> but I truly believe that Mr. Edwards is only waiting for an opportunity to declare himself. I think Mary would be very happy with him, for he is a bit of a scholar, which would suit her, and with his gentle character and hers, I believe that they could be as happy as you and I and Jane in the marital state., but as I said, do not say anything to anyone until we know from Mary herself, and then it would be her news to share as she chooses.

Thank you so much Lizzy, for the beautiful baby clothes you sent me. My baby will be the most beloved child and the most handsomely dressed in Kympton! Did you really knit that beautiful shawl yourself? It is magnificent; I shall use it for the child's baptism. Speaking of which, Lizzy, would you consider being the child's godmother? Edmund and I are hoping to have you as the godmother and his brother Thomas as the godfather. Please let me know whether you wish for the charge and responsibility. If you prefer to decline, I shall ask Mary, for I truly believe that she will be in the neighbourhood in the not too distant future. Or does that make me sound too much like my mother? Do not take me wrong Lizzy, for I love Mama very much, and know that she loves us too, so then is it so wrong for her to wish for the very best for her children, as do you and I? I am beginning to understand her better, now that my own child is soon to be with us. He or she is very active, kicking most robustly, but you would know how that feels.

I have recently received another letter from Lydia, she seems happy but she did ask if I could send her some monies, for she thinks that they do not have quite enough to get by. Edmond said that I could send her five guineas, but no more, explaining that you, Jane and my father also send her money, so she should be able to manage on Wickhams income with what you are all helping her with. She did not even ask how little Jane was doing, but perhaps she may enquire of my mother for more pertinent news, since none of us are at Longbourn."

The rest of Kitty's letter spoke of local events and persons, which were not of any interest to anybody else except Lizzy, who as the wife of Mr. Darcy, the major landowner of the area, would expect to be kept informed of them.

Lizzy felt very content as she folded up Kitty's letter. She of course was going to speak to Fitzwilliam about the possibility of Mr. Edwards asking for Mary's hand, for he, as his patron, would be morally obliged to assist him in his career. Kympton, the best living in his gift, having been given to Kitty's husband, consultation would be required; perhaps he could speak to Sir Thomas, for he had held Mansfield for Edmund, the best living in *his* gift, but Edmund had declined it when it finally became available, so it had gone to some young person, to hold until the right person came to Sir Thomas's attention: yes, that was definitely a possibility, for she felt that Mr. Edwards was just the man for the living. Sir Thomas and Lady Bartram being quiet, withdrawn persons themselves, and Mr. Edwards and Mary being equally calm and quiet, they might do very well together in the same parish.

The third letter Lizzy read was in a hand that she recognized from several years ago, that of her cousin, Mr. Collins: it was announcing that his dear wife, Charlotte had finally given him the long-awaited son, heir to the estate that he himself was privileged to be heir to; Longbourn. Lewis Henry, in honour of the late Sir Lewis of Rosings, and of his own dear father. All Lizzy could think of was that perhaps *now* her very dear friend would *not* be obliged to provide him with a child *every* year. She did sincerely hope so, for Charlotte had seemed very tired, the last time they had met.

Chapter 62

The Darcy's returned to Pemberley for the summer, relieved to leave the hustle and bustle of London behind, for the calmness, coolness and verdure of Pemberley. They had passed through Longbourn and Gaddesley on their way, catching up on all the news and the various children's progress.

"I never tire of the drive up to Pemberley, my love, it is just so beautiful" remarked Lizzy to her husband, squeezing his arm tenderly.

"I am glad you feel so, dearest, for since you have been mistress of Pemberley, I feel the same elation as you when we approach our home" replied Darcy, "it never felt quite so welcoming before you graced me with your hand and then blessed me with our children."

"I agree," said Georgiana, who had accompanied them north, "I have always loved the place, but before you came, Lizzy, it echoed; it was too large for just two of us, each occupied with our duties or occupations in separate parts of the house or grounds, only really meeting for meals. Since your arrival, Pemberley is so much more alive!"

"Then why are you in such a hurry to leave it then?" asked Fitzwilliam, who was referring to her growing attachment to Tom Bartram, with whom he had nothing to really reproach, apart from trying to gain his sister's heart and thus tempt her away to a new home.

"Fitzwilliam! You know that is utter nonsense! Georgiana has been remarkably cautious in bestowing her consideration on people in general, and even more so with her affections. Thomas Bartram is a very personable young man, who has clearly gotten over the foolishness of his youth and is now a very steady and sensible young gentleman, with the advantage of being related to the family, and being heir to a baronetcy certainly does not *lessen* his qualities to being considered as a very suitable candidate for her affections" exclaimed Lizzy, with a smile in her eyes, for she knew that Darcy was slowly resigning himself to the idea of such a match, but his long habit of being very protective of his sister had come rushing to the fore with his remark.

"Yes, my dear Elizabeth, I realise and concur with all of what you say, but you cannot bear me ill-will for being so concerned for her future happiness" was his reply.

"Really Fitzwilliam!" Georgiana burst out with a laugh, "you can be so ridiculous; you talk of me as though I was one of the children, to be cosseted, seen and admired, and possibly, the poor darlings, never allowed to grow up. Well, 't is too late, my dear brother, I grew up whilst you and your 'dear Elizabeth' were blissfully happy in each other's company, and there is nothing you can do about it, and besides, perhaps nothing will come of it, for although Thomas *says* and *shows* that he admires me greatly, nothing has been declared, though I suspect, *Mr. Darcy*, your haughty frown, whenever I was in his company, might have something to do with it!"

"I am truly trying to let you be a grown up young lady, Georgiana" he replied "I did not flinch, well not *much*, when you asked me if I would object to you corresponding with him whilst you are at Pemberley; you cannot imagine how difficult that was for me!" he finished with a wry chuckle.

Changing the subject, for she considered it had gone far enough for the comfort of both her husband and sister, Lizzy wondered aloud how the children had travelled, for they had left Gaddesley the day before, whilst she, Darcy, and Georgiana had stayed on an extra day for a dinner that Jane was giving for some of the more important of her neighbours. The Darcys being known to be related to them *and* present at the dinner gave the occasion the cachet of the social "place to be seen" to any aspiring families, and great satisfaction to those who felt quite satisfied and content with their own position in the neighbourhood. The Darcy ladies, dressed in the latest fashions from Town, inspired many a lady present with ideas to update their own wardrobes, whilst Mr. Darcy had been very congenial to all: nothing like the haughty gentleman, above being pleased, that rumour had somehow made him out to be, for many years.

"I am sure that they are well, Lizzy, you know how well Gwen looks after them and ensures that their nurses behave properly" said Georgiana.

"I know that, but you know how James can feel ill in the carriage, and Anne was a little sniffly when they left yesterday, but as you say, Gwen will manage everything perfectly, she is a gem" Lizzy replied, who wasn't really worried about the children, but was happy to have introduced a new subject of conversation, for the Bingley children followed in the discussion, as well as little Jane, who was an extremely pretty child, the delight of her grandparents and Aunt Mary.

This in turn brought inquiries as to how the Wickhams fared, which Darcy could answer, for he had his agents in the north keeping an eye on them.

"They do as well as can be expected, still spending above their means and living together in perfect indifference to each other. They have just moved to other quarters, Elizabeth, so I suspect you may receive another request for assistance."

Chapter 63

The rest of the summer passed pleasantly, with frequent visits to or from Kympton to see Kitty, for Mary came to Pemberley to stay, to peruse through the library and to practice her playing and singing in the music room, when it was not being used by Georgiana.

As Kitty had said in her correspondence, Mary's singing had vastly improved, and continued to do so under Mr. Hemmings weekly instruction, and with Georgiana she learned some finer points of how ladies should sing in company: not too loud, not too soft, with a natural air, not trying to show off against other young ladies etc., all of which had been detrimental to her efforts in the past. Mary was delighted with her progress, as were her sisters, for they knew how much she had always striven to do her best with all of her learning and accomplishments, and were pleased to have had the opportunity to help her achieve her aims, quite apart from the fact that she could now be listened to without fervently wishing to be elsewhere.

Mr. Edwards was now a frequent visitor to Pemberley, allegedly to consult Darcy on some parish matter or other, so Lizzy took to inviting him for tea or dinner on a more regular basis. She was hoping to draw him out a little more, and to give him and Mary more opportunity to decide on how they wished their acquaintance to progress.

One particularly fine day brought Lizzy and Mary walking in the vicinity of the Pemberley parsonage, and they found Mr. Edwards working in his garden, tending to some very fine strawberry plants. He looked up as the ladies approached, scrambling to his feet and apologizing profusely for his dishevelled appearance, for he had removed his jacket and had rolled up his shirt sleeves.

"No, Mr. Edwards, please do not apologise, for we came to you without warning and no-one can expect you to work in your jacket in this fine weather" said Lizzy, "and you do not need to stop your labours on our behalf, for I know that your garden produces better strawberries than the gardens at Pemberley."

But he still stopped, wiping his hands, picking up his jacket and inviting the ladies into the house for some refreshment, "For I was about to stop for some myself" as he called to his housekeeper to request that tea be made and brought into the parlour, or out to the table and chairs that were set up under the shade of an old oak tree, if the ladies preferred.

Thinking that Mary would like to see the inside of the parsonage, Lizzy said that the parlour would be preferable and they proceeded into the house.

The parsonage was not as large as Kympton, it was in fact quite small, but well set up, with furniture that was well cared for, rugs on the floor and had a general air of tranquillity, more like the Collins's home at Hunsford, under Charlotte's care. Whilst waiting for the tea, Mr. Edwards asked if they would like to see the rest of the house. This was very agreeable to them and he proceeded to show them the kitchen and pantry, a small entrance at the front of the house, prolonged by a corridor that divided the house effectively in two. Opposite the parlour, which was at the front of the house, was a room that he had set up as a study, the walls lined with book shelves and a large desk with a comfortable old chair. Mary said nothing but her eyes lit up.

"Mr. Edwards," started Mary, "Would you mind if I just look at your books? I see that we have similar tastes."

285

"Most certainly I do not mind, Miss Bennet, I am more than happy to let you peruse anything in my paltry collection, I am only sorry it is not more extensive" he replied, as Lizzy continued to another room, obliging him to leave Mary alone and follow his patroness.

"Exceedingly well set up, Mr. Edwards," said Lizzy, "and having the dining room and breakfast room at the back, near the kitchen, is very sensible; it means that your dinner will still be hot when it gets to the table! My dear friend, Mrs. Collins, could not have set it up better."

"Thank you for your approval Mrs. Darcy, my housekeeper has done her best to make it a home for me, bless her, but I will be happier when it receives a lady's touch" which remark would have thrown Mary into paroxysms of embarrassment had she been within hearing.

"I am sure you would be Mr. Edwards, but it seems that you are in no hurry to find such a person"

"I would not say so, begging your pardon, Mrs. Darcy, but I am afraid I have so little to offer to a lady; this is a small parsonage and perhaps a lady would understandably expect something better, having been used to a finer life with her own family."

Understanding his dilemma, Lizzy tried tactfully to suggest that happiness in the marital state did not always depend on a gentleman's income, but more in the compatibility of character. She also mentioned that should he feel he had possibly found the right lady, he should speak to Mr. Darcy, who would contrive to make his situation more suitable for a married clergyman of his excellent capabilities. More, she felt, would be tactless, so she left the conversation at that point, to admire a particularly fine piece of china; a soup tureen serving as a centre-piece on the dining table, whilst wondering to herself whether she was not stooping to use such manipulative tactics that her mother would consider as quite justifiable in the acquisition of a husband for Mary. The housekeeper saved her from further reflection by announcing that tea and refreshments were now ready in the parlour.

Chapter 64

September was magnificent, having lost the extreme heat of summer, with balmy days and rain at night. It also heralded the safe arrival of Edmund Thomas James Bartram, Kitty and Edmund's firstborn child. A healthy child and Kitty being safe, the whole of the family was thrilled. Mr. and Mrs. Bennet duly came up to Derbyshire, with little Jane, who had insisted that she most truly wanted to meet her new little cousin and to see her beloved Aunt Mary again; Mrs. Bennet could not refuse such a plea and Mr. Bennet did not see any importunity in the dear child's presence in such a family event.

All the visitors, including the Bingley's and their children, who had arrived first, stayed at Pemberley, so as not to crowd the new family group at Kympton, because Sir Thomas and Lady Bartram were staying there, to meet Edmund's son.

The only family members who were not present were the Wickhams, who, according to Lydia's letter of congratulations to Kitty, said that they could not afford the journey, her husband being in Bath for some reason, and herself being stuck up in Newcastle by herself.

Knowing that Kitty would be delighted to see her youngest sister again, Lizzy consulted with Fitzwilliam and it was decided to send the head footman up to escort Lydia down to Pemberley on the mail coach. Nothing was said to the rest of the family, because they could not be certain that she would accept the offer, so it was an immense surprise to the rest of the family when Lydia drove up to the house in the family coach, which had gone to meet her in Derby.

The reunion was exuberant, Lydia being Lydia, and Mrs. Bennet was beside herself with delight at having all her daughters around her; Kympton being close enough to count as being the same as being in Pemberley. Mr. Bennet was somewhat less joyful, being constantly reminded by his daughter's behaviour that she had not changed one whit, and had learned absolutely nothing from the past.

"My dearest Lydia," exclaimed her mother, "shall we not go up to see the children? You have not had the opportunity to meet most of them, for it is so long since you have been away!"

"If I must, mama, but I am not fit to be seen, my gown is at least two years old. I will try to acquire something more fashionable whilst I am down here, but you must lend me the money" which response sharply reminded Mrs. Bennet of the circumstances of the last time she had seen Lydia.

Once they had arrived at the nursery, accompanied by Jane, Mary, and Lizzy, Mrs. Bennet was totally absorbed in greeting all of her grandchildren. Jane and Lizzy were taken by their own children, who were delighted to so unexpectedly see their mothers, little Jane leaping into her Aunt Mary's arms, squealing with delight.

Lydia looked on, with a nonchalant air, looking thoroughly bored, waiting for all of the mater and child reunions to subside. She supposed that the child clinging to Mary was a niece who happened to favour Mary above her own mother, but who would possibly prefer Mary? A very boring person, who preferred books over bonnets.

"Lydia!" exclaimed Mrs. Bennet, "do you not wish to greet your own child? Jane, come here to grandmamma, see here who this is? This is your mamma" as she presented the child to Lydia.

Shrieking in fear and trying to escape her grandmother's hold, Jane would not have let Lydia come near her, had Lydia actually made any move towards her, but Lydia hadn't moved, just staring at the child with a repugnance that she could not hide.

"I thought she was in Longbourn! How could I guess that you would bring her with you? I had hoped never to see her again when you took her away, so why did you bring her here with you?" was her response to her mother's query.

Total silence followed. Mary took the child and hugged little Jane, consoling her as best she could, hoping that she did not truly understand what had just occurred, Aunt Jane standing up with a horrified look, Lizzy equally appalled, but it was Mrs. Bennet who responded.

"Lydia! How dare you! How dare you speak of your own child in such a way, and in her presence too? I consider you no longer as my daughter! Mary! Take Jane down to the kitchen to fetch biscuits and milk for herself and her cousins!"

As soon as the child had left the room with her beloved aunt, Mrs. Bennet seemed to explode with a fury that none of her daughters had ever suspected she was capable of. "Begone with you! Get out of my sight! Elizabeth! Order your coachman to take this unworthy creature away! I cannot bear to be in the same room, or even the same house as her! How could she be so cruel? She is no longer a child of mine! Oh! my poor heart! Such palpitations! I can barely draw breath! The pain is crippling! My poor nerves! I need to sit down!"

Seeing their mother's genuine distress, and fearing for her actual well-being, Jane and Lizzy ordered the nurses to take charge of the children whilst they carefully assisted Mrs. Bennet down the stairs to her bedroom. They were truly alarmed for her health and sent a servant to fetch Mr. Bennet, and to send someone for the physician, immediately.

With such a commotion, it was not surprising that the gentlemen were quickly made aware of the situation. Darcy had a quick word with Mr. Robson, to arrange the rapid removal of Mrs. Wickham and her trunks, Mrs. Reynolds was asked to attend to whatever her mistress required, and to keep him informed of the physician's arrival.

Mr. Bennet had immediately gone to Mrs. Bennet, sensing that this was not one of her usual attacks on her nerves, and that his presence would possibly assist his daughters to settle her until the doctor arrived. He was furious that Lydia had yet again ruined what was supposed to be a happy occasion for her mother, and silently washed his hands of her. He would of course respect the monetary settlement made for her at the time of her marriage, but as far as he was concerned, she would not receive one penny more from his household, and he would insist on Mrs. Bennet respecting his decision, but first he wanted to see his wife calmed and settled. He might have lost respect for her many years ago, but as his wife, she had a right to his care, and to her eternal credit, she had given him four daughters of whom he was very proud.

The physician came as quickly as he could, examined his patient, and then spoke to Mr. Bennet, saying that he had given her a draught to make her sleep, which in turn would help settle her heart, which had been beating at over double of what it should have, hence her palpitations. Her nerves had obviously had a rude shock, and she was to be treated with the utmost gentleness for the next few days. He had left instructions with Mrs. Darcy's housekeeper, to administer more draughts whenever Mrs. Bennet awoke, to make her sleep and let her own body heal itself with the induced rest. Mr. Bennet was made aware that his wife was in fact seriously unwell, and had been very near to having an access of heart flutters, which could have been fatal. He felt the irony of the situation, for she was always convinced that he would be the first to die, and had bemoaned the fact frequently, that she would be dependent on her daughters once the Collinses threw her out of Longbourn. Most definitely was Lydia going to be left to reap the fruits of her abominable behaviour.

Once their initial fears had subsided, the family agreed that Kitty should not be told of Lydia's arrival and rapid departure at all, simply that her mother had become unwell but was now recovering with rest. Georgiana would be told the whole truth when she came home, for she had spent the day with Kitty and the new baby.

Lizzy, Jane, and Mary would sit with their mother, and Mrs. Reynolds would do so when they went over to Kympton to visit Kitty. Sarah, little Jane's nurse, also offered to sit with her mistress, who had rescued herself and Jane from the evils of Newcastle, so she held Mrs. Bennet in great esteem. The offer was accepted, for Mrs. Bennet knew Sarah and was fond of her.

With such care and daily visits from the physician, Mrs. Bennet slowly recovered enough to be able to visit Kitty and her latest grandchild after a sennight, but she was definitely quieter and much more subdued than before, having been seriously frightened at her real mortality, as opposed to her imaginative frailness and weaknesses of the past.

Chapter 65

The incident, and its subsequent impact on Mrs. Bennet's health had a surprising consequence, with Mr. Edwards suddenly making an offer for Mary's hand. He had in fact feared that should Mrs. Bennet not recover, he would not be able to make an offer for her hand until after a substantial period of mourning, so now, whilst Mrs. Bennet was still of this world, was the only time he could declare himself.

Having spoken with Mary and received her shy acceptance of his offer, he then proceeded to her father, who also, to his surprise, agreed to his proposal, for he was convinced that the father of Mrs. Darcy would want a better fortuned man for his only remaining daughter. What Mr. Edwards did not realise was that Mr. Bennet only wanted Mary's happiness, and that personal fortune, although most useful, was just a secondary consideration in his eyes.

Two hurdles having been overcome with an ease he could hardly believe, he then went on to speak to Mr. Darcy, who as his patron, must be informed, and preferably agree to his choice, though surely, he could not object to such a woman as Miss Bennet.

The interview, which took place in the Pemberley library was a revelation to him, as to the regard in which Mr. Darcy held him. Not only did he agree to the marriage, he even spoke to him of what he planned to do for him, to advance him in his noble profession.

"When I offered Kympton to Mr. Bartram, Mr. Edwards" said Mr. Darcy, "Sir Thomas had not been able to offer his best living of Mansfield to his son, for it was still held by another. When the incumbent died, the living was offered to Edmund, as had always been planned, but he declined it, preferring to stay in Kympton. Sir Thomas and I had a discussion at the time, and because he was so grateful for what I had done for his son, he offered Mansfield to me to offer to whomsoever I thought worthy. We agreed to this and have the agreement in writing. Mansfield is currently being temporarily held by a young man, who will vacate it and move on to another parish once we have found the right person for Mansfield. What I propose, once I have spoken to Sir Thomas again, is that I will recommend *you* for Mansfield, and I will take the other young man for your position here in Pemberley, until he obtains a better preferment. Does this suit you Mr. Edwards?"

Mr. Edwards was struck dumb with this incredulous stroke of good fortune and amazed at the esteem in which Mr. Darcy apparently held him, for his shy nature had not allowed him to think he was so worthy of such a great man's regard. Mansfield! He had heard talk of it when it was being offered to Mr. Bartram, it was worth at least a twelve hundred a year!

"I will take your silence as a wish to discuss this with Miss Bennet, Mr. Edwards, so please do so at your leisure. I will in the meantime inform Sir Thomas of my choice. And welcome to the family, George" as Darcy shook his hand warmly, fully understanding that the look on Mr. Edwards face was more of shock, rather than a disinclination to accept the offer.

"I think a drink is called for, do you not? A brandy will be the best for you at the moment methinks" chuckled his patron, as Mr. Edwards accepted the glass offered.

"I am simply so surprised sir! I have been happy here in Pemberley, but I realised that my income would perhaps be too low for a lady to accept, but my Mary did so! And then her own father said that he was less interested in my income, than he was in my ability to make his daughter happy, and now you, sir, have just offered me a living with an income which is beyond anything that I had even dared hope for, so I was indeed somewhat speechless Mr. Darcy!"

"I understand, Mr. Edwards, indeed I truly do; I recall my own amazement when Mrs. Darcy finally accepted my proposal and then Mr. Bennet, who initially did not want to do so, I am certain, thinking me unworthy of his daughter, finally accepted too. It does tend to take your breath away and you cannot believe your own good luck!"

Afterwards, Mr. Edwards joined Mary and walked with her in the gardens for above an hour, discussing their plans and hopes for the future, before going back to the house, where Mary went up to her mother to announce the news. Nothing could have been better for Mrs. Bennet's health:

"Oh Mary! How delightful! Mansfield Park! Sir Thomas and Lady Bartram! Twelve hundred a year and maybe more! When is the wedding? I must dress and go to Kitty to tell her the good news! Lizzy! Jane! Have you heard the good news? Mary is to be married! To Mr. Edwards! They are to have the Mansfield living! Five daughters married! Oh! how Lady Lucas will be jealous! Order a carriage Lizzy! We must go to Kympton to tell Kitty the good news!"

Jane and Lizzy congratulated their sister and wished her well, knowing that the young couple were well suited, and each privately intending to do all they could to help them, but they would first have to let their mother absorb the information, and settle down to organise the wedding. It would, after all, be the last one for her to organise, but knowing Mary, her two elder sisters knew that their assistance would be required to curtail the excesses that Mrs. Bennet was sure to want, and that Mary would prefer, as they themselves had done, a quiet family affair.

Mr. Edwards was as a matter of course invited to as many dinners and suppers as he could attend, whilst the Bennets remained at Pemberley, whose stay had been prolonged due to Mrs. Bennet's ill-health. Mr. Bennet did not wish to travel until his wife was fully recovered, and he insisted on obtaining the physician's approval before even considering a return to Longbourn.

Mary had acquired a glow of contentment which made her appear quite beautiful when accompanied by her smile of happiness. Via her sister's connections, fortune, and genuine love for her sisters, both she and Kitty had found happiness, thanks to Lizzy having married Fitzwilliam Darcy, and from things she had heard, even Jane owed her happiness to Lizzy and Darcy, as did Lydia.

Chapter 66

———•———

October was not only the month of great joy for Mary; several days after the Bennets had returned to Longbourn, taking Mary with them, Georgiana took great pleasure in informing them by letter that she was to marry Thomas Bartram,

After having corresponded with Georgiana throughout the summer, with Mr. Darcy's approval of course, Mr. Bartram felt confident enough to think that Miss Darcy might reciprocate his feelings, enough hopefully, to accept an offer of marriage. His offer having been accepted by Georgiana, Mr. Bartram then wrote to her brother to ask for her hand; he did not wish to see Georgiana and then have her brother refuse his permission, it would have been too upsetting for her, and he wrote this in his letter to Mr. Darcy. It was this consideration for her feelings that had led Darcy to agree to the marriage, with a little more assistance from his dearest wife, who had been for the match from the start.

Here was a double joy, for it meant that Kitty and Georgiana were to be doubly sisters as well as friends, and of course there was the wedding to plan! This was to be Lizzy's responsibility, as the matriarch of the Darcy family. There was much to discuss, including the date of Mary's wedding, for they would not wish to have the ceremonies too close together, and of course the venues, from where were each to be married from? With so much to consider, there was only one thing to do: in spite of their habit of not going to town till the spring, they would go down now, to be closer to Longbourn to discuss the plans for Mary, and to pass by Mansfield to discuss the young couple's future, and to finalise the gift of the Mansfield living to Mr. Edwards.

The Darcy coach left Pemberley on a chilly morning towards the end of October, carrying Lizzy and Fitzwilliam, Georgiana, and Mr. Edwards, who was to travel with them to Mansfield for the signing of the papers with Sir Thomas. It had been decided to leave the children at home, where they were happy in their familiar surroundings and routines, for the trip to London would not allow their parents much time to spend with them, with so much to be organised for two weddings.

"Oh Fitzwilliam! I can hardly believe that I am to be married!" cried Georgiana, "and that I am to see Thomas in person again. It has been months since we have seen each other, but it is perhaps because of our correspondence through the summer that we got to know each other as well as we do! No interruptions by dinners and dances, just talking to each other through our letters."

"Unconventional my dear Georgiana, but in your case very successful," replied Darcy, "I shall certainly be recommending it when our daughter Anne is of an age, Lizzy, remember that all courtship is to be done by correspondence."

"Oh my dearest, please let Anne at least meet the gentleman first; it is easier to write to a person one has actually met and possibly danced with at an assembly or two" laughed Lizzy. "Georgie, you have set a difficult precedent for your poor niece!"

"I will be her advocate in her defence should her father insist on courting only through letters, Lizzy, for I had actually had the pleasure of meeting, dining and dancing with my dear Thomas, before the correspondence part" replied Georgiana with a broad smile.

"And what are your thoughts on the matter, Mr. Edwards?" enquired Darcy, "Would you not also wish to protect a daughter from the assiduous attentions of gentlemen whose respectability and intentions you are not entirely sure of?"

"Until I have a daughter of my own, whose happiness will be my very real concern, I cannot honestly say, but your question leads me to request your opinion, Sir, on a matter close to my heart. As you are all aware, Miss Bennet, Mary, is exceedingly fond of her niece, Jane, and it will be a sore parting for them both when we marry, so I was wondering, Mr. Darcy, about your thoughts on the possibility of Mr. and Mrs. Bennet allowing Jane to come to *us* to live, once we are settled in Mansfield. I will treat her as my own daughter, which is not at all difficult, since I have known her almost since her birth, and it would make Mary so happy."

"Why I think that is an excellent idea, Mr. Edwards, for as you say, Mary is very much attached to the child, and the child regards her as her mother. It may be difficult to get Mrs. Bennet to agree, but I am certain that Mr. Bennet would see the good sense in such an arrangement, so you will have my full support, so long as my wife agrees. What do you think, Elizabeth?"

"I agree with you, my dear; my parents are not getting younger, and as my niece grows older, they may not be able to attend to her as well as they would wish. They of course always will remain her beloved grandparents, but I too think that Jane would be happier with Mary. It is a generous gesture that you are making Mr. Edwards, I laud your benevolent spirit for considering it, for I know that Mary has been worrying about the separation."

With so much to discuss between the four of them, they arrived at Mansfield well before they had thought to be half so far. The reunion between Georgiana and Mr. Bartram was as warm and tender as a greeting in front of everyone would allow, but their smiles of joy left no-one in doubt of their mutual affection. Sir Thomas and Lady Bartram met the guests in the entrance hall and the pleasure in greeting each other as relations was genuine. Mr. Edwards was warmly welcomed by Sir Thomas, and as warmly as she was capable of by his lady.

"Mr. Edwards, I am pleased you were able to come down to Mansfield, to see your new living. We will visit the parsonage in the morning, and if there are any alterations you wish made, I shall ensure they are done before you come here to live once you are married. You marry in April, I believe? A month before the marriage of my son to Miss Darcy. I am truly delighted at having another two connections to the Darcy family."

"You are so generous Sir Thomas, I hardly know how to thank you for your preferment, for you hardly know me!"

"Nonsense young man, I know you very well indeed, from what my son Edmund has told me of you, and of course if Mr. Darcy can recommend you, then why should I doubt of your merit? I know that Mr. Darcy would not have spoken of you for the living of Mansfield if he felt you were not worthy of such an attention. It will be with great pleasure that I sign the papers with you after dinner" before leading his guests to a drawing room for refreshments whilst their respective servants saw to their trunks and unpacked what clothes and jewels were required for dinner and the following day.

Dinner was a happy affair, Georgiana and Thomas delighted to be together again, Darcy making an effort to get to know his future brother, and conceding to Lizzy that he was indeed the right man to marry his dear sister, but woe betide him if he ever made her unhappy! Lady Bartram was as quiet as ever, but her niece Susan, her companion, was much more talkative and had much to say about her delight at the thought of the wedding, and to enquire after her cousins Edmund and Catherine and their baby son, whom she had met when she accompanied the Bartrams north when they had come up after his birth. Susan had even more to say of her delight when Georgiana asked her if she would be her attendant for her wedding.

"Oh Miss Darcy! How very kind of you to ask me for such an honour! I will be truly delighted to assist you!"

"It is not so much a kindness, Miss Price, as a pleasure for me to ask my future husband's cousin to assist me on such an important day, for we are to become family. If it gives you pleasure also, then I assure you that I shall be doubly pleased."

Chapter 67

After breakfast the following morning, the ladies, excepting her ladyship, who was too fatigued to make the exertion, travelled the short distance from the main house to the parsonage in a phaeton, while the gentlemen chose to walk.

The house declared itself as the residence of a gentleman, a noble building with gabled attics and quite large rooms, almost as big as Kympton. Mr. Cresswell showed them around the house, the generously sized rooms; the dining table was quite large, being able to seat twelve people comfortably, the handsome and spacious front parlour facing south, contained a piano, and a smaller parlour facing west. There were several bedrooms and the attics had rooms for several servants. There was also a small library, which would please Mary immensely.

Deciding to make inquiries on her sister Mary's behalf, Lizzy addressed the current occupant, "Mr. Cresswell, I am curious as to whether or not your housekeeper will be accompanying you to Derbyshire, or would she prefer to remain at Mansfield? I know it might seem impertinent of me to ask, but my sister is not here to ask for herself," she smiled, "and these things must be thought of at some point. I know that Mr. Edward's housekeeper would prefer to stay where she is, as she knows the house and the neighbourhood, so she would be able to see to your comfort in Pemberley, should your own housekeeper prefer to remain on here."

"Why, Mrs. Darcy, ma'am, that would be a splendid solution, for I have to admit that Mrs. Scanlon is not looking forward to moving up north, she seems to think they are all heathens, begging your pardon ma'am, and has in her own way made it very clear that she would accompany me under sufferance, only to ensure that I was adequately taken care of! She is my old nurse's sister and seems to believe I am still eight years old, and need to be looked after and fed on a regular basis, so it would be ideal if both housekeepers can stay where they are. In fact, most of the servants could stay, if that meets with Mrs. Edwards approval, as well as your own, of course, Mrs. Darcy!"

"A very practical idea indeed, Mr. Cresswell," replied Lizzy, "though of course my sister *may* wish to choose other servants, but knowing her; if the household is running smoothly, then she would feel no reason to change things at all."

Mary would feel quite at home here, thought Lizzy, as they walked around the house. In spite of Sir Thomas' earnest enquiries as to any changes needed or wanted, Mr. Edwards would not presume to make any suggestions, and Lizzy simply said that perhaps once she was living there, her sister might like to change some curtains or wall colours, but the house was perfectly well set up as it was. The current occupant, Mr. Cresswell, was to move to the parsonage in Pemberley when the Edwards' were to move to Mansfield, so he would not suffer any disruption by painters or carpenters for the rest of his stay. Darcy spent quite some time talking to the gentleman himself, offering the same to him, as Sir Thomas had offered Mr. Edwards; any changes required etc. to which Mr. Cresswell responded the same as Mr. Edwards had done, preferring to wait until he was settled in his new abode before making any changes.

The grounds were well set up to cover the family's needs for the kitchen, with a substantial brick wall surrounding that area, for nothing was worse than suffering the sight of a rotting vegetable garden during the winter, and other areas around the house were set up for a lady to walk around pleasant hedged gardens, providing shelter from the wind, rose arches, and here and there were pretty cast iron benches to rest on, with thatched structures over some of them, to protect one from the harshness of the sun or from any sudden rain showers. The gardens still had chrysanthemums in bloom, asters, the last of the roses, and some very determined summer annuals. The trees were ablaze with the colours of their autumn leaves, which were only just starting to fall as a carpet on the paths and lawns below. A very pretty setup for a gentleman's residence, the previous occupants had obviously very good taste, relations of the Crawfords she believed, for Sir Thomas had informed them that much of the garden improvements had been done by the previous lady of the house, Mrs. Grant.

Sir Thomas was just mentioning to the other gentlemen that the family would also be able to use the park grounds for their exercise, and should the future Mrs. Edwards feel inclined, she would be a most welcome visitor to the ladies of the house, for Lady Bartram did not go out very much, so Susan would love to receive the occasional visit from their nearest neighbours at the parsonage. There was a sheltered path between the two houses, making walking quite pleasant in the warmer months and still practicable in all but the worst of the winter months.

Lizzy felt that Mary would be very happy here, and felt proud of her husband's involvement in the whole situation, for if he had not offered Kympton to Edmund, and Edmund having to preferred to stay there, Mansfield would not have been available for Mary's husband, and Sir Thomas and Lady Bartram were very quiet, unobtrusive people, just the sort that Mary would feel comfortable with, it had all turned out very well indeed!

Chapter 68

Everything having been settled and signed by Sir Thomas and Mr. Edwards, the family left Mansfield the following day for Hertfordshire with very satisfied feelings: Lizzy and Georgiana would be able to describe the house to Mary and Mrs. Bennet, and Mr. Edwards would of course be talking to her of their future together there. The only slight issue would be convincing Mrs. Bennet that her grand-daughter would be best off being raised by Mary and her husband in Mansfield. Lizzy would try to address her mother's sense of vanity, to convince her that she would be able to boast of Jane being raised, almost, if vicinity had any influence, by a baronet's family, and should Georgiana have children, they would be Jane's cousins and brought up, to a degree, together, without Jane being a regarded as a subject of charity.

They arrived at Longbourn in the late afternoon and were greeted with great enthusiasm by Mrs. Bennet, and in a quieter degree by Mary and Mr. Bennet.

"It has been an age since we have seen you all at Longbourn, my dears! Come in! Come in, before the rain starts! How I hate autumn! You never know what the weather will be like! Miss Darcy! Mr. Edwards! How delighted we are that you both came too! You must be chilled to the bone! But no, perhaps not, for the Darcy carriage is so large and comfortable, and with hot bricks and the furs, you would have all been as warm as toast!" cried Mrs. Bennet, "Come inside, do!"

"They would, Mrs. Bennet, if you would remove yourself from the entrance!" said Mr. Bennet, "It is quite chilly so please do come in and warm yourselves. Your servants arrived an hour or two ago so your rooms should be ready for you by now. Welcome to Longbourn Mr. Edwards, and congratulations on your preferment to the Mansfield living. Mr. Darcy, I know you will not stand on protocol, so make yourself comfortable in either the library or the parlour. Miss Darcy, you know the way, and Lizzy my dear, you are looking very well" as he hugged his favourite daughter.

Mary stood back a little, waiting for Mr. Edwards to be freed of the civilities of first greetings by her father and mother. Once free, he went to her and gave her a warm hug and greeting. He would have to wait a while before he could talk to her properly of the idea of taking her dearest niece with them to Mansfield, but they could safely talk about the parsonage and tithes and servants and such things with the rest of the family, for Mrs. Bennet could hardly think of anything else.

"Oh! how well done of you, Mr. Edwards! I have heard that the house is quite the gentleman's residence, and with such neighbours as Sir Thomas and Lady Bartram, you will be very comfortable indeed! Who would have thought that Mary would do so well for herself! But then again, if there is one thing I do *very* well, it is raising handsome and accomplished daughters, so really, it is not much of a surprise after all, for Mary is the most accomplished of them all!"

"Ma'am, how is little Jane? Can we have her brought down? She is such a pretty child, I cannot help loving her" exclaimed Lizzy, who thought that Mrs. Bennet was a little too rapid in her exultations of Mary's forthcoming prospects at Mansfield, so asking to see her niece was a total change of subject, especially knowing what the future of the child might mean for her grandmother, but she refrained from making any mention of it, for Mr. Edwards needed to speak to Mary first, then Mr. Bennet, before anything could be mentioned to Mrs. Bennet, for it was most likely that she would suffer at least a *mild* attack on her poor nerves, and after her previous indisposition at Pemberley, nobody wished to stress her unnecessarily.

Whilst waiting for the child's appearance, Lizzy felt that the approaching nuptials was a safe subject, since it concerned most of the party present, for of course Mary's wedding was to be closely followed by Georgiana's to Mr. Bartram.

It had been decided that Mary would marry from Longbourn, where most of her acquaintance lived, and where Mrs. Bennet could make the most of the last of her daughters' weddings. It would not be as grand as Jane and Lizzy's wedding, but she was determined to make it as grand as she could, and she was very eloquent in her plans for the wedding breakfast, even though it was still several months away, but one cannot be too well prepared, thought Mrs. Bennet.

She had already been to Town with Mary, staying at Gracechurch Street, to buy the wedding clothes, and get Mary's wedding gown made by Lizzy's modiste. There had been some animated discussion whilst there, for Mrs. Bennet had wanted something that Mary felt was totally unsuitable for herself, not at all to her taste, and it took the admirable skills of the modiste to come up with a compromise that suited both ladies, although it involved much less lace, frounces and frills in Mrs. Bennet's opinion, and rather more than Mary would have liked.

The arrival of little Jane changed the direction of the conversations again, she was delighted to see her aunt, uncle and cousin Georgiana, and of course there was Mr. Edwards, who was going to marry her dearest Aunt Mary. She was not sure if she would like that, for it meant that her aunt would go away to live in his house, instead of staying at home with her, but both Grandmama and Sarah had told her that it was a happy thing, so she did her best to smile and be happy.

After the child had been returned to her nursery, the guests went to their rooms to change for dinner, where their servants had made everything ready for them. Mrs. Bennet loved finery, so the ladies dressed in a manner which was more suited to London than to a small town in Hertfordshire.

Mary had been to first to arrive downstairs, so she was able to talk to her fiancé, who broached the subject of taking Jane with them when they moved to Mansfield. The smile of joy and happiness that illuminated Mary's face was worth more than gold in Mr. Edwards eyes, but he did warn her that Mrs. Bennet might not be quite so happy with the proposal. He asked her not to mention it until he had spoken to Mr. Bennet.

"Did I hear my name being mentioned?" inquired the gentleman himself as he entered the drawing room just at that moment. "What is it you wish to speak to me about? If it is about changing your mind about marrying Mary, then my answer is no, for Mrs. Bennet has almost ruined me in wedding clothes!"

"Father, please, remember that George, I mean, Mr. Edwards, is not used to your humour; he may think that you are being serious!" reproached Mary.

"No Mr. Bennet, I most certainly do not wish to withdraw my offer, but I *do* have a request to make" interposed Mr. Edwards, who then proceeded to explain his wish to raise Jane as his own child, and take her to live with them in Mansfield, finishing with 'It would make Miss Bennet so very happy, and her happiness means all to me" as he held Mary's hand tightly between his two own. Mary did not know whether to blush, cry from trepidation. or laugh with joy and happiness. George was such a kind and considerate man and she was overjoyed at the idea that their future would soon be bound together, and should her father agree to Jane going with them, then her happiness would be indeed complete, so she was subconsciously holding her breath as they awaited for a response from Mr. Bennet.

"Have you spoken of this with Mr. Darcy and Sir Thomas? If they do not object, and I see no reason why they would, I think it is altogether an excellent suggestion!"

"But Papa, what of my mother? Will she not think it wrong of us? She truly dotes on the child and might not wish to let her go" asked Mary, who had drawn breath again, after hearing Mr. Bennet's opinion.

"Leave your mother to me, my child. We are not getting any younger: we have had our opportunity to raise our own children, as best we could, and Jane sees you as her mother figure, you see her as a daughter, so it is only right that she should go with you. I am happy to let her go, under such circumstances, although I shall miss her, for she is a very tranquil, well-behaved child, something she obviously learned from your influence, Mary, for she certainly didn't get anything from Lydia!"

At this point Lizzy entered the room, and seeing Mary's happy countenance, surmised that Jane's future had been discussed with Mr. Bennet and that it had gone favourably, so she warmly hugged her sister and congratulated her, "It is the most sensible solution for all of you. Mary, the child has really only known you as her dearest Aunt Mary, but she looks up to you as she would a mother, so I think it will be better for everyone that she remains with you, in fact it would be quite unkind of us to separate her from you, considering how she ended up in Longbourn in the first place, being rejected by the woman who gave birth to her!"

"Oh Lizzy! I am so completely happy now, for it had been a sore point with me, thinking I would have to leave her, although this *is* her home, but I would have missed her so much! How kind of Mr. Edwards to have known this and to offer to take her with us! Not every man would accept to raise another man's child as his own, I realise that, so you can imagine how much I appreciate his worth!"

The rest of the family had now descended and dinner was announced, during which Mr. Bennet announced his decision; that his grand-daughter would be going to live in Mansfield. Mrs. Bennet's initial noisy protests simmered down to a much quieter level after Darcy announced that he had agreed to the idea, and that Sir Thomas had had no objections at all. She was still in awe of her son-in-law and would never think of contradicting him, and since Sir Thomas had also agreed, she tempered her complaints to a quieter lament that she would be left completely and utterly alone, once they moved to Mansfield, and that nobody had consulted her, or had asked her regarding her wishes, but that was always the way, when one refrained from putting oneself forward.

Chapter 69

———————•———————

The Darcy's only stayed for two days at Longbourn, then travelled on to Darcy House, whilst Mr. Edwards returned to his duties in Pemberley, a happy man who was not only going to gain a wife, but also a daughter!

Lizzy and Fitzwilliam had been kept informed on Lady Catherine's health throughout the summer, and Anne's last letter had asked them to come to town, to be close at hand should her mother take a turn for the worse, which was expected to occur quite soon, certainly before the end of the year, according to her physicians, who were very surprised that her ladyship had held on to life thus far, contradicting their prognostics of the previous winter. It had been decided that whilst Lizzy and Georgiana settled down into their London habits, Darcy would go down to Kent to see his aunt, knowing that it could be the last time, and to give support to his cousin Anne, and to his aunt and uncle Matlock, who had been at Rosings with their sister the whole spring, summer and autumn.

A call in to Gracechurch Street was the first social call made, then on to others of their London acquaintance who were in town. There were visits to some warehouses, to start buying linen for Georgiana's wedding the following Spring, a visit to Storrs to select some plate and jewellery from the family collection, Darcy having insisted that his sister had as much right to it as he did, consulting their modistes to discuss her wedding gown, ball gowns, and other such feminine pastimes, considered necessary to most women's happiness. They even ordered some mourning clothes, for they knew they would be needing them soon, once Lady Catherine passed away.

Several days passed before Darcy came back, bearing the expected mournful news: Lady Catherine had passed away peacefully, surrounded by her daughter, brother and sister Matlock, and Fitzwilliam. Her funeral had been planned earlier in the Spring, and only the gentlemen would attend. Letters were sent express to Lord Matlock's eldest son, Henry Fitzwilliam, Colonel Fitzwilliam, the Bennets and the Bingleys, the post office being deemed to be quite adequate to notify anyone else who needed to be informed.

Within a very few days the Bingleys arrived with Mr. Bennet. Jane would stay with Lizzy and Georgiana for the first night, so that she would not be alone in her own house, whilst the gentlemen went down to Rosings. From what she could glean from her husband, Lizzy learned that Anne, Lady Matlock, Mrs. Jenkinson and Charlotte Collins would be the only ladies present at the funeral. She was relieved that Anne would not have to face the ordeal alone, that she would have the presence of such females as had proved their ability to support her in difficult times.

In accordance with the late great lady's wishes, the funeral was private, the service done by Mr. Collins, so the ladies in town would have to await the return of the gentlemen to hear of the details, or unless Charlotte could find the time to write.

Lizzy wondered aloud, when a letter from her was delivered the following morning, as to how her friend had found the time to write at all. She retired to her dressing room to read the missive.

"My dear Eliza,

I write whilst the children sleep and Mr. Collins is gone to pay his respects, again, to the gentlemen across the park.

You will be relieved, I am sure, to learn that her ladyship's passing was as peaceful an affair as could be expected, laudanum having relieved her of almost all of her pain. She astounded all of her physicians with her longevity, having lasted twice as long as was expected by anyone, except, I suspect, her ladyship herself. She was surrounded by those she loved and simply went to sleep, not to awaken again.

Considering the circumstances, Anne is well. She has borne her loss with great dignity, and is much changed from the shy and withdrawn young lady we both first met. She has learned much from her aunt and uncle, Lady Matlock teaching her how to run the household, and her uncle was surprised at her interest in running the estate, or at least to attend meetings with the steward, to better understand the way things are run. Mrs. Jenkinson has continued to be devoted to her charge, and will be retained as a companion to Anne, which I think is an excellent idea.

The funeral service itself was the quiet affair that Lady Catherine had requested, though Mr. Collins drew out the eulogy to over a full hour in his efforts to laud her greatness, whilst expressing his own humble gratefulness. I could see the gentlemen glancing at each other as he drew breath again to praise her benevolence, understanding, skills etc. so Lord Matlock harrumphed loudly to give him a hint to be done, and even more loudly after another five minutes of Mr. Collins not seeming to have taken the first hint. Had you been present, Eliza, you might have had to restrain at least a smile.

The gentlemen accompanied her on her final journey to the mausoleum, where she now lies next to her husband, Sir Lewis, whilst we ladies returned to the house. Once the gentlemen returned, we had the attorney read out her will, where, as was expected, Anne inherits everything. Mr. Collins and Mrs. Jenkinson were each left one thousand pounds, most generous of her ladyship, and Mr. Collins did not have sufficient time within the ensuing hour to thank the attorney enough, and to my own great surprise, she bequeathed me a gold brooch that I had once admired, and a small string of pearls! I was never more astonished! I have never owned anything like them and shall treasure them, for once one got to know her ladyship, she was not really as unpleasant as first impressions gave one; she genuinely did care about people, but her forthright manner, which would have been much admired in a gentleman, grated when exercised by a woman. The world is not ready for opinionated women.

In spite of her being of age, to do as she pleases, Anne has asked that her uncle, Lord Matlock, and your own Mr. Darcy, continue to advise her in the future. She doubts her own abilities, knowledge and skills in running the estate, but her steward is an excellent, trustworthy man, employed many years ago by Sir Lewis, so I do not think she can go far wrong. Her biggest fear is that she will become a target for unscrupulous suitors, for she is not wise in the ways of society, having been kept secluded in Rosings for so long, but Colonel Fitzwilliam has promised to protect her by his presence, whenever she does go up to town, and Mr. Darcy has insisted that she stay at Darcy House whenever she does do so, so I think she will be well looked after.

Perhaps it is because of Mary's and Miss Darcy's upcoming weddings unduly influencing my judgement, but I do think I perceive the beginning of an attraction between Miss De Bourgh and her cousin, the Colonel. She could do a lot worse for herself, and the irony of it would be, that Lady Catherine would have got her wish of her daughter marrying her cousin after all, although not the nephew her ladyship had originally intended!

However, I think it would be a good thing; the Colonel has no estate, being but a younger son, but he has the breeding that Lady Catherine approved of, and I am sure that Mr. Darcy has quite enough to do with Pemberley, without having have to concern himself with Rosings. Should it be a match, Miss De Bourgh will be safe from a bad marriage to an inconsiderate or unscrupulous husband, and the Colonel will finally have an income suitable for his station in life: yes, I think it would be an excellent solution for all concerned!

I must go now, for the children have been wanting me for this past half hour, and Mr. Collins has just returned from Rosings, so he will be impatient to tell me all about every expression, turn of face, and opinion from the gentlemen at Rosings, as well as your father's current state of health, in which he takes a great deal of interest, as you can imagine, although I sincerely wish Mr. Bennet continuing good health.

Fare thee well my dearest Eliza,
your true friend, Charlotte

P.S. I have just been informed that the gentlemen return to town tomorrow morning.

Folding the letter with the smile that her friend had anticipated, Lizzy joined Georgiana and Jane in the breakfast parlour and read them the letter.

They were all relieved that the end had been so peaceful for her ladyship, and impressed at her remembering that Charlotte had once admired the brooch, that Anne was bearing up well was good news, and even Jane gave a wry smile upon hearing of Mr. Collins' behaviour, as obsequious, ingratiating and pompous as ever, thus ensuring Mr. Bennet's continuing entertainment.

Chapter 70

Charlotte's letter having been written the day before, this meant that the gentlemen were returning today, so Lizzy notified Mrs. Clayton and Mrs. Appleby of the expected increase to the household, to ensure rooms were ready and to add some more dishes to the day's dinner. Mr. Bingley would go on to his own house in town, where Jane was staying, but perhaps Lord and Lady Matlock, having been down in Kent since the spring, would prefer not to have the trouble of opening their house, since she knew not whether they would remain in town or carry on to Matlock, so rooms were made ready for them, as well as for their eldest son, Henry Fitzwilliam. Mr. Bennet was of course to stay in Darcy House, and the Colonel would most probably return to his barracks, but everyone would come for dinner, which had been agreed upon before they had left for Rosings.

Lizzy smiled to herself, wondering whether they had changed horses at Bromley: she still vividly remembered Lady Catherine's recommendation at the end of her very first stay in Kent, to visit Charlotte, newly married to Mr. Collins "If you mention my name at The Bell, you will be attended to" were her very words, how strange to remember them just at this time. "And we must invite Anne to Pemberley for Christmas, it will not do for her to be alone in that great house, so soon after her bereavement; I will speak about it to

Fitzwilliam tonight" were her next thoughts, as she climbed the stairs to go to her rooms to change for dinner.

The gentlemen had arrived an hour earlier, without Lord and Lady Matlock, who had preferred to go to their house in town, along with their sons, but to Lizzy's surprise, Anne and Mrs. Jenkinson had also arrived at Darcy House. The ladies, fatigued from their journey, had gone straight to the rooms that had been prepared for the Matlocks, Anne announcing that she would not come down to dinner, but could she please have something sent to her room. Mrs. Jenkinson said that she would do likewise, to ensure that Miss De Bourgh was settled.

It turned out that Anne had wanted to get away from Rosings for a time; the house was too full of unhappy, even oppressive memories, and her cousin had insisted that she come to Darcy House, where she would always be assured of a warm welcome, whether the Darcys were in town or not. Georgiana and Elizabeth being currently present would surely help raise her depleted spirits.

This being discussed over dinner, it was decided that the Darcy's would stay in town until the spring, so they would send for the children, to be brought down from Pemberley, for they could not bear to be separated from them for so long. This also meant that the wedding preparations for Georgiana need not be as rushed as was originally thought, which would have been the case if they had remained with the initial idea of staying for just a month. The Matlocks were returning to their home in Derbyshire, having been at Rosings since the beginning of the year, when they had first learned of the seriousness of their sister's illness. Colonel Fitzwilliam was to remain in town with his regiment, and offered to be his cousin's escort whenever she wished to go anywhere, and Henry intended to stay at the family house in town with his wife and children, so Anne would have all of her cousins around her, something she had never experienced before. It would certainly be a change from the quiet seclusion she had always known at Rosings.

After dinner, Lizzy went up to see Anne, who was sitting quietly by the fire with Mrs. Jenkinson, doing some needlework. Settling herself in the comfortable chair opposite, she explained what the family had decided, and reiterated her husband's offer that Darcy House would always be open to her, but that they had thought that she might prefer to have some familiar faces around her whilst she was in town, which was why the Darcys had decided to prolong their stay this winter, to keep her company.

"Oh Elizabeth! You seem to understand how lonely I have been! It will be delightful to me to stay here with you and my cousins. I will not be going out in public, for of course I am in mourning, but I also still find it somewhat intimidating. Today, I did not feel equal to coming to dinner, but from tomorrow, I will, but would you mind, Elizabeth, if Mrs. Jenkinson accompanied me to meals?"

"Why on earth would I object to her presence, Anne?" replied Lizzy, who then turned to the lady in question, "Mrs. Jenkinson, over the years I have had the pleasure of knowing you, you have been a most attentive, caring companion to my cousin, attending to her every need, just as a mother would do, so for *me*, you are as welcome to my table as Anne is. I would in fact be most offended if you took your meals separately or with the servants."

"Thank you most kindly, Mrs. Darcy. If you permit me to say, ma'am, her ladyship always mentioned how perceptive you are to the feelings of those around you. Although I am her *paid* companion, I have been with Miss Anne for so long that I do indeed consider her as I would have done my own daughter, had she lived."

"Mrs. Jenkinson, how sorry I am to hear that you lost your daughter! I had no idea that you had had a child! How terrible to lose her! May I enquire as to how, if it is not too painful for you?" cried Lizzy.

"She died of smallpox when she was three, at the same time as her father, from the same cause. It was very painful to me, as you can imagine, and it was only thanks to her ladyship's benevolence in engaging me to be Miss Anne's companion, that I did not end up a pauper, for my husband left me with almost nothing, his monies going to his son from his previous marriage"

"Oh! my dear Mrs. Jenkinson! how terrible a time it must have been for you, losing your daughter *and* your husband, and being left practically destitute! I cannot even begin to imagine how dreadful that must have been for you! Lady Catherine rises even *further* in my esteem, for noticing your plight and *doing* something for you, without it appearing as a charity." replied Lizzy, feeling a little emotional, trying *not* to imagine losing her daughter *and* her husband.

"Thank you, Elizabeth," interposed Anne, with teary eyes, "for yet again being so understanding. I know that my mother, when she first met you, may have appeared disdainful towards you, and overbearing, but believe me when I say that later, she held you in the highest of esteem, even telling me that you were an example that I should try to emulate, and believe me also, when I tell you that that is my earnest intention."

"Oh Anne!" cried Lizzy, rising to hug her grieving cousin, "please, never feel that you are alone in the world; we are here for you whenever you need and you *must* come to us, wherever we are, whenever you feel the inclination, and I am so very glad that you have Mrs. Jenkinson with you, watching over you. Mrs. Jenkinson, should you *ever* have any concerns about my cousin Anne, no matter what, I insist that you keep me informed, please."

Leaving the two ladies to their needlework, Lizzy returned to her other guests, a little subdued, but determined not to let anything appear changed in her demeanour, intending to speak to her husband in the privacy of their rooms.

The conversation in the drawing room was still about Lady Catherine, and they had been discussing the information, obtained from Lord Matlock, that, although *not* included in her will, because she had arranged it before her death, her ladyship had left a thousand pounds to each of Mr. Collins' daughters, as their dowries, to be held in trust until they married, the interest of which was to be added to the original sum each year, until they either married or reached the age of twenty-five, the monies not able to be touched by their parents. They all concluded that this was in fact for Mrs. Collins' benefit, to secure to her the knowledge that her daughters would be provided for in the future, not including whatever Mr. Collins might be able to do for them once he inherited the Longbourn estate, without them feeling obliged to marry somebody, anybody, simply in order to obtain an establishment, as Charlotte had felt obliged to do when she married Mr. Collins. Lady Catherine was still surprising them with her well-hidden understanding of human nature, and her benevolence to those less fortunately placed in life than she herself had been.

Chapter 71

The Darcy children arrived down from Pemberley, Christmas was for the first time celebrated in town and the weeks passed, quietly but happily for Anne de Bourgh, and a little more animated for the Darcys, with private parties, dinners, concerts, and such, but only with close friends and acquaintance for they were also in mourning for their aunt.

March arrived, bringing Mrs. Bennet and Mary to town, for the final visits to the warehouses for yet more wedding clothes and linen. Mr. Bennet had been so frightened the previous autumn, by Mrs. Bennet's ill-health, and the very real prospect of actually losing her, that he had allowed her a generous sum for Mary's wedding, knowing that she was the last daughter to be married. So theoretically, he should be able to recuperate the expenses within the next twelvemonth, having no more daughters to provide for, and even his own dear grand-daughter Jane would be taken off his hands when she moved to Mansfield; not that he objected to the expense of her keep, but with Mrs. Bennet's total lack of sense of economy, every little helped, and he was hoping to achieve for Jane, what he had not been able to do for his own daughters: to set aside an amount each year so that she would not be beholden to relations when she married, but would have a dowry worthy of the word when the time came, should he live long enough to provide sufficient funds. What he and his son Darcy knew, that the ladies did not, was that Darcy himself was setting aside a hundred pounds a year for his niece, for the same purpose.

April brought fine spring weather and Mary's wedding. Just as with her eldest sisters' nuptials, she was married in the church in Meryton, with Mr. Powell presiding again. She was radiant in a lilac gown and bonnet, her pearl necklace and earrings, and a very pretty amethyst brooch, a gift from Kitty and her husband. The gown was a lot less ornate than fashion and Mrs. Bennet dictated, but more than enough for the bride, whose natural taste had always tended to the more subdued. What was original, in the eyes of the goodwives of Meryton, was the presence of a pretty young Jane Wickham, dressed very daintily in white, walking in front of the bride and her father, scattering petals in front of them, from a sweet little basket, instead of an older attendant.

The wedding breakfast was at Longbourn; a small party, for the groom had lost his parents some years previously, and he had no brothers or sisters, so it was just the Bennets, their daughters Jane, Elizabeth, Catherine, and their husbands - Lydia wrote to say that she was unable to come, hinting at the need for funds, which the recipients chose to ignore - and the Philipps's and Gardiners, and of course Mr. Powell. Mrs. Bennet's now famous silverware was on full parade, filled with spring blooms and the best wax candles. According to Mrs. Philipps' information, which certainly could be relied upon, for she had been present at the time, it was not as grand as when Jane and Elizabeth had married, but there were so many dishes that the wedding breakfast had lasted a full four hours! Mrs. Bennet knew how to provide an excellent dinner, she always had done so, and her wedding breakfasts would be difficult to surpass.

The bridal couple left for Mansfield the following day, in a small but elegant carriage, provided for them as a gift from the Darcys and Bingleys, along with a matching pair of horses. How well the Bennet girls had done for themselves, in spite of the scandalous behaviour of their youngest sister, Mrs. Wickham, whose notoriety had only increased over the years, especially when the Bennets had been obliged to take their grand-daughter into their care.

Later visits, to and from Mrs. Bennet, informed Lady Lucas and the good ladies of Meryton that little Jane was to go and live with her Aunt Mary, the new Mrs. Edwards, how well that sounds! in Mansfield, to relieve Mrs. Bennet of the concerns and responsibility of her care, for at her time of life, especially after her health problems of the previous year, nobody knew what a strain it was on her poor nerves, but as the child's grandmother, she could not have done anything less at the time, so it was an excellent thing that she was to be raised at Mansfield, and since next month, Miss Darcy was to marry Mr. Bartram, and he was Sir Thomas's heir to the baronetcy, Jane would be raised more or less with any cousins she may have through them. Much as she would miss the dear child, she would be better off amongst such elevated relations, so Mrs. Bennet was prepared to make such a sacrifice, for the good of the child. What an excellent grandmother she was! That she certainly deserved the good luck of marrying *most* of her daughters so advantageously, was the general consensus.

Chapter 72

April was swiftly followed by May, leaving only so very few weeks before Georgiana married Thomas Bartram. The young couple were to live in the Bartram family's house in town, since Lady Bartram never liked to go to town, and therefore the house was practically unused. In preparation for the new incumbents, Sir Thomas had ordered that the house be completely refurbished, from top to bottom, with Miss Darcy's taste to be consulted in all matters. How fortunate that the Darcys had remained in town!

Another slight adjustment to circumstances, was the decision for the wedding to occur in London, as opposed to Pemberley, which had been the original intention. Most of their acquaintance were still in Town, and since the children had come down, there was no pertinent reason to have the wedding in Pemberley, as Kitty and her husband would of course come down for the event.

Lizzy accompanied Georgiana everywhere, especially for the all-important matter of her wedding gown. Georgiana had decided to dress all in white, with a veil to be held by a tiara, made for her at her brother and sister's insistence, of silver, diamonds and sapphires. More gowns were ordered, for her wedding was the event of the season, and she and Thomas would be invited everywhere by people of the Ton. If Lizzy had thought that her husband had been somewhat over-zealous with his showering of gifts to herself since their marriage, it was nothing compared to the extravagance he lent himself to for the nuptials of his sister. Nothing was too much for her, and he was going to hand her to her new husband with as large a flourish as money could buy.

Lizzy wondered how they had possibly thought that a month in Town would be sufficient to prepare for the wedding, because they were out every day to peruse through fabrics and furnishings, dress fittings, milliners, shoe makers, visits to inspect the progress on the house, and so forth, followed by evening engagements almost every day.

"Lizzy, I can hardly believe how generous Fitzwilliam has been for my wedding! I am having to constantly refuse his offers of procuring me this or that, should I inadvertently admire anything in his presence!" said Georgiana as they travelled in the carriage to visit the Bartram's town house.

The painters had finished, the window dressings and wall hangings hung, and new furniture arriving daily, to add to the already substantial quantities that had furnished the house previously. The young couple had selected which pieces of the old furniture they wished to keep, and ordered new to replace the old that was deemed too old-fashioned to remain. Lizzy's Aunt Phillips could hardly believe her good fortune when some very elegant pieces arrived at her house, in a style admired previously during one of her now regular journeys to town to visit her nieces, and her brother and sister Gardiner.

"You should hardly be surprised Georgie," replied Lizzy, "he has always done whatever he could to please you, you just had to take a liking to a room and he would have it refurbished to your taste, even if it was only a whim on your part! And considering that he will no longer have the pleasure of spoiling you quite so much once you are married, I think he is doing as much as he can for you whilst you are still under his care."

"I know, I have been very fortunate to have such an affectionate brother and guardian, I could not have wished for better."

Arriving at Bartram House, the footman assisted the ladies out of the carriage as the newly appointed housekeeper came to greet them at the front door. The previous housekeeper had decided to retire to her sister's house in the country, having been generously offered a very respectable annual stipend by Sir Thomas, after almost fifty years in the family's service. Mrs. Ann Gregory had come highly recommended by Mrs. Georges, Jane's town housekeeper.

"Welcome Mrs. Darcy, Miss Darcy, you will be pleased to learn that the main drawing room is now ready for you, if you would care for some refreshments there" showing them to the room as she took their gloves and outer garments, handing them to a maid.

"Tea would be most welcome Mrs. Gregory" answered Georgiana, after a slight hesitation, for Lizzy had held back from answering, wanting her sister to step up and be the lady of the house, which she was to be in a few days' time. Georgiana was not as shy as she had been when she had first met Lizzy, but she still had a natural aversion to appearing forward.

Once tea had been served and dispensed, Mrs. Gregory lead the ladies over the house, making notes of any changes or additions Miss Darcy wished for in the placement of furniture, paintings, and ornaments in all the rooms. Her dressing room was already quite well filled with her new clothes, jewels and accessories. Lizzy smiled, recalling her own first visit to her dressing room in Darcy House, when she had wondered how ever she was to fill it with her then comparatively meagre wardrobe of gowns: how changed were her circumstances since then! Her younger sisters were the happy recipients of gowns that she no longer wore, Lydia begging for the ball gowns so that she could outshine the other ladies at the regular dances and assemblies that she assiduously attended. Wickham still had not yet made his fortune, so should their circumstances become too dire, Lizzy felt sure that her sister would always be able sell some of the gowns to the wives of the other officers.

Having been through the house, where Georgiana's good taste could be seen in the decoration and selection of old and new furniture, Lizzy and Georgiana thanked the housekeeper and left to go to the dressmaker for the final fittings of their gowns for the wedding, which would be sent to Darcy House when finished, from where Georgiana would be married.

Chapter 73

The day finally arrived when Darcy would hand his beloved sister over to the care of Thomas Bartram. He was still not sure of whether he liked the idea, but had resigned himself to its inevitability, albeit with the assistance of both Elizabeth and Georgiana.

Neither he nor Lizzy had slept much the previous night, himself because of the realisation of the change about to occur, and Lizzy from worrying as to whether she had forgotten anything, this being the first wedding for which she had had the full responsibility of, and it was a major society event whether she and Darcy liked it or not, for the young couple were very popular and being the nuptials of *Miss Darcy* to the heir of a baronet, everyone wished to attend.

Colonel Fitzwilliam had gone down to Rosings to escort Miss De Bourgh back to town for their cousin's wedding, accompanied of course by Mrs. Jenkinson, who was more like a mother to her mistress and loved almost as such. They were staying in Darcy House, whilst Mr. and Mrs. Bennet stayed with the Bingleys, along with Mary and her husband. Kitty and Edmund were naturally staying with Sir Thomas, Lady Bartram and their niece Miss Price, in their house in town, now completely refurbished for the reception of the soon-to-be-married couple.

Recalling her own wedding day, especially the pangs of hunger beforehand, Lizzy had organised an early breakfast for the family, for the ceremony was to take place at one of the clock, to be followed by the wedding breakfast at the best hotel in town, for even Darcy House could not hold the number of guests invited. Mrs. Appleby had initially been most put out, but had been somewhat appeased when Lizzy insisted on discussing the menus with her, before asking her to accompany her to the hotel in question, to continue the conversation with the maître d'hôtel, Mr Bradley, and the head chef of the establishment, Mr. Vincent.

"So, Mr. Bradley, Mr. Vincent, any questions you may have, please address them to Mrs. Appleby here, who has my full authority to deal with all matters concerning the menus."

"Certainly Mrs. Darcy, I am sure that between us, Mrs. Appleby and myself will ensure that all runs as smoothly as in your own household" Mr. Bradley replied most courteously, for he knew that he was responsible for the biggest event his establishment had held for many a year, for the breakfast, with over one hundred guests, was to be followed by a ball in the evening, to be attended by everybody of note in the Ton. The reputation of the establishment could be severely compromised if he failed in *any* attention to detail for this wedding. He was in fact relieved that he could count on the assistance of Mrs. Darcy's staff.

After their early breakfast, the family retired to their various dressing rooms to prepare themselves. Madeleine was extremely occupied, first dressing the hair of her mistress, then Miss Darcy and Miss Price, who had been brought over earlier that morning from Bartram House, and finally Miss De Bourgh, and Mrs. Jenkinson. Georgiana and Anne both had their own very efficient ladies' maids, but it had been agreed by all concerned, including the maids, that Madeleine was the most dexterous and talented in dressing ladies' hair.

Lizzy had chosen a pale green ensemble with lilac trimmings, not too elaborate but superbly made, as befitted the sister of the bride. Her jewels were of amethyst and silver, again so as not to outshine the bride, but in keeping with the bridal bouquet, which was to be of lilac and white blooms.

By noon, everybody was dressed and ready, assembling in the drawing room for some refreshments, whilst Lizzy went to Georgiana's rooms, to assist her in the final touches to her attire and for a sisterly talk.

At the appropriate time, the others left for the church, then Lizzy, travelling with Miss Price, followed, preceding the bride and her brother by a few minutes. Everything had been planned and prepared with military precision; Colonel Fitzwilliam's influence of course, for he had been involved in the preparations, as his cousin's other guardian.

As was hoped by Lizzy and Fitzwilliam, and *expected* by the Colonel, everything went smoothly during the ceremony and everyone agreed that Miss Darcy looked quite ethereal in her beautiful gown and was not her tiara the most divine creation? The bride's maid looked very pretty in a lilac gown, quite matching the lilacs in the bride's bouquet, a cousin of the groom did you know? and did not Mrs. Darcy look *quite* the part in her choice of colours? and did you notice that even Mr. Darcy had a lilac coloured waistcoat under his dark green coat?

Much to Mr. Bradley's relief, the wedding breakfast had gone without a hitch, the plentiful food much admired and the servants had worked very efficiently, getting all the dishes to the scores of guests whilst still hot, for Mr. Vincent's possible wrath would not allow them to let the food get cold before being set down before the guests. All the said guests had now left for their respective residences, to rest and then dress in readiness for the ball in the evening, for which grand event his staff were now putting the finishing touches in the ballroom. He himself was keeping well away from the kitchens, for he could still hear the chef shouting at his minions from the depths of his domain as he supervised the final preparation of the evening's supper. "Best let the man do what he does best" thought Mr. Bradley as he checked the card room one more time, "and no wonder he's nervous, poor soul, with Mrs. Appleby in there with him!"

He was a much happier man, in the early hours of the morning as he supervised the arrival and departures of the multitude of guests' carriages, under the watchful eyes of Mr. and Mrs. Darcy and Colonel Fitzwilliam. Not a single incident, not even a hint of disaster had occurred, that is, if he chose to ignore Mrs. Bennet's attempts of criticism, given under the guise of 'advice' which Mrs. Darcy and Mrs. Bingley had very quickly put a stop to. Very perspicacious ladies, the Mrs. Darcy and Bingley, a pity not more ladies of the Ton were like them!

Chapter 74

———•———

It was agreed by all that the wedding was the highlight of the season, as most of the guests returned to their country estates soon afterwards, many having stayed in town a little longer than they usually did, in order to attend.

The bride had looked positively angelic in her white bridal gown, the short veil held by a splendid diamond and sapphire tiara, her bouquet of lilac and lily of the valley, with trailing ivy was quite beautiful but her ballgown surpassed everything they had seen all Season. Brussels lace, satin, flounces and frills, pin pleats across the bodice, and her train, embroidered with silver thread and seed pearls, pinned to the shoulders of her gown with amethyst brooches, was truly the work of a very talented seamstress and modiste. Rumour had it that Mrs. Darcy's *maid* had something to do with it, but it was not certain, for the family had said nothing to that effect, and the modiste herself had also kept very quiet about the design, in spite of numerous, skilled efforts to obtain information. The happy couple were gone off to the continent, Italy had been mentioned, but everyone wished them well for the future.

"Well my dearest" said Fitzwilliam, in the carriage driving them finally back to Pemberley, "I think that went very well. You did a magnificent effort with the wedding, I am sure Georgie and Tom told you so, and even Sir Thomas himself said as much."

"I am truly thankful that it is over and that it *did* go so well, I am glad that I have quite some years to go before I have to repeat the performance," replied Lizzy "I think we agree that we are in no haste for our daughter to marry!"

"No haste at all!" laughed her husband, "but I must warn you that there might be another wedding soon, for which your assistance may be requested."

"Are you referring to our cousins, Anne and Richard?"

"I am indeed; you more than likely will have noticed that most of Anne's dances at the ball were with Richard, and he has confided to me that he has become warmly attached to her, no longer in the way of a cousin, and he believes she returns his affection to an equal degree."

"Well then I am very well pleased, for she deserves some happiness at last, and he is a very kind and considerate man who will not treat her at all unkindly. I think it will be an excellent match; they have always known each other so they have an idea of each other's character, and should have no unpleasant surprises later."

"As you know, my dear, that our biggest fear for her was for her to be sought after for her fortune, by every impoverished gentleman and fortune-seeking scoundrel in the kingdom, so although Richard has not much of a fortune of his own, we know that he is not seeking her for her estate."

"That is so very true my love, I have seen how he has been courted over the years by every mother in Town with a well-endowed daughter to dispose of, yet he has never taken the bait and married for money. Do you know if he intends to ask for her hand?"

"He does; he will do so when the flurry of the past weddings in the family has subsided, and propriety decrees it respectable for the offer to be made, after my aunt's demise."

"Well I am certain that we shall be among the first to know, should she accept him, and I see no reason why she *would* refuse. It seems to be the most sensible thing for them both, though I would never condone a match for purely practical reasons, but since they appear to have developed a sincere attachment to each other, we really could not wish for better for either of them, and Lady Catherine will at last have got her wish, in marrying Anne to her cousin" laughed Lizzy "albeit not *quite* the one she had in mind!"

Chapter 75

———————————

Whilst enjoying the clean, refreshing summer air of Pemberley, the Darcys were delighted to learn that their surmising had been correct; the Colonel did ask his cousin for her hand in June and was accepted, though only the close family were made aware of the betrothal, and they projected to marry in October.

Anne wrote to ask her aunt, Lady Matlock, if she would be willing to organise the wedding, with Elizabeth's help, because the family were all up in Derbyshire and she would like to marry there, from Pemberley, which was a suggestion Lizzy had made in their correspondence. There was no need at all to marry from Rosings or Town, and she felt more comfortable being close to the family for the occasion. Lady Matlock was touched by her niece's request, and was truly delighted that she was going to become her daughter, and although not of a naturally mercenary nature, she knew it was a splendid match for her son: an estate bringing in more than eight thousand a year was certainly an excellent alliance by anybody's account, even for a *first* son, let alone a *second* son, even if he *is* the son of a lord.

He would of course have to retire from the army in order to look after Rosings, but since peaceful times had made his military duties less rigorous, he had become somewhat bored, so running the Rosings estate as well as looking after his new family should fulfil his need for purposeful activity. Lady Matlock was very satisfied with the outcome indeed.

The rest of the summer was spent in the northern counties, with regular visits to Gaddesley, the Matlocks and a fortnight's stay in Scarborough with the children, accompanied by Anne and Mrs. Jenkinson, who had moved up to Pemberley after a short sojourn in Town to buy her wedding clothes. She was staying with her cousins so that she could be married quietly, by Mr. Cresswell, the new clergyman at Pemberley, who had previously held the Mansfield living until Mr. Edwards received it from Sir Bartram in the spring.

In August the Darcys were equally delighted to learn that Jane had been safely delivered of another daughter, Caroline Mary, which had greatly surprised Miss Bingley, having the child named after her, which gave her boasting rights over her sister, Mrs. Hurst, and she became much less proud and conceited in her manner with Jane.

The Edwards' were very happily and contentedly settled in the Mansfield parsonage, living quietly with little Jane, and regular, though unobtrusive interaction with the family from the park. Mary was granted constant access to the library, and could not but be most delighted that she could discuss whatever she had learned, with her husband. They were regularly invited to have tea or dinner with Sir Thomas, Lady Bartram, and Miss Price, where Mary was always invited to play and sing for the company.

Kitty was equally content in her home in Kympton, surrounded by her gardens and homely comforts and expecting her second child. She was totally different from the silly, ignorant and petulant girl she had once been, having spent most of her time since Lydia's marriage and subsequent move to the north, with her elder sisters, learning the social graces and consideration for others that she had sadly lacked before.

Lydia remained Lydia; as insouciant, boisterous and ignorant as she had ever been, retaining all the claims to reputation which her marriage had given her, continuously moving from place to place in quest of a cheap situation, and always spending more money than she had. Her husband had become totally indifferent to her, but since Darcy continued to assist him in his profession, he realised that abandoning her was not in his best interest.

Mr. and Mrs. Bennet continued in good health, perhaps to Mr. Collins' disappointment, but to their daughters' continuing relief. Mrs. Bennet had gone up in her husband's esteem, but not quite sufficiently for him to actually *enjoy* her company by himself, so they were frequent visitors to their four eldest daughters, where he was sure to be able to converse with sensible people, escaping to the nearest available library when the need was felt, and Mrs. Bennet could visit all of her grandchildren. Having so well disposed of her daughters, it gave her the all joys of being a grandmother, without the responsibilities of being a mother, but her daughters knew well, and remembered with fondness, that she had *always* done her best for them, albeit though her 'best' manners and general ignorance had caused all of them some highly embarrassing moments and heartache in their courting years.

THE END

Printed in Australia
AUHW022235160521
345641AU00001B/2